AXEL

BO

CARPELAN

𝄞

AXEL

A Novel

Translated by David McDuff

CARCANET

First published in 1989 by
Carcanet Press Limited
208-212 Corn Exchange Buildings
Manchester M4 3BQ

Axel A Novel published by Bonniers, Stockholm 1986
Translation from Finland-Swedish © David McDuff 1989

British Library Cataloguing in Publication Data

Carpelan, Bo, *1926-*
Axel.
I. Title
839.7'374[F]

ISBN 0-85635-808-8

The publisher acknowledges financial assistance from the
Arts Council of Great Britain; and warmly thanks the Finnish
Literature Centre for a translation grant.

Set in 10½pt Bembo by Bryan Williamson, Manchester
Printed and bound in England by SRP Ltd, Exeter

Derjenige, der mit dem Leben nicht lebendig fertig wird, braucht die eine Hand, um die Verzweiflung über sein Schicksal ein wenig abzuwehren – es geschieht sehr unvollkommen –, mit der anderen Hand aber kann er eintragen, was er unter den Trümmern sieht, denn er sieht anderes und mehr als die anderen, er ist doch tot zu Lebzeiten, und der eigentlich Überlebende.

The person who cannot cope with life while he is alive needs one hand in order to protect himself a little from his despair at his fate – he has little success in this – but with his other hand he may note down what he sees among the ruins, for he sees other things and more than others; he is after all dead in his own lifetime, and is the true survivor.

Franz Kafka, *Diaries*
19.10.1921

Contents

Foreword   9

I
15.1.1868   11
From the Diary 16.1.1868–30.5.1870   15
July 1870   19
From the Diary 26.9.1870–2.8.1872   21
October 1872   25
From the Diary 12.1.1873–24.5.1877   27
31.5.1877   35
From the Diary September 1877–5.10 1880   38
7.10.1880   47
From the Diary 15.1.1881–June 1882   51
23.7.1882   54
From the Diary October 1882–6.1.1884   58
5.4.1884   65
From the Diary 5.4.1884–3.11.1887   69
2.12.1887   78
From the Diary 15.1.1888–16.5.1891   85
22.5.1891   95
From the Diary July 1891–15.1.1893   104
27.1.1893   112
From the Diary 3.2.1893–3.5.1895   116
26.5.1895   127
From the Diary 29.5.1895–17.9.1896   135
22.9.1896   145
From the Diary 24.9.1896–19.7.1897   149
24.8.1897   157
From the Diary 3.9.1897–4.7.1899   160
13.7.1899   171
From the Diary 14.7.1899–31.12.1899   175
1.1.1900   183

II

From the Diary 1.1.1900 – 2.7.1900   189
3.7.1900   196
From the Diary 5.7.1900 – 1.7.1902   203
22.7.1902   221
From the Diary 13.8.1902 – 10.3.1904   227
16.6.1904   236
From the Diary 18.6.1904 – 23.5.1905   241
1.6.1905   248
From the Diary 4.8.1905 – 20.4.1907   254
21.4.1907   264
From the Diary 3.9.1907 – 8.4.1909   270
25.4.1909   281
From the Diary 26.4.1909 – 1.1.1911   286
26.1.1911   296
From the Diary 28.1.1911 – 16.8.1912   299
4.9.1912   305
From the Diary 7.9.1912 – 24.9.1914   312
3.10.1914   324
From the Diary 16.11.1914 – 26.6.1916   326
5.7.1916   334
From the Diary 8.7.1916 – 28.8.1917   340
22.9.1917   345
From the Diary 28.9.1917 – 23.1.1919   349
8.2.1919   355
From the Diary 14.2.1919 – 15.3.1919   359
Epilogue   363

Translator's Notes   367

FOREWORD

I came across the name of my great-uncle, Axel Carpelan, for the first time at the end of the 1930s, in Karl Ekman's *Jean Sibelius And His Work*. There, in a brief note following the bibliography, the author stated that the quotations from letters which appeared in the book were addressed to Axel Carpelan, 'who belonged to the master's most intimate circle of friends and was his regular confidant in all things musical. Sibelius celebrated their friendship by dedicating his Second Symphony to him.' I never heard Axel's name mentioned in my own family.

The real stimulus towards the writing of the novel came to me – many years after my reading of Karl Ekman – from Erik Tawaststjerna's biography of Sibelius, where Axel appears as a fully-fledged figure in Part II of the Finnish edition (1967), his death being described in Part IV (1978; Parts I-II inclusive of the Swedish edition, 1968). At the beginning of the 1970s I began to jot down Axel's fictional diary covering the years from 1868 to 1919 (whether Axel himself ever kept a diary is not known), basing it as far as possible on the available facts. These grew more numerous when I was given access to the correspondence between Axel and Janne from 1900 onwards. What I wrote turned into the story of a very sick and lonely man's hidden strength, and of a friendship in which the give and take on both sides was far greater than Axel himself could ever have guessed.

Bo Carpelan
Hagalund, June 1985

15.1.1868

Axel stands in the homespun coat that is far too big for him,
stooping forwards as though the ice-cold earth were drawing him
downwards. Or is it the woman cowering in the snow there who
is trying to tell him something, to call him with her open mouth
into whose blackness snowflakes are finding their way like insects?
He stands with his arms sticking out and his hands hidden away,
as though he had no hands at all. The sky is so low that it is almost
touching the earth with its clouds. A freezing wind is driving the
people southwards in hunger and fear. The dead woman is lying
with her eyes half-shut, in her clenched fist the rope of the Lapland
sleigh in which two bundles of felt lie silently. Or are they complaining? Perhaps it is only the wind moving through the black
treetops, making the branches and trunks creak. Over the fields
the squalls move like mist; in the hedge a flock of sparrows sits as
though it had grown there. Under the coarse-knit woollen hood
his eyes see something unknown, primordial, something he has
not seen before but which he has been waiting for, something that
has always been a part of his life. He did not know what it was
then, and he does not know what it is now; it is drawing him
down to itself with half-closed eyes, he cannot move. It is something that draws him away from his body, that breathes like a
mist through the heavy layers of clothes, gloves, neckties, the mist
of his terror, and he feels curiously calm, drained. He says nothing;
she is, as he is, beyond words and utterances, and the death that
until now has been concealed from him she shares with him as if
it were the bread of the last supper. She lies felled and beaten, and
he stoops over her, has to support himself with his hand against
the icy road: I forge a thin thread between his eye and that of the
woman, I lean forward, have for years been wearing out his coat
and his hood, tensed his old man's face in front of mine, looked
into this thing that is changing him and nourishing him, for the
second time, now on his tenth birthday. In the emptiness a curiosity is growing; if he had a stick he might perhaps prod the end of

it gently into this thing that is lying huddled up before him, inside him. The narrow spectacles, like lenses of ice in front of his motionless eyes, burn on his heavy head. Neither his brothers nor his sisters, neither his father nor his mother know anything of this. He saw the dark figures from the window, from the warmth in there, he crept out to the darkness and the blinding snow, and now he is leaning forward as if he were being sucked into the dead woman's mouth; he brings his breathing close to her. But the clouds come thrusting forward in the whirling vortices of their invisible magnetic fields, and the landscape is beginning to softly glow. Bushes freeze like crystalline corals, people rise to their feet and look up to the sky at God's threats and signs, the land lies forsaken by warmth and even the sun hides its ice behind driving clouds. Some unknown power is forcing him to his knees. Then from the sleigh he hears the soft clamour, as of newborn puppies; when he gets up, the lightning strikes.

In the hall with the two gently burning oil-lamps and the bracket candlesticks on either side of the tall mirror, the Referring Clerk turns to the two delegates and says: 'Thunder in January?' He looks at the window. Darkness has already fallen, the six wooden pillars are powdered with a string of snow that glows white, with a peculiar brilliance. For a moment he catches a glimpse of himself in the Empire mirror; the men say nothing. He goes over to the window and casts his gaze towards the church, but trees are concealing with violent movements the order and method in nature he is used to, and on the way he sees dark figures and his son rising to his feet and looking at the sky. How has Axel managed to get out there? He is opening his mouth in order to shout when the lightning divides the night, swiftly tears it asunder and cuts a bleeding score in the lime, the memorial tree by the iron gate. The snow is smoking and the heavens are thundering, attacking the earth. Axel raises his arm, stands there, blinded; he calls out but no one hears him, he is his father and beyond him back to some primordial state of being: he has seen the sign and doesn't know what it means; he is lonely. His senses are growing confused. All that is left is a faintly singing tone, as if everything – trees and fields, the woman with the clenched hand and the half-closed eyes, yes, even the wind had been drained of its contents and then quickly filled with an invisible music, like the sap of trees, like the resin in their limbs, like the honey of flowers and the lingering subterranean wells deep in the earth, silvery, alive under the earth's dead shell, the snow and the black sky. As if a requiem had been struck up in his praise: he was alive! And the voices alternated within him, low at first, then rising in indomitable power, only to sink back once again, as the wind sank, at last merely ruffling the dead woman's hair. He was outside himself; later he would experience it in the arch of nerves that is formed by the fingers against the strings of the violin, in his elbow, his shoulder, his chin against the resonating vessel of wood, the movements of his right arm, his wrist, the bow against the strings, the circle closed but at the same time free: a sense of happiness that lasted for one fleeting moment, in darkness and death. He had been waiting for it without knowing it. His mouth is filling with a bitter taste of metal. The woman is lying motionless. 'Wake up!' he shrieks. 'Wake up!' Fields, wind, fear now begin to flow into him and drive out the singing, he turns round and starts to run towards his sister Fanny who takes him in her arms, drags him along with her as if he were a log, a sack, makes heavy work of it and cries out in fear and anger: 'What have you been up to? And on your birthday, too!' Now he knows what it is: he has conjured it up: the woman, the lightning-flash, the vengeance of the heavens; his face closes, his arms dangle deadly, he is borne up the staircase to the entrance door and the kitchen. But when mother holds his head, he whispers: 'There are children, I heard them.' 'Oh, baby, baby,' she whispers back, rocking him in her warm embrace, 'you're my little boy,' and she holds his big, heavy head, pulls the hood off and puts her hand on his thin forehead, against his light, blond hair. The Referring Clerk stands there helplessly; through his head, like well-ordered sparks, flash pieces of conversation about corporal punishment, equal rights, the Empire as a way of life: meaningless abstractions, polished and elegant, disappear in the face of a great uncertainty, as if Axel, his son, had upset a pattern. 'Now, Axel, calm yourself!' But Axel is calm, he is empty, used up and reborn, alone, to a world of unfamiliar faces and mouths: they are speaking to him, but he can't hear what they are saying. 'We didn't see him go out!' Hjalmar says, and the Referring Clerk places one hand on his shoulder, he is one of the regular visitors. Then he turns and goes into the hall where the two delegates are standing like candelabras: some peculiar things are happening here. Those who say that there are ghosts in Haarla are perhaps not entirely wrong. From the kitchen cries are heard: 'Rub them with snow! They're alive!' But once again a fiery chariot of rocks and barrels passes over Bjärnå and Haarla and disappears in black echoes to

13

the south, or perhaps it is rolling down to Strömma. 'While the present circumstances last,' says the Referring Clerk, and the gentlemen take their leave, hurry to force themselves into their ankle-length overcoats, the wind whips the door open and then they are gone into the whirling snow. Sofia carries Axel up to his room, sits with him in her arms, the big boy, his body so small for such a heavy head. As though there were echoes inside him, he senses and listens to and repeats meaningless words, my boy, my big boy who has reached his tenth birthday, and what a lot you have to tell that diary I gave you, haven't you, eh? And those children, they're alive, that's a miracle, isn't it? She rocks him and sings to him, he is filled with sleep and images: the dead woman who is dead no more but is a snow queen, the children who are floating like dandelion puffs. He feels the warmth of summer. There, deep inside, there is a darkness where sounds and tones belong, as in the piano's interior; but the light is too strong, he complains, he feels ill, he can't eat, can't take his clothes off, can't sleep, look, the lightning has struck him: a red stripe on his arm, barely visible. She is singing something in Danish, the words fall soft and red into one another, and then she croons goodnight; have you said goodnight to them all, to Fanny and Hjalmar and Elin and Anna and Olga who left us and Ida Sofia who died; she stops rocking him, leaves him sitting on the bed, he manages with difficulty to take off one of his stockings, indecisive and vacant he continues to rock himself Olga used to come in and just look at him with her bright, cold eyes. He lies down and looks at the ceiling, the wallpaper, the lamp that smells of mercy. He holds his fingertips gently against his temples. There is the note that the landscape contained and that forced its way into him. He hums faintly, but can only imagine the height of the note as it rises and rises into the infinite. There is a thought in his throat, a narrow, burning fork, a whirlwind of snow against the dark. So distant, all of them.

14

From The Diary

1868

16.1

Their eyes are buttons sewn on to their faces and the snow is falling on them. One of the children died of hunger and cold; the cold has lasted over a year, and there has been no summer, no spring and no autumn: nothing but freezing wind. We too have begun to go hungry, but only 'on a small scale', as Mother says. We have had bark that is crumbled and dried and which comes out like clotted blood, all brown. I have now seen four dead people. Father has had the school opened for the refugees and suffered ignominy as a result, but he hasn't taken it badly. People shy like horses when confronted by the dead.

23.2

Mother and Father never smack me, but if they did I would turn into a Bengal Cane. It's too narrow to be smacked, but can give a good smack itself. Kindness is sufficient, says Father, but he says it sternly.

19.3

Now there is light in the sky and spring is coming early to drive away our distress. I am ill in bed and can't sleep, such strange pictures of those faces keep floating by, and they are all trying to tell me something. Then beyond that there is a great music, as of many choirs in an endless church.

24.3

Father's hat has watered silk inside, like the inside of a coffin, and it's prettier than the outside. It smells of jasmine while Mother's tulle hat smells of Héliotrophe. These are spirit-beings, and they accompany our thoughts.

3.6

Now the hot weather is here and people walk as though they were asleep, with pale sweat on their foreheads. I have only grown two centimetres in the past six months. Am I a dwarf? Could I join a circus? Still have trouble seeing as the light dazzles me. Since I cry out at nights I have been given my own room. Hjalmar says I'm a loony. A dim lamp is kept burning in my room, so that if anyone comes in I hear it, silk, homespun, leather, tulle, each with their own sound. This autumn I'm enrolling at the Elementary School in Åbo. So that will be the end of my home on Södra Esplanadgatan.

25.6

Towards evening the birds hide their songs in the thicket, and from them grow radiant flowers, all white and fragrant in the night. The leaves have opened quickly, and the chestnut stands looking like a Christmas tree, only different. In the evenings the horses' hooves echo on the road, I draw one line for every cart that passes. I hear them at night, too.

2.7

The colour blue is that of heaven, but red screams, it is fire. It forced its way into my eye, that kind of thing is a sensitivity, the doctor says. I remember how they lay huddled up piled on top of one another, like tree-trunks. It hurt and still does, and I can't forget it.

16.8

Olga Stierncreutz has come back in order to prepare me for school, but she spends most of her time talking to Hjalmar; they whisper together. To me she keeps saying: 'Speak up!' Then I finally lost my temper and said: 'In our family we honour the proverb "Deeds speak louder than words"', she shut up for a second, but then burst into long and heartfelt laughter: little marmots have claws, too! I saw her teeth when she bared them. When she plays the piano she hits it. Then it hits back. Crop failure – that's what's the matter with me, too.

1.12

I have no friends at school. I have asked Hjalmar for help, he rushes away, runs and leaps and throws snowballs at me.

13.4

I stood in the water and a fish came out and stationed itself there and looked at me as though I were standing underwater, yet only half awake. I didn't dare move in case the water rippled. Then the fish slid away. It wasn't a dream, and I went on screaming. Now I shan't write any more.

1870

February

Read Pinello's *Puff's Almanac*.* Nature inspires the Finnish tenement soldier* to poetry, but the principal voice of the human spirit is music. Best thing in the almanac is the description of a performance of Mozart's *Don Giovanni* at the Stora Teatern in Stockholm. That's where I want to go, away from all this.

4.4

I am going to the Elementary School in Åbo. My Headmaster's name is C J Arrhenius. When he walks past me at morning roll-call he smacks me on the nose with his Bible, I don't know why. He has spectacles like mirrors. The pupils go skating on the River Aura, but the ice has gone now. The classroom smells 1mo) of stoves 2cundo) of kerosene lamps. Hjalmar is here too somewhere, in a higher class. A school orchestra has been formed, and I crept into the hall, but they discovered me and interrogated me so that my spectacles steamed up. I was forced to play the violin on which I have my lessons from Miss Petrelius. We played a piece called 'Evening Cloud as my Sun Goes Down'. They told me to come back again in a year's time. It is Sunday today, so this morning we will walk in a crocodile from the school to the Cathedral. I borrow books from Kurre's Library, they have Topelius, *Robinson Crusoe*, Marryat and a book about J.S. Bach. I don't play him yet, but am looking forward to it. I don't like it when no one will speak to me, but it does happen sometimes. This summer we are moving to Odensnås in Masku, to a tall, yellow house with potted palms on the banisters, and there are a lot of rooms. Hjalmar and I are to get one. I am reading diligently, but my eyes often smart and sometimes I have difficulty in breathing. Last night I dreamt that the lime-trees down by the fishing harbour fell down, and that dwarves climbed up towards the school, all of it by moonlight. I shouted but very quietly in case Father and Mother should wake up and be angry, but they weren't there. All night the dwarfs scrabbled at the outer walls, sharpening their claws, so I couldn't get any sleep, and today I have lain in bed reading, have done my homework in bed, too. When I stick my foot out from under the blanket it looks as though it were severed. Then I fancy that the pain is soothed by the music which I summon forth within me and which resounds there purely, not like in my violin. When I practise scales they all shout: 'Stop that screeching!' They screech themselves. I like Latin best, but mathematics is hardest. I am scared of it and much else besides.

30.5

We have had our spring term exam and the teachers have been wearing dress suits, and we were examined in public, but I wasn't asked any questions; then the orchestra played (Pacius*) and the violins missed their entry in the second movement and came in at least a fourth too low, so that I got painful lights in my eyes during it. Then we all traipsed off to the Hall of Solemnity where there was singing, and the basses roared. The day after tomorrow we are going to take the steamer to Nådendal and then to Odensnås, and I am looking forward to it very much. I won't be so lonely there. There I shall build a leaf-house.

18

JULY 1870

Axel is sitting motionless on the edge of the bed, listening to the happy voices that are mingling with the cry of the swallows in the evening twilight. In the darkness of the room his face glows palely, like a lamp that is misted over. On his left foot there is a sock, on his right there is none; his nightshirt is already damp with sweat. He is sitting with the diary on his knee, but doesn't know how he ought to begin; he presses the pencil against the paper and its point gives way and breaks. Should he try another pencil, or a pen instead? What if the lead's too hard, will it also break? Ought he to put his clothes on again and go downstairs and out into the garden and into the park and play with his ball, and even if the ball gets lost no one will find out? He could, of course, ask Anna for a softer pencil. Should he shout from the window or go down to her? He did say he was ill, after all, and Mother said he ought to go to bed, but now he is well again, almost. It was something to do with the food, the jellied bream whose dead eye looked at him through the gelatine, so that he had to put the knives and forks in a row. The evil spirit vanished at that sign, and the dining-room was lit by a gentle, mellifluous radiance. 'What do you want, then?' Mother asked, but Father said that everyone should eat the same, regardless of age, sex or class. That was the way it ought to be, at least. But the bream lay still on its dish, full of bones. He knew it. He was going to get them all. Ought he to choose the horseradish sauce or the dill sauce? Now the strains of an accordion can be heard coming from the head gardener's cottage, and Axel lets the diary fall without noticing it. Perhaps someone is dancing over there, swaying in time to the music like him, each beat accentuated with a kick that makes the dust come swirling up from the floorboards, rise into the evening light like white, transparent veils and through them he is dancing, his eyes closed, floating with arms that rise and slowly fall again, and they see him, all those silent faces, barely visible in the darkness; but their eyes follow him, light up as he moves, he is transformed, he con-

19

jures the heat and the summer, the flight of the swallows and the water that lies quiet in the bay. And he grows, it gets darker, he is King Fjalar* and he dies, mighty, with outstretched arms, and all the poor people weep and bend their knees before him, and he expires, he yields, he dies, and everyone mourns: nature grows silent, the birds sing no more, all the voices die away, the silence listens to his last breath, and a quiet music leads him into the eternal realm; he lies down with his eyes closed, one leg still swinging a few last times over the edge of the bed, the red sock almost black in the gathering dusk. Then the door opens and Sofia comes in, her white dress rustling. She sits down on the edge of the bed, bows forward and takes her son's sock off, stuffs the naked foot back in under the blanket, gets up, tucks the blanket in, sits down again, but now turned towards him, puts her hand on his forehead and says softly: 'Are you asleep?' He shakes his head. 'Do you want some fruit-juice? Or a glass of water?' He lies silently, not knowing what to reply, everything is difficulty and remoteness, relief and unease, pain and pleasure in each other's presence, and he sits up and throws his arms clingingly around his mother: 'I don't want to go to school any more! I want to stay here!' But she cannot promise that, cannot answer, something heavy, like a shadow or a premonition, is bowing her down over him, she can only say: 'Sleep! Forget the horrible things, remember the nice ones, cherish them! Try, for my sake, Axel.' He says something into the material of her dress, into her warmth, is it 'Help? Help me?' But what is she to answer, she knows nothing of his sorrow and desolation, only that he is weak, an invalid, the last, the most sensitive, the strangest, the most beloved; she guesses her way to the loneliness in him but doesn't understand it: she herself is everywhere, a part of everything, protecting, talking, soothing; as always, she holds his head, as if she were trying to stop his words, not hear them, just sitting here, in the room, for a while, in the evening coolness and seeing the curtain slowly moving and the tops of the trees grow still. She frees herself from him and says, firmly: 'Now you must sleep. I've got other things to do. If there's anything you want, just shout.' She kisses him on the forehead, gets up, closes the door silently after her. He lies motionless, awake, and hears, far away, the unreal booming of a gathering thunderstorm. He huddles up, pulls the quilt over his head, then lies there in the warm, familiar darkness of his anxiety.

From The Diary

1870

26.9

My violin teacher Mr T-nder has thick, fat fingers that move across the strings like worms. He wants me to play 'precisely' but my fear keeps coming up through the bottom of my violin, making me play out of tune; I hear that out-of-tune playing when I am trying to get to sleep. Music cannot live like that. This morning we have a Latin test and I have done a lot of swotting, but am ill because of this sinister thing that gives me migraines and makes it necessary for me to lie still in the dark, where I slowly shrink and grow petrified, so that soon they will be able to add me to the school's collection of stones and then I won't be scorned any more, least of all by my own brothers and sisters. No one, no one must see what I have written here, and whoever does see it will fall down dead on the spot, struck by a beam of light as vengeance!!!

3.10

Kauko came by with the waggon and we set off, via the cemetery where they lie behind the church at Masku and so have shade while other people are getting scorched in the sun. If one looks up, the treetops cross the sky with so many leaves that one can't count them. There, the roof can be seen behind the hill, I feel happy: now I can hide myself away from other people and read in silence and listen to all the sounds the forest has to offer.

23.11

I have a smooth, high forehead and thin hair, and I wear spectacles; so they call me 'old man' or 'Ho-Hum' because I often hum to myself.

4.4

Have not written anything for a long time, since I haven't had anything but misery to relate. I am trying to stay silent in order not to annoy others, and then my pen stays silent, too. I wish I could transform myself and make myself invisible, then I'd show them all! Written by The Avenging Hand. Sealed in solitude with h-s blood.

5.5

My schoolfriends walk up and down outside the Girls' School in order to attract attention. They strut and swagger. This is for the benefit of the seniors, and they chase the younger boys away. I have been in bed with a temperature for a week.

29.8

Now the summer is over, and I have been fishing with Hjalmar and have grown three centimetres. The aunts have been playing duets by Lithander, then only the Magdalena Variations on a theme of Haydn: very pretty. The square piano is called Engelbrecht Norberg and comes from Stockholm, where Father bought it. I am allowed to turn the music. Sometimes I play the violin and practise in the hammock in the forest, but I was found out by Elin. I lost my temper and tore down the hammock. And again the school with its black mouth, waiting to swallow me up.

3.10

It's snowing: the snow is covering all the houses in white, and this morning there's no more school, and the teachers are standing in the empty classrooms looking out of the windows that are covered in snow.

23.12

The Christmas tree is gleaming in the big drawing-room, and everything glitters, and everyone is a different person for a day. I have been given a better violin, it is bigger and I had to play it. They all listened. There is a circle of sound that passes from the fingers of my left hand to the finger of my right, with singing wood in between. It is my life.

31.1

The toe which the hole in my sock cannot hide watches the rest of the sock like an eye. Perhaps they talk to each other like everyone else – or rather – sing to each other. There is a gentle radiance in these things, as if they wanted to get to know me but can't, whereupon they lose their temper and knock against me, so I get covered in bruises. That's a peculiar thought.

16.2

Dreamt I was flying and saw myself quite tiny with an ugly body like that of an insect, was freed from it, and felt light and happy. Expected a catastrophe, but the dream ended, and I lay relieved and not forsaken as I had been in the dream.

21.5

Dr Mullman reminds me of a bumblebee with no honey, making a loud buzzing sound and with a black bag dangling from one hand; he is very fat yet seems to hover, while thin, yellow weaklings such as I move heavily upon earth, only liberated in dreams (see prev. note).

12.7

I have scarcely grown at all this summer. I am fourteen years old, my youngest sister nineteen, Elin twenty-one, Hjalmar twenty-four and Fanny twenty-five. All together we are a hundred and three, that gives us twenty and a bit each. I have six years left. Olga S. has been saying that Hjalmar is going to marry her. She has her hair in a bun. When it's hot I prefer to be in the shade, deep inside the forest where no one can see me. Have read about the great battles and their arrangement, it is strategy that gives courage, and one can plan one's life that way too. (?) Thermopylae and Waterloo are my favourites. Yet not everyone died honourably. It's important to die an honourable death. My promise shall be kept, even though the enemy rings me round on all sides. Then I will fire quickly, with confidence, and lie down to die, as if to sleep and no longer suffer from insomnia. Then I will hear my own oratorio growing louder and louder, even though I can't hear the words, or perhaps just because of that. I am: weak, frequently ill, can't compete, and Dr Mullman says that my nerves are not as strong as they might be at my young age. For that reason my blood is of the thinnest. Many of the items on the meal-table fill me with disgust. I listen to Father, but Mother listens to me. I sit by the Big Rock, fishing and waiting for the steamboat, and then go home. On father's advice I have read Caesar's *De Bello Gallico*, as the school is now to be changed to eight forms. Not only are the hostages piled high in the rivers, but I am also so nauseated by these victims of Caesar's that I find it hard to breathe, as when on cold nights the log fire smokes into the room. I have read about Crusoe. Oh, would I be able to look after myself that well? And have a Man Friday too? My music is secret, and I think a great deal about my cantata in my head, where a glorious female voice sings the first subject (in C minor). My arm has gone to sleep, and I am going to stop here.

2.8

Have been bedridden. It has been warm outside and the trees have been motionless, growing black towards night.

OCTOBER 1872

The autumn sun moves restlessly among the fishing smacks below Pinellan*, and the brown river flows sluggishly past burning trees and the wharves where the women in their white kerchiefs and black dresses haggle over prices in shrill voices and the men in their bowler hats raise glistening fish up towards the light blue sky. It is the recess, but Axel doesn't have to go out into the yard. He has been convalescing; he is pale, he leans his big head on its body that is far too thin for it against the window. People are moving to and fro, as though his thoughts were leading them, now here, now there. He receives a blow on the back and turns round: it is two of his tormenting spirits, sent to harden him. Silence is his weapon, his strategy, his armour, fragile yet still there, like an inner skin. 'Why aren't you outside? What did you say to the teacher? That you're ill again? You're not ill. You're just a coward. You don't dare to go outside in case you get beaten up. Look, he's sweating. Have you lost your voice now, too? You can hardly hear and hardly see, if we so much as point a finger at you you'll fall down. Look how he's shaking. You're a coward and a hypochondriac, that's what everybody says. Say it or we'll beat you up: "I'm a coward and a hypochondriac." Say it again.'

But Axel sinks down against the wall and they get scared, run outside. He can feel the taste of blood in his mouth. As if snow were falling he lies huddled up on the floor with its big, broad wooden boards. There is a square of sunlight that is just about to make his thin hair shimmer. But he is in his darkness, where face after face alternates, says something, shouts something and then changes as though it were being dissolved in water, and their voices swell and grow louder, a chorus of lamentation that makes him press his hands to his ears and close his eyes against the light from the bursting dams. This takes place in the interval of a few burning seconds, he doesn't know where he has been, he gets up staggering and dusts himself down, sits down on the bench. There is complete silence, broken only by the scream of seagulls outside,

25

everyone has either gone home or died, he is the only person left. He looks towards the Cathedral, it is still there. The clock says eleven, strikes with brittle chimes. There is a rumble of feet, a quivering of shouts and cries, a flood is rising, the recess is at an end. With white knuckles he clutches the desk lid, looks with blind eyes towards the door, his heart flutters as it tries to find a way out of the day, out of the light, out of life.

From The Diary

1873

12.2

Dreamt that I stood at the head of an army which consisted of musicians with their instruments. When a trumpet sounded the general fell from his saddle among the enemy, who had formed themselves into a line in the great, wide valley; blood streamed from his mouth. Then from their side a long, intense cello note could be heard, which caused me such great pain that I fell to my knees, and someone also bent my head down against the ground. Unbearable! I thought, but struggled up with all my might, as though I had drowned and was now rising towards the water's surface with an almost blind gaze. Then knelt on my bed with sheet and blankets in a mess, and Anna came running in in her nightdress, they had heard my scream. I was ashamed then and had to write this down. There is nothing I can do about it, just keep silent.

23.4

Another confession, for only in them can we be truly honest, and perhaps this helps when there is no human assisstance to be had. Yesterday I was summoned to a musical soirée at the home of the Misses Montgomery, Charlotta and her sister whose name I've forgotten, who played my accompaniment. I have a horror of playing in public, but Mother went there with me and had told them glowing things about my violin playing in advance; I had begged with tears in my eyes to be spared, but she stood firm. There were mostly ladies in the salon, they sat as though they were at the gardener's house, all squeezed up together, and in between some gentleman in spindle-leg breeches and pince-nez. There were potted palms and a proliferation of chairs, statues and draperies. Miss Montgomery put us in the first row, and I sweated so badly that the room seemed to go dark. I had my violin on my knee and could feel how light it was. Tried to remember the great heroes of famous battles, and how they went to meet the enemy with courage. Miss Montogomery's sister played on a square piano that reminded me of our own (which reassured me a little). *Für Elise* (of course) with great force, so that an icy breath almost rose from the open lid of the piano. Then there was applause, and a gentleman shouted 'Da Capo' and 'Bravissimo' and looked round, the donkey, as though he were trying to take the applause for himself. Then Miss Montgomery got up and said that a gifted son of Baron Carpelan of Odensnäs was now going to play on the violin a solo composition he had written himself. Mother whispered in my ear that I should say what the piece was called, but I felt completely empty, and had death in my heart. I got up and went to the piano hardly seeing a thing, and turned round. There they all were, the faces I had seen in my dream, and they were beginning to dissolve as though in water, and I had to shut my eyes so tight that a beam of light passed through my head. Then I quickly put my violin to my chin and as I did so was seized with rage and terror, had forgotten the name of my composition, could feel that the violin was alive, that it was producing sound, a long, dark sound that demanded more and more of me, in the way a fish-hook demands the entrails of the fish in order to be used again. At first I managed to get out a simple melody on which I was going to play variations, it was a folk melody in a minor key; but it taunted me, it cut towards my inner being, it forced me to expose myself because it was false. Then, Mother told Father afterwards, I was seized by some kind of madness, so that I played faster and faster, more and more wildly, and the music grew agonized and the keys changed like water over faces (sic! my own expression) and got twisted up, and my face twisted too and became a death mask, and the composition could easily have been called 'Death', but certainly not 'When I Walk in the Garden'. The more wildly I played, as though I were trying to hurl a taunt, an expression of contempt towards the gaping faces around me, the livelier my movements became, so that I bent my knees, stamped in time, turned and twisted like a buffoon, kicked my legs out the way people do on country dance-floors. There was a sound like cloth being torn or cats howling, like crazed swarms of bees and the imminent approach of the end of the world; I played myself into darkness and obsession, I grew and conquered, people did not concern me, they could no longer torment me, like a bird I rose from the fire, a prehistoric bird that swallowed everything:

28

people and furniture, antimacassars and smiling geraniums, tore down curtains and velvet draperies, and people ran away screaming and naked and Åbo stood raging in flames. But this happened inside me and inside my eyes, and Mother said that I ended with a terrible, jarring cadence, then stood still and finally rushed out of the room, with her at my heels. It was a scandalous scene and there were shouts of 'Doctor!', and there was Dr Mullman standing in front of me laughing with his big yellow horse-teeth, saying: 'Hypochondria!' And I heard him wheeze in my ear: 'The more you suffer while you're young, the stronger your mind will be!' I was breathing like someone who was drowning, I stood there, on Biskopsgatan I think it was, surrounded by the warmth of a spring evening, I felt a great sense of relief and thought: 'They can say what they want, that's the way I am and I shall bear my destiny!' Mother came running out, and so did Miss Montgomery, and they encircled me with cries and questions, lamentations and laying on of hands, and Mother led me away, and someone came running with the violin in its case, and I tore myself away from Mother, I absolutely had to have silence, complete silence, and I climbed the steps to the cathedral, went in, Mother pulled at me, but I went in, sat down and let the silence flow into me like a great echo. It was twilight under the vault and there was a calm there which had nothing to do with human beings; and it was as if I had finally understood that I possessed no other life than this poor one, which even in its poverty could be great without anyone seeing it, and in its sickness healthy, and in its weakness strong, and that when I complained it was the worst part of me that complained: deep inside I could see, feel and was conscious of my destiny, deeply alone and yet not alone, as though something in me was seeking a final reconciliation and a paradise that I knew existed, in spite of everything, in spite of all the bad things. And I knew that I had something to say, but must suffer, because I had no words, no tones, no creativity with which to say it: I was a servant, one of the lowliest. And they don't see me, they think I'm a child or only half grown-up, and therefore I must keep silent about all this, and I was led away and put to bed with a temperature, as though I were sick. As I write this it is dawn, and I know that in some part of my being I am now invulnerable, even though I may receive many wounds, and they may bleed. But it is quiet, in both town and country, and there are flowers and trees, seas and forests and all that the earth bears, and music which is the greatest tree, embracing heaven.

18.5

I looked at him and told him he ought to stop tormenting me: it was unworthy both of himself and of me, and the advantage of the stronger is self-assumed and cheaply won. Had *he* never been lonely and unhappy? He was so astonished that he turned his back on me and went away; and ever since then I have been left in peace. Why is it that I must be alone when I feel lonely, yet when I'm with others must immediately transform and alter myself and turn away from my loneliness as though it were infected with the plague, that I do not understand.

12.6

The leaves are spreading everywhere now, and in the shadow of the spreading leaves I want to live, dream and work.

1874

31.12

An empty year has run to its end. I have not been living but existing, have read, tried to learn the language of music, but have not penetrated its grammar; it doesn't divulge its secrets to just anyone. Yet I know how music could speak through me. But it defends itself, is silent within me, I myself am silent, act only if I am compelled. Two more years of school, and then freedom, if such a thing exists. Excursions to Runsala, visits to cafés. Have not played in the school orchestra. Spent the summer in solitude, how else? Have studied the oaks, how they spread out, grow, how they move (they are for the most part still: hence the impression of might they give?). High wind is likewise seldom heard in their tops, unlike the poplars and alders which respond and sough at once; so I listen all the more attentively to the oaks. Would like to compose an orchestral work dedicated to those dark trees, those trunks, branches, leaves, with the sap moving through them all, and their striving towards the light only made possible through their bond with the earth and the darkness: how deep are the oak-tree's roots? Perhaps the year hasn't been completely empty after all? Now the snow is drifting over the living and the dead, and in the cemetery we visited today the covering was everywhere the same and the gravestones were powdered with snow.

10.1

Father gave a speech in memory of Alexander Armfelt,* mentioning his impartiality, moderation and honesty. A cold wind made the candles flicker. When my aunts and sisters get up there is a rustling like that of a deciduous forest. Ague, sleeplessness, and in the darkness the two glowing eyes of the stove.

Easter

Home for the weekend had a scene with Father when I was unable to finish my buckwheat porridge and felt violently sick, as though I were a child again. Hjalmar has married Olga, they were sitting at table and Olga noticed me. To overcome my terror. The final exams still lie ahead; I won't come through them alive.

12.5

Wrote my exams at home as my nerves were bad, and have now graduated from Åbo Academy. What if there are others who are born with the photophobia I have, too? Then we shall form the loneliest of brotherhoods.

23.5

The weakness is in Hjalmar too, entering blindly into marriage; he is saved by his lack of solitude. Tried to explain to them the essence and significance of music. Olga made such a noise clattering the dishes in the kitchen at Lilla Odnesnäs where they live that we went out into the lilac bower, where the first green shoots are appearing. Hjalmar gives me kindly looks, from a great distance.

22.6

We watched the snorting locomotive that was leaving for Toijala. A woman fainted. Grand Duke Alex. and Grand Duchess Maria were present incognito, shouts of 'hurrah', flags.

July

All this will disappear, even the most beautiful things alive, whilst nature will continue on her way, unconcerned, past us, paying no heed to the longing we have to hold on to it all. If we could give up our longing, would not the plants and the objects, the fields and the shadows be even dearer to us?

14.9
Nothing can arise out of nothing.

— — —

I still remember the journey to Helsingfors in July, when the imperial couple were greeted with triumphal arches and the flying of flags, when I paid my respects at the Imperial Palace together with my fellow students. Measured entrance. Empress Dagmar waved as we sang 'King Christian'. Great red sun slowly sinking in Tölö Bay, singing from Alphyddan.* Loneliness is sometimes more difficult to bear when one is surrounded by life and movement. Have cut out Martin Wegelius's letter to *Helsingfors Dagblad* from Bayreuth about Wagner. Something turgid, like a fountain of German beer, about his music. A great mass of overflowing emotion. How far will it be able to grow before it bursts like a balloon, or is slaughtered like an overfattened pig?

All this merely observation, not growing inner life.

20.9
Pouring rain. The carriage gets bogged down in mud. The fields and forests suffused with grey light. A throng of peasant carts and staring children outside Masku Church: a funeral? Go up to the dark churchyard where no one is waiting to receive me.

13.10
In Helsingfors I went to Opris and managed to get in, then also to Kapellet, likewise to the music hall and Brunnshussalongen* where I listened to the girls: sparrows for hawks and an eagle or two, this observed by an owl.

20.11
Concert yesterday at the Swedish Theatre at which the moral rearmament enthusiasts whistled and shouted and were then led away from the lewd and shocking depravity of *Die Fledermaus*. This was the music of joy, something that much so-called serious music unfortunately lacks. In all great music a vision that also has room for joy.

7.12
Within the space of a week sister Elin's children Gunnar, John and Ingrid have all died of scarlet fever. Only Ragnar – who asked for pea-soup in a faint voice and got it – survived. Have You only prepared us for death, and not for life, O God? Odensnäs lies in

32

silence, Father's door is locked. Mother is knitting socks more than ever before, has become deafer if such a thing is possible, and no one wants to shout in her ear-trumpet. Father went up from his room to see her just now, but there was nothing but silence.

10.12

Father corrects misprints in the newspapers, which are then gathered into thick bundles and kept in his wardrobe. 'Anyone who spills eats at the little table', Mother said today at dinner, then spilt something and went to sit at the little table; but we found it hard to laugh.

1877

15.1

I am now nineteen and young no more, that's simply all there is to it.

18.3

Dreamed of a forest that was being pillaged, trunk after trunk, and of people who were carrying the trunks amidst burning flames. Their teeth and eyes showed white in this darkness where the heat arose from their own breathing.

21.3

Angry and repulsive, comical and lonely; and how is one to keep one's rage under control when the goal is missing? Feverish, faint and exhausted by months and years of sleeplessness, every year I age ten and understand little of life.

22.3

Perhaps the meaningless also has a meaning, like a pause in our lives, necessary and demanding, the way when the music is beginning I can already hear it, even before it has started. Perhaps the expectant mother has a presentiment of her child's entire life, without knowing it, yet conscious that nothing can be changed. How does Mother see me? As a child. How does Father see me? As an unfortunate accident. And my brothers and sisters? As the silly youngest brother.

28.3
Sleeplessness, death's antechamber.

7.5
Johan Ludvig Runeberg* has died. Grief and sadness and gathering darkness. The motherland in tears! O thousand lakes!

18.5
Conversation at Samppalinna with my classmate X. He told me the most intimate and dirty things, as I did not interest him and he was therefore able to blurt out his confidences to me, and then afterwards make me swear an oath of silence, while he watched me with curiosity. Mustachioed man-about-town. Felt like a drain. Had he any idea how old, indeed prehistoric, and at the same time childish I was? Had he ever tried to observe himself? Or do most people go through life without observing themselves, without any desire to change anything about themselves?

24.5
I remember things that other people call unimportant, and find much that is considered to be important quite the opposite. The images I see are often accompanied by feelings that conflict with them. Thus the most brilliant summer landscape often gives me a sense of the deepest distress and terror, while a storm can give me a feeling of joy. All this is totally fruitless and confusing, and only a steady honest routine for my life can now save me.

31.5.1877

He runs into Hjalmar as he is crossing Trätorget. Student caps are gleaming in the sun, he has a flower in his buttonhole, a Bengal cane in one hand, his eyes are bright and filmy. He takes Axel by the arm. 'Now you're coming with me, we're going to celebrate now. Haven't you got a woman? We've got a room at Börsen.' He is nearly a head taller than Axel. Everyone is wandering about, jostling against clothes and faces, and songs are born suddenly, at street-corners, in the mass of people, in the general restlessness. Hjalmar shouts across the street, Axel keeps to the walls of the buildings as he walks in order not to collide with all the revellers, but gets pulled down, walks arm-in-arm with Hjalmar, the cigar-smoke is rising like the cloud from a steamer. He is being led along rather than walking independently, and the city is shimmering with spring and the day is declining with a sun that is scurrying among the clouds and will soon disappear behind roofs and spires. Has he no programme in front of him? 'Do you want to be a hermit? Do you think you're better than us poor mortals? Still saying nothing?' Hjalmar laughs, his wet lips gleam. 'And Olga?' 'Olga's at Odensnäs and I'm a free man, I'm enjoying myself, don't you know, and with good reason: I now have four sales accounts.' He stops, pokes his walking-stick into Axel's stomach as though he were about to run him through: 'Four! Finest brandy, whisky, sherry, what else? But you – you don't drink, you're not interested, you keep yourself to yourself, you're sufficient unto yourself, brother, brother, what's going to become of you? Do you still play the violin?' But he doesn't wait for an answer, they are pushing their way through the vestibule, there is a hubbub of voices, white tablecloths, laughter, tables so close together that the mass of students is steaming with sweat and revelry, Axel is dragged and shoved forwards, suddenly finds himself sitting next to a woman who is leaning back impetuously as she talks to some-one at the next table; there is a stain on the white arm of her dress, the scent of violets mingles heavily with the smoke, the greasy

35

sunlight that gleams on glasses and bottles. He begins to eat mechanically. The babbling dies away and the Toast to the Motherland is followed by shouts of 'Hurrah!' They get up. Axel drops his table-napkin and looks for it under the table. Someone is slowly crawling by. The Toast to the Memory of the National Bard. The Toast to the Tsar, hear, hear! The Toast to Woman, a sigh, breasts rise and fall, gazes search, kissing of hands, waitresses trying to push their way forward, someone gives a cry, someone is asleep in a corner, someone is being raised aloft on strong arms, songs are being sung, by quartets, solo, out in the garden, in here indoors, someone whispers in Axel's ear but he can't make out the words, a soft mouth, a breath, so caressing, provocative, free and disordered, he looks into her eyes and turns his gaze away. 'Are you shy? I'll cure you! I'll be your sweetheart. Then you'll have a heavy burden to bear'; but she laughs, and he has to join in, the *brännvin* is flowing like fire in his veins and he describes for her, in a tremendously amusing, a tremendous parody of an opera performance gone wrong: the *primadonna*, the conductor, the principal lover, the villain, the orchestra, he leans forward and she laughs! Laughs! Little white pointed teeth. 'You're too amusing for words!' 'Am I now?' 'Carl, do you know this tremendously amusing and gallant man? Is he a baron? Well, hello there! Hjalmar's brother? And how old is the boy? New and fresh and innocent? Does the Baron suppose that I'm innocent?' Punch and coffee, and the flower arrangements like giant eruptions on the ever more soiled table. The rector's address. The rooms, the halls, the corridors, now in light, now growing dark. She turns his face towards her, bites him on the lip, Carl laughs, his starched collar loose, his Adam's apple moving under the pale-grey gooseflesh. Axel begins to sing, it bursts forth: 'Alas, O thou, my mother!' He sings louder and louder, more and more shrilly, the people sitting round him fall silent, the sweat is shining on his forehead, he takes off his student cap, his hair, his hair is in a mess, he can't get enough air, he loosens his collar, pulls and tugs, sees Hjalmar in the doorway, he leaps to his feet, away, out towards his brother, but his eyes have tricked him, he trips over chairs, voices flutter by, the hope of the Motherland, a new era of greatness, the railway, buying and selling, silk and tails, saddle-backs, mouths and eyes, he tries to find his way through the darkness of the hall, sees a stranger stumbling in mirrors and plate-glass windows, there is a staircase, a passage, a silence, the babble like ocean breakers far away, he knocks upon a door, there are two bodies there, trousers unfastened in haste, knees, a shrieking mouth, quickly he staggers back, the door booms shut and the walls collapse on top of him, he tries to shield himself, holds his hands to his face, sinks down on the red carpet, someone is coming, a waitress, her white apron, someone touching his forehead, bending over him: 'Are you ill, sir? Can I help?' And he whispers: 'Yes! I don't feel well.' She supports him, she helps him along, he can vaguely sense her warmth, she opens the door to the men's room, he stands there alone, white tiles, coolness, 'Gaudeamus igitur,' he mumbles, 'hope of Finland', and sees in the mirror the features, the familiar features of death, the white, rigid eye-sockets, the old, unlovely, forsaken, lonely mask, the death-mask, and the water flows cold over his hands, flows and flows, as if it were his blood that had turned pale and was now abandoning him, so that he is drained of everything, all feelings, all life, and merely remains, a jacket and tails, a face-mask, a grotesque white cap on something that blindly, out of empty eye-sockets, beats against the mirror, beats and beats until a wound opens. There is blood, he is alive, he is really alive, he shouts, he sees his mouth shouting, he can't hear anything, and the white lamp on the ceiling high above him goes out, swings, flares up again with intolerable light before at last it slowly fades, until in the darkness there is only a glowing thread, a nerve, a pain, distant, inevitable.

From The Diary

September

Ill all summer. In August visited Dr Berg in Stockholm, who recommended cold rub-downs, fresh air and healthy food, and warned me against masturbation. Met a finely-educated young man there. A ray of light, when the prisoner who has been flung into the dark discovers that friendships can arise. Axel Tamm. So there is still something human left in me, after all.

11.11

Ague; but calm. In my kind of situation what else could I do? My fever makes the room and the objects in it soft. Life becomes distant and tolerable.

14.11

Dreamt that Father and Mother had left a dark room, and that I was looking for them; there was food on the table which had been hastily abandoned. Looked for them in a big hall where old people were sitting, men on the left, women (in kerchiefs) on the right, according to rural custom. Went out into an overgrown garden, where people in light-coloured clothes were moving away, but I realized that they were all dead. Looked for Father and Mother but could not find them. When I turned round a tall, dark man was standing with a raised axe. I looked up at him and understood, and woke up at the very moment the axe was about to fall.

3.12

They go dressed in rags and dirt, which out of necessity they scrape off themselves in the sauna on Saturdays. Was offered a round loaf soaked in water or blue-milk. Their flower is the nettle-flower which grows everywhere. The old are broken by resignation and illness, the young have hatred in their eyes under the obedience. I feel it and understand it. I don't belong with them, but don't belong with my own people, either. I could join the company of the travelling people who move along the country roads with their squeaking carts, and then quickly go to my doom. I haven't even the strength for that. Just daydreams.

1878

15.1

On my twenty-first birthday I remember the young Wolfgang: 'Little Wolfgang has no time to write because he has nothing to do. He wanders up and down the room like a dog with fleas.' Yet that dog created a paradise. He has taught me another piece of wisdom, too: 'It is my habit to deal with people as I find them: that is the most productive way in the long run.'

23.2

Father says, apropos of our country's development and future wealth: 'Even if they are allowed to do with their forests as they please, they ought to remember that the forest too has its morality, which is to live for the generations to come, protected in the same way that it protects the landscape with its beauty; a modest thinning is what is required.' I ponder the expression: 'a modest thinning'.

4.4

The violin. Animal sinews forced to labour, and to utter shrieked protests.

Whitsun

Enrapturement's time. It is not ascent but submersion. Schubert's *Death and the Maiden*, the slow movement: not ascent, not resignation, dilation, wide expanses. There is still light even after the sunlight has taken its leave. In its very leave-taking: light. Not the lightning-bolt variety, which destroys, but the light of suffering and hope. Is the finale a contradiction of this fervent calm? Perhaps only a confirmation of the wholeness that is: acceptance of life.

18.5

Around Alexander Square horses like a mahogany frame, passing water in such ample volume that there cannot possibly be any fires while the voluntary fire-brigade holds its celebrations; creeping over the tableau, already soot-black ladies and gentlemen like fly-specks, parasols and brass-band music like the smoke from a conflagration. Fat, slow clouds hanging over it all...

9.6
Not a single star in the sky, not a single guiding star, no matter how hard I look. So life goes on, making me old before my time. Most foods are repugnant to me. Letter from A.T.; a beacon. Viktor Rydberg.*

September
One more summer gone – where? Watched the pair of swans that are returning to the bay, their loyalty, their contemptuous view of all that lies outside their circle. So: be careful of life, it can hurt you. Resign yourself! Be a stranger; then perhaps you will be able to bear your fate. Empty words.

24.10
The old do not change, they are simply – old. The sanctity of the law, the triumph of justice, the well-being of the motherland, loyalty and honesty, the keeping of a promise. Being punctual. Order and method. I must get rid of the last vestiges of slackness within myself. But there is one thing I cannot get rid of: music. So the (passionate), unpredictable, disordered, passionate still remains, in notes and scores, and in the violin, that tortured creature. The 'old' music ought to be *read*!

6.11
This must become the diary of my inner life; I must endeavour to avoid non-essentials and not be afraid to have my own philosophy, even though it be a childish one. It must be my wailing wall, but there close by will be my cathedral, the one I myself must build, even though it may subsequently lean askew or grow as confused as life itself.

1879

6.6
The whole of my life has been filled with falling snow and

ice-cold wind, and streets, towns, roads, all things have been drowned in snow and cold from which there is no escape. The warm lights on New Year's Day, the bright voices, and I an icicle.

February
Nothing to write, nothing, nothing.

23.5
Summer has come like an avalanche of miraculous warmth and sudden verdure, the lilacs bear large buds! The cough-weed is already in flower, the bird-cherry is wafting its scent, the grass has spread everywhere. Was seized by a great sense of happiness on my way down to the landing-stage, and then without paying any attention to where I was, performed a triumphal dance, emitting shouts and swinging my arms, as in a Red Indian story-book I finished recently. It is a war-dance or a sorcerer's dance or perhaps a dance of joy, in a sort of radiant dream, and surrounded by warmth. Then, exhausted, I see Olga standing beside the bathtub at Lilla Odensnäs and looking at me as though I were a madman. She says nothing, the eldest boy's back shines, he is crying gently and pitifully. I pull myself together and go away, whistling. Can feel her eyes in my back.

10.6
Was walking past Aningaisgatan, heard singing – it was half-past six in the evening – recognized a voice, stopped: on the veranda behind the lilac bushes with their glorious blooms a company sat carousing, among them Hjalmar, and his happy, lively voice struck up 'By a Spring'; and how his joy and the sorrow the poem gives utterance to and the scent of the lilacs and the smell of leather from the tannery close by mingled together and seemed perfectly natural, so that high was not high, low was not low, heavy was not heavy, light was not light, but all was a part of the same pattern, however much it changed. Thought of Olga with her children in the country, and it struck me that the innermost, secret kernel of this age is concealment. The body is concealed by a lot of fabrics and starched shirt-fronts, collars, shawls; furniture is concealed by antimacassars, lace; the poor are concealed by the rich by means of the rich people's politics, and emptiness is concealed by rituals, regalia, awards; finally naked power is concealed by uniforms, and all perspective by objects, bric-à-brac, pedestals. Even in music the real kernel can be concealed by external decora-

41

tions; that is even more the case when it is merely a void that has to be filled, by happy singing. Having embarked on such deep thoughts, I silently walked away from Hjalmar's home and garden.

14.7

I grow and shrink at irregular intervals. I am reading: Goethe (*Werther!*), Rydberg (*Singoalla*), Scott (*Ivanhoe*). I am drawn back to my childhood, when I see my leaf-house, now not a house at all, only a leafless skeleton, and feel like building a new one, as really very little in my external circumstances has changed.

18.7

Leaf-house finished. In an even better place than before. My sisters stroll right past it, prattling away, and the summer shines. I go deep into the forest, play the violin there. Perhaps my playing could have a future, if only I had the strength to show what I'm capable of doing, what I want to do, in which direction I want to go. In which direction *do* I want to go? That's the crux of the matter. To become someone when one is many people all pulling in different directions, despising one another. And don't I conceal my inner growth, or is it just that they don't see it; but one day they will see it, like a mighty Sunflower that is rising out of suffering!

23.7

In the library, in front of Father, Mother, my brothers and sisters and aunts, I did an impression of a concert which my violin teacher conducted, and they folded up with laughter, while I, at the same time as I was showing off, saw myself showing off, and overdid it to such an extent that in the end Father said: 'Enough!' And I recognized the intonation. Afterwards I lay on my bed and of course did not get to sleep until daybreak; listened to the cries of birds and the wind in the trees and felt that there is no silence on this earth; yet it might be worse if all our concealed pain were formed into plaints and cries, as with the birds. One wouldn't be able to live without earplugs then.

27.7

As if the children understood that I'm an old man disguised as a youthful student: they go quiet, laugh behind their hands, throw stones and disappear laughing and shouting into the undergrowth. Their bare feet covered in mud, shreds of clothing, swift and supple in the art of survival. And in the hot air with the rank and poor tang of nettles – cat-like creatures, silent and lurking; suddenly wild battles, and the animals crying like children in fear; until a woman, ageless, in a shawl, uttering curses from ancient times, chases the combatants away with a broom. In all this there is much earth, mud, gravel, stone, seed, diluted milk and *brännvin*. When one enters there is a smell of babies, sweet and penetrating, and the flies go crazy; on the long bench the pail of water covered with a cloth, and up in the rafters, on sticks, round loaves like stunted cartwheels for sharpening one's teeth on; but most of them have few teeth, and those they have are black. In the heat some of them are asleep on the sofa bed, and the sleep-drunken sun moves slowly across the worn and shining tiles of the floor. It is only the very young and the very old who stay in during the day, all the others are out in the fields, or in the cowshed. In all this there is a stillness which the town smothers. Had I the physical strength, I would be happier here, where I can conceal that I do nothing and am nothing, except that which is concealed from everyone.

10.9

Viktor Rydberg possesses a great consoling strength. He struggles with his suffering which is the suffering of all. The Flying Dutchman! And there is in him, too, a childlike, innocent essence that strengthens and deepens what is radical in him: a being that listens to the voice of an inner morality. One senses a great openness in his poems. Thus he gives me strength for the future. A.T. agrees with me about this. The liberation of the tormented individual!

20.12

When there's a draught in the stoves their doors rattle with excitement. Magdalena and Carolina are sitting motionless in the library, each with a book on her knee, asleep. Mother is talking to Father in the bedroom, suddenly she laughs. I don't know if that has any significance, but perhaps any image of time stopping is significant, as in photographs that quickly fade and shrivel up in the flames and turn black, like memories.

1880

1.1

On the first day of the year I can confirm that I have my centre of gravity in the wrong place: it is situated in my head, not in my back. That's why I stumble so often, and why the lower part of me is weak and poorly developed. But occasionally I move this centre of gravity, so that at some times I'm standing on my head, and at others on my feet, and lean violently to one side, now to the right, now to the left. If anyone tries to touch me I bend over to one side, if anyone tries to hit me I lean violently backward, tears start to my eyes and it is I who feel both humiliated and the cause of the whole thing. If anyone boasts, I feel a sense of personal anguish, as though I'd been giving myself airs. But most of these imbalances can't be seen from the outside; when I stand on my head, I do it solely for myself. My body has increasingly grown accustomed to not showing on the surface what is going on inside. In that way my body betrays me by constantly giving a false impression. Yet if I had no centre of gravity at all, how would I be able to live and move through rooms, and talk, read, play? How do people who have no centre of gravity manage to live? They do it by not being conscious of their loss.

4.3

The Sunday quiet ghost-like after unprecedented festivities on Friday to mark the occasion of Alex. II's 25th jubilee as Regent. Åbo in an intoxicated fever of flags, rich and poor in the same delirium, parties and dinners, the Phoenix lit up like some rich madam of a brothel, all evening the stink of gas-oil from the Voluntary Fire-Brigade's burning torches, from Sampalinna a 101-gun salute, the shots aimed at the sky for the time being, the scraping of feet in church and other holy places, cries of hurrah from patriotic shirt-fronts, tableaux and privately-written plays in which the ladies can show off their *toilettes*; champagne and cognac, producing the same headache, irrespective of social rank. A transparent banner had fallen down on to Auragatan, putting the traffic in total disarray; horrible natural sounds from the Fire Chief's horse mingled with the shouts of hurrah for the Tsar, at which point the horse grew wild and started to kick, a healthy reaction in itself. Highly-placed persons, gaped at by the mob, were seen staggering into their carriages after the patriotic display, making abusive remarks; the whiter their shirts, the dirtier after-

44

wards. Slept in the pantry at Hjalmar's house; he returned late and tired. More shouting even after it was dark, but no more greetings to His Majesty. The Grand Duchy of Finland is asleep.

4.4

Into me now and then flows healing, soothing music; nothing flows out of me, and my beloved violin rests silently on my chin or speaks, indistinctly, falsely and stumblingly, whereas my inner voice is clear, seeing and passionate. Of that which fills the heart the mouth speaks crookedly. That is the worst kind of loneliness.

20.5

Remember as I lie awake how as a three-year-old, with Father and Mother, I saw the Esplanade lit up for the first time by gaslamps. They even cast their strong light into our house on Södra Esplanadgatan. Poor Wecksell* used to come on visits, as one of his friends had board and lodging with us. Now it is light and merciless spring, which hollows out my eyes and paralyses me.

3.7

As I was lying on the shore I saw the clouds suddenly grow still while the earth continued its movement that was making me dizzy, and it seemed to me as though I fell into eternity accompanied only by the cries of birds and the wind's vague movements in the trees. Oh, if only that had been so.

4.7

Inwardly created for friendship and altruism, I have been branded with solitude's mark of Cain. Derision, contempt encountered at school, facetious indifference from my brothers and sisters, yet not always. What it is that irritates them isn't easy to see, but it must be the mark of Cain that frightens them, and my defencelessness.

5.7

Perhaps I will find myself in what I am writing here, in my secret book? Perhaps the last line will become an answer to the first question, and if it doesn't, even that will be an answer: that my life can't be summed up for as long as there is a heap of debris at which someone else may be able to warm themselves. I'm jumping the gun a little, however. Yet I have a premonition that everything is going to continue the way it is now. I am paralysed by nerves,

45

tormented by shyness, and when I strain myself I collapse. The letters to and from Stockholm help.

20.8
Have been ill in bed with severe headache, curtains drawn. In order to survive I must live in darkness with all sounds muffled.

5.10
At the soirée met a Miss H. who invited me to her home for tea; warm and friendly, young and radiant, her father a businessman. If only my life could now take a new and brighter turning.

7.10.1880

Axel comes down the staircase from the attic where he has been
practising the violin. Hjalmar meets him in the hallway: 'Ill again?'
But Axel shakes his head. He dusts himself down and adjusts his
bow-tie in the mirror. It is time to be off. Hjalmar thumps him
on the back: 'Good luck, Don Juan!' In the gloom his features are
luminous – tense and unreal. He nearly forgets to take the violin
with him. Hjalmar hands it to him, smiling: 'Bring light to their
simple souls, as you bring it to mine.' It is damp and still, the
dusk is softening the town, and the trees are glowing yellow. He
crosses the Cathedral Bridge and looks up at the clock, stops and
sets the pocket-watch he received on his birthday: yes, it is time.
On the stairway, which smells of floor-polish, he stops and draws
a breath. Is it the watch or his heart that is ticking with such brittle
haste? Someone is practising the piano, possibly in the Holm-
ströms' flat, perhaps it is Greta herself – Czerny. It is she who
opens the door to him; her large, brown eyes look so gently into
his, he kisses her hand quickly and self-consciously, bows to her
mother and father who are standing to attention in the sitting-
room. There is a warm scent of fresh baking, and a canary is
twittering in a cage. Would the Herr Baron care to be seated in
our humble home? Axel clears his throat and exclaims admiringly
at the painting that hangs above the Gustavian sofa: a moonlit
landscape of wild forest and rapids, reminiscent of Marcus Larsson.
Director Holmström says he finds it quite interesting, while Mrs
Holmström imparts the information that it is a copy. Miss Greta
has her eyes on Axel, but he is looking at the silver plate, a decanter
of madeira; oh, it is familiar to him – why is it all so familiar to
him, why this feeling of sympathy and loneliness precisely now?
He talks, makes conversation, tells stories about his estate, it suddenly assumes exaggerated proportions. Director Holmström
talks about the upturn in the textile trade, about Finland's future,
about the newly-opened factories, ever-swifter communications,
about the green gold of the forests and the power of the rapids,

47

and Mrs Holmström inquires if the Herr Baron would not care for a little more? It is all exquisitely delicious, Axel replies, but he is satisfied – not only that, but overwhelmingly content, if he may say so; but Miss Greta's eyes are radiant. It is something about Axel's collar, which is too tight, or perhaps the room is too hot; a magnificent shawl with embroidered roses on it has been spread out on the grand piano; 'Oh! of course the Baron plays the violin, you promised to play for us, Greta told us about it, to us music is the elixir of life'; and Gottfrid Holmström adds that for him Bach is one of the finest representatives of the old, honourable kind of music – not long ago he attended a Bach organ recital in the cathedral. 'Yes, he's a builder of cathedrals', Axel says, and Gottfrid Holmström finds that interesting, he wishes that some of the new stately homes that are sprouting from the earth like mushrooms could have been built by Bach and not by building contractors with no sense of style, even though the house in which they are now sitting is not one of the ugliest, but has qualities that do not always demonstrate themselves in terms of façade and ornamentation, but rather in the height and vastness of the rooms, and in their joint proportions. They make a viewing-tour of the library, the study, they walk past bedrooms. Axel obtains a quick glimpse of the kitchen regions, where a housemaid in white curtseys and disappears; even the floors of the passageways are inlaid with parquetry. But of course it's not like living in a manor-house out in the country, is it? Now Greta raises the cry that Axel must be allowed to play – 'We've been waiting for him to' – she runs to fetch the violin and hands the case to Axel, and he takes his beloved instrument from its red velvet box with trembling hands. Greta asks what music he is going to play from, but Axel shakes his head. 'Oh! He plays from memory!' Yes, Axel plays from memory. He leans his head heavily on the violin, tests the strings and tunes them; the pegs squeak, from the staircase comes a dog's loud barking and the sound of a door banging. They sit watching him, as though the music had already begun, materialized, taken shape in him, Axel, his glasses slightly misted-up again, Fru Helene is already nodding in time to a soundless melody; Axel closes his eyes, the chaconne flows jerkily, tentatively out into the room. Axel is struggling with enormous shadows, they tower up, scatter in glimpses and flashes, the bow weighs heavily in his hand, Bach is dumb, he wanders onward, blind, deaf and dumb, or is that Axel standing there playing, poor man, for a copper coin and a cup of coffee? . . . tries to build a cathedral, but it hardly amounts to a dwelling-house, only a hovel, an outbuilding perhaps; blasphemous thoughts pass like lightning through Axel's heavy head, sweat breaks out on his steep, bare forehead... the curtains will soon catch fire, a wind will get up and whip all the cakes, plates, decanters, the entire universe, into a lofty, whirling autumnal dance; and what is the bow doing, is it trying to burn like a magic wand among things that are safe and secure, among flowers and vases, palms and pier-glasses? What is this music trying to do? Create a new, even more progressive Finland, weave a skein of textile from township to township, person to person, furniture-suite to furniture-suite? The grand piano stands speechless with its gaping lid, in which Axel's already balding pate is mirrored like an eggshell in a sea of tar, behind his closed eyes tears are gathering, even Miss Greta has tears in her eyes, and her mother Helene is furtively dabbing her face with a small lace handkerchief she keeps up her sleeve. He brings his performance to a close, almost on the point of fainting, he has done violence to himself with the music, he is desperate; but they gather round him, thank him, and Director Holmström says: 'Excellent, quite excellent, a real achievement – but hardly a lucrative profession, eh?' 'Papa!' cries Miss Greta. 'Axel owns a manor-house and an estate, he's a Baron!' There is an embarrassed silence during which Axel notices one of his headaches coming on; he has to rest palely on the sofa, no, Axel mustn't move, the exertion has been too great for him, Axel has taken too much out of himself! For our sake! But it is Axel who feels ashamed, he has deceived them, he is unable to tell them about it, he has betrayed both them and the music, he is nothing, a sham, a clown, an impostor, soon he is sitting up and managing to stammer out that he thinks it best he should go home. They are full of solicitude, he looks at them with unseeing eyes: all their warmth, all that he is has observed and judged with irony, what right does he have to judge them? With their bare hands they have created a home, a life, an atmosphere of security. And he – that he should be able to take Greta away from all this, and give her – what? Axel is shrinking inwardly, at the last moment he succeeds in making a joke out of it, 'I am one of those textiles Director Holmström would never be able to approve for sale, my fabric is neither strong nor unshrinkable', and Gottfrid Holmström laughs, with his round, good-natured face, but Greta is silent, her brown eyes are full of sorrow as he takes his leave, as if she knows that he will not come back to renew their acquaintance, he would so much like to put his arms round her, warm her, protect her, but he has nothing to give, only a kiss on the hand; he gropes his way downstairs like one intoxicated, holding his violin in a lifeless grasp; the door slams shut like a stone coffin-lid.

Outside the gentle gas-lamps are already lit, and the mist is making footsteps and voices sound remote. He doesn't really know where he is going, there are no roads, no directions, only a strange town shrouded in soft mist; and the river gliding motionlessly by, its water almost black. The old, yellow houses – he peers into them, somewhere a room is lit up, two people are sitting at their evening meal as if it were the holy sacrament; he notices that it has been raining, that the paving-stones are glistening, and he makes his way down to the river. There there is no one, no one to demand what he cannot give. Now he knows. He can build no cathedrals, cannot even express their shadows, cannot make the music speak. He sits on a bench. It is cool, a wind is moving through the trees and wet leaves are falling around him. He opens the case, looks at his violin; it is not an expensive one, but very ordinary, so dark, like a burnt-out corpse in its coffin; it has a long, narrow neck, no head at all, in other hands it would be able to sing, to take wing into space, to build cathedrals, to give solace and joy, but not in his; it rests there so silently, no more than a shell here on this bench beside the river. Protectively he spreads the velvet cover with its gold embroidery in the shape of a treble clef over the weightless body and closes the lid, stands, he knows not how, on the lowest step of the landing-stage, pushes the black vessel out on to the water; for a moment it seems as though he too is about to fall into that darkness, that coolness, then he kneels down and watches it float away, surprisingly far, until it sinks beneath the surface and there is nothing, no eddying, only the silent water flowing by and himself leaning back against the wet landing-stage with his eyes closed, feeling how cool, how lonely the world is, and experiencing a great sense of relief.

From The Diary

1881

15.1
Born, to what kind of life?

2.2
It was Hjalmar who found me and led me away or home. Explained that the violin got lost when I had an attack of my illness. Best that way. Lonely.

4.2
Loneliness; offensive. In insomnia the larynx tries to follow a rising scale that constantly repeats itself at a higher register; like a needle being slowly forced into one's temple.

5.2
Solace: that something is formed, rhythmically, out of the poorest material.

8.2
Do I hear the music I imagine? Or is it silent, since it can't be written down?

23.2
Must write this down. The horrors of school whirling by. Am taking the preliminary exams, beaten by pointer on hands that are bleeding, can't go on, the classroom dark, icy cold, have to stand up in front of the class, the animal faces, the wolf-grins, the bleating, the mooing, the neighing, I clamp my mouth shut but a big white bubble comes out of it, expands, bursts, I wake up bathed in sweat.

7.3

Freezing wind, out for the first time in ages. The Swedish Theatre is on fire, Åbo Voluntary Fire-Brigade are performing the folk comedy *The Hosepipes*, the commerce on the square continues, white snow, soot-black people. This world will be bargained away in flames.

14.3

Tsar Alexander II killed by assassins' bombs, his legs torn off, the country has lost a pillar and the darkness is settling in.

15.3

Appears every night with holes instead of the eyes he has lost. Rather stout, obliging, large hands which are every bit as white as flour take my pulse and press my head back until, my neck almost broken, I see a black sky. 'You haven't any pulse.' He shoves me away, departs in contempt, can be seen far away by the door in the dark room, and the windows are completely white, burning in my eyes. Pain.

2.4

How hard people are growing, yet I'm still defenceless. So is Hjalmar – though in a different way. Something vegetating, empty; with me, on the other hand, it's waiting!

22.10

To organize my pens, paper, effects, clothes, furniture in such a way as to build up a front-line against the days of wrath. Contact with objects that are indifferent is what is painful. A faint glow in the dark, whether from the stove or from something else I'm not sure.

December

Mother usually reads to me, Cooper or Fritz Reuter. This evening Father did it, making pauses and clearing his throat, when he sounded like a corncrake, but a completely heart-shaped one. The words say something but indistinctly, the music rises towards the heights but I can't capture it: my oratorio! The *Dies irae* as an everyday occurrence. Am I not sufficiently empty as it is?

15.1

24 years since my birth, and look: the ageing in life's cracked mirror is held up to my near-sighted eyes. God's creation! The rich years! And all the blows that have been aimed at me haven't hardened me at all, but have made me insecure, confused, and withered me away. Whoever attacks me sees my weak spots and comes back again. Getting used to that makes me completely alone.

23.2

Mother got me the score of Schubert's B major Trio, the slow movement of which says farewell, radiantly and painfully, always farewell; and there is in it a necessary poverty, it has a purity that goes well with my room, with the bed, the chair, the table, and not much else except twilight and long, sleepless nights; 14 years ago struck by lightning and pierced by death. And yet: the dream of paradise! The finale with a great, overwhelming desire for things to go well and a burning faith, which I don't possess. And everything locked in, unused, unexpressed, like the child paralysed with terror in a locked cupboard.

June

Like a shadow wandering through the streets. There was the graduation ceremony – the hum of voices, sunshine and happiness. I met Miss H. in Alexandersgatan and saw her young, radiant features, withdrew to one side, and she was passing on a young man's arm, saw me but didn't say hello, looked me in the eye but didn't say hello, then turned her head away as one does when faced with something ugly, offensive or contemptible. Sat in my room doing nothing. Am writing this and don't know what it means. Slight giddiness.

23.7.1882

Eternity... eternity, merely repetitions, the grass grinding its small knives, soaking his trouser-legs with its hidden dew, the sun rising over the bay as it had done since he was born and would continue to do after he was dead... and clear, echoing axe-blows brought forth a new era of miracles, forests that turned into paper, mighty bridges that connected country to country, blast-furnaces swallowing up whole areas of the country, and always the smell of something fermenting... a brewery perhaps, a river of mash finding its way without resistance through rock and gravel... and the spies, the informers, the disguised enemies of the people in small innocent towns where jasmine and violets bloomed and one could scarcely hear the sea rising... the rustle of silk, stockings against stockings, the blinds drawn down... between the crenellated stone houses with their balconies supported by blind giants, wooden houses with grimy windows in which a cold dawn glimmered; they had hoisted the jubilee flags, the triumphal arches, ships steered past with black smoke – were they burning wood or coal, human beings or animals? – he stumbled onwards, out towards the road across the fields, down to the shore, predatory seagulls screamed loudly towards the land, the smell of mud and sun-warmed waters enveloped him like invisible clouds in childhood and wordless seeing, who was that walking there under the leaves, was it one of the farm foreman's children, what was she doing up so early, curtseyed, stood still, he hurried by with pounding heart, would she give him away, were there in the wood, in the thicket several pairs of eyes observing him, the trees bending suddenly and straightening as he walked past, and the water silvery ... the white light that flowed in through the blinds at the window and woke him, the white light that flowed out like water from invisible sources, the untouched white light of a morning in the hall when the clock struck short, distinct chimes, cut grooves in his skin so he could count the years, and inside, in the casing, some decayed forefather, the general, perhaps, observing him where he sat, motionless, merely a body. Above the treetops he saw a narrow, white cloud, it also white, an arrow-tip. He took the road along the shore, inside the bay there was a smell of dead fish, the bream had come flowing in, the Referring Clerk had entered them in the ledger, the cart had not been able to reach them, the men leapt out into the water, there was a splash of light, a flailing, boiling mass of dying fish, now all was quiet, only here and there among the reeds – how had they managed to get so far on to dry land? – half-rotted fish, scales on the surface of the water, the dawn cold and all of it inside his head, landscape and ditches, roads and trees, rocks and thickets, he ran through them, panting he looked out over the bay, out towards Merimasku Sound, could have thrown himself over, was unable to throw himself over, an insect, or a stone thrown by someone, God, perhaps? down into nothingness... Last night the dream about the lightning again as from an infinitely dark distance, like a ball or a pupil, hurrying towards him, and he takes a step back into a bubbling marsh, someone is holding his feet as in a quiet but immovable vice, it is God the Invisible holding him like that, he is one of His unwanted children, he bends out of the way in order to avoid being struck, but the teacher's ruler lands painfully across his knuckles, he has nothing to say to that, he who seeks liberation must be punished, and Axel stays in after class, he stays, he goes, he begins to run through the wood, over the moss, rough at first then as he gets near the dell softer and softer, he sinks into it, the moss, it contains dampness and oblivion, his hands are quite intact, after all, he can push them in deep towards the ground, he is a vessel filled with brown marsh-water, he totters back, frightens a grouse, with booming wing-beats it tugs his heart from his body, he remains there standing, quivering, he is almost awake, while terror fills him his ear listens to the rhythm, the whistling, a swiftly-departing roar, then suddenly silence, as though all movement had suddenly ceased, hammer-blows, wheels and shovels, pistons and streaming water... He is standing in a streak of light among the trees, his linen jacket is glowing there and the youngest child can lead him home... it must be autumn now, or winter, they are like each other, the same great empty sails unfold and boom towards the rocks, suddenly the people have abandoned farms and fields, they are running like ants over the great squares, he sits in the grass and shuts his eyes: 'Dear God, let me live, dear God... let me have the peace... that passeth all understanding... I have no under-standing... I am too young for all this...' He strokes a wet, earth-scented hand over his forehead, feels the fragile bone enclosing the roving, wandering, worn-out thoughts ... eternity, merely repetitions, like a simple theme played over and over again and groped after dejectedly on an out-of-tune piano ... everything stunted, the dream of the stunted world, tight as the twisted sheets on a bed without sleep ... it's going to be a warm day, each and every one is going to their tasks, people are born and die, grass grows and cows die ... he looks at his feet, the felt slippers disintegrated, clinging, like fetters ... he scrapes them off against a tree, leaves them there, goes out on to the road barefoot, sees the farmhouse, tries to take a shortcut across the field, slips, reaches the ditch but can't get over it, has to take the road past little Odensnäs, where Hjalmar is sitting in the arbour, it's summer, it's summer, after all, Hjalmar is there beckoning to him, stretches his arm out to Axel, but there is something wrong somewhere, it is getting dark, the plaster is falling from the house-walls, it will soon be more than he can bear, the trees are positively dark-green and are getting darker and darker, yes, Hjalmar is dead, it's only his eyes that are studying him out of his white head that is glowing so horribly that he wants to press it against him, hide it, protect it, warm it so it might speak to him again ... he jerks his arm away but Hjalmar supports him again, makes him sit down, there is a glass and a crystal carafe, and something burning runs down his gullet. Olga is standing there looking at them, children can be glimpsed behind her, round faces, pigtails, scrofulous knees, young children, he would like some children like those, he opens his eyes wide ... 'Ah, so the marmot has burrowed its way out of its hole ...' He turns round but there is no one there, no one at all, says: 'There's no one there', and she: 'He's mad, stark staring mad, get him out of here!' and he gets up obediently, it is very early, he hasn't had enough sleep, Hjalmar is there and helps him, he looks at his brother in surprise, his face inclined, heavy with sorrow: she never speaks directly to me, and he: 'Cheer up.' Hens are strutting about and a cockerel crows angrily and challengingly. 'I'm such a failure', he mumbles, but that too is without content, his mouth empty, his spirit flown away, 'The little spirit flew up to heaven!' he mumbles, the mumbling marmot, there's a tune for it, he puts his hand to his face and tries to brush away the cobweb that has caught on it, he stands up and Hjalmar is unable to set him off balance. I don't exist. I don't exist. I don't exist. He is agitated now, has to take Hjalmar's arm, there is Anna running, the aunts are standing there, the whole reception committee, he goes up to them, shakes his brother off, says: 'What a nice morning, I've been out to Big Rock, Big Rock, a very big rock!' and goes past them and up the staircase, inside it is silent, as silent as he is silent, he must walk silently so as not to wake those who are sleeping, sleeping and sleeping, and have been doing so for such a long time. He opens the door very softly, he goes to bed very softly, he can look after himself, he doesn't need anyone and no one needs him, he is quits, he smiles, lies there and smiles, he is waiting for no one, yes, they're all going to die nevertheless, all of them, just as lonely as when they arrived, they come up the staircases, hesitate behind doors, it doesn't affect him for he is invisible, yes, completely invisible, he pulls the blanket over his head, voices and birds grow distant, finally die away; when he wakes up he has forgotten it all, 'useless stuff', as he calls it, more of my muddle-headed dreams, his mouth says, and they turn away, don't want to talk about it, what is there to talk about? He appeals to Hjalmar, and Hjalmar stays silent. Hjalmar hasn't seen anything. And Axel himself? He has merely slept, been exhausted, dreamt, like some hibernating creature, he nods his head, but everyone is sitting in silence and he doesn't know whether it is in acknowledgement or whether it means he is an outcast; at any rate, he has his own room, and there he sits, there he is left alone, there no one goes near him, there he is, if he is there, yes, there he is, he can see in the mirror that there is someone sitting there looking at him, a very long way away, but not so far away that he won't ever be able to reach him, perhaps not in his own room but in some other room, perhaps in the room next door, when it falls vacant.

From The Diary

1882

October
Cold soothing autumn, which is taking place outside

Trying inwardly to listen to music in which the individual speaks
to me, as in Mozart, Beethoven; but there are some who are not
at home, like Berlioz

29.10
Sister Elin has married Fredrik Färling. Was present at the wedding.

Oboe, bassoon and shawm pursued me in my dream, and I danced
a grotesque dance to them, with movements that set my limbs
free so that they were scattered far and wide with smoke and
flames.

4.11
Deepest vulnerability, frozen by winter; I don't move about at all.
Piles of scores: if they could all give voice at once, what a cacophony
there would be – even I might be woken up.

15.12
Thirty years ago Ingelius wrote to Cygnaeus* that in Åbo 'poetic
thinness increases in direct proportion to bourgeois fatness.' He
dreamt of a poetic calendar, I dream of a musical one.

18.12
Extreme irritability, went to Dr B, feared for my sanity, attacks
of weeping in the silence, insomnia, asked for a sedative, he looked
at me suspiciously and prescribed healthier living! I, who neither
smoke nor drink, merely – disintegrate.

25.12

Was given a copy of K.A. Tavaststjerna's *Before Morning Breeze*.*
There is a note of hope amidst all the immaturity. Remember the
sailing trips of my childhood, all the things that did not become
– me. Closest to me to me is 'The Guest of the Skerries', its quiet
hopelessness, the resignation.

1883

1.1

Try to live in what you observe, in what is most simple – and in
music what is most intimate and cannot be expressed. Not simply
to experience, but also to *understand* this!

4.2

The peculiar (lightning-like!) exhilaration that can seize me in my
deepest lethargy, as though I possess something important that is
my more unique uniqueness and is valuable not only to myself,
and this in spite of the fact that I know I have no one who will
listen and accept, perhaps just for that very reason! Because I know
it. Joy in the concealed. The pearl in the sick mussel. Reading my
children's books over again: Marryat, Defoe, Cooper, old newspapers lying in the warm attic in the sawdust between the rafters.
I often sit up there, it's quiet.

23.4

Karin, Tom and Bertel stood in the doorway looking at me, as
though I were a first-class children's entertainment. Something I
did, perhaps smiling at them, scared them into flight; loneliness
renders one ghost-like.

2.5

Uncle Fredrik: 'Not everyone is made for the highest achievement'
(as a consolation)! Great watery eyes, looking at me appealingly.
'Not everyone is made for drawing total blanks either', I felt like
answering; the latter stink to the heavens and ought to be avoided
or despised; the former attract a great deal of hatred and envy.
Therefore: the peace of the middle way!

23.5

He – my robust old classmate – has had a great deal of success: has always judged people not by what they are but by how they can be used, and he has countless brothers and sisters. Fruitless to argue with them. He is said to be unhappily married –.

2.6

Now they are lying in closed rooms with ice-bags after the great bacchanalia, and I lie in mine, motionless.

12.6

In every summer room there is *one* fly that makes life unbearable; however much I try to escape from it or pull the sheet over my face it finds eyes, nose, mouth, face; and is devilishly on its guard, it can't be killed. It is everything detestable gathered into one little creature, the eternally obtrusive, dirtying, inquisitive, purposeful, industrious, don't-give-up, life-affirming, ambitious thing that makes life into an unendurable agony. It crawls on one's neck, on one's hands, in all the hollows of one's body. It is the indestructible, the ignoble.

15.6

Elma was sitting in the upstairs kitchen with her hands outstretched and the palms turned upwards; there was warm spring sunshine in them, it fell so beautifully into her hands which are already those of an ageing woman, while her body is young, agile and soft. Stood watching her, and she didn't notice me. It was as though the moment possessed a special significance, and it had, and has: gratitude. My skin was also touched by that warmth, so that it felt alive. Then she sensed my presence, turned towards me and looked at me earnestly with her slightly slanting eyes, putting her hands behind her back. 'I'm sorry, I'm intruding', I stammered out, and withdrew, and closed the door. And stood there for a moment, my heart thumping.

17.6

There is in music something extra-human that is capable of inspiring fear. I was told after the first concert I attended – in Åbo – that I went stiff with terror during the *forte* passages, so that my body grew tense and my features distorted, and I think some of this still persists in me, even though I conjure it in the name of all that is human in music, so that madness does not break out. It is said that when Tolstoy listened to music his face bore an expression of panic. There he, the great fisherman, had found a fish that was too big; and here I see Dostoevsky smile knowingly; here we have not merely light but also a darkness which no powers can master except the very greatest, for the darkness has itself been called into being by those powers.

20.6

Today I observed what goes on in nature, but understood little of it. Yet it was restful to observe the raspberry patch, in which swarms of bumblebees and wasps excitedly buzz around: good and evil united. And the aunts, now over seventy, alongside with their fragile voices, and unstung; if the wasps came near they (the wasps) would probably fall down dead.

23.6

The swallows hurry so lightly round the house, over and over again, sink down towards the garden, rise up again, and not one of their flights seems like a repetition – each one is as fresh as the air and the wind, as though they were imparting tokens of love – or rain.

27.6

Reading the Bible, its overwhelming words, and seeking peace in it.

Life a torment – but how continuous, how persistent! So the days roll on, unaware that they are being plundered. From books and scores the extra that one needs if one is not to sink.

4.7

Incredible, the way the Messrs Penpushers' ignorance of Music is seen by them as something taken for granted, as though language were not founded on music and rhythm. The beautiful has *meaning*. Lack of musical sense in poetry produces poetry about nothing. The vulgarity of such one-sidedness: all eye, no ear. Giving rise to the most superficial banality: 'realism'.

14.7

Patience. Wait out this sense of distress, even if it takes the whole of my life. Something deep inside, a feeling that it's worth it, *quand même*. These recurring thoughts of death are perhaps spells to conjure life – telling it to take a step nearer.

15.7

Haydn's universe, as yet undiscovered. The idea of him as some kind of elderly 'papa' in a dressing-gown, a father to child geniuses (Mozart), is mistaken. In many ways a revolutionary (the symphonies of his youth!) he develops towards ever greater depths; the harmonic richness is manifest and free. His world is not a castle chamber but a starry sky. Suppleness and innovation even in his old age: the London symphonies. *The Creation, The Seasons*: mighty boulders so lightly hurled. Not to mention the chamber music in which he speaks so penetratingly. The Russian quartets, and the piano trios!

2.8

August bestows something dead upon nature before the arrival of the great liberator, autumn. Half-waking dreams, feverish and confused; then I stagger to my feet and try to interpret Haydn or Mozart over by the window. Music is a language (Quantz).

13.8

Suddenly see a picture hanging crooked, a window-sash on the point of falling, notice that the ground is shaking. But no one else has noticed it. Then things change and return to how they were before: they were merely testing me, as if to see how much external chaos I can put up with before the chaos inside me comes trickling, like darkness welling out, like a haemorrhage.

September

Father says nothing about the Fennomanes' leaning towards Russia and the Governor General's proposal concerning the language of the courts;* he turns away in order to go off into agriculture, the fishing industry, the garden and the economy. Heavy brooding and unease; the number of visitors has grown less. He raged at the Tsar's shameless humiliation of our representatives at the coronation, he had treated them like a group of soldiers and roared at them: '*Napravo*'! An air of rigor mortis about him, and also about his claw-like right hand, Pobedonostsev.*

22.10

If only a new music could rise up out of our own land! Building my invisible, un-written-down symphonic work, in my head, where there is plenty of space, as in a country drawing-room. In this way I can build it as mightily as I please, between A and E flat with the finale in C.

11.11

Clear winter's day. Was standing in the street talking to Hjalmar when suddenly all sounds ceased. The houses turned white and drew away. A large, black carriage was driving past at the intersection (Universittetsgatan); but the iron-rimmed wheels were striking sparks and screeching with pain. Moved my head, looked to right and left, and received the world back again, I was in a cold sweat, leant on Hjalmar who took me to the nearest café – or was it the Phoenix★?

23.11

My time is strictly measured. I don't have time to throw away. So: I get up early, read the newspaper, take a short walk, buy the newspaper, write letters about my condition, read scores and music journals; it gets dark early, I feel ill and go to bed early, but can't get to sleep. Then I compose as I lie awake, and write statements on various subjects. It can't wait.

26.11

Woke up with clenched fists, traces of blood on my hand; had dreamt that Dr Bengtsson laughed in my face: 'Hypochondriac!' Then at the same moment saw a great bird of prey which he conjured forth with his black, burning beard, his piggy eyes, his chubby hands which he raised emperor-like to the skies where sooty clouds scudded by, saw a condor and said so, and it sought my eyes in order to tear them out, and I defended myself, and struck at it with my fists, and at the same time there was groaning, a group of people with white faces, who were calling to me, but I couldn't hear the words; woke up exhausted. Quiet day with falling snow.

3.12

The only link with Stockholm via the steamship *Express*. Now what if it should be holed by the ice in the darkness of night, so it sank soundlessly with all its passengers asleep on board, to remain on the seabed for another hour like a bubble of air, and the people who had been trapped inside could do nothing but slowly suffocate, and the people up there in the light hear them beating on the walls, hear their cries, and could do nothing – a murmur for large chorus and string ensemble. And if I could divide the chorus on the church gallery in such a way that the cries were hurled across the interior in a 'Libera nos! Libera me!'

26.12
Unbearable sounds and snow mixed up together. Rigor mortis.

1884

4.1
The music rises, grotesque cacophonies overwhelm that which is most precious: the sound of silence, gentle and appealing, within me.

6.1
Sacred light, when the silence is followed by distant music, scarcely audible, and I myself invisible, listening, merely. Perhaps it is precisely from this emptiness that victorious life will some day arise?

5.4.1884

The ice has not yet gone. It beats against cabins and hovels where Axel moves like a shadow. There is boarding coming away like skin from its simple skeleton. Inside now and then one glimpses legs, bones, the whites of eyes. Far away out at sea the snow is drifting like mist over the floes. In the twilight the people move slowly. A glimmering lamp in a window like a bloodshot eye, and the wind working its way through the alleys between herring barrels, coaches, piles of firewood. He stands up and listens: didn't someone shout just now, didn't someone bang something, and why is it all directed at him? Three Russian soldiers are coming his way, he holds his breath and makes himself invisible, stands in the snow in his black overcoat, they don't give him a second glance, go laughing past. Footsteps, and then sudden silence. Uspensky Sobor, a shadow, heavy as a thundercloud. He strokes his hand across his face, it is lifeless, it is a thin mask, there is nothing underneath it. Now he crawls in the snow, now he stands still again, now he hears voices, now they have gone and left him, he is either forsaken or free, he doesn't know which. Here is a door being opened, an inn with long tables and benches, here there are yells like raw mist from mouths and décolletages, the dead things stumble about or stand still, observing him. They stand askew. The city is shrinking around him. There is only this table, only this bench to sink down on, and someone tapping him on the shoulder: 'Sir, sir, will you buy me a drink?' No detours, no sick mother, just this grin and this toothless thing, and he fumbles about for small change and is suddenly gripped with terror: 'They're going to kill me.'

He produces a few coppers, the man snatches them to himself, he is huddled up in an old military jacket, while he is looking at the coins Axel gets up, makes a crouched exit, no one throws anything after him, he slithers and slides down the alley, the city is glimmering there, the market-square deserted, the Esplanade deserted, only a droshky rounding the corner of Högvakten and disappearing. What has he been doing here? Who is it roaming around like a stray dog with a collar that bears no name? He tears and pulls at his long scarf, Mother knitted it, snow-peace, snow-sleep, the eternal kingdom and I – the son of sadness! In my mother's eye – he stands up, blindly, can scarcely see the sea, the ice-field: in my mother's eye into eternity I did spy. Yes. And woe unto you! Who art weak. Yes. I have many brothers and sisters. I have a father and mother. I'm not alone. I have music. People are moving about. A lady in a long coat, she looks at Axel, he raises his hat hesitantly, she hurries past; it is already twilight and the gas-lamps are being lit. Warm rooms open up, murmur of voices, the head waiter bows, he is nearly snow-blind, someone takes his arm: 'Axel!' It is Edvin, his schoolfriend, with the red, cropped hair, the moustache above the large mouth, the small, amicably blinking spectacles. He used to play the cello in the school orchestra. He never persecuted me, there was an unspoken agreement, as though we could have become friends. Axel is led to a table in the corner, flickering candles glimmer in the glass panes. 'Where have you been, you look frozen stiff – waitress, bring us some hot punch, and quickly! No, toddy!' 'I've been out on Skatudden.' 'Axel! People don't go there in the evening except on certain errands.' But he sits still and quiet, and Edvin leans forward: 'You're not ill, are you?' 'I've been to see a doctor here,' Axel says, 'and he recommended fresh air, the way they usually do.' 'And you were looking for it on Skatudden?' Edvin leans back and laughs, his starched turn-down collar rubs against his throat, a pearl gleams in his necktie and he smells of toilet water. 'Eau-de-cologne', Axel says to himself. 'No, toddy!' says Edvin, 'but while we're on the subject of Cologne –'

Edvin talks and Axel listens, it is good to listen to someone else talking, good to sit silent and listen, and Edvin has been to Switzerland, he has visited the Fraumünster in Zürich, he sat alone in one of the pews, someone was playing a mighty fugue, he describes how he found his way up to the gallery, there was the organ, it was gleaming, he raises his glass and screws up his eyes, Axel is almost sucked into all this, into the silence, the gleaming music, the thundering, swelling organ, no, there was no one there, the sheet-music open, the music still quivering for a moment in its own echo, so mighty – and the fugue unknown, the player departed, the organist gone, no verger to be found, everything completely silent: 'but someone had been playing, you know.'

Edvin looks at Axel as though Axel had the answer inside him.

Perhaps he knows a thing or two about the supernatural. The music was getting louder but no one was playing. 'Perhaps it was a self-supporting organ?' Axel says, making his voice sound as dry as possible. For a moment Edvin is confused, then he leans back again and laughs, he laughs so infectiously that the people at the next table turn round smiling, and Axel says: 'It reminds me of a dream I had, if you're interested.' 'Of course, perhaps what happened to me in Zürich was also a dream, waitress! Another toddy, please.' And the landscape, the city, the air so blue in the twilight, Axel sees it and doesn't see it. 'I'm standing in a church,' says Axel, 'in my nightshirt, I look up and see the starry sky, there is no roof, and from the sky musical tones are falling, a strange music, pale, remote, but there is also a face that is looking at me from above and is getting closer, it's not unlike the Tsar's face, actually; I begin to run, find a dark staircase that leads not down but up, rush up it and find a gallery that consists only of a few loose planks, and far below me there are people with white faces in the darkness.' 'Awkward situation', Edvin comments. 'Yes. A strange scent of flowers surrounds me as I walk out on to the springy board, in front of me an old baroque organ with pipes like silvery tree-trunks glows and gleams, and then the organ begins to rumble, it roars out, it booms, you see, like the very worst of thunderstorms, and it isn't Bach, it's music just as strange as that which you heard in the Fraumünster, threatening, demanding, as though it were about to – and there I am on my board, it begins to sway, and I get down on my knees, shuffling along, oh God! Who will save me, and the faces below me are shouting but I can't hear them, I can see that one of them belongs to Olga my sister-in-law, yes, you know her, Hjalmar's wife, and finally I grab hold of a sort of beam that's hanging over the abyss and –'

'And? And?' Edvin hisses, leaning forward across the table. 'What happened then?' 'And I'm flapping about like a fish suspended from a gory hook, I stare upwards, heave myself up with the last of my strength, like this, my face rises over the edge of a table, and there I am sitting in dear old Kapellet with my dear old schoolfriend Edvin right opposite me, I'm rescued, liberated, at peace: all's for the best in the best of all possible worlds. Everything. It's all over.'

Axel leans back, Edvin observes that there is sweat on his brow, but can't decide whether he has been the victim of an outrageous leg-pull, he doesn't know what to think, he stammers: 'What? What?' then leans back, stares almost blindly out across the sea of white tablecloths, clients, waiters, gleaming glasses, then turns to Axel who is sitting in silence, almost threateningly so: 'I see! All's for the best in the best of possible worlds. Well, that was a strange story. I think the gentleman's having a little joke, isn't he?'

But Axel is sitting there so pale, his lofty forehead gleaming, he smiles and looks at Edvin: 'The dream is a true one, but the ending was – poetic licence. I woke up in my room, it was dark, and that was all. When need is greatest, help is close at hand, they say. In dreams, at any rate. In reality things can be rather different.' They sit in silence for a moment. 'Waitress!' Edvin shouts. 'The menu!' And the trio begins to play something by Strauss, the first violinist's face is globular above his instrument and he plays routinely, loud and clear, 'I could at least have been an inn musician,' Axel thinks as he closes his eyes, he is running in the whirling snow, he turns back, continues running, there is an eternal darkness to overcome, so wearying and so indifferent to most people, why torture them?' And he raises his glass to Edvin and says; 'To music! Its health! Long may it live, even though it makes mincemeat of us!'

They both smile simultaneously.

From The Diary

5.4

Strolled around Skatudden, hovels, poverty, fear and hatred. Alleys, and the shadow of the Uspensky Cathedral. More dead than alive shuffled into Kapellet where I met Edvin W. and exchanged talk about music and dreams. Or something of the kind, double loneliness, my own, and that which I receive from others.

12.5

Today was able to look at myself in the mirror and saw nothing there. Deep sense of relief. A face among many indifferent ones.

12.7

Overflowing summer in which I can merge and disappear, like a blade of grass in the meadow; sat with my trousers rolled up on the end of the landing-stage at four o'clock in the morning and fished for perch that glistened like the cool, newly-awoken air. Rest during the day, in yellow twilight behind the curtains.

15.7

People avoid the failure for the same reasons as they avoid the person who is sick: in order not to be infected. Yet for the sick there are nursing homes, while the failure has no recourse but to walk in silence amidst the jeering crowd. It demands and frequently exceeds the whole of one's strength.

9.8

Perhaps there are no unmusical people, only those who can't understand music they hear, external music, but have a musical structure, a kind of inner language of which one can obtain some idea when they're a) sitting in the sauna or b) singing songs while gathered into groups, usually under the influence of alcohol. Without these little safety-valves many of them would go insane. And my safety-valves? Musical scores.

26.10
So seldom is there the glimmer of an idea in this book. Insomnia and darkness. What kind of a world is it that is drowned in the smell of decay, that lives like a corpse but dies at every second? Maybe I'm protected from that world by my poverty and loneliness. Even the happiest person suddenly displays blemishes. Don't ask for justice from Grotte* or Nemesis. So the world is merely a blemished picture, a testimony, a proof, but not a deed.

1885

1.1
I count years, look at death-notices as though I were Methuselah. In two weeks' time I shall be 27. I shall withdraw into myself and stay there; there I will listen, eat healthy food, study strategies and scores, and shun all the outer world; diamonds aren't found in the dark!

7.5
Prof. Johann Ludvig Runeberg stood unveiled. Pacius conducted. Rapture, emotion. The only dissonances in the orchestra. But the winds of springtime are always inconsiderate.

12.8
It is said that when attending the student vigil at the Castle, Tsar Alex. II refused to take off his helmet during the singing of 'Our Land'.* Father said at the dinner-table: 'He didn't want to show how little there was under his bonnet', and added: 'This is an omen, and not a good one.'

15.8
Olga was standing over the washtub at Lilla O—näs, washing her children, there were at least five shiny seal-like bodies which she was scrubbing in a kind of assembly line. The shadows from the maple-trees ran across the grass and the children. They shouted to me but she made them be quiet; in the arbour sat Hjalmar with glass and bottle of Madeira, he beckoned to me, but Olga gave me

the cold shoulder. Hjalmar stretched his arms out, a picture of health, but with some shadow attached to him, spoke, now in a loud voice, now whispering. It was than that the sky seemed suddenly to go dark, the bathed children to gleam like white ghosts, and the narrow old house to move spasmodically. The trees stood black, disheartening the summer, and I saw Hjalmar's face like that of a dead man; for a brief moment this was unbearable, I found myself on the grassy field with a wet cloth on my forehead, being steadily looked after by – Olga. Her great firm face with its strength of will. If only I could obtain some of it. But in her eyes I'm just a 'marmot', a sick creature. And Hjalmar? Heard her say: 'I wish we lived up there; one day it'll be ours.' She's waiting for that day. The children in the scrubby lilac hedge are twittering like birds.

14.11

When the rabble laughs I feel like crying. When solemnity's tall hat is flourished I feel like laughing. What I see confuses me. What I don't see but think gives me my only happiness. I can crow because the world is full of fear. If there were no caracoles nothing would stand firm. Those I only make inside myself, but dress in a morning-coat. Painful vomitings and evacuations, but one ought to construct a routine for one's life that possesses at least some kind of quality. Honour, duty, willpower, the last-mentioned of which is what in my own case is burningly, consumingly absent.

1886

1.1

Everything is changing and growing old around me: people, Father and Mother, my brothers and sisters, the rooms, the overgrown 'park', the streets, only in the towns ostentatious new houses everywhere; the sound of axe-blows in the forests; chimneys and shops. Must try to get something down on paper on every first day of the month, so that I don't go to my ruin entirely speechless.

1.2

In the carriage the young man is just on the point of declaring his warmest feelings to his beloved. There is frost, and the trees are glittering. The hooves stir up snow, all is silent. Then the mare lets out a rhythmical series of explosions, and the two young people in the coach avert their gazes from each other. The moment has passed forever. The young man will become a lonely bachelor, dried-up and bitter, the young woman will become a veterinary surgeon, or it will happen the other way round; subject for a novel.

1.3

In every inhuman action there is always something all too human. Same complaint from the woman in childbirth and the woman in love, from the born and the dying, the same lonely lives. A man approaching you along the road in the dark inspires fear, but greets you cordially. Hands that are placed on a table in the circle of light from the lamp often rest helplessly and tenderly, even those of the strongest. Lullaby behind the closed door, even from the hardest mouth. The helplessness of the sleeper.

12.3

Feel that in my innermost being – in spite of everything! – I am taking a step forward which I want to conceal from everyone. This happiness, of seeking the pure and the genuine in that which is desperate. I complain and sense my inferiority, but deep inside – the kernel, the striving, the gentle, not burning, light. Like resting on a summer morning in calm and limpidity. I long for the summer the way I long for the best things in my childhood.

13.3

Were the great masters able to hear whole, completed movements with their inner ear, whole works, or did they simply pick up something (the way one picks up a child without being conscious of it – ?) which subsequently, unknown to them, developed in a given direction? Towards wholeness. Are there people who are able to survey their life and understand its meaning?

16.3

The cry of the true artist: 'This is not what I intended! But now I must do it!' Even though I've no time for Wagner, it was he who said it, to Liszt, back in 1851, in connection with the horrible *Ring*. It's the work that commands, not the artist. The work is all.

21.3

Julius Caesar piled up corpses in the rivers in order to cross them in chariots which crushed the bodies but were able to continue, thanks to the dead. Cooper speaks of how 'the sun had hid its warmth behind an impenetrable mass of vapor, and hundreds of human forms, which had blackened beneath the fierce heats of August, were stiffening in their deformity before the blasts of a premature November' (*The Last of the Mohicans*). What do children see in their sheltered lives? They read this, and each and every one of them is marked, perhaps forever. And all this is repeated from generation to generation.

18.4

Came to me quite silently in the night, called herself a faithful old servant, but was an angel. The harsh scent of pine soap and sweat, but an angel. In the morning I heard her voice from the upstairs kitchen, she sang. My heart listened, and my Oratorio soon came sounding through, choir and soloists, just like a fleeting day of sunshine, even behind my eyelids. Pain and happiness, united. Later, when I went out into the kitchen, her little son was there. Wanted to go down on my knees and take it by the hand, but stood observed and myself observing. The red face, the spasmodic movements of the limbs, and the mother –. As though she could hardly see me or was embarrassed. Driven out, I turned and went. Later a doctor from Nådendal called, as the child had a fever, but it died in the morning without a sound. It was buried a few days later in Masku. The mother only a shade more silent than usual, she is one of the shadow-folk.

27.4

Mozart as a 'darling of the gods'! The suffering, the painful journeys, illnesses, humiliations, the indifference on the part of the world both in Salzburg and Vienna (where they now boast of M.!): out of all that – music. Goethe speaks of the 'lifegiving power' that dwells in M.'s compositions, with his usual perspicacity. To him it is clear that only M. could have composed the music to his, Goethe's, *Faust* with its 'repulsive, disgusting, terrible' features, to use Goethe's own words. Don Giovanni! How strange to imagine the 14-year-old Goethe when he saw the 7-year-old Mozart, 'the little man with his haircut and sword'. The little man, the two children: childishness as genius and permanently retained. For all that, the starting-point for those children is that of the discerner, the adult – the eye of a wise man looking out from a child's features. From Goethe's economical words one can gain more understanding of Mozart the genius than from hecatombs of false rapture about the 'darling of the gods'.

7.5

Yesterday Aunt Magdalena died, today Aunt Carolina, both of pneumonia. That was the way Aunts Sofia and Louisa died within a few weeks of each other, in 1869; I never saw them. And now the rooms are quiet. They used to sit in the library, the centre-partings of their hair showing white in the twilight, the voice of one of them shrill, the other tentative, and when they walked there was the rustle of their wide dresses. Something eternally stunted. In this house everyone moves as if according to some fixed routine. Mother walks through the drawing-room past the slanting sun-light. Magdalena gets up and goes to her room, when I approach I meet Mother, she smiles, goes about her business, we sit silently for a while, Carolina with her sewing, we are like insects that communicate in a large, invisible, silver-gleaming cobweb, deriving nourishment from the meagre dewdrops that cling there. O-näs full of resistance and rooms in each of which someone has died and now lies supine under white sheets. And these two who lived all their lives together, who regardless of the season moved from one room to another, ever more slowly, ever more stiffly, and looked at me with eyes that followed me the way eyes of dead people in portraits do. When they played the piano it was as if nails were being hammered into it with great precision. In the end they came to resemble each other like two withered skeletons, and are now motionless, silent, after years of existence, not life. I can't grieve; there really was something transient about them from the very beginning.

12.5

My family really belongs to a middle class that has a varnish of aristocracy – in former times a bourgeoisie, but with fighting gen-erals and governors, even further back law-speakers at the assemblies, now something ossified on its way down, something uncertain, doomed, in a land on its way up; and our axe that makes the tree-trunk sing also brings about the death of the tree. The future belongs to those who active; the quiet, or the paralysed, are the ballast. If you've got any ideas, throw the poor fellows overboard! But without the ballast the balloon will vanish up into the sky, without it the ship will go down in the storm. To believe oneself at one and the same a balloonist and a man of action, while one is really the ballast, that is a comic situation that cries to the heavens in terror.

20.6
Something violent, life-threatening in a storm through the reeds, when the grey sky stands immobile but this belching forest rises violently with darker flecks, a mass, a crowd of people, still shackled in mud, but year by year approaching further up the shore, under the dark sky, in a scarcely presaged storm. From *pianissimo* to a hard, cutting *forte*. A fugue of hatred. And yet there are those who say that music is a picture-book. It is the invisible storm that is able to change that which is innermost, it is creative, not carbon-copied life. Against this no decrees or laws are of any avail, not even Father's arranging of his pens in rows, or my own symmetries, the ones I secretly demolish in the night.

21.6
Love your neighbour as yourself. Even if you despise yourself –

22.6
Blind He was, God, when I was begotten, and blind He will be when I die. From time to time I see, sometimes even with His eyes, how unimportant that blindness is when compared to the music in the trees, above the land, above the morning mists, a clear, light, elusive tone, a grace, a blessing.

27.7
At the end of July when the summer grows dark my life darkens, too.

18.8
Friendship between men perpetually misunderstood in the most sordid way by the lustful. In Brunnsparken yesterday, warm evening, student caps glowing in the dark like lanterns, and behind Badhuset the surge of the open sea, waves in a salt wind. G. said: 'If this were to be my last August, I shouldn't be sad.' My happiness, wordless.

19.8
Attempt to find the other person in myself who can survive and

give me dreams and mature in spite of me. The will to live. But who is the dreamer? I or the one whom I seek?

23.9 (on the way from Nådendal to Åbo)

Suddenly felt deeply and happily at home in the drifting mist, alone on deck, when all directions were dissolved. A few words, a sentence accumulated and were repeated in my inner being: the tall trees with no shadows, themselves shadows. If there were a music that could express this, which is dead and yet alive and will continue to live.

25.9

The melody is simply the cloud in the sky, the movement, the filling-out. Ducts and air passages, the displacements of the clouds, are the symphony. One starts to feel dizzy as one watches masses of cloud moving into one another at different heights. If the symphony does not have enough space it is misconceived. The great architect of clouds: Bach. The great creator of space: Mozart. The expert on storms: Beethoven. And Haydn? Remember that clouds can be filled with light even when the earth is already dark and inclining towards night.

28.9

Hanslick has shown that music of sufficient intensity can equally well be interpreted in a tragic or an optimistic manner, that the text of a song can within certain limits be changed without the music itself being changed. Music is like day and night, it *is*. We the listeners are responsible for the interpretation.

1887

15.1 My birthday (29th)

I am a temporary arrangement. Someone else is going to come along and be the real, living Axel. And how could it be otherwise? For if that Someone Else were to appear while I was still alive, I should die.

6.8

Everyday existence lulls us into believing that the difference between joy and sorrow is a great one. We don't notice that life, like music, is full of little alterations, that within the space of a moment joy may pass into melancholy, light into twilight. A mere semi-tone, and colours change, conversations die, the music in its entirety is altered. And even if we could keep track of all these changes in our lives, would it make us any happier? More attentive, yes, but happier? Would we not despair of ever regaining the calm of the everyday, the safe haven of monotony, and be tossed, ever more feverishly and miserably, between the varieties of sensation? And if we never acquire a grasp of the music of our lives, how can we ever command our inner orchestra?

25.10
Winter early, making the window white, and opening on white fields and black trees. Those two colours. Experienced a bolt of lightning, and when they strike it is not a brain haemorrhage but a haemorrhage of feeling; after a moment like that, everything is all the same. I function, live as before, if this can be called living. I wake up, go to sleep and wake up again, and even though things are turning white outside the window and the pure snow is falling, the darkness continues within me. And I'm not yet thirty!

3.11
Extremely seldom have I been changed by my experiences – perhaps because they are few in number? The things that change me are unreal impressions, swift, violent moments of emotion, above all from music. Through the demands music has made on my emotional life this tendency has been strengthened, often deepened, and has even filled me with terror, so that in the utter-most extremities of my sick nerves I have none the less become clearer, more sentient. Thus can the music that is newly born from such experience make loneliness into wealth. *That* is the experience which can enrich us, not our beating our heads hundreds of times against the same door-frame.

2.12.1887

In the becalmed town the river slid darkly past white trees and mercifully snow-laden shanties on its way to the paved city that lay over there, closed to his gaze. He stood on the Cathedral Bridge with his collar turned up, his long, grey overcoat like a monk's robes around his stiff form. How agitatedly his heart was beating. Was this a sign? In the woollen mittens that were far too big for him – grotesque! childish! – Mother had knitted them, Mother had surrounded him with yarn and cloth, hoods, scarves, stockings, belly-warmers, waistcoats, so that he should not bump too hard against the hostile objects around him – with his gloved hands he gripped the bridge's parapet and looked down into the slow-moving blackness: there were no violin-cases slipping past, all was quiet there now, and as he stood there he felt a slight giddiness, followed by relief. To free oneself from the temporary. To view all actions, movements in various directions, scenes, external figures, drozhkys, cabmen, sleighs, striking clocks, flowing water, shores, houses motionless under a blue-grey sky, his clothes, his gloves, all his failures as temporary – he stroked his hand across his face, it refreshed him, his pince-nez – was it in his pocket, why wasn't it there, had he lost it? Then he could see nothing, only the mist, there: he sighed with relief, dried the lenses absent-mindedly with a handkerchief, two ladies walked by, stirring up a little cloud of snow with their wide coats, ought he to have greeted them? They were looking at him. Even his body, shut up in all its clothes, habits, peculiar, uncontrollable movements, even it: temporary. And beyond all these accidents which gathered together were called life he was in search of – what? Mechanically he began to walk across the street, down along Slottsgatan, conscious of the motionless, pure, gentle reality around him, streets and houses, the old yellow-painted houses, a town for small ideas, mellow family happiness, confidence in the future; and did not all these new buildings, so massive, heavy and ornate, bear witness to the majesty of the future, did not the Hotel Phoenix stand there as a testimony to solid respectability, and was not the punch steaming behind frosty window-panes, and were there not pedestals, palms, porcelain figures, draperies, plush, yes, plush, all these 'p''s in order to encompass the temporary –; he kicked a hard, black stone in front of him, it disintegrated: horse-droppings. That is how everything one has believed in disintegrates.

He paused in his progress and looked across at his old school: years of humiliation. The hard, echoing corridors, a hand twisting his head, a chorus of voices forcing him in against the wall, the smell of kerosene, sweat and urine, and only the books, the words there as a deliverance. There is something unredeemed in my life which I must try to redeem. Must. I cannot have sustained so much injury that I have no strength left. Try to redeem it. In order to redeem it I must, like the doctor, seek the cause as well as the healing remedies. And what if the cause is the absence of healing remedies? There must be defenceless souls who, like haemophiliacs, cannot tolerate the indifferent onward rush of life. He turned round and watched a sleigh that was driving in his direction, the horse steaming with sweat, someone shouted to him, an arm was stretched out, he stretched out his arm, too, the sleigh swerved and disappeared up on to the bridge, he had no idea who it was, and could anyone have recognized him when his face merely protruded like an accident between his collar and his fur cap? He undid a button and hauled his watch out of his waistcoat: he was still in time. I'm not yet thirty but am less and less convinced of there being any permanency outside music. There are those who know what their goal is at twenty, and who by the time they are twenty-five have turned existence into a routine and a game. Yes.

He looked in the window at a clothes' shop, there hung fabrics, dresses, the feminine – and under the clothes? Fear, transparently white and fleeting, and humiliation: that was not how it was supposed to be. Somewhere in his body a small creature stirred. Had he not groaned and wallowed, behaved like an animal, and had she not found it natural? After he had paid had he not fled like a wounded creature? No – he had felt eased. The heavy, sickening fragrance of scent – he drew in the fresh, cold winter air, bells ringing like music, Mrs Edelstam went by and he greeted her, she smiled at him without recognizing him, bowed her head, her hat floating forward like a tray of crystals, her face that of a horse, the eyes glowing violently, only for a moment: was she inviting him? Should he follow her, she had turned round after all, but then disappeared, he had been a guest at their house, porcelain cups, the left leg over the right, the hum of conversation, he had started to feel slightly unwell, had groped his way along, opened the door of the servants' room by mistake, three beds squeezed into a room with no window, someone sitting on one of them looking up at him in fear – life a series of such moments, in between streets and squares silent, the winter mild and overcast. Here the snow was full of footprints, and none of them could be interpreted; out in the snowy fields of the manor one saw hare tracks. In his pedantic, needy life wasn't he like the hare that runs aimlessly, in eager anxiety, trying to escape from its persecutors by rushing around in a circle, in order to collapse at last in total exhaustion?

He looked about him – yes, he was still in Slottsgatan. To live, stubbornly, that was what it was all about. In an inner courtyard, through a gateway, he saw a wooden hovel, dark smoke coming from its chimney, someone lying like a bundle on the ground, a woman screaming, but the snow muffled her rage into gentleness, or as if he were seeing it at a distance. Behind the façades, drunkards, poverty, the dead things that were used up and absorbed the impress of those who lived inside, so that the hovel looked as though it might keel over in the barely concealed stink – was it fish? Rotten fish?

He took a few steps into the yard, turned round, this was not his town. His town was a city by the sea – Helsingfors but without the poverty, without Skatudden, the shanties of Sörnäs, without the restless, nervous, *nouveau riche* quality. A great clear river falling in quiet floods down into the sea. On both sides of the river old, terraced town districts with alleys, houses, gates opening on wonderful gardens: holy trees, acacias, rhododendrons, but also scented country lilacs. Gentle, green spaces, and people talking with one another in them. Open squares with wells, parks filled with music, above the town a wide-horizoned cemetery, where I too shall rest. Mild early spring, high summer, autumnal splendour of leaves, in the winter skiing parties with torches, and the beloved blushing like an apple, her gaze so clear and promising. Little shops with fragrant bread, outdoor cafés with gaudy parasols, through carved doorways entrances to panelled restaurants with glowing glass and porcelain, lightly scented white wine...From an open window the sound of a harpsichord – Scarlatti. In homes with light-coloured furniture simplicity, dignity and quiet conversations, children and grown-ups listening to fairy-tales and music. A face gently turned, and then – the altered reality, the darkness, the white teeth, the voluptuousness, a wind sweeping along the street, a voice screaming: 'You bastard!' and the bundle lying there motionless. Peasant carts and jades, blue flecks in the sky above Observatory Hill; Axel stands blackly on the street corner, not knowing which direction to take, can he move, is he nailed fast in snow and ice, doesn't Hjalmar live nearby, couldn't he go there for safety?

He looks hastily around him, but there is no one there. Someone is mimicking him, his short steps, his stunted life, his childish dreams, yes, someone is mimicking him even in his dreams! When he turns round the other person steps right out into the light, that is the terrible thing, he is completely black and unrecognizable, and is then obliterated. And everyone keeping their distance. He goes quickly into a dark stairway, it is quiet. Only the gentle sound of hooves in the street. They, too, stop. Someone has got his cart out in order to come and fetch him. The aunts travelled side by side, each in her coffin, the hearse shuddered forwards. But no one opens the door; he plucks up his courage, goes out, the air fresh and the sky clear now. To bring some order to his thoughts, an imperative demand. Fanny had got married when he was – let's see – eighteen, to Ernst Börtzell. The following year Elin had married Malmborg, become a widow, and got remarried four years ago to Fredrik Färling; only Anna and he were left. What were they? Nothing. And Hjalmar and Olga – how many children did they have? Axel stopped outside the theatre. Six. Karin, Tom, Harry, Bertel, Åke, Ove. The oldest ones at school. The sun came out, crystals whirled like sparks over the black-clad women in their shawls and aprons, eyes and red gills, fish-scales, scales falling from red eyes; he looked at the clock: he must hurry.

On the stairway the smell of dust and printers' ink, the rattle of a typewriter, doors banging. Axel took off his fur cap, knocked it against the door-frame, asked for 'Editor Cygnaeus',* was led to a door, he was practically shoved inside, there wasn't much time, it grew quiet, they looked at each other. There was from the very beginning a peculiar mutual understanding, as though they had known each other for a long time. The one, who lived right in the middle of events, and the other, who stood in the wings. The heart that grows calm when someone takes the time to listen. 'We have heard about your deep interest, yes, your knowledge in the field of music. The post of music reviewer on the *Åbo Times* is vacant. It would give us great pleasure if you felt able to accept it –'.

He leans forward, as if to egg Axel on, but at the same time as if he had already seen, as if he knew and was merely waiting. Axel clears his throat, undoes his overcoat, Cygnaeus hurries to help him off with it despite his protests – 'I'm not planning to stay long, actually' –; and he sits down, slowly, heavily, as though his soon-to-be thirty years were weighing him down, now, as he is arriving at his first decision regarding the question of regular work, some lonely pictures of rooms, years, snow go past. 'I have given your friendly, indeed flattering letter my careful consideration. Believe me, I don't receive many like that – but let me get to the point. I've come to tell you that I am compelled to decline your offer. There are three reasons. The first is my mental invalidity, which renders practically all kinds of work impossible for me. The second is my meagre and insufficient competence, and the third is the fact that early in the New Year I shall be moving to Helsingfors.'

He bows his head, then looks straight at Gustaf Cygnaeus again. As though he were waiting for an attack, resistance, attempts at persuasion. He could have stayed quiet about the third reason; he feels a slight sense of uneasiness. The other two remain firm. And behind all this the darkness, the motionlessness, the listening walls, the wasted years, old age hidden like a mask in the still bright morning light – he adds: 'My existence is –', and is seized by a powerful desire to weep, bends forward, his hands twisted together with their thin, ridiculous wrists, and hears Cygnaeus saying: 'I understand you, I won't prevail upon you, but hope that music will always follow you –'

He cannot speak. He is half blind. He has to get up and stand at the window, there is a carrier, a waggon, a horse with lowered head, birch-trees in their most transparent winter attire, motionless, and the bright sky, 'almost like spring', he says and receives a mumble of assent in reply. The dream of a ridiculous man, he thinks, the whole of my existence, only solitude will save me, and as he takes his leave he sees a look of recognition. Cygnaeus follows him all the way out, stands looking after him, in his shirtsleeves, his brown and red striped waistcoat, his steel watchchain, he has noticed that. As though he were saying goodbye to some dear and cherished friend he may never see again. Who knows? He turns round, lifts his hand in solemn farewell and receives a farewell greeting in return. It was necessary to tear some leaves from the calendar on the way out, it was showing the wrong date. That amused Cygnaeus, as though that was something he understood, that despair needs as a counterbalance the most extreme carefulness in diet and living habits, in one's view of life and moral attitude, in constancy and routine, in orderliness and faithfulness to one's word, in matters of punctuality, if it is not, like an opened black mouth, there, in the woman with the bundle of firewood who is staggering out of the gateway, to find expression in confused cries, laments, curses. Black bodies dug up out of the earth, kicked into life, nourished on *brännvin*, sunk back into the earth again – but in him a freshness in spite of everything! Yes. He hadn't been laughed to scorn, hadn't been mocked. A cold wind glitters through him, quickly he crosses the street, down towards the river, almost weightless, his legs move fast, his buttoned boots stir up snow, cold light-blue sky, the cold like sweat from the big patrician houses that lean over him with dark shadows. Bent down to the ground the willow rises up again –: he smiles. Was what he said really true? Mental invalidity? For all the inner world he has created, will the outer one strike back in revenge? Inside him this longing to stand plain and upright, in liberating solitude. As though Cygnaeus understood this, and had received something from him. To render oneself free of all confusion and, from one's inferior position, see clearly – the water with yellow, broken ice-floes, the cart-tracks, the black trees on the banks right opposite. Here, in the water, it glided away, the music like the voices in his oratorio, he stops and hums, yes, the final coda intensified from *forte* to the very utmost degree of volume, then extreme *pianissimo*: the triumph of the human spirit over all shabbiness, all successful fortune-seeking, all exercise of power, the camaraderie, the privileges, the whole sordid game! To elevate oneself!

A man in an overcoat is standing there, he raises himself on tiptoe, he spreads out his arms, suddenly a child is standing alongside him, the child, too, in a long coat, of grey rough home-spun cloth, his face white under the knitted cap, it could be Bertel, or Åke, the boy mimics him, flings his arms wide, he is a shrunken Axel, he is mocking him, didn't you hear it, Axel shouts, didn't you hear it, the music? Or is it only an inner cry that he hears, the boy backs away, takes to his heels, runs up towards Slottsgatan, past the horsedrawn cart with its jingling bells. Axel stands there with turned-up collar, his face almost hidden in the shielding over-coat. Quiet, he tells himself, quiet. Is he not happy at moments when he forgets himself? Yes, there is something at the same time comical and frightening about a person who forgets himself. His breath is like a column of cloud from his mouth. Dressed in his breath – that ought to give them something to be horrified about.

Isn't everyone in the last analysis alone with himself? The cathedral answers, strikes two. He pulls out his watch and checks it: yes, the church is right. He takes off his spectacles, wipes them absent-mindedly. *Vox humana*, the chariot of the freed, like the lightest snowfall in sunlight! Like crystals, gleaming in the light winter breeze. The town surrounds him like the most fragile bell of glass, chimes in his heart, for a while he is alone and at home in himself.

From The Diary

1888

15.1

My thirtieth birthday. There is nothing to enter, no balancing of the books. What I experienced as a ten-year-old, that innocence that was betrayed, that despair that surged in when all the dams had been burst, and that light intensified until it became unbearable, so that only in the most reserved silence could I follow and create my own world, concealed from everyone – this world I must live with until my death.

16.1

If all the great successes were to be set alongside all the great failures, what a brilliant assembly we should have to learn from then! Then our self-sufficiency and our scorn for *les hommes ratés* would have a slightly different tinge. No one ever talks about the people who went to their ruin in the States, yet it was they who made life possible for the successful ones.

23.1

To experience everything the way one did as a child, but in the knowledge that now one cannot grow out of it. Perhaps even then my growth had been arrested. Not all are born as children, growing up and maturing, but perform an inverse development, from being an old person at birth to someone who is ever more naïvely helpless. All the same, I was often lively and happy in my childhood, so far as I remember, and even then music made an indelible impression on me: the song of a bird, Mother's lullabies, my sisters' plunking on the square piano, and the wind great in the treetops. Then death entered and set the theme.

12.2

Promenade in Åbo. Father and Mother very old now. Their strictness is becoming helplessness, their gentleness confusion. Those who greet us hurry by. Tea at Olga and Hjalmar's house. She watches me with a cold gaze.

2.3
De Vogüé on Dostoevsky: 'small, thin, extremely nervous, worn down and oppressed by the misery of sixty years, he looked more faded than old.'

12.3
The most valuable of all that is human must be the good teacher. Does he exist within me, unborn?

19.4
Have seldom been addicted to self-overestimation, unless the very fact of declaring this counts as such. In every context, not least the artistic ones, it leads to a reduction in the sense of one's own intrinsic value. Instead I vaunt my self-underestimation. Illness, pain, insomnia have worked together to build up my life. Would it have been richer if I hadn't been ill so much of the time? Illness can teach us much about vigour and good health. It can also crush a great many things.

20.4
Intense desire to talk confidentially with a total stranger, someone completely free from family ties. Here the dead people walk around from room to room, through the big drawing-room, and when one sits down another starts to move, all of them old, as though they had crept out from behind the wallpaper. Only when Hjalmar's children rush around does the house acquire life. Father, who cannot bear disorder, withdraws at such times, Mother turns up the palms of her hands resignedly, her blue eyes fill with tears. I lock myself in my room. Hjalmar is in Åbo. He is now an 'inspector' – of wine and spirits – down to the very last drop. Anna is 'resting' her way through life, wants nothing more. And I want the music of heaven!

20.6
Weakness, fever and dreams. In music there is no link between facts and their significance, for they have a significance that is different from the one that is expected: they involve instinct and rhythm. When the rhythm is broken, madness breaks forth, just

as in life. I think of Wecksell at Lappviken, who in my earliest childhood used to have coffee at our house on Södra Esplanadgatan, chattering away as lively as a bird. He remains silent. What does he hear? Nothing? And if I didn't have music to listen to, and these pages to fill –?

22.6

Man wants to believe and therefore believes. It's a flight from hopelessness. To have breathed in, absorbed the hopeless, that is, to have seen to the uttermost limit, to the void, is to have been bound forever to a clear vision, which sees everything out of its context and yet longs for a context: it is music.

22.6

They get dressed while they're having their baths. Wet-gleaming borders and puffed sleeves, little screams and spasmodic limbs, the older ones chalk-white and slow-moving. In the evening when the people from the Kankas estate are here they dance in the drawing-room, undressed with bare shoulders and chests. A punch-glass knocked over: little screams and spasmodic limbs. Children, dolls and pregnancy that never ends: Hjalmar pale, his eyes closed, on the balcony, and Olga coming out like a thundercloud with concealed bolts of lightning.

13.7

Hot summer's day with no wind. Reading the poet X's latest production. It's considered *'comme il faut'* to have him in the bedroom. Even composer Y. is considered 'salon'-able. For those who do their best to attain the smörgåsbord of culture, 'moderation' is the rule. Moderate realism, moderate romanticism, moderate genius – as though there was ever any moderation in great art! Moderate passion, moderate suffering – what crassness!

15.7

Can you feel how you are no longer answerable to yourself but go your way even though it leads sheer downwards and you may be lost, fall and die like an outcast, while you feel you want to shout: 'This isn't me! It's someone else!' Horror, and at the same time you are speechless, denying all this because this other person is like you, is your twin brother. 'The last refuge of the silent and the chaste: mockery.' Dostoevsky.

14.8

The person who lets himself be carried along on the casual tide of success is ground down and smoothed away by the current. There must be something hard and resistant there to be fought against. That which has no foundation is worth nothing except for a season.

20.10

Stood like a famous conductor and accepted ovations for my symphony. Had this been real and not a dream, would I have been able to stand so much reality? Most likely not. For to have one's dreams fulfilled demands a robust disposition, spiritual health, a belief in 'what was it I said?' and 'I knew it' which renders one's success meaningful. Success with one's uncertainty preserved – 'I've failed, but they can't see it', 'What shall I do after this?' – leads to paralysis, fear, isolation and silence. So: be content with your solitude, your dreams, if you can. But I would not wish this sickness of the nerves even on my worst enemies, if I had any. It is remedied to some extent by a regular routine, which the ignorant call pedantry. A routine protects one against chaos and disintegration. And whoever cannot imagine that chaos and disintegration, he is the cause of it.

22.12

In Åbo today met Mrs K., who asked after my health. Low voice which I had difficulty in hearing, but in her gaze something wild, a violence breaking through and then disappearing again. Outwardly she was calm, narrow features, brown eyes under a big dark surge of hair, and her mouth sensual, bitter. Phrases, and inner solidarity unarticulated. The two children tugged and pulled at her, Christmas was drawing near; am spending it with the old folk, am one of them.

23.12

When I was eight years old I was given as a Christmas present a toy violin from which I was able to entice a few scraped notes. Wept bitterly, as I had been expecting the music of the spheres. Ten years later I coaxed from a real violin an infinity of dead notes that cut against my ambitions like knives against sinew. And all those people who were expecting something from me! I struggled, but all that came from the instrument was fear, conflict, dejection. The same as had come from the toy violin – yes, it changed, grew hard, until it was dead and had to be buried.

Later:

The music that can be completely explained – is it music at all? There must be an irrational vestige, something alien that makes the whole, like a figure that resembles and yet does not resemble oneself; and this figure also resembles everyone else who truly listens, and to everyone it gives this inexplicable thing that is each person's innermost uniqueness, and shares it with others. Thus loneliness becomes deepest communion, and those who mock at the lonely person have never listened to themselves, nor, consequently, to others either, and music has never given them anything but yawning in chorus. Quite simply. The candles have burnt down. It is night.

25.12

Grace, as a result of hard work. Mozart's music soaring above its creator, while with Beethoven the creator with the sweat of his brow stands digging in his own earth, and can only turn inwards when he is freed. With Mozart the inner world is a gleam of light, even in its darkest timbres; but its foundation is the hardest work. Beyond the complete mastery of the means of expression there is a great simplicity, lightness, and a limpid soaring. I like to think that his pauper's death was just such a soaring away in light from the heavy earth.

26.12

Brooding over a new system of musical notation – an alphabetic one, which might bring music and language closer to each other. Have rejected several different series as being far too complicated. Great joy in the abstract. Yet already a resistance in my larynx is making the idea of encompassing five octaves with the alphabet an impossible one. But as an idea!

30.12

Mother sees that I have come to nothing and tries to fill each empty space with love. In this all too constricting fluid I live and have difficulty in breathing.

15.1

On my birthday, over thirty now, I give myself this advice: cut off the music! Look at reality! Don't count on any underlying mysticism. Look at what is visible! Perhaps from that will come music, reality, mysticism, as in this instance.

20.2

My usual nervous complaint, incapable of doing anything. I doubt, therefore I am. But if I doubt even that thought, am I alive at all? I see myself running but don't move. There is a light in the forest, a long-ago extinguished star. And two Topelian trees with their branches touching one another, each with their deep roots, and the landscape obliterated by rain.

3.4

That which the sculptor hews away so that the essential shall remain. But the essential could not have been created without what has been hewn away, the unessential – we, the fragments.

12.4

To sit with the frame and the canvas not filled up, empty. So much bliss forced upon one that it can't be expressed. To find a notation for a music of silence.

20.4

Violently ringing its bell the red omnibus drove along the Esplanade and in front of the Grönqvist House ran down a young lady who was badly lacerated. Black stains of blood on her light-coloured dress. The treetops cast transparent shadows. Wandered away, kept thinking I could smell blood all the way along Konstantinsgatan; towards me came swaggering officers stinking of horse.

1.5

They're celebrating. I had a dream: with one swift incision someone cuts open my breast and draws its surfaces aside like a stage curtain. Then the hard work of pulling my heart out. But it won't come loose. Finally rage, like tearing the entrails from a fish. Afterwards I am rinsed in clear, cold water.

13.5

Quiet music from a quiet temperament, lively music from a lively one? What does an artist's life have to do with his art? The most bourgeois environment may produce the most fantastic creations, while Bohemia may simply produce false fashion. Balance out of the deepest need. Mozart: demanded knowledge and education of his listeners. If he could see our public now!

14.5

Common sense an admirable quality in everyone except the artist. Shakespeare with common sense! And yet: in every intense experience the most universally human, the most common, the most humane, a common sense of human value.

23.5

Insomnia, the days of tiredness dissolved, the nights of wandering thoughts.

26.5

The swallows have come, sweeping low along the ground, the way my thoughts do, while the darkness is falling.

30.5

The drowning man's cabin-mate, who is to take the news to the man's wife, who is unaware of what has happened: 'Are you Widow Överman?' 'Yes, but I'm not a widow.' 'Would you like to bet on that?' This may be elevated into a general rule: 'No misfortune has befallen me!' 'Would you like to bet on that?'

July

The Imperial Fleet has been on manoeuvres in the Åbo skerries. The Tsarina has been out walking in Slottsgatan, has bought a parasol, some knives and a coffee-pot, so the family ought to be able to manage in the short term, at least. Enthusiastic cheering, flags, singing and brass-band music, light-coloured linen suits on the deck of the *Tsarevna*, the ship still afloat for the present, anyway. I grew up under Alexander II, at the time of the thaw, and must have absorbed some of the stormclouds of '61 and the representative assembly of '63 at which Father was present. Only four when *Daniel Hjort* had its première, but remember conversations about the play in our home. The forward march of the Finnish language, Snellman's language ordinance, the censorship that began in '67, the conscription question, the gleaming new coins at Christmas '65,* and behind it all a scarcely-suspected darkness. What are they thinking, those people there on the after-deck, and what are they thinking, those people gathered on the shore? The next thirty years should provide the answer.

12.9

A good score possesses a graphic airiness. Dark air, light air, rain, fog, sunlight, yet jointly: airiness. The notes rest on the staves like swallows on telegraph wires. They are permanent and yet they fly. Observe that one cannot see air, only hear it, like silence or wind. Under all this, rhythm. Perhaps I could even use the expression 'space' which gives more sense of depth than the 'airiness'. The earth-bound person's dream of soaring.

15.9

Bogus distinction, snobbery, contempt for one's fellow human beings are not merely privileges of the upper class, I have found them among the most ordinary people, though in their most unbearable form among the philistines. What is an 'ordinary' person, anyway? That which is genuine receives equally short shrift in the fields as in the streets, honesty follows the plough no more than it does the secretary's pen, and the folk element is concealed in all honest striving irrespective of social class. Where chauvinism spreads its wings the genuine is in danger. Neither dress-coat nor folk costume can conceal bigotry. Where there is true nationalism, there also is the source.

17.9

There is something about me that repels other people even when I am trying to please them. Yes, precisely then. So –. Follow one's path, not hanker after goals, endure, accept one's life in the margin, a name carelessly dropped by an unknown master. Or his helper. 'Could we draw any conclusion from the darkness that surrounds us on all sides other than that we are unworthy?' says Pascal. Unworthy to live? I didn't ask to be born.

20.9

Wonderful autumn morning of great clarity. A light between the trees where already single leaves have begun to change colour. The silence of an early morning. Walked carefully, while everyone was still asleep, down through the lilac avenue, past Lilla Odensnäs, from where a low murmur could be heard coming from all the children and a deeper bass-note from Olga; Hjalmar is in Åbo. Strong scent of reeds and mud, fog still drifting over the bay. Reflection of treetrunks in the water and the echoes of seagulls. Old and young are asleep, on or under the earth, in heavy dreams. The lightest puff of wind will blow us away.

31.12

All autumn laid low by illness, and now winter is here, and a new year is standing outside the door. The most difficult thing about loneliness is the urge for self-observation, like self-abuse. Like trying to construct a life out of a few, perhaps just two or three notes, repeated until they become intolerable.

1890

24.5

Deep silence, like Mozart 100 years ago. Did approaching death silence him temporarily?

11.7

The postal decrees* are a disgrace, and the beginning of something ominously bigger. The Russian language is being forced upon us. The professions are not being consulted. Father silent, with anger. Soon the hide will be flayed from the Finnish lion, the two-headed eagle is already aiming at its eyes.

12.9

The thief talks of honesty, the liar of the importance of truth, the libertine of pure love's supremacy, the murderer of the sacredness of life. The butcher talks of the body's subtle beauty, the usurper of freedom, the hangman of justice, the family oppressor of harmony, the miser of generosity, the general of peace, the rich man of the importance of poverty, the social climber of making do with one's lot, the politician of the importance of culture, the professor of the poor who are blessed in spirit. The master of the household talks of the happiness of being a farmhand and the fox of the happiness of being a hen, the great artist talks of food and money, and I talk of illness and of music.

Christmas

Everyone has aged, and in the conversation there is suddenly a silence that is not silence but a void. A dark year that will soon be over. Sense of powerlessness, increased Russian antipathy.

1891

15.1

My birth coincided, true to form, with the publication of Goncharov's *Oblomov*.

January

One of Kajanus's popular concerts in the Fire Station. Old Topelius in the audience, as well as Edelfelt, Ville Vallgren, Gallén, Tavaststjerna.* Kullervo March received with enthusiastic cheers and encored several times. The days in Helsingfors exhausting, came back more dead than alive.

25.2

'Our land' wonders what the Swedes can do for Finland and comes up with the answer: pray!

2.4

When I'm dead someone – if such a person is to be found – will say: 'Did he really exist?' And from the grave I will shout: 'No! He didn't!'

16.5

Light in the darkness. Greetings from V. Rydberg, letter from Axel Tamm, inviting me to go and stay with him. I'm going!

22.5.1891

Ladies' hats floating on hair done up with hairpins gleaming in
the last rays of the sun in an atmosphere of the most delicate
cigar-smoke; couple after couple, stiffly expressing their greetings
with bows and curtseys as in some inexorable dance; faces under
parasols, pale and luminous, lips almost black like eyes, gleaming
as gentlemen's hats gleam and clothes rustle; the gas-jets are lit.
Behind him the silence of Riddergatan, the heavy buildings, the
great empty marble staircase with windows like glowing mosaics,
heavy oak doors, the fragrance of dust and ground coffee in the
hall where the darkness lingered among gleaming brass tables with
flowered vases and a pale, swelling, dead-gazing plaster bust by
some unknown hand. The servant helped him off with his overcoat, the lining torn, tangled, in his nerves, in his nothingness, he
tore himself free, wiped his forehead in a tall mirror, was led in
to see Doctor Wargentin, light-coloured curtains in front of a tall
window, the man dark, with a dark beard, perfectly clear blue
eyes, of indeterminate age, narrow white hands like those of a
woman; and the silence, the silence in a new, heavy rich house
where the rooms had not yet grown accustomed to voices, resisted
them, thrust against them, gathered themselves around thousands
of objects, clung tightly to the furniture, the stuffing, the plush
velvet, the tassels, the fans on the wall –: bright, simple and clean,
as though he had returned to the summers of his childhood where
the silence was full of expectancy, simple things, sea and bright
verdure –; and the simple questions, about the voyage (the safety
of a narrow cabin, where he could be alone, as in a coffin, had
met no one on board, had scarcely moved from his cabin, later,
in the twilight, on deck, he had looked out across the sea, a liberation). Yes, Doctor Wargentin, too, loved the sea, was shortly
about to go to Dalarö with his wife and children, a modest villa;
but he had received a message from Foundry Proprietor Tamm
about Axel's arrival, and was prepared to listen. Would he examine
him, listen to his heart, his lungs, take his pulse –? He would rather

listen. What did Axel have to relate? Years of sleeplessness and inferiority, inability to act, how far back in time? He couldn't measure it, there were endless days, summers that had slipped by, thirty-three devastated years, his youth as though he had never had any, his brothers and sisters, the school, everyone laughing, and the dreams that kept recurring: the faces, perpetually changing, slowly fading the way the memory of a death fades, he sat there describing it all, it seemed to him as though the room were echoing and expanding, he was sitting in a corridor, light was streaming somewhere far away, another life, how could he talk about it to a stranger when he didn't even know himself? Doctor Wargentin leaned forward, do we ever know ourselves? But he had had the finest, the most burning ambitions, had seen himself as a violinist, a composer, had he done any composing? No! Never! Only – only in my imagination.

He drew a breath, wiped his forehead with a handkerchief, the man behind the desk lit his green lamp, the shadows fell onto the table, his face in shadow, who was he, who was this he was telling his life to, as though he had seen him before. And his parents? His father a public official, a pedant like himself, a good speaker, uncompromising, order and justice, honesty and duty, and punctuality, he had that, too, he had inherited it all, and his mother? Axel was silent, sat for a moment hunched forward with his hands clasped, yes, she had listened, she had tried, he knew the dreams and hopes she had entertained, he had dashed them all, she had sat by his side on the edge of the bed and he had not answered her, had wanted to lean in against her but had stopped himself –; somewhere far away on the same floor a door closed, then footsteps were heard, they stopped outside the door, then turned away. They both sat quiet. What tormented him most was a stubborn, heavy, sometimes dreamlike, sometimes brutal fear. Of what? Everything! People, their meaningful looks, the things they said about one behind one's back, their inconsiderateness, their way of distinguishing between sickness and health –. How would he distinguish between them, then? There is strength in shyness, too, there is insight in fear, too!

He did not notice that he had stood up, walked across the worsted shag rug, the only soft thing in this room, no, the light, the lamp, the face of the listening man, they were soft, too, and the cleanliness of the room which lacked all objects other than the most essential, that was how he wanted to order his life, too, only that which was essential, necessary, helping it to be born, yes, he was an idealist in fetters, a dreamer, a hypochondriac, a civil servant like his father, but unemployed, unemployable, was there something in the air that made the weak grow tired, shrivel slowly like soft wood in fire, what was this resignation when it thundered around them, on every street scaffolding, magnificent new buildings, like this one –; yes, said Doctor Wargentin, he had only recently moved in, didn't feel at home himself, but his clients did, the rich ones –. But he wasn't rich, he was poor, hadn't Foundry Proprietor Tamm –? Doctor Wargentin leaned back into the shadows, his hand made a deprecating gesture, the whole thing had been cleared up, the Baron had nothing to worry about from a purely financial point of view.

Axel bowed his head, and there was another pause. If I don't pay my own way I shall feel humiliated. He could understand that, he had taken it into consideration, he had seen that Axel was made like that, uncompromising, life deals harshly with those sort of people –. Some long-concealed sorrow, perhaps over his own misspent life, was trying to force its way out in the form of tears, he succeeded in mastering it with a violent blowing of his nose, it was hot, warm spring weather, yes, Doctor Wargentin got up and opened the window, a glimpse of Nybro Bay with smacks and rowing-boats shone through the gentle twilight, the silence, the pompous façades. Would he please come again, Doctor Wargentin would not at this stage recommend medicines of any kind, oh, some harmless sedative for his nerves, perhaps, but the important thing was his childhood, dreams, the things he had experienced –; Axel began to think about the dead woman, the lightning bolt, all that had pursued him, here in the silence it all seemed unreal. Doctor Wargentin wanted to continue the conversation the following day if possible, he could not promise anything, he would have to travel back, he had meetings, suddenly he was gripped by the fear he had just described, he must go, how much was he owing? He paid. Doctor Wargentin was silent, as though he were still listening down the long corridors, as though Axel was the building, the passages, the unexplored rooms, there was a darkness that was welling towards him; he must go.

Doctor Wargentin followed him out into the hallway, tried to help Axel on with his coat, in utter confusion he managed to get the arm wrong over and over again, sweat broke out on his forehead, he stammered: 'You see! What use am I? What can I give you –? A most valuable insight. The human, yes, the human is composed of so many weak threads, so many glowing ones! –'

Axel was already on the staircase when he said, in his turn: 'I didn't tell you about my aversion to daylight – in your consulting-room there was a healing twilight, for that I thank you –'; he stumbled down the stairs, his knees shaking, the umbrella quivering in his hand, he came out on to the street: it was growing quiet. Quiet streets, quiet houses, mechanically he began to walk uphill, a gentle murmur arose, he'd made a fool of himself again! Masochist! He hadn't made a fool of himself, he had set out his life as honestly as he could, what more could he do? He turned the corner and there was Storgatan, shops, stores, a photographer's: there they were in the window, the portraits, all looking as though they were dead, all motionless, brown, leaning against pillars or caught against the background of an Alpine landscape, the children as grown-up as the adults, the precocious eyes gazing straight at him out of something timeless and forgotten; outside a pawnshop he stopped, took out his wallet, yes, that wouldn't be enough, he went in, the bell above the door rang, towards him came a warm, still scent of abandoned hope, everywhere things, objects, gold rings, pocket-watches, clothes on wooden stocks, glass and porcelain, in the darkness the round, self-luminous face of a short, flabby man who cast an eye at the proffered ring, held it in the flat of his hand as though he were weighing it, examined it with a lens, named a sum, always an insufficient sum, Axel was familiar with this, it was not worth arguing, he took the money and left, was sucked into the stream of wanderers, on the corner of Östermalmstorg a man was selling newspapers, but he didn't buy anything, went into the brilliant electrically-lit market-hall, into the odour of food and bakeries, stood looking at the women, heavy and dark behind the counters, in the shimmering light, he was almost blinded, almost frightened, secretly he was enjoying it, enjoying the sight of all these people, and none of them knew him, he need greet none of them, he was a nobody, he could move freely; for a long time he stood in front of the cement basins and watched the fish in their depths slowly moving, as though they were free, did not know they had been captured, condemned, squeezed within their prison, where they could only move with violent, abrupt strokes, the water eddied black in the gleaming light. Behind cut-up carcases and dead red meat stood the butchers, there were misses and madams, and there were servant-maids doing the shopping, he heard words he had never heard before, he heard dialects he understood not a word of, he moved as though in a trance, was churned in a slow, dignified manner out towards

Nybrogatan, wandered down towards Nybroplan in the mild spring air and then on through Berzelius Park. A murmur arose like a flock of birds towards the darkening sky, the trees were shot with the most transparent green and in front of Bern's Salons the numerous gas-jets were flickering, and the same old sense of unease had gripped Axel; he stood tense with his umbrella, looking inwards on a world from which he had been forever excluded; people were moving there between the tables, faces were raised, female profiles calm and smiling, matches glowed, through the open windows the orchestra could be heard playing Offenbach, the first violin a semitone out of tune, with a sad, scrapy sound, he could have done that, could have played recklessly and happily out of tune, been a member of a little restaurant band and lived happily with a wife and two children –; he turned and went, made his way through the King's Gardens, watching, listening. A thousand footsteps, a thousand rustling dresses, gentlemen's hats which were now spreading out here from the calm, gleaming whirlpools of Sturegatan; and scarcely had the music from Bern's grown thinner and died away, than from Strömparterren came the sound of the Hungarian boys' orchestra impetuously and enticingly hurling a czardas out across the water of Strömmen, while the sun went down like a dark-red orange behind the black scenery of the house-fronts in the west.

He stood watching the light's reflections in the water and remembered a poem, a verse, whate'er your pain, one day you will forget it, but seek your gaze, look down, look down, into the waves' swift current –. What he saw was the white eddies of foam, the façade of the Castle, the white swans, he heard the babble of the people but could not see his own gaze, why was that? 'I, melancholy's son' –: he smiled slightly, and began to make his way up towards Humlegården: it was time. The voices of the old churches could be heard in the clear air above the scaffolding, dead houses and dark alleyways where suddenly a swarm of children might come running out in order just as swiftly to disappear again; the city was rock being blasted, something reckless too in the women's laughter and coquettish glances, in whirled parasols and glowing white cuffs, or in the blind man's outstretched hand, the toothless darkness of the open mouth, in Hotel Rydberg's sparking horsedrawn omnibus as it swept up to the entrance on Gustaf Adolf Square! Everywhere rattling, voices, and always, as though muffled under the spring's light broadcloth, the deepening veil of the twilight.

He made his way through the streets, up towards Humlegården where in the morning he had delivered his suitcase to Tamm's house; Tamm was already out in the town. A card inviting him to supper – with good friends! – was waiting there for him, and the maid had taken his suitcase and carried it to his room, she bore it lightly, lightly, and he followed heavily after, had then rested on the bed almost dead from exhaustion, got up, gone out, wandered in the verdure of Humlegården amidst children at play with hoops and nursery maids, stood for a while looking at the shanties north of Tamm's house, was swallowed up by the thundering building sites of Östermalm, where the dust hung like smoke over the gaping pits and the suddenly appearing alleyways with their wooden staircases, their gutters, their women in aprons, their barefoot children. Blackest of blacks and whitest of whites! Cowshed plots, tobacco patches, wooden shanties crouching as though they had been expecting a beating and were going to get one, cobblestones glistening with sweat were now being wrapped in twilight; along Sturegatan officers who had been delayed still wandered on their way to Bern's, approaching ladies enveloped in white dresses and veils bowed white necks faintly before dandies and dignified manliness, and the scents of the springtime rose like a faint mist between the tree-trunks. Axel wandered alone uphill on the empty side of the street, turned off into the park, pulled at the heavy door on Engelbrektsgatan and stood in the silence, listening: a faint murmur of voices, closed lives, heavy walls and, far away, the quick cries of the swallows.

Blue-grey cigar-smoke streamed towards him, white turn-down collars gleamed above dark waistcoats with gold chains, he was greeted by laughter and swept into an irksome and unreal warmth; titles were flung around and dissolved like bubbles in Vichy water –: 'What shall we call you, we can't just say Axel after all, we won't know whom we're addressing! We'll call our friend from Finland Axel, and we'll call Axel Evald!' The brothers are gathered, there are Director Adolf Vilhelm, Foundry Proprietor Per Gustaf, Comptroller Claes Oskar, Doctor Fredrik August, Director Carl Wolrath, Lieutenant Christian Teodor, there is the youngest of the sons, Axel Evald, and all of them gleaming with abundant, expanding time: Axel looked at them, stood inside their circle and was yet outside it, something in him grew smaller, a fear and a foreboding bound him, he had difficulty in finding words. Axel T. made a speech: my grandfather took part in the Finnish War, at Fredrikshamn, Björkö, Svensksund, and General

Vilhelm Carpelan helped Ehrensvärd to build Sveaborg: a toast to our common past! 'Our long-gone past', added Axel, and they laughed, what were they laughing at? To table, gentlemen! There were the plates, the flickering candelabras – there was finest salmon, cut into slices, vol-au-vents, they sat down at table, two servants – from Finland! 'Like the wood in the stove', called a man with black, twirled-up moustaches, like the horns on a provincial devil, thought Axel, his pince-nez was misted, he had to take it off and wipe it with his damask napkin, suddenly there were silences in the babble of talk, a brewer's waggon could be heard rumbling by, and the conversation slipped over to the subject of the May Day demonstration. Eight hours' work, eight hours' free time, eight hours' sleep, it might just as easily be eight hours' work, eight hours' drunkenness, eight hours' unconsciousness, the Director said as he opened his mouth to put his soup-spoon in it, his cheeks blushed red like ripe apples, something warped, bitter gave each word, each gesture a dark, distorted undertone, he sat there listening to something wild and threatening. I, melancholy's son! But the babbling spring is not silenced, no chalice is drained, the toasts go down, the soup gives way to roast meat, cheese and fruit. The maids are seen dimly, filling up the stoves and going swiftly and silently away, the company moves into the study, Axel stands at the window and sees the sparks from hooves between the trees, the horsedrawn tram on its way up Sturegatan, the three jades like dark shadows. Axel! What would you say? Music – after all, it talks to the feelings, directly. Then isn't it mostly for pleasure, isn't that what it's supposed to be, it says nothing to the intellect, does it? Pleasure – but use, what use is it? None!

He sees: the black-blue stubble, the glistening forehead, the hair combed over the bald patch, horrible! And this brother's opinions: the cross-cut blocks of the timber-merchant, all of the same length, his lips shining, fleshy, his happy countenance, a jovial boon companion, a jovial time, full of hopes for the future –; he sits motionless, he is barely smiling, Evald calls to him: 'Defend us! General!' But Adolf Vilhelm leans forward and says: 'Music may be a sign of beauty, but in real life what is needed is action, purposeful action, science, facts! Isn't it?'

As though he were being taken down a peg or two at school. They don't know him. Do they think he is a chess-piece, a little bookkeeper, or just an obliging ear? His collar is tight, the arms of his jacket are too short, he looks at the wart on Adolf's upper lip, the dark wisps of hair from his nostrils, he gets up, leans forward, supports himself on narrow wrists, in the silence that follows there is heard a faint, cutting sound that grows gradually louder, he can hear himself talking; but there was in the busy, grotesque, eddying room something motionless, fixed, clear, inside him; behind it all, the absurdity, the uncertainty, the quivering voice, the shrillness, the increased volume, it was there: the silence, the calm. He noticed it, he lowered his voice, what had he said – empty phrases! He had to say it:

'My life wouldn't be worth much without music. But my life is only a part of a greater one. What would we be without music? Where words end, there music begins – it, and silence. What would we be without music? Gormandizers, charlatans, inhuman fortune-hunters, empty shells on the whirling surface of success! Where your words die great art continues to live. Bach gave us a cathedral of the inner world, Mozart a garden of light and shadow, Beethoven –'

'Beethoven a saw-mill!' someone shouts cleverly; 'Yes,' Axel continues, he has so little time left now, something dark and desperate is trying to force out the words that are his own and rob him of them, he struggles against it: 'Yes: Beethoven has given us a saw-mill, a bigger one than yours, and the din from that saw-mill will awaken, has already awoken a world, a world inside us – great works of art carry us along with them like spring storms, they change us, we sense the presence of a power that we call God –'

'Hear, hear!'

On the white tablecloth there was a spreading of stains: sauce-stains, grease-stains, remnants of food, they were spreading out, flowing towards him, he stammered: 'In the end there is only – silence, calm and silence –'

He was silent, raised his head, was he crying? He couldn't show it, he walked out quickly, tottering, half-blind, rushed through passages and darkening cloakrooms, out on to the staircase, down the thundering steps, out into the already silent street, in among the trees, the twilight, the lamps that sparingly illuminated the lawns still bright with spring, but everything was already black, as with soot, in the darkness a light bench gleamed, he sank down on it, rocked with his hands in front of his face, it was alive, tears flowed, what was he crying about? That everything was dissolved in confusion? That no one understood the lofty, the inexplicable, the great longing that must exist for us to be able to live, the inexplicable life that bows us, crushes us, extinguishes us and continues as the waves of the sea continue, with roaring in dark trees, with wind and storm –: always this craving, this emptiness that must be filled up inside him, inside them all, before something inhuman, unfeeling and loathsome to the mind forced its way in and replaced the music –

He heard his breathing, a woman had stopped in front of him: 'Doesn't the gentleman feel well? I can make you feel better –'; in the white-powdered face above the plume collar a black mouth, was it a smile or a grimace of distaste, he shook his head, made a gesture, how helpless we are, how we fumble our way across life's surface and grow frightened, how we seek freedom where all is barred; he drew a deep breath, the very twilight, the May night breathed its fragrance as it had once in his childhood, he heard her footsteps grow distant and the silence which was never silent, leaned back, closed his eyes. So cool the fumbling breeze. If voices could take up that theme, the theme of irresolution, fear, anxiety, in a middle movement, build slowly with contrasting chorus, each on a gallery of its own, the way the great masters used to do it, long before Bach, the Gregorians, Ockeghem, if he could only find a musical form for all the hidden fear of this age; there was a face before him where he sat, the face of Wargentin, it was saying something but he could not hear it, only the mouth was moving, it changed, twisted, there were the gaping mouths, 'music's a pastime!', someone springing to his feet, his fists clenched so hard that the table almost followed along with him when he ran out, like a dog that has been given a beating, no, like a victor, a victor! That which is deepest, most intimate, most pure – that shall triumph! But they were empty words. There were empty rooms. There were silent trees, a strange city, and he, poor, insignificant, overstrained, alone. See it. Live with it.

He heard quick footsteps on the gravel path. Tamm's voice: 'My God I was scared! My friend!' He sat down beside him, put his arm round him: 'Don't sit out here on your own. Come on. They've gone. But I'm still here. I won't say anything. Come on!'

They looked at each other. For a while yet they remained, in the silent May night. They did not speak. In the deep sky a faint, radiant brightening. Axel merely a weightless shell, a touch.

From The Diary

July
The first Swedish music festival in Ekenäs: now Finland-Swedish folk-song is beginning to sound, from forgotten chambers, the chambers of the heart. Only hope that they're not full of dead objects, bric-à-brac! Behind the joy in the folk-element there is a sense of melancholy, perhaps it is the precondition of that joy, and they unite the two languages, the two songs in our land. Melancholy: how could it be otherwise in a country where person is distinguished from person by so much dark forest?

13.8
That which is palpable in music is said to be a fruit not of thought but of the logic and warmth of emotion. *La musique, le moins intellectuel et le plus sensuel de tous les arts*, says Lamartine. Hence, no doubt, Tolstoy's fear of it. Yes, perhaps this is true, and perhaps that is why music with its sensuality fills the void within me that yearns for another kind of sensuality. Yet I would still lay stress on the importance and significance of the mind, the architectonic element in music, the thoroughgoing and essential form which must be created not merely by the heart but also by the clear, deep-burrowing mind.

22.8
Read Adolf Paul's *A Book About A Man*, dedicated to Jean Sibelius.* A kitchen midden of semi-digested insights into the artist's work and frenetic life. Little Hans's sufferings are decadent, Sillén's egoism that of an unsophisticated child of nature, a being whose existence I doubt in the world of art, which demands more than naïveté and refinement. Paul also proposes a theory: 'The moods which struck him and made an impression on him were identified in his brain with certain nuances of colour, and it was only when

he had a clear idea of what mood and colour he wanted that he began the real work of composition.... There existed for him a wondrous connection between sound and colour.' Herr Sibelius emerges as something of a gifted apprentice in a paint-shop. The egoistical creep of a hero later meets the child prodigy in Berlin and the plot thickens amidst cigar-smoke and rubbishy chat. The child prodigy improvises at the piano: 'rearing up to a cry of distress and agony at a conscious lack of freedom, before dying away again in silent lamentation' – not a bad description of me reading Paul's book. Sillén sleeps in until twelve and is then in the grip of idleness. The hero finally goes crazy; to that I have nothing to add. Bang is supposed to have translated this as a feuilleton in Copenhagen!

24.8
The magical element in music is concealed in certain reiterated themes which have a consolatory function, as in a mother's lullaby. In that which is tragic and at the same time sublimely reiterated there are also to be found a ritual, not a language, gestures, not spoken sentences. Music dispels that which is 'I', O happiness! Saul's melancholy is dissolved; thus music can never interpret death, only sorrow, suffering, and courage, the flame of eternal life. No music can arise from self-hatred. For my life's having acquired any meaning I thank the singing of the swallows and blackbirds of my childhood. I listened, was purified by their song, as self-evident as nature.

12.9
Fever dream. The thieves on the cross shouting at Christ, their words obliterated by the storm. Were they given vinegar to drink, they also? Who took care of their bodies? Perhaps they were not laid down, but fell down, into an eternal darkness. This dream only lasted for a moment. These horrors that are being played out in reality – I see them in dreams. What's the difference, then?

20.9
It is only by chance events that I have occasionally been brought closer to myself. One passes a mirror, stops and gapes: who is this comical clown, this shabby-looking fellow, this murderer? One hurries onwards with one's secrets. The non-recognition of one-self! Is not that what I have been occupied with until now? Or have I recognized myself only too well? Hurried onwards, with my own image burned into my brain forever.

24.9

On a visit to the capital took a tram from the Student House to Brunnsparken! The horses labour blindly, like so many of us –; remembered Stockholm and the three horses struggling up Sturegatan. I struggle and pull, am less than a horse.

13.10

Most great battles are shapeless masses of straggling troop formations in a mist of blood (Lützen, Borodino, Leipzig). Thermopylae was quite uninteresting from a strategic point of view, it was an imperative necessity created by the landscape. On a great plain, or in a desert, strategic patience is put to the real test.

15.10

As though there were no complexity in music long before the great nineteenth-century giants. The motets, Dufay, Monteverdi: what a web of beauty! The worst flattener-out of these depths was Beethoven, in whose music the Napoleonic celebrates its orgies. Now the task is to re-attain, by means of a deepening of popular and national consciousness, a sense of balance, a flame of self-restraint!

12.11

It sometimes seems to me as though my life were not taking place in the time in which I live, but in some future time when a person will be free to seek among his many selves, be free to leave his class and language in order to speak a language of community, where external poverty will no longer be of importance and hereditary rights unknown. I spend a part of my life in this other life, inside my head. Here I am mummified, fettered to time; there I am in a boundless realm.

13.11

Not to find oneself: can that be a way to self-enlargement, a sense of the universal, or is it simply despair? After all, light cannot exist without darkness, a landscape without shadow, day without night, music without silence, which must be broken.

14.11

Those who cannot tolerate loneliness feel sorry for the person who sits in a solitary room. For that reason they pursue him, beat down doors, surround him with sympathy and lead him gently but firmly out into the rich wide world with its intrigues, idle chatter, self-assertion and boasting, its blind faith in success and strength, climbing and power. In solitude I find the way to the human and living, sometimes in glimpses and flashes, lit up as by a bolt of lightning in darkness, intolerable and inevitable.

16.11

When I consider this circular course of accidental occurrences which we call life and which we believe is directed by fate towards our own 'I', I can find only one way out of the trap: to become less 'I', create another 'I', and then yet another, let them float on the wind like dandelion puffs, and continue the passage of chance without making any demands. From such a course of action sweet music may arise among the dissonance, and a pure sound may become a theme in the 'I'-less playing under the indifferent clouds. It will all be forgotten soon enough. May the chill day receive it, for there is nothing to see but frozen fields; and remember that even in July the autumn wind was there and that which forebodes deepest winter.

22.11

A wife would sit beside me in the same silence, for words would not be necessary.

23.11

To seek God and discover Him to be just as lonely and unhappy as oneself; following from this, a deep friendship. How I long for it!

26.11

The difference between 'alone' and 'lonely'. They alternate, life and half-life, and that undular motion gives rise to seasickness, and the seasickness gives rise to insomnia, days in mist.

29.11

An angel with a nakedly cutting sword: what a terrible image! Mercy like a bolt of lightning one cold winter's day, life and death intertwined with each other. To endure, see clearly. My faith – the faith of the erased?

3.12

Children, how we seek to mould them in our image, and they fade, wither, except the strongest ones, who grow up to mould their own children in their own image –'

5.12
This desperate little Ivan Ilyich of Tolstoy's – does he grow in spite of everything through his fear?

13.12
My environment: Biedermeier, contentment, hidden spiritual poverty, life precisely measured out in little things. Clothes and scent, something warm and motionless. Then may the axe-blows fall!

24.12
Mother ill, did not take part in Christmas. Reading passages from Fröding's 'Guitar': 'for in myself the iron bars are forged and fixed, and only when I too am crushed, will they be crushed as well.' I can well imagine that the iron bars will continue, hovering like a grid of iron above the world even after the time when I too am crushed.

1892

1.1
The New Year is coming in with silence; Mother in bed with a high fever, and I worry, can do nothing.

4.1
Mother died early this morning. I sat by her side to the end, Father had fallen asleep from exhaustion with his hand under his head. Was not aware when she passed over the frontier. A light in my life extinguished. Woke Father and we sat mourning together, until Olga came and took command, Anna silent in her room. Went out walking on the icy roads. A flock of crows was cawing, but golden reeds are rising up from the snow, perfectly still, and the sky clear. Father is alone now, and there is a bond between us which wasn't there earlier. Every door is silently closed. The darkness falls too soon, however late it falls.

5.1
Slept deeply and peacefully. In Mother's room a suffocating heaviness, everything was irrevocable, the sheet dazzling white and the yellow, bandaged, shrunken face.

8.1

'Nothing, nothing!' my soul cries, but doesn't know why or to whom.

27.1

Brother Hjalmar died yesterday of pneumonia only 44 years old, leaving Olga with 7 children, scarcely two weeks after Mother's burial. Father said nothing, just closed the door after him. Gurli, the youngest, is only 3.

3.2

Hjalmar was buried at Masku Cemetery, only the eldest children were there, and Olga supported herself for a moment on my arm. Icy cold in the church. Anna and I supported Father, and we were like black shadows stumbling along the narrow pathways through the snow. At Odensnäs silence that smites the eardrums.

12.5

The spring warm and overflowing, the garden is getting overgrown and Father doesn't go down there any more now, sits in silence for the most part, looking out of the window. Olga has moved in downstairs with her children; a strict regimen. Violent conflicts with Anna. My oratorio has faded and died, its last voices disappearing like a flock of birds. Yet: woken in the night by a theme for string quartet, followed the four voices as though they were intimate friends, and from this happiness managed to get a few hours' blessed sleep.

22.7

On this warm July day registered the silences in the following order: on the staircase up to the cloakroom warm and sunny, scent of flowers; in the cloakroom listening, and cooler; in the big hall as though someone had just gone out leaving table and chairs standing to attention; in the upper hall something long abandoned, sunbeams along the floor, the piano silent; in the library warm smell of books and dust, there it's possible to live for a few hours. Went up to the attic, looked at the great rafters, swallows flew crying in and out the broken windows, in a clothes' chest Mother's clothes, in a corner our skis, Hjalmar's and my own. Sat there for a while, mourning.

12.9
It was Robert Kajanus who brought me to the *Kalevala* and Finnish music through his Aino Symphony; Jean Sibelius has him to thank for *Kullervo*, which shows signs of genius.

13.9
Behind *Kullervo*, do I hear a peculiar sound of gothically-constructed terror? Of fear so deeply hidden in myth and legend that it can only be squeezed out in deep blocks of decorative folklore? Perhaps all 'folk' art contains a fear of growing into something international? Look at the darling little composers in Sweden.

14.10
Father broke a long silence and said that Heiden's menus come, dirty and thumbed, from some shabby civil servants' eating-house in shabby St Petersburg; and we are forced to eat what is offered on them.

Christmas
Reading Tavaststjerna's *Hard Times*,* and am seized by memories. The pure atmosphere of Kotkai is not unfamiliar to me, I myself have walked like a stranger through the rooms in this house. Atmosphere of the midsummer bonfires, and this about Thoreld: 'He knew neither himself nor his fellow human beings properly. He did not know that a person who isolates himself or goes his own way is always viewed with suspicion by society at large, and that only the person who allows his virtues to be weighed and understood by each and every one can count on approval, while the person who because of shyness or pride has not managed to attain favour never has any good sides which the world has been able to confirm. It is an insult inflicted on those nearest to one, to go one's own way outside the orbit of their lives.' Yes! The scenes in the book lead my thoughts both to Tolstoy (Levin-Thoreld) and to Chekhov. The depiction of T. listening to music: the man of the pastoral idyll! Who does not cherish in his heart a yearning for the idyllic! The purity and calm one must fight for in one's inner being. Lehtimaa's imagination a poison that leads to ruin; only the greatest can put the imagination to use and tame it for creative work. My own imagination merely of the reproductive variety, sterile and useless. Also wonderful description of how the peasantry 'heard with surprise their own songs being sung by the gentlemen in many-voiced chorus.' But the folk-element will die,

if the gentlemen do nothing to help. What it's all about is the genuine, to seek and find the genuine, prompted without compulsion.

1893

15.1
Walked in silence into my thirty-fifth year.

27.1.1893

Early in the morning Axel stood by the window and watched the snow quietly falling. The sky was of an even greyness and the light soft. Even in what is apparently dead, pure, and shrouded there is consolation. Yes, perhaps precisely there, in that which is slowly falling and being obliterated. From across the hall, from his father's room, he heard a cry: 'Hjalmar! Hjalmar!'

He turned round, his heart thumping. But the cry was not one of fear; it was firm, demanding. 'Hjalmar!'

He opened the door and hurried through the silent hallway, knocked. 'Come in!' And there, in the dimness, was Father standing on his bed, his long, white nightshirt glowing in the dimness, the yellow blinds lowered, a sweetish scent of eau-de-cologne hanging in the room. 'There you are, Hjalmar.' 'Father, it's Axel.' 'Come, Hjalmar, support me.' He went over to the old man and helped him down to the floor. He still had so much strength left, a bone-hard, sinewy resolve, his bright eyes now hidden deep in his dark eyesockets, his beard completely grey; he helped him over to the writing table where Karl Johan sank down on to his work-chair. He spoke with agitation:

'You must send word to the Tsar in St Petersburg that this cannot go on. This cannot go on! Law and order must not be broken, justice and mercy must come first. Do you understand?'

He looked at his son, his face was so open, appealing, an old man's anxiety, it touched Axel deeply, it was a part of him; yes, he understood. And the old man whispered 'Kneel! Kneel!' He knelt, felt his father trembling, father and son, alone, he felt how cold the room was. 'You must swear and promise to resist evil!' He gave him such a searching look, he said: 'You're not Hjalmar, are you? You're Axel. Yes. You're the only one. Do you promise?' 'Yes, Father.' They both got up, with creaking effort, he saw how the old man's eyes wandered, closed, saw him support himself against the writing table, he rushed to his side, was about to take hold of him, but his father pushed him away and continued in a hoarse voice: 'Here, here's the table, it ought to be at right angles to the window – look, my hand's casting no shadow. Here's the decree, you must make a personal application for an audience. The peasantry is behind it too. Our eleven-man committee was unanimous about it. Our decision remains firm.'

He clutched at Axel's shoulder, held it in an iron-hard grip: 'You realize the necessity of order. Listen. You must be up at seven, milk and porridge, farm work until half past eleven, bookkeeping, stock control, the leased-out fields – you must keep an especial eye on them. Don't forget the daily inspection.'

He lowered his voice, whispered in Axel's ear: 'They'll try to rob you. They'll listen at the doors. Don't talk about important matters at the meal-table, they'll rehash it all in the kitchen, got it? Hjalmar?'

In despair Axel said: 'I'm Axel!'

He looked at him, his eyes slowly filled with tears, his old, red-rimmed eyes, with the bags under them, the long, narrow pale face: 'Yes – you're Axel, aren't you? Axel. Hjalmar let me down. So many are dead, I can't keep count of them all. Little Ida – she was only eleven. How old were you?'

He didn't know what to reply, he whispered: 'Thirty-four.'

His father nodded: 'Yes, that's right. Keep records of everything. Do you know what I am? I'm a law-speaker, and a law-speaker never lets anyone down.* Do you understand? The important thing is to keep everything clean. Look here, stains on your shirt, dust in the corner, the windows dirty –' He looked around him in confusion, pulled up the blinds, a soft white light filled the room and its disorder. 'No one's looked after me since Sofi! They've murdered everything that was dear to me! They don't know that death doesn't exist!'

His father laughed, a faint, croaking laugh, began to cough, sank down on the chair in the corner by the bed, Axel didn't know what to say. 'Father – shouldn't you go to bed, so you don't catch a chill?' 'Me? I've got the strength to outlive you all! Bah –.'

It grew quiet, far away someone was singing in the kitchen, Axel went over to the old man: 'Come on now, Papa, go to bed!'

But his father slowly raised his head, looked at his son, and said: 'Do you remember? Do you really remember me? Help me up. That's right. Follow me.'

They walked through the room, opened the door to the hallway, there was no one there, his father whispered: 'They were standing outside the door, but they run away at once in that cowardly way of theirs! Sometimes I've caught them in the very act, and then let them go. The bird knows the hand, oh yes.'

They wandered further, Axel more dragged along than supporting, the old wall-clock in the big upper hall struck a few rusty, brittle chimes as they went in, as if in response to some command. White curtains, light yellow furniture, the piano silent, and the big family portraits, the full-length one of the general smiling, in a full-bottomed wig, his eyes attentive and awake. The old man stammered: 'What's Vilhelm smiling about? Can you tell me that, boy? What is there to smile about? Pride goes before a fall.'

He turned round with surprising swiftness to face Axel, who stopped at the door:

'Do you know who God is? Him over there, does he know? Is He here, do you suppose?'

Axel didn't know whether his father meant the General or God, but his answer applied to both of them: 'Yes, he's here, Father.'

A smile passed like a shadow over his father's features. 'Good! I've never been able to understand all that stuff about heaven. It's all here, here, on earth, here, in the beams, it all goes back, you'll see, it sinks down into the earth, just as we do –.'

He beckoned to Axel: 'Don't be afraid, come with me, I'll show you!'

They wandered across the light carpet with its red border to the library, his father's legs under his nightshirt so thin, so fragile that Axel almost expected him to fall, he tried to take his arm, but he shook his hand away, walked slowly over to the lectern, opened the Doré-illustrated edition of Dante's *Divina Commedia* which always lay there, searched with quivering hands, turned over the pages, searching: 'I can't find him. He was here, no, that's not the right plate, I can't find him –'

He closed the book, his frame collapsed, his shoulders, his head. Axel hurried to his side, and now the old man seized his arm gratefully, whispered: 'I couldn't find him.' 'Who?' 'Jesus. I want to go to bed.'

Silently they walked through the library, faint coughing could be heard coming from Uncle Fredrik's room, from Anna's room silence, as usual, thought Axel, their steps were so slow, cautious, as though they had finally arrived at their destination after a long journey, from the kitchen a distant clattering was audible: early morning.

He helped his father into bed, laid the bedspread over him, the old man at once turned towards the wall with his hand under his cheek. Axel was just about to turn and go when his father said something, mumbled, indistinct. He turned, bent down over the old man: had Father said anything?

'Yes,' the Referring Clerk replied. 'Remember: moderation in all things. And order, keeping one's word.'

'I'll remember.'

'One more thing: don't you think it would have been too big and heavy for anyone else to carry? The cross?'

'Yes, I think so.'

'I want to rest now. Off you go. Not far away now. Mind.'

'I will.'

He closed his eyes, his breathing so light as to be scarcely noticeable. For a moment Axel stood quite still in the room, then turned, silently closed the door, and stood leaning his head against its chill.

From The Diary

1893

3.2

Father died peacefully in his sleep today at the age of 82. Within the space of a year I have lost Mother, Father and my only brother. The hard earth must yield again.

10.2

In the churchyard watched the people standing round, their faces with those assumed expressions of solemnity, even the priest's. Only the children were unable to keep up the pretence. The sun broke through and hoarfrost gleamed on the trees. Olga kept opening and closing her mouth. Father's brother Fredrik not there because he was indisposed. Anna somewhat theatrical with gestures she had seen at the theatre? My ears were cold, my top hat was rubbing, the bell in the tower on the other side of the road was tolling, and fifteen-year-old Tom is now the head of the family and Olga the head of the head.

28.2

Had a nightmare about the room being on fire, through the burning doorposts rushed the dead, leaping past me as I was impatiently waiting for – whom? At last, slowly striding his way, came Dr Wargentin with a smile, while I screamed at him to hurry up; behind him the mighty oak rafters were falling in thundering vortices of sparks. Then I was alone and was being forced backwards towards the deep, dark staircase behind me, I was merely two eyes, merely a child, and woke up with Olga standing in the doorway shouting in an angry voice: 'Axel, you mustn't scream like that! The children will wake up!' She bangs the door shut with more noise than my cries had made, and I sit in the darkness, no longer knowing where I belong.

3.4

The northern spring requires nerves which I lack. Pale, ice-cold light, everything dirty, drawn-out, wind-torn, especially in the towns. Read a long obituary of Father in the *New Illustrated Gazette* for 18th March, where the most important things are included; rather moved by his long speech at the Representative Assembly of 1863-64: 'A people that is working on its own independent development will not threaten, will not mock another people undergoing the same process –; it will rejoice in every step forward that another people, in whatever land, may have made and be making on the great arena of mankind. Thus at any rate the Finnish people have rejoiced at every step forward the Russians have made on the path of civilization and independent development, and one may therefore hope for a similar feeling from the side of the Russian people.' Where did Father get this idealism from? The legislative revisions, equality between man and woman in the question of inheritance, impartial birthright, the fight against high excise duties – all foreign to me. Can it be that some people grow up from birth with sunlight in their lives and receive sunlight back, while others remain in darkness? Is not darkness capable of giving strength? Both Father and Mother were originally of the light, Mother until the last. Whence all my darkness, in that case – or, more precisely, my photophobia? Or is it rather that people create their own darkness? And are unaware when they have taken the step into the dark.

4.6

Olga summoned us together and told us that we must leave the family home. We knew this and yet did not know it; Anna burst into tears. Uncle Fredrik has already gone to live in Åbo. Said nothing, went into my room. There are people who only perceive what others can be used for, not what they are. Now it is Olga's turn. The children stood, watching. All the rooms quiet, someone was hushing a child who was shouting.

7.6

Went and said farewell to the faithful old retainers. Even in the hallway this smell of staleness, sour milk, soot and warmth. In the big servants' room darkness, two or three men sitting along the bench to the right, to the left beside the whitewashed stove women and children, over by the end-wall with its little window the long table, the sunlight chequered on the polished floor with

knotty chunks of wood like the joints of legs, and the light pro-
jected along sunbeams charged with the finest dust. Only here did
I feel great sorrow for the first time, wanted to sit for a while, but
it was no good; they curtseyed before me, Axa with her apron
held to her face, as though they had been punished, or as though
they were mourning, not me, but an era that was now at an end.
Once outside I crossed the road and walked into the woods. It
was cool in there, and the sky above me clear and bright, and there
I said farewell.

12.6

The surrey has taken Anna, myself and our luggage to Nådendal,
where we are living in rooms that have been let to us by Dr Branders. You, my book, are all that is left to me now! As a consolation,
for what I say here is of no account. It has also now finally dawned
on me that for the defenceless person every attack has its own
justification. Sketched the beginning of a quartet which before
long foundered in confusion and emotional storms. Wandered
down to the harbour, an evening calm rested over ships and masts,
and there were no stars in the sky. Am now reading the *Kalevala*.
Kullervo's shout asking not to be born! The creator of the Kullervo
Symphony has given a performance of *En Saga* – I wish I had
heard that, as legends, *sagor*, are full of consolation.

14.6

In my boyhood I used to imagine that I lived inside this unsuccessful, stunted figure of mine as in a disguise; that behind this façade
magic forces were concealed! Dreams that could move mountains!
Unheard-of music of rare strength! And perhaps there was some
truth in that, then. But now I can see that 'le façade, c'est moi',
and no power protects me, no one sees my agony, because it is
the poverty of the age, of the earth and of society that has formed
me. The important thing now is to form my lament into praise
and exultation: music which, originating in sorrow, is always
triumph, homage, human spirit. And consolation, the way a
mother consoles. And in this there is not so much aesthetic sense
as moral strength, though in great art these are united, and are
one and the same thing.

12.9

The summer has gone, and I have done nothing; Anna has seen
to my food and the other most essential things. How quickly a

whole life is demolished by ambitions, dreams, actions, words, writings, marriage, company, travel, experiences; suddenly one day all the objects one has gathered are abandoned, and a body sinks quickly into the earth, within a few years to be forgotten, as though it had never existed. But Mozart's *Requiem* exists.

15.9

Mörike: *Einem Kristall gleicht meine Seele nun, den noch kein falscher Strahl des Lichts getroffen** –; but I *was* struck, and my soul was never allowed to rest again.

18.9

The Branders family most delicately considerate. Against this, Anna's rather crude demands, which I attempt to tone down; together we make a fine couple, well-accustomed to attending funerals. My black overcoat with the fur collar is starting to get worn out, as the bodies and clothes of elderly bachelors do.

21.9

Leisurely walk in the cemetery, so beautiful and quiet. The dead extend the sense of melancholy in the way dark shadows extend the landscape. As in Schubert's Op. 99 Trio, the andante. These dark, weightless shadows in the clear September light, as though one were looking up into the foliage of a tree; and the summit deepens, arches towards the stars, as in the voices of Mozart's G minor Quintet: pain, oblivion! And in that, a sense of freeing.

3.10

Could bear it no longer, travelled to Helsingfors. While there saw Axel Gallén's 'Symposium' painting. Reproduces some of the chaotic loneliness that is always there when artists gather together in order to try to destroy darkness and the men of darkness. What would our art be like if moderation were to be observed (as it often is)? It would be – moderate. Where Edelfelt has given brilliant displays of champagne, Gallén has given the bitter aftertaste. Yet even here there is the creeping suspicion of a certain fashionable worldliness, something self-pitying. How well I recognize it. Those dark eyes, the demonism of a small country glowing by itself in the darkness, which cannot yet thunder into fire and flame!

12.10

Those who reject what they do not understand should remember

Mozart's pauper's grave, obliterated, gone. How Salzburg and Vienna scoffed at him and humiliated him, and how they now honour him, call him their own. People's coarseness and superficiality contributed in bringing about his death. And we sit over our glasses of punch, and lament.

13.10
Mozart's early Symphony in G minor. Life great in its suffering and greatest in its shadows. The winds give an impression of sunlight in a gloomy park, a momentary opening that is closed again. This concentration upon suffering by someone carefully continuing his work. What this age needs is art of depth, clear and – haloed. That which exists at the very heart of this 18-year-old's perception of suffering. As I write this, autumn is aflame; the expanses are great and free, the fields are growing hard.

18.10
We ought to possess more symbols for that which cannot be articulated, in the way that music has its own notation; perhaps then people would get along better with one another? Everyone would speak the same language.

22.10
V. Rydberg in a letter to Heidenstam concerning 'Pilgrimage': originality but not naïveté. 'What I love in poetry is simplicity and honesty; and showy phrases, unnecessary displays of language are what I detest.'

14.11
Snow, ice-fields, and a town that is closing around my neck like a blinding white double collar; the people black, if there are any. I and the world in opposition; all that's left is to live, to grow!

5.12
The part of me that is alive scrutinizes the part of me that is dead and discovers that it occasionally gives signs of life and begins to live in separation from me. This thought frightens me: must I go into the shadows, at last?

24.12
Christmas, outside the house, people, life. Gentle, white snow.

3.1
Ill, sleepless.

15.1
Birthday with cake baked by Anna. Ah, ah, ah! Life's all right, I suppose!

22.1
This cheap demonism, these excesses on the part of those who have not perceived in earnest that the giddy depths really do exist, and that their darkness can only be vanquished by keeping oneself afloat on a steel point of light. The G minor Symphony.

3.4
In the dream my room altered, the things in it became hollow and menacing, there were echoes as though the wind had blown through the windows and shattered them. Then dead, unfamiliar faces passed through this world of sound, and streamed in appalling multitudes right through my eye from the left-hand door to the right; they quickly turned their empty faces towards me, baring their teeth; I remember that then I cried out, but nothing was audible except the whisperings and laments of those who were streaming by; I have not encountered their singing in music, they require a new tonal system.

4.4
They have a way of talking past me, as though I were not there. And, as usual, they are right.

10.4
Hypochondria, real torments, martyrdom, self-pity, apathy, fear – and in contrast to this the abundant life that teems in alleyways and among the trees, at sea and under the sky around me and which I would not see with such burning clarity if I were healthy, strong and took everything for granted.

12.4
Fell asleep and woke up in the middle of the night with my knees drawn up to my neck and my pince-nez still on my nose. Saw myself from above as though I had been put in a grave and then

set free. Old fossils, remains, dead relics from the Stone Age. Got up, stood at the window. Moonlight on the big oak-tree in the courtyard, completely black, and the light like a mist.

30.4

Yesterday the statue of Tsar Alexander II was unveiled on Senate Square in Helsingfors. In the old days they were loved. Now, to be endured.

5.5

Was asked to play in a string quartet, but refused. There are enough happy amateurs in search of a pastime.

22.6

The rats have performed their seasonal coupling along streets and alleys. The notabilities of the town in mottled coats with vibrating whiskers, the she-rats, too. The pink darlings of the bathing establishment in striped bathing-suits à la prison. The town's gendarmerie with sabres straggling askew beneath their bellies. Female posteriors in tulle swaying beneath little parasols, stained by seagull-droppings. Oh me, oh my! A red-gleaming brass band playing out of tune, what a terrible shame! *Brännvin* on ice, soul on ice, water in exceptional circumstances, and air there's none, it's all run out. Soon we puppets will be dead, but the seagulls will scream as before and the jackdaws dart laughing out of the church wall.

28.6

The dying Keats in one of his last letters to his friends. 'I can hardly say farewell to you even in a letter. I always make such an awkward bow –'

13.7

On the café terraces there is sentimental enthusiasm for lofty and unattainable ideals, while the gaze voluptuously absorbs itself in others of a more lowly nature. Condoms in marriages of convenience, servant girls as mattresses, illegitimate children boarded out – like presents! – to grateful crofters, which bondsmen, moreover, receive a gratuity every six months!

16.7

What is degradation? We perceive it as a threat to ourselves. So it is when we forget ourselves, pay no attention to mockery or sympathy and outgrow them. I know that I am 'outside' myself the way music is, the way the air, the city, the alleys, the water, the boat-rigging in the twilight, the voices are; I go there and am soon vanished in the shadows. But it would naturally be a consolation if someone were occasionally to turn round and watch me go, and remember me, with love.

5.8

If you felt you were shut up inside a mountain, deep inside its darkness, would you call for help all the more?

14.8

After so many corpses, have entered upon a new solitude. I am not a man of imagination, hence my tormenting dreams, which I cannot control. Dreams are one thing, imagination another: it demands action. The bane of this age and of mankind is lack of imagination; formerly this sickness was concealed and hushed up with money, possessions and power. Now it stands exposed.

So: out into life, sluggard! The only power I can muster lies outside myself: the belief in freedom from tyranny. For I do not belong to the old ruling class in which I have my origins, but neither do I belong to the new one, which is composed of men of action running riot in pursuit of power. Increasingly there is a type of person to be found who no longer pays regard to his brother for what he is, but for what use may be made of him. This is a pestilence of the soul, invisible even to those who carry it. And in this air we breathe. By day negators, at night enjoying our prerogatives, double in our souls. Father's civil service honour is being crumbled away between dirty fingers. Each man the architect of his own happiness! Each man a sledgehammer!

Some are rescued from this by embracing an idea which slowly emasculates them or corrupts them. They become performers in a single key, walking mouthpieces; they have stopped creating.

The only way for me is towards solitude, genuineness of thought, even if overshadowed by death. Only that can save me from lack of self-respect which is the most extreme humiliation.

The obverse side of this age is Dostoevsky's theme of degradation.

22.8

My body rejects even the strength of alcohol. Most sober of torments, driest of despairs, most pedantic of lunacies, most comic of tragedies, saddest of visions. Music the only consolation, the only language that will protect us from despair. The fact that it is at the same time the language of eternal spring, of hidden paradise makes it none the less rich a source of consolation for those who live as shadows.

3.9

Dreamt of my childhood's manor, a stone's throw from here, as the crow flies. The city is losing its inhabitants. Life the song of an idiot, according to Euripides, but how beautiful sometimes – clear, cool, ethereal, like the fragments of the great idiots – Hölder-lin, Kivi*, Wecksell. Good to live with them, when one's gaze takes in the people of everyday life. Anna's care-worn features. My own.

12.9

Mild September days of soft light. Feel how the elements carry one. Some people move all their lives in this life-giving water, sink, rise up, think perhaps they are drowning, but are ever surrounded by the vision that bears them along. For the others the elements are merely the bitterest of afflictions; but when these unprotected ones are occasionally vouchsafed the chance of being borne along by happiness, they hear, more clearly than those who are protected, the transcendental, playful melody of the Magic Flute. Where the music of the protected is a landscape, at happy moments a heaven is theirs.

22.10

Nightmares, of being pursued, running through the alleys, down to the harbour; woke up in a fever. Autumn gale outside, the last leaves being torn away like embers for the soil.

Christmas

spent with Anna. Fatal year, nothing out of nothing, horsehair screeching against gut, rigid eye. Bleating sounds, lapping, moaning, voices raised and lowered, behind the walls, like a cacophony of rubbish. Spying and deceit of the authorities, sordidness and intrigues, the throat-clearing and pestilential pompousness of the academics. Rage in the flesh, pedantry in the spirit, fear and helplessness. Out of insomnia I walk without substance.

15.1

Am now thirty-seven years old, not grown-up but dried-up. And at every moment I must choose: post-chaise or train? Egg gruel or nothing? Nothing. Cake from Branders, with punch. Told stories about ski journeys on glazed frost; remembered the creeks of my childhood.

23.1

Anna was sewing. I sat rubbing a stain on my overcoat, the one with the fur collar. It was quiet, only the stain gleamed towards me with a dimly phosphorescent light, and the more I rubbed it, the more this radiance spread, began to glow like a bloodshot eye. I wanted to call out to Anna but sat with my head bowed, in order not to disturb her. The stain spread up my shoulder, resembling a continent. Rubbed desperately, felt like a Jew in the diaspora, persecuted by an unknown external force. Had to push the overcoat away from me, and it slid down to the floor. Perhaps my face, too, is a stain like that, which God is finding it difficult to rub from his overcoat; he could hardly find it difficult, when there's so little to which I cling – Anna, but she can't hear me.

28.1

At any second to be exposed – for having done what? For having lied all one's life.

3.4

During my illness, an inspiration – heard a string quartet in which Father, Mother, Hjalmar and I were talking, Hjalmar was first violin, I was second, Mother was the 'cello and Father the double bass. Tranquil, from darkest minor to major, as we never talked in real life, in unreal life.

26.4

The spring has come, and the little gardens behind the fences are beginning to turn green. Have moved my bed to the other wall and am looking at the window and the shadows on the curtain, they are moving as though someone were moving them.

27.4

Keats mentions in a letter to his brother and sister-in-law in America his joy at drinking claret on summer evenings in a garden, how refreshing it is, how it slips down his gullet cold and feverless, down into Keats's 'sore throat'. How touching this joy in coolness, on the part of one whose lungs are diseased.

4.5

Small fires have been laid in the town and have caused an enormous sensation. As though everyone had been expecting them! The good citizens are not so hypocritical as not to be able to imagine that the mighty, concealed volume of rubbish could catch fire and whirl a course of devastation across shut-up houses. And now of course poor retarded Pauli H. is suspected of the misdeed – for no one with any sense would bother trying to destroy such a diminutive Sodom, would they?

26.5.1895

When Axel came down into the kitchen the new kitchen-maid was standing by the stove in a beam of morning sunlight, there was a clattering of stove-rings, a crackling of firewood, the air was warm and fresh and a breeze wafted the fragrance of lilacs through the open window and mingled it with that of the coffee. Axel stood in his stockinged feet and breathed deeply. A night spent in semi-wakefulness was slowly dispersing, the ghosts and chimeras were giving way to the listening and quiet objects, the table, the chairs, the rag-rugs, the daylight, and the girl who was turning round and watching him without fear. Her dark hair was combed back, its parting gleamed white and the brown eyes in the radiant, sunburnt face were watching, smiling. 'I haven't been able to sleep,' he said, 'I had such terrible dreams.' He felt like a schoolboy. 'Am I disturbing you?' She shook her head, pointed to a chair, he sat down. Her checked dress was so tight for her firm, round figure, her apron was freshly-ironed and dazzling white, when she turned round there was a gleam of down at her soft, slender neck. She stroked her hand over her hair, a quick, girlish gesture, she could scarcely be twenty. Some almost forgotten childhood memory, something painful passed before him, an image of someone consoling, long since vanished, and with it Mother's face, but now young, alive. He leaned his head in his hand: 'The faces, I can't cope with them any more' – and noticed that he had spoken aloud, in despair. She stopped in the midst of her tasks, turned round: 'The gentleman should tell me, if things are hard, I'm listening –'; the words came softly but firmly, as though she knew him, as though she possessed some special wisdom; and bless him if she didn't come and sit down right in front of him, looking at him like a doctor at a patient, or perhaps like a mother at her child, or simply like someone who wants to come close without doing harm. His self-pity welled up like a wave and he began to feel a burning sensation behind his eyelids, he had to rub the ridge of his nose, his face felt long and narrow, rough and dead, an old object forever fixed to a heavy, clumsy body. Why was he sitting here on an impudently early morning when the town was not yet awake and only a few solitary cockerels were clamouring and crowing, the May warmth slowly rising out there in the sun, with a girl he did not know who sat there looking as though she were listening – was she really listening? He looked into her eyes and turned away; there was a purity there which he recognized – why was he unwilling to accept it? Because he so seldom encountered it? Because he believed there was compassion there: compassion smothered him, degraded him, he wanted to turn aside, run away as a child would do; he asked her: 'What's your name?' 'Rachel.' He said: 'I had a long nightmare. I saw the faces of my father and mother, they had their eyes shut, I knew that they were dead, they came close like ice-floes in a dark sea, they knocked against my cheek, I cried out to them but they didn't answer, their mouths – had changed, they laughed or bared their teeth, they shrank and disintegrated, disappeared, there was a white door that struck my eye, and Father came out of it, almost threatening, and I shrank back to being a child out of fear –' He could feel how exposed his face was, how naked, he had wanted to say something quite different, but the words had dispelled the dream, also his father's gaze which said: 'How insignificant! How easy! Too insignificant! Too easy!' He had a weight of his own, after all, he was alive, here, she, Rachel, was listening, Rachel! She sat quietly, then said: 'Mother used to wake me up if I cried out, she'd put her hands on me, then I'd sit up, pass my hands over my eyes, that used to help –.' She fell silent, a scent of soap came from her, was it pine soap, how pure it smelt, they were like brother and sister, he couldn't explain it, he closed his eyes and she got up, walked round the table, stood behind him, laid her hands on his eyes, they were utterly cool, he placed his hands over hers and she did not draw them back, time stood still with all its sounds, even the wall-clock beat in time to the pulse in her slender wrists, he wept for a short while in her hands but stopped, felt only calm, lowered his hands and laid them on the table. She turned hers and stroked his eyes with them, then laid them on his shoulders beside his neck, massaged them slowly with her thumbs, then stood quietly with her hands on his shoulders. Then the moment was past, she went back to the stove, he sat for a while following her movements, she smiled towards him: 'Did that help?' And he smiled back: 'Yes, Rachel, your hands made me feel better, it's strange, it's as if we had known each other for years

128

and years, it's all right if I call you Rachel, isn't it?' He got up, went over to her, she did not turn away, but for a moment there was fear there, in the calmness, in her eyes; he put his hand against her cheek, went back, stopped near the door, looked around him, she stood there with her back to him, her slender neck, motionless, her hair, her dark hair gleaming in the morning light. He closed the door silently, stole up the staircase, lay down on his bed, it was completely quiet, the morning so warm and summer-fair, the foliage young and listening, the air light, and he fell asleep the way one slides into the shadows without effort on a cool, mirroring sea, the oars soundlessly grazing the surface, making no demands whatever, full of happiness, dark treetops raised towards the light of the firmament, the sleep, the dreams there, like a gentle light behind the eyelids, and the singing of the birds remote, then vanished.

He awoke to an empty house, slowly and carefully put on his white summer suit, donned a soft collar and his wide-brimmed hat and took a stroll down to the harbour. Low windows looked for a long time after him, every so often someone would greet him and he would return the greeting, hurriedly, as though caught unawares. Carts, old men and women, black and white, boats and the water itself as if covered by fish-scales in the clear sunlight, and up there crying swallows –: he stood for a while in the shadow of trees and watched the trading, saw how the gulls fought over ripped-out entrails that were hurled in the water, how the keen shadows fell between the low, wooden shanties, heard the singing from the veranda of Socis: this is a wonderful place to be! And on his way out to the steamboat pier he saw her again, but she failed to see him, moving so lightly, so naturally among the stalls, had her white headscarf on, he drew back, bumped into a parasol, said he was sorry, and a deep, rough voice answered: 'Oh, for goodness' sake, everyone bumps into everyone else here.' He turned round and saw a thin, pale face beneath a broad-rimmed hat, clear-blue, ice-blue eyes and a mouth that was only just smiling, he had met her at Anna's: Mrs Döhr, the piano teacher, the widow of a wealthy timber merchant. She took his arm impetuously, flung herself into a conversation about music, about Beethoven's piano sonatas, about the amusements offered by the town, about the latest scandals, about the possibilities of the Finnish opera. The birdlike, nervous element in her was balanced by a peculiar, intense strength: was she desperate, perhaps? Was she in search of contact by any means, even with someone like himself? The couple was observed from the verandas of the restaurants and was thought bizarre, there was a stroking of moustaches, a twirling of parasols, a polishing of bootflaps, a stealing of glances, a nodding from one to another, silently, in tacit mutual agreement. 'Call me Julia,' she said, 'I'm sure I'm older than you', and she smiled, but her lips contracted over her teeth, and the general effect was more like a grimace, as if what she had said was: 'I'm acting under a compulsion, something inside me demands it.' Axel listened yet did not listen, walked along with his eyes lowered, saw lawns, flowers, white bench-loads of summer visitors, children running past with hoops, in sailor's suits, it was all a remote murmur, and closest to him was a name: Rachel. How had the girl got that name? From a mother who knew her Bible, of course. Was Axel talking to himself, or to her, Julia? He had to ask her to excuse him, his thoughts were filling him to distraction, just as the music did her when she played, he expected, or was there something else as well; she laughed coarsely: yes, the sight of her pupils' hands, fingernails, the jarring of an untuned string. But when she herself played? She narrowed her eyes, looking out at the bay, before answering: she was beside herself, out of herself, as they say, the way one is when in love –; she gave him a quick look. He felt beneath his fingers the cool, shiny cloth of her dress, the wrist white and covered in veins, saw the small wrinkles at her throat, the blonde hair around her ear, she pressed his hand: 'If Axel wishes, I'll play for him! Whatever he likes!'

To be sure, he was excited, as by a painful heat, quite the opposite of the one that surrounded them, he had to take off his hat and mop his face with his handkerchief, wipe his pince-nez, he said: 'I find Beethoven the symphonist hard to stomach – there's something pent-up, titanic and convulsive about him' – but his thoughts were closer to her, followed the movements of her shoulders, her back, her legs, and she turned halfway round with her cold, clear eyes directed towards a point immediately beside him, beyond him: That heaviness was too great for her, she loved the swift passion in Mozart, the lightness like that of a bird flying over deep water –; he said that was what he himself thought, she had the soul of a poet, had she done any writing? Only a few love poems, and nothing after the death of her husband. She lowered her head, and they walked on in silence. The narrow alleys, the gravel that crunched so hard and loud beneath their feet, the door creaking open, the entrance-hall with its motionless, honey-yellow warmth, the drawing-room; he waited while she went to fetch refreshments, she had taken off her hat, her face not beautiful but alive, mobile, as she was standing right up against him he had to touch her, support himself against her, seek her mouth, she was breathing so violently, moaning, almost, clung to him, half-blind over palms and draperies he saw a far-away reflection of two strangers, almost submerged in darkness. Was it he or she who led the way to the bedroom, the silence, the violent cries, the eyes and hooks, the desperate, almost cruel coupling, he was not there, he bit, the sweat streamed, he was truly out of himself just as she was, meaningless words whirled around in his head, it was grotesque, not worthy of human beings, he could not go through with it, he had to throw himself on his back, panting, half-dressed, a total defeat, a humiliation that penetrated to his skin and his nakedness, she flung a blanket over him, she got up from the bed, never saying a word, disappeared, he heard the splash of water, quickly sat up, dressed, everything was soiled, sticky with sweat, through the window he saw a garden littered with dandelions, he did not know what to do, he sat down and waited. If he raised his hands, they quivered. The flypaper on the ceiling was black with dead flies; still they flew in here, into the warmth, the heat that smelt of some heavy, almost intolerable perfume. Only now did he notice it, saw the uncovered bed, had to get up and pull the bedspread across. 'Is that you making the bed?' she asked, with an ice-cold, frozen smile, a scornful voice. Axel mustn't exert himself. Axel might get tired.

She sat down by the window, her hands in her lap, she twisted them, looked at him: 'I didn't mean to frighten you. I wanted to make love to you. But perhaps you didn't want to in the first place? Say something.'

Yes, he had wanted to. But that was how he was, fear attacked him, he was alone whatever he did, he hadn't meant to hurt her, he would so much have liked to – but his clumsiness, his inexperience –

He bent forward, as though he were in pain, but she smiled at him, began to laugh, a shrill, high laugh, she couldn't stop, he took her hands but now she drew him towards her, now she pushed him back, her tears flowed, she pummelled him with her small, hard fists, he tried to stop her, tried to calm her, he put his arms round her, they rocked together until she pushed him away from her and screamed: 'Go! Go! And don't come back!'

He had wanted to explain, to tell her about his darkness, his photophobia, about everything that weighed him down. He walked through the rooms, slowly, kept his self-control, closed the door quietly after him, he stopped and listened: was she crying? But nothing could be heard. Should he go back? What more could he do. It was over, like everything he touched, everything he hoped for. He took a long route home, stopped for a moment and saw the sea in a haze, the merciless sun, the town crouching under the heat; at home he stripped naked, washed, then lay on his bed and looked at the ceiling where the damp had left marks, wandering marks like the ones on old maps, undiscovered continents, meaningless profiles, satyrs and dead people. Someone was singing in the kitchen, was it Rachel? Whatever he touched became twisted, silent and death-transfigured; but the singing was coming to him from a cool, healing distance. He saw that he was living in the house of music.

As Axel sat in the very furthest dim room where only the milk-white triangle of the window spread a mysterious light he saw Doctor Wargentin coming through the suite of rooms with a violin in his hand. It flamed glitteringly each time he passed one of the windows in the big hall, and each time the bells intoned their Te Deum as though they were people with voice and passion, and the light fell in such a manner that the dust-particles formed streets through which the man walked with a smile. Each room was like a song, Axel listened but could not make out the words, they were lullabies or folk-songs, melancholy, clear, but he saw he was bleeding, that from his wrists, so badly cut, blood was coming; how would he be able to play with hands like those? There was a fragrance of childhood and summer, he was perhaps thirteen years old, someone had hurt him, but Doctor Wargentin had white bandages in his hands, they billowed after him as though a wind had passed through the halls. Axel sat in the library, and it was from Uncle Fredrik's room that the stranger, the saviour, the consoler came. Axel stepped towards him, his arms outstretched, and they stopped shedding blood, and he found himself in a big attic where crying swallows flew about. There were beams and the fragrance of wood and sawdust, gentle sunlight and a static warmth, and Doctor Wargentin was now only a listening face, his eyes fixed on him so that he had to meet his gaze and do nothing but mechanically move his fingers over the strings. The faintest music arose, a most intimate voice, almost silenced but clear and welling forth, like the resin from the trunk of a damaged tree. There was no one in the attic now, he could play as he liked, from the rooms below a mighty darkness came flooding up, so that he stood as in a phosphorescent light surrounded by invisible listeners, and he raised the violin, it almost forced its way beneath his chin, so wild was the cadenza, so tall the building, so clear and daring the arch, so lonely the person before the music that only grew in intensity. By glimpses he saw the rafters cross, whirl around one another, as in Piranesi's *Carceri*; to the captive he gave voice, to the sufferers meaning, to the lonely joy – and there, among the rafters, in the middle of the attic floor, stood Rachel, motionlessly listening, and it was for her that he was playing, no one had ever played as mightily as this, and the music rose like a wave, it broke, there was suddenly bitter, corroding pain, one by one the strings snapped, twined around his hands, he tore and pulled, and Rachel's face changed, grew narrower, paler, there were black lips opening and a laugh bursting forth, that was Julia, her shrill voice cut through the rooms, echoed, redoubled, he stood against the wall in the big hall, then he walked on like a blind man and brushed his sleeve over his eyes, it smelt of napthalene. In the rooms in the flat upstairs they were playing quartets, he must creep softly so as not to disturb them, his tears as a hindrance. If only night would come soon!

In the lower hallway he stopped: everyone was asleep, he was alone. Or had they died? Such faintly murmuring voices, how had he not heard them before? A table was laid there, they had not left it, his father and mother, was it they who were singing? His hands, he must show them his damaged hands, he would never be able to play again, they would surely see to that, all of them, those who were alive. When he went down the wooden staircase past the urns with the monogram CEC and the still, dead palms, the meadows spread out with frost and chill, and the trees gleamed with a sound so high-pitched that only he could hear it, a white sound against his eye: nothing was forgotten, the dead woman lay in the snow, watching him from beneath half-closed eyelids, the children got up out of the Lapland sleigh and fell back like black skittles, the low-scudding clouds with their soot were gathering and moving in his direction and he shouted: 'No! No!' in fear and terror, and awoke, wet with sweat, not knowing where he was.

When he came down to the kitchen old Mrs Anne Winberg was standing there talking to Rachel. They looked at him, as though they had been talking about him, secrets, plans, decisions. Shyly Rachel returned to her tasks, the table had to be set for dinner, the smell of frying fish and boiling potatoes warmed him. 'You look like a ghost, Axel,' Anne said, and Rachel turned round and looked at him, and he replied: 'Yes, that's what I've always been. A ghost. And I move freely in time and space, and when the table shakes at Anne's seances, that's me, and when the piano plays all by itself in the drawing-room, that's me.' He laughed, he had to take out his handkerchief and hold it against his mouth, then he turned and went. He felt their eyes in his back, but that was his life: to endure, conceal, and in pain and humiliation grow, independently of himself, of the living, and the dead. On the staircase he met Anne, she had aged, her hair was thin and mouse-coloured, she said: 'You were shouting just now. Couldn't you ask Doctor Branders for something to calm you down?' He looked into her pale blue, worried eyes: 'I've got some pills, I'll take them, I'd forgotten about them. Don't you ever have – nightmares?' 'Very rarely', she said. They went their separate ways. He sat in front of the window. His diary lay open. He leaned his head against it, it cooled his forehead. He clenched his fists, put them against his temples. It seemed to him as though behind closed eyelids he was looking with forced-open, wide-open eyes into a heavy, dark depth that had no end, and that from this depth there flowed a coolness that embraced him like a blessing.

From The Diary

1895

29.5

Where the race-horse shies and, wild-eyed, takes a leap and breaks his leg, the cart-horse lumbers sweatily and unimpressively onwards – under the whip. He has learned his lesson.

2.6

The town full of summer visitors and bathing enthusiasts, members of the authorities, officers; there are also a lot of Professors with a rather special form of personally-manufactured worthiness, for they imagine that they have drawn a ring round reality in the way the theologians have drawn one round God. The pattern of social intercourse is embroidered on canvas, the prevailing language clichés, authoritatively delivered. Boasting, punch and whist, among the ladies coquetry and ouija boards (the gentlemen also take part in the seances). Now and again the highly-tensed, concealed erotic game-playing of which I have perceived a glimmer in myself. No Strindbergian storm could ever substitute for this warm breeze of mud and refuse –. Against a smiling sky the grey sails of the fishing smacks, the gaff-rigging, the men and women dressed in black, fish-scales on the red, swollen finger-joints as the meagre coppers are exchanged; here a spark of hatred could ignite. When the steamer from Åbo arrives everything is jumbled into a muddled brew of eagerness and indifference, outward status and inner fear, silk and refuse, and married men still flushed from borrowed embraces devotedly kiss their white-clothed wives and doll-costumed children. Is this the small-town format, or is it a universal one? Even their souls are of small-town format and their opinions are coffee-rolls and pastries. There I sit in the arbour talking with Selma and Anders, scarcely aware of what I am saying, unless it's about music, to which they're benignly indifferent. In the morning I observe that something about the

135

daylight destroys what the night has developed in its quiet dark-room, where I wake and listen: note after note. Sign after sign grows pale and becomes meaningless. The music is taken from me. My Quartetto Notturno! Allegro-Adagio-Allegretto, in F minor, in my inner ear, forever within the devouring proximity of Schubert, but also with echoes from Chopin's Nocturnes. All this I must build up again, in the darkness of night, in my head, while by day a terrible erosion destroys nerve after nerve! My programme: to listen with my inner ear to a scale, growing louder and giving the illusion of a never-ending ascent; while at the same time allowing two voices to rise and fall against one another, keeping them separate, at once expressive and distinct, woven together and yet in free relation to one another. Bach.

10.6

Mrs D. Letter, another rendezvous. The attractive in her the ugly: the sweat of her skin, her hair falling over her forehead, her worn sleeve of dove-grey silk, her hands the nails of which are bitten down, the harsh wrinkles along her neck, the severe rustle of her dress as she walks, just as severely, the hem of her skirt muddy, her lips that open and close as though no words wanted to come out, her sharp eyes which suddenly look past me with an expression of disgust, her hips that sway in a peculiar rhythm and remind me of those of a horse pulling a cart; when I kiss her does she bite back out of passion or is it for want of anything better, keeping her eyes open, constantly expecting to be discovered? The simultaneous hardness and indolence of this already somewhat thickset woman, playing *Ständchen* like a regular man. Passion of the flesh which pushes away my nervous love (lust). Physical contact almost destructive, refuses to let 'someone else' touch her clothes or remove them from her. Many layers of them, like an onion, and demanding brings on tears. Was none the less seized with fury when she said: 'You are nobody!' Held her tight, until she fell towards me with open mouth. Clung to each other like brother and sister. This is shattering all my peace; I must go away.

14.6

The twelfth chapter of Part VII of *Anna Karenina*, where Levin goes out hunting alone in the early morning, gives me the same feeling of happiness as the clearest, deepest music, something which writing seldom does to me, and also a heightened sense of presence, a sense of something truly greater than reality itself.

What is realism, after all? To see not with a sharp but a sharpened eye and to give the recipient a wholeness, a beauty that is the highest morality. And this frequently, as in Tolstoy, through the most delicate transformations of nature, the most wonderful everydayness, the most natural and most difficult-to-perceive nuances. Add to this Levin's moods and those of the dog: here is the gesture that embraces all, calmly and full of confidence: 'this is the world!' And meanwhile human beings move around in their circle, are ground down on their treadmills, destroy one another, and night reigns. So too in literature, hence Tolstoy's greatness. *Hunger*, *The Father*, all this dying, and these men who died by their own hand, Nietzsche, van Gogh, Wolf, in madness. Yes, the soul of this decade is sick. Decay, and convulsive activity. This bitter, stagnant taste of blood.

25.6

Stayed on my own for the most part over midsummer. Self-contempt, bottom reached. She has gone. The rat stays in its hole, as before, despised, with hairless tail. What do I care about Moonlight Sonatas and Lays of Grotte? I am my own darkness and am waiting for autumn.

2.7

Contacts with human beings interesting. Supreme Court Judge Paragon strolls along the shore, finds the view 'exquisite', the life of the harbour, too. His wife maintains that she derives less from closeness to the wild Finnish nature than she does from closeness to the wild, authentic, upright, natural inhabitants of Finland, to the rugged fishermen, the honest farmers, the hardworking (this particularly, and cheap, too!) old women, the splendid if occasionally somewhat unruly children; indeed, all who out of blue eyes watch the summer visitors the way one watches something necessary and bizarrely evil from the forest of masts and fish-laden stalls. Frans from the manor is there with his bream, shy as usual, greeting his customers self-consciously, selling the fish for the subsistence that a miserly day's wages denies him. From the drinking-house a man who is somewhat over-refreshed steers a course towards the judge and his wife – this is no longer quaint and is far too wild, and they flee. He tries to take me by the arm, but I say to him, quietly: *'Jätä rauhaan! Etkö tiedä: rikkailta ei tipu?'** He looks as though he had turned to stone, and staggers away.

16.7

Uncle Fredrik died in Åbo yesterday – the last of Father's brothers and sisters; now everything is scattered to the winds.

21.7

Perhaps – one of the words I'm fondest of. Offers no solutions, offers – perhaps – some hope, but leaves the darker door open. Perhaps a paradise awaits us. Perhaps: doubt as the hope of the hopeless. Perhaps that most merciless light is capable of transforming the landscape into an enchanted garden, not the landscape of death. Perhaps.

29.7

Faces that have no beauty dissolve into vacuous parts. A fat nose with the red marks of a pince-nez, an open mouth, double chins, sunken cheeks, wrinkles, eyes that have lost all brilliance, straying wearily hither and thither with no firm focus; add to this an element of rosy, easy-going naïveté. Poor, characterless face. Would it not have been better if it had not been enticed by hope?

5.8

In contemplating my sock with its toe poking through there, I find that my attempts at darning the holes in it have been in vain. I already suspected as much earlier, when I noticed that the darned patch looked as though it belonged to a completely different sock. Going around with holes in one's socks can in the long run make one more uncomfortable than a good many sufferings and misfortunes of metaphysical, social and abstract origin. Neither can a hole in one's sock be concealed in the long run, and arouses pained attention in society. Holes in one's soul might be more easily concealed, but how is one to darn them? There, too, the sharp-sighted person will soon observe that the darning belongs to another sock. Sooner or later an ugly toe will always stick out. This on the occasion of very hot weather (+29°C in the shade at 8 o'clock in the evening).

6.8

Continued reading Emerson.

10.8

Can one really talk of form in music at all, when it is forever a matter of a forming process, the way nature forms trees, landscapes, people in light and shadow; with open eyes you enter an occurrence which constantly changes you; even though you may not be aware of it, you become another person. But this is not seen by those who merely look at the externals: the 'facts'.

12.8
Every time I walk through the bath-house gardens and pass the music pavilion I expect to find the Poet Wennerbom.* But the town cannot rise even to this, only to snobs in uniforms, gout-ridden minds wrapped in linen.

4.9
Saw her, but she did not see me, was living another life, one of the many set-pieces in the play she is performing. They think they are superior when they follow the pattern.

10.9
So tired of these eruptions, these shrieking choruses and daughters of Elysium, these titanic furniture removals, these starlight dreamers, these Russian cloaks; so tired of this constant seeking to be original: give me a straight, whole line of music, a single world held together by a striving for objectivity by virtue of its accumulated personality! Not a star for the moment, but a universe, even though in sections. Wagner – if only there were not all this pernicious, fat-bellied symbolizing. That which is human is anonymous and can be learnt. Not to renounce tradition, not to be bound by it.

27.9
Made acquaintance of local police authorities and was present at interrogation of woman who had murdered her children. Pale, skin transparent, very thin and bony, gave an impression of strength. Daughter of an alcoholic and a mother who kept quiet about all the blows she received, she had married an elderly carpenter and had two children by him; she had had one child outside marriage since the carpenter's death; tried to kill herself with a pair of scissors after smothering her children, but succeeded in inflicting only minor wounds, after which she gave herself up to the police. Complete apathy – or calm? – as though she had found peace. Sat with her head bowed, peculiarly radiant smile; black buttoned boots, her hands, restless, otherwise quiet, submissive and reticent. To the question why she had done what she did, she replied in a toneless voice that she had not been able to stand her

children's loud, shrill screams which gave her a headache so bad that she needed to have darkness and complete silence around her, whereupon she would feel great relief. The desire to sleep. At that point felt as though I had fallen, and because of this moment of dizziness had to bestir myself, and returned with effort to my room.

2.11

All October ill and sleepless, so that nothing has been done but nothing undone either. Perhaps when we seek nothing and there is no hope every experience is one of the most gentle light?

14.11

At a coffee gathering in the basement yesterday met a poet who wants to do away with the established order of society. Well-fed, he is said to have inherited a lot of stocks and shares from his father, who was a rentier; has had much success with a few risky plays which are being performed in various theatres. A phenomenon of the times: no one sees through him, not even he himself: hence his self-confidence. He has not been damaged by life, either: hence his mocking superiority.

3.12

What atrocious developments in the field of clothing I have been compelled to live through! From grotesque wasp-waists, shamelessly emphasized hips and bosoms in a cloud of morality, in an era of 'virtue' and 'maidenliness'! While in the meantime the young gentlemen in frock-coats bed shop assistants, operetta actresses and peasant girls with a kind of stupid, sanctimonious cockerel's pride that is merely crudity. All the clothes, all the waistcoats, all the top-hats that are flourished in a bow and which as in case of indisposition could be used as sick-basins, or as chamber-pots in 'piquant' situations. These surface-lacquered gentlemen in checkered waistcoats and gaiters, and the peacock cries from their noble, virtuous consorts. Frills and plush velvet and the witticisms that smell of corruption.

15.1

I have survived.

24.1

Visit to Stockholm, met A.T. Nocturnal conversation with him about V.v. Heidenstam's* poems, about the new colours, the courage to live, the death of Viktor Rydberg – a tremendous loss, a light that has been extinguished. 'I cannot love, but help!' About here, on earth, trying to create a glimpse of eternity.

28.1

The bitter thing about a loving emotion is that it blinds; something is close to me, so close that I cannot see it. An acrid flavour after such encounters, a straining of the nerves which my psyche will not tolerate. Then I go smashing down into self-contempt.

16.2

In the clean, snow-drowned city move the dirtiest of people.

18.2

Looked at Anna. Her cheek-bones more marked nowadays, her wrinkles, too, her narrow lips pursed up as for a smile or a grimace, her heavy eyelids and the scarcely feminine chin – Father's chin. Her eyes large, watery and blue. Veins standing out on her skin; and she probably views me in a similar way.

3.3

Dr Branders' fortieth birthday with general paying of respects. Stood in my frock-coat in a corner, and was spoken to by strangers as though I were a butler. The serving brother. Garlands on the ceiling, in the evening grand supper, which the worthy Anders fully deserved. Have seen more of what is hidden in this town than the most frightened potentate would ever suspect. So it's probably just as well that they're pawing the ground.

12.3

This is the era of concealed illnesses, the ones people 'don't talk about', and which consequently swell like suppurating boils. Behind the intoxication with beauty, desperation, behind the home-made folk melodies, confusion; only the strongest could go through this twilight withthe tendencies of the age laid bare, following his own genius. Sibelius' *Kullervo*: not free of flaws, but the concentration, the energy.

14.3
People gather in groups and argue, their gazes fixed obliquely on the person next to them. Group photographs are taken in a rust-brown tint, and I am supported by a pillar and an Italian landscape – a glorious country! Have often dreamt about it! These are merely pictures which conceal the naked truth; perhaps if it came to light it would be a disappointment for many: neglected, scabby complexion, shameless and evil-smelling, and worst of all: robbed of all its privileges.

20.3
We have not learned in our darkrooms to develop that which we have seen.

9.4
If only I could live life as it is! Look into its expressionless eyes, observe the play of its features, judge it by its actions, define day as day, night as night, and experience pain at the transience of all things and speedy death as a liberation and a calmness. The sun is no longer low on the horizon, but looks one in the eye at the day's beginning and at its end; the rest is moods. If I can then separate them from nature, I have come closer to the music that is silence and listening.

2.5
Headache. Red mark on my forehead from student cap, hoarse from songs that died a long time ago, gratuitously dug up.

12.5
Crept under a bathing-woman's white broad-cloth. Reborn in water pouring out of the darkness, then slag and mud removed. Steam and burning skin. Exhausted, empty and now have nothing to say, as though language too had been rinsed away or ripped out of me, like the entrails of a fish.

18.5
Verdure which has not yet stiffened but surrounds me with new hope. From the hill with a view out over the sound and the town; the mind's horizon expands.

27.5

Helsingfors. Wandered through Kronohagen. In spite of the fact that I have lived a large part of my life in the country, I can recognize, in the back yards and among the hovels, all the pale poverty, in which I see myself. A flaking window-sash, a darkness from which the people emerge like drowning souls from a cruel sea, a face pressed palely against a dirty window-pane: that might be me. All those who have lost the struggle for bread and the juicier morsels. Here I could melt into damp mortar and mouldering wood, never to see myself again. In those warm, small-town drawing-rooms I am a stranger, for among those cushions and ladies I am like an accountant among prostitutes. And why not?

30.5

If all the horses on Salutorget were to neigh in chorus, that would be preferable to the flock of students who, fuelled by liquid oats, sang (falsely) patriotic songs in Alphyddan yesterday. A bigger crowd of tail-waggers has not been seen for a long time.

2.6

The so-called 'educated' class views both the worker and the artist with the same contempt and incomprehension. Both seek their own worth and will find it long before I lie in the ground.

13.6

At the turning, the familiar one, after which each bend in the road is familiar and where at last the house comes into sight behind the fields, up there on its hillock, we drove straight past as usual and I had to turn my head away. Anna sat with her lips set, the dust swirled up with the steam from the horses.

15.7

After dinner at Phoenix. How oddly people's mouths move, most oddly of all when they are laughing, eating or singing. These wide-open holes from which sounds come, where teeth are bared, into whose empty darkness the food is shovelled. And the blind, staring eyes above this grimacing aperture! The quivering jaw and fluttering tongue of the female singer! These violent efforts to be merged in the song, to become nature! If this is art, only – the birds – know!

Addendum:

The hypochondriac suffers from his hypochondria and the embittered man from his bitterness. Now I remember Mozart. *Voi che sapete*, Cherubino's love song: the song, when it has passed through life's stages of birth, suffering and death, in order to return to the gentle sorrow we all feel when confronted with the fleetingness of our experiences. The song of consolation, the words of which no longer mean anything that matters but the wholeness of which they are a part, the eternal, breaking wave that moves through the generations and their dreams of love. And the man who sings can become his song and his voice the voice of all. *Voi, che sapete*. But on we stumble in the dirt of suffering and the everyday. O God, why must I walk, crushed clown, through these hard streets?

15.9

The summer has vanished somewhere and the clear, cool autumn is here.

16.9

The older I grow, the more of a stranger to myself I become. This is a law people try to hide from themselves. They think they grow more mature from childhood onwards; it strikes me that they often merely grow coarser. Driven sufficiently far from childhood we commit desperate acts, sever dear bonds of friendship, flee from our homes, plunge into mental illness or business affairs. You who are called naïve – thank your Creator! To be a stranger to the universal rigor mortis of the adult world! It has to be concealed, like an illness! But the man who reveals a living childhood and thereby matures to humanity, he shall suffer: Mozart.

17.9

She spells her name Rakel, of course. Looked me in the eye so fearlessly, as though she were expecting something of me, waiting for me to say something. But I stood there in silence.

22.9.1896

He pulls the black felt hat lower on his forehead and turns up his overcoat collar. The track meanders up towards the rocky headland, passing right next to low wooden shanties and inquisitive windows. Can anyone see that he is tottering, as though the wind might sweep him away with it? He isn't wearing the right shoes for this kind of terrain. He is panting. The wind is so strong, carrying with it the smell of salt and the open sea. The maples, which have already received splashes of gold and blood, are giving way to pines, but right at the top it is cold, and the grey granite glistens with rain. 'As if we could do anything against this,' he thinks, 'as if we could change anything to conform with our will! If we blast the rocks they will reply with deeper rocks, higher rocks, a greater, more contemptuous silence. What can I learn from this?' Far below him he can see the water, grey and full of waves with white foam, they move and yet do not move, and the water flows into eternity, from something, to something, and the shores stand silent. Nådendal is crouching down there, as in fear, the alleys, the houses, the foliage to hide the little stage-extras that crawl around in and out of rooms, up and down Alexandersgatan, and the boats cling to one another, and when they go out they are a grey sail scarcely visible against the water, a dark shadow, a soot-flake, a grain of dust driven by the wind.

He took out a folded newspaper and spread it carefully on the knob of rock. He sat down, drawing his hands up so that they could not be seen in the stiff sleeves, his gaze searching among the clouds: lights were splitting open in the grey, mobile expanse, the wind was getting up and the water in the rocky crevices was moiréd. They were small mirrors that refracted the light from the sky. Was not a sea always necessary, he thought. The greater his longing for people, the greater his longing to be alone: that was his problem, like a weak but stubborn fever in his blood. He was driven onward, he drew back, he tried to beat against the wind, he tried to maintain his own course; but didn't that imply that he

145

knew who he was? Splashes of rain made the view through his spectacles blurred, he took them off and put them in his pocket, closed his eyes. What was this meagre happiness that he nursed and cherished more and more as he cowered and huddled up his shoulders, like a child bent double in the warmth of its bed, unwilling to open its eyes and see that it is morning and time to wake up and a new day? He chewed on his thumbnail and followed a hovering seagull that lay motionless on the gusts of wind, sank only the merest way, rose again, resting on the squalls and the growing light. 'There veers no height to heaven's edge, there sinks no vale, there bathes no shore', he murmured, shivered a little, suddenly turned round as though he had been observed: someone really was coming there, could be glimpsed through the tree-trunks, between the knobs of rock, his heart beat powerfully – it was her! He had said he was going to come up here, that here there was a broad outlook, here he could live, here he could hear what he wanted to hear, it had almost been an outburst back there, in the kitchen, and she had listened and understood. She had draped a grey cloak around her, her face shiny and a healthy red, the rain like tears of joy, he had to tell her that: 'Rakel's crying tears of joy, or is it the rain?' She smiled and sat beside him, and he let his hand steal out, and pointed from left to right: 'Look! Isn't it wonderful!'

To that she made no reply, perhaps it was only the silence she had come to see, the one they had in common, said merely: 'You're getting wet, oughtn't you to go home?' Otherwise might not he catch another bout of his pneumonia? She looked around her, as though his pneumonia were lurking somewhere behind the rise. He had to look at her, she looked past him, but then their gazes met and fixed, she was looking into him so candidly that he felt old, deprived of strength and consolation, but still strangely grateful, he took her hand and warmed it: 'You've got wet! Are you willing to consider me your friend? Your closest friend? In spite – in spite of the fact that I'm so old that I could be your father?' 'You're not old', she replied earnestly, searched across his face with her eyes, he took off his hat, laid her hand against his cheek, she did not pull it away. She was like a child, and serious. He had to kiss her cool hand, her slender hand, wet-cold, a paw, with bitten nails, he saw that now, and his tenderness pressed forth tears. 'Are you crying?' He shook his head: it was the rain, it felt so beautifully cool against his face. And if she needed help, could she not always turn to him, could she not give him that promise?

146

She bowed her head, he caught a glimpse of her thin neck under the headscarf, so defenceless, a thread was hanging down, he pulled at it, then she turned her face so that it came right up to him, he leaned forward and pressed his mouth against her cheek, beside her ear, so cool she was, so young. For a moment he closed his eyes as though in that brief moment he had cancelled out years of sleeplessness, he smelled her fragrance and it was the fragrance of the wind and the sea, and the rain's, but only for a second, a fragment of eternity, then he had a pain in his back, he noticed the screwed-up position in which he was sitting, the way he was bearing down on her, they were on the point of falling, and he drew himself up, tried to pull her towards him but she took his hand and put it on his knee: 'No, Axel, not here, the whole town can see us.' 'Let them see us', he felt like saying, but he was anxiously aware that she was right, that he could not expose her to their eyes and gossip. There had been enough of that already, and he had to ask: 'Is Rakel afraid they'll talk? About us? They've so little reason to. So little. Oh, if only there were more!'

He did not dare to look at her, examined the lichen on the stone, patterns, heard the cry of the gulls, the sun flashed out down the sound, cutting silver in the water. She answered: 'I'm afraid, for Axel's sake. Afraid he'll be lonely. And that they'll drive me away – it's happened before –'; but the words died away, he kept his hands clasped, his face bowed down, he was looking for it; 'Lonely,' he said, 'without Rakel I'll be even more lonely, can't imagine being without – my friend – if Rakel is willing to be my friend –'; he tried to take her hand again, but she got up quickly, there was the Grönwall woman walking along with a basket, she gave them a long look, strolled past, did not want to look round but did it nevertheless, he got up and followed Rakel, in the alley they parted, he tried to detain her, but she shook her head, gazed at him fixedly, then turned and went, her rough shoes crunching on the gravel, her grey skirt swinging. He stood for a while between the shanties and the fence, holding his hat in his hand, the hair at the back of his head completely wet, he walked slowly downhill, had anything at all been said, had he understood her clearly and distinctly? Had she the same expectation as himself? He walked along the shore towards the harbour, the church was swathed in mist, and between the clouds stars gleamed briefly and were hidden again. Now people were starting to light their oil-lamps; Rakel would already be home, in his thoughts he followed her, but she was gone, he had to give her up, she had become almost unreal, so painfully gone that he had to support himself against the white railing of the landing-stage, had to sink down there on to the bench, he could hear, but only remotely, singing inside him, as though she were addressing him and him alone, this child, this young, beloved girl.

From The Diary

24.9

Walked past me and smiled; at the dinner table there were some who looked up and, like me, followed her with their eyes. Later, after the washing-up was done and all was quiet in the kitchen, I talked to her, and she had got over her uncertainty, or shyness. Said that music is almost my only consolation in an otherwise empty existence. She raised no protest, merely looked at me. I: 'I often hear you singing, Rakel. What does music mean to you?' She looked at me uncomprehendingly: 'It's singing.' 'When?' I asked. 'What do you mean – when? When you're happy, or sad, or want to be happy or sad.' 'Which is it?' 'What do you mean – which is it? Both of them, they're the same!' 'Is it that you're sad and want to make yourself even sadder through singing?' 'Oh, Axel, you are the limit! No, it's because I'm sad and want to be happy, of course!' Then I put my hand on hers, and she didn't draw it away. That is how our conversations go, and they are a great joy to me. And she tells me about her life, so unlike mine in the question of external poverty, which has been her lot since birth, mine only since I was driven out. When I see what a rich, living personality she has, I am amazed. I asked her about the future, what her expectations were. A cloud passed over her features, and she said: 'I know I'm not much.' Then I stroked her soft hair and said that she possessed great value, in herself, and for me, and that she was the only person in whom I could confide. Heard footsteps, and Anders came in, Rakel got up and went out. He warned me, as one friend to another, about the chatterboxes in Nådendal, but I said that Rakel was my *friend* and that nothing unseemly had passed between us, which he said he was sure was true, but dropped some bitter comments about the old men and women in the town. Sleeplessness and aching heart.

3.10

Mozart: light above the depths. Beethoven: stubbornness in the vertical; Brahms: longing for home. That is to say: life-longing, death-longing, united.

4.10

When I used to remember Mother I never saw the whole of her, only a few details, painfully clear, or recalled a mood: how she sat at the piano in the big drawing-room and was so alone in the music that the image remained. I thought then that there is a life protected from the view of others and even from one's own sufferings. For there, in the music, she was so quiet, so remote and happy. That, I decided, would be my world. But that world is still not wholly open to me. Yet, when I hear Rakel singing, I receive a gleam of happiness. Just as when today I sat on a bench by the harbour and thought of nothing, and there was just the harbour, the houses grown pale and the trees that were magnificent, and nothing more was needed; sat quite still and saw that. It has now struck me that there is a difference between *looking* and *seeing*; looking is what we do in face of the habitual, and we find nothing new in it; but if there is something new that we discover, we *see* it. The same may be said of *hearing* and *listening*. Good music forces one to listen, listen and gather into a whole. The autumn now burning, and intensely, before its extinction and the snow's funeral pall. Have not spoken to Rakel for several days, but don't suffer because of it, as words are not always necessary.

18.10

Anna read aloud from Tavaststjerna, and I was so moved that I had to go up to my room. 'Answer me, swelling sea, do I still live?' And this: 'It is so quiet around me, quiet as in some place where life has faded away.' That is giving in, and I won't do that!

26.10

The first snow is whirling, and people are turning to shadows. My love is longing through and through, so it is what is closest to me.

27.10

When Rakel came to make the beds, I asked her to stay. Asked her to tell me about her mother and father, and her childhood. Her mother dead, her father alive, a fisherman, a strict man who often beat the children. Of this she wants to talk as little as possible. I held her hands, she sat with her head bowed, her black buttoned boots turned with the toes towards each other, wiped her apron over her eyes, said: 'Axel is too kind, I can't pay him back for this.' Said she had already paid me back a thousandfold. She said she was afraid for my sake! Then got up quickly, when we heard Anna coughing in her room. Left alone I was seized with despair. Now it is night, and after all that I am trying to free myself from every thought and simply listen to the gale outside.

3.11
People of originality and genius are usually discovered by 'the experts' after they have been laid to rest in the grave; then come the commemorative speeches. Their works survive. That is why the sacrifice of quality is a betrayal of the human spirit. This true not only of art, but also of human feeling, which each and all of us are free to develop and cultivate.

5.11
All is pure and white outside. There is a smell of snow. 'And it seemed that I saw a gable stand white / and a window that opened to me, / that a piano did sound and a merry sprite / of a song with a bold melody' (Fröding*). The white piano, in the big drawing-room, when mother used to play. Rakel thought the poem beautiful when I read it, but didn't want to touch the book. Said that my life, too, was mostly 'Daubs and Patches'*, and she said I shouldn't talk like that, it made her angry, and I promised not to bother her any more, and she replied that I wasn't bothering her, she couldn't explain it, turned red and left the table. Reproaches and warnings from Anna; people's faces grow so ugly when they are delivering a reproach.

13.11
In her room there is only space for a bed, a chair and a little table; she says she is content with this, as the greater part of her young life was spent with her brothers and sisters, father and mother, in the darkness of their cottage and the summer twilight, around and on a whitewashed, smoke-blackened fireplace. She sits on the bed, I on the chair. She told me a nasty dream she had had in which she was pursued; I talk about my dreams, which are few but troublesome. In them I find a kind of wealth, for in them I act, don't know what I want and therefore act. In them there is play

and horror, and the bizarre aspect of my life appears in them as something self-evident. Yet dream resembles reality in the sense that in neither of them do I participate, even though I act: in both I observe myself, my clothes, my shoes, which inspire wonder or horror, but I never see my face. Neither do I ever hear anything. My recurring dreams are 1. Faces that change expression and appearance and look without seeing, and 2. The depths of the heavenly vault from which a terrifying ball of light (a fire-ball) is rapidly approaching in order to kill me, but I step aside and instantly wake up. Twice I have also dreamt I was conducting a large orchestra in a composition of my own which the audience laughed off the platform in no uncertain terms, and a few days later that I was talking to some men in dress-coats, when they suddenly seized me under my arms and dragged me away to some room, locking the door on me; then I stood alone among silent old men who were ranked along the walls of an unbearably brightly-lit room, at which point I had to close my eyes. Went out into untained nature, everything happened in semi-darkness that flowed out of me. Shrivelled from child to old man, saw with staring eyes that had no eyelids and then woke up, don't know if I'd been dreaming with my eyes open or closed or where the boundary between life and dream passes. Pain and terror, which in the dream can change into recklessness and lightness, in reality never. Often in my dreams I am humiliated, forced into begging, debasement and abject servility, and what happens in them is pre-determined, there is nothing to be done about it: in them the most bizarre things are just and right, for I have forced my way into life, where I have no business to be. My life, and life, are two completely different things, or parts of a whole where there is no whole. For what are the events of my dreams aimed at? Nothing. Then I wonder: what are the events of life aimed at? Nothing.

23.12

Am giving her a present, some dress material, not least as thanks for the help she gave me when I was ill, in spite of Anna's attitude; when I close my eyes her voice is closer to me than anyone else's, yes, like a song. And perhaps she is part of a larger chorus, a youth that must leave its hypochondria behind it like something unknown.

27.12

See before me Prince Andrei, his eyes, his thoughts. What lies there, one step beyond the fields, the trees, the roof lit by the low sun, hunched up behind the town like an embryo? What lies there, on the other side of that which we see and hear? Perhaps other landscapes with other trees, sunlit roofs, small towns hunched up between hills, other poor folk resting with open eyes, on beds and on deathbeds.

1897

1.1

Through the frost-patterns on the window a cold, springlike sky with light-blue depth and clouds. Rakel gone, said she would return, but when? As though I were homeless. Worked on the quartet, made from it a quartet for crows. 'The Crow quartet, by inspiration abandoned'; pain within me the like of which cannot be expressed in any language. Ought I to appropriate the sweet little folkloristic murmuring of the birch-trees? Or write variations on 'Down the Hatch'? Modern music: rhapsodies on drinking songs. Lied to Anna that I had finished the composition as the crowning of the year now passed, but am inclined to allow it to mature. Sense of having turned my back to her and of this being irrevocable. Then had to get up and support myself against the table, whereupon Anna thought I was ill. Shouted at her, told her to be off with her! Was it I? Have torn up the Adagio, it was airless, heavy and clumsy, hopping along on a damaged foot, picking up the leftovers others had spurned.

13.1

Prof. A. on a visit. Nonentity, squeezed into a dress-jacket and department. Produces theories with an air of complacency; the creative person for him contemptible, a threat to decency and the sacred temple of knowledge. Dissects art like a corpse. Tried to bring the conversation round to the subject of music, which for this expert is merely a surge of emotion that fails to observe the requirements of objectivity. Pointed out the connection between mathematics and music, whereupon he smiled as one might to a child. Anna in raptures. Dirty fingernails, smell of naphthalene. Best just to play along, displaying the same deadly earnestness. Can't afford any form of superiority except the spiritual kind, which ought to be checked and concealed.

153

15.1

Perhaps even a sparrow can teach something of the art of survival. People should watch a curious bird splashing in the mudhole that belongs to everyone, and from it learn the name of failure. If one knows it, one can stand on one's head and still hear a music that surpasses rational understanding. I kick my heels in a small town, but at night I have Alpine dreams, and in those I rule the wind and the echoes, in those the symphony of my life is played out, which is the symphony of all, for we shall all be forgotten and come to nought. Usual birthday cake.

18.1

Rakel back, crept in to see me and told me of how she had almost had to flee from her father, and said we could not meet often, said I was her best friend even when I wasn't there. Same with me. The snow fell so gently in the alleys, wandered for a long time and thought of nothing.

23.1

Ten years since *Sensitiva Amorosa* was published. Afraid, as though I had dreamt of my own death, I abandoned the life-agony of my rendezvous with woman's primordial power which seeks him out but from which he recoils. Have I not received sufficient proof of my unfitness for life? Against this burning text I set listening, coolness, Rakel! And they blend with one another!

4.2

Stiff as the winter is stiff, the snow gleams at night and towards morning grows subdued.

14.2

I find it impossible to be moved by the plot of an opera when it is merely a catalyst for the music, and the words can seldom be heard. The events that take place are arbitrary, while the music is definitive. So perhaps also in the great opera of life: the plot wretched and arbitrary, the action confused, the protagonists the wrong age, the scenery set-pieces that can be dismantled, the words inaudible, the music from God.

15.2

Perhaps music is a language that has been cleaned of impurities and has turned into waves of sound with a meaning, direct and clear, for those who truly listen. A centre, a world language, an all-embracing pattern. Even the simplest song sung in the kitchen by Rakel is a part of this language which speaks directly to one's innermost being. Told her this, but she gave me a shy look and said nothing.

16.2

The more often a word is used, the more diluted it becomes. We skate about on the surface of words that have been devalued, believing that we understand one another. But the surface gives way, we fall down into the darkness where we are compelled to seek the words that have meaning – for ourselves. To 'be of the same opinion' is meaningless. We are unique, and so our language ought to be, too – and our music.

18.2

I can easily accept that these young people who walk past me will still be alive when I have been laid in the ground; but the thought that the trees in this park which now stand black with mighty summits throwing their shadows over the white snow will still be here when even the young folk – Rakel – have withered and died, gives me great pain.

3.4

Have been ill. Felt Rakel's presence. *Wer immer strebend sich bemüht –:* towards what? This envelope that is 'I' occasionally sees Paradise, but mostly in dreams, and in them Beatrice is so near.

8.4

If only, even in my dreams, I had a child that would listen to me now that I am old, a child that knew everything in advance; but that child is myself, it is old as I am, bowed down and concealed, its gaze turned away, it is no longer listening.

27.4

Wanted to talk, but she fled. What did I do wrong?

3.5

Went to her room, we talked, she said she had been frightened when K., the Consul's wife, had stopped her and told her that it would not do for her to be seen with me. All I had done was to walk with her to the harbour, carry her basket. Didn't want me to stay, and cried with distress. I held her hand, promised not to put her in jeopardy, but told her that being close to her was something of value and importance to me. 'Why?' she asked. Had she not noticed that we were able to talk to each other even when we sat in silence? That I didn't have many people whom I could talk to. Was she not lonely herself? When I came out of the room Anna was there, said this had to stop. I asked her what was on her mind. She said nothing was, but that this wasn't suitable for either me or R. I asked her what 'suitable' meant. She went to her room without answering.

6.5

Her father came and took her away. When I rushed downstairs, he shoved me to one side. Rough and heavy, eyes hidden by growth of hair covering the whole of his face. Rakel lugged away the basket that contained her personal belongings, the cart squeaked, it was a spring day and I shall never see her again as long as I live, the mob watched with greedy eyes. How can I go on living? When I have nothing to live for?

2.6

Crawled up to the surface, saw that it is summer.

22.6

'The Fates with implacable breath / mankind's laws in blindness engrave. / Tones that today make us brave / give us bravery also for death!' writes Mikael Lybeck* in 'The Young Summer' in Western Finland, apropos of the Åbo Music Festival, but everything in me is silent, only in the most extreme need do I hear the singing of her from whom people have cut me off. 'Life must go on?' Why? Autumn follows upon summer, winter upon autumn, another spring comes, everything continues, and we are born, live and die; and if I were to die now, they'd mourn me for two or three weeks, perhaps, and at the same time feel relieved that I'd escaped from my misery. Where is the meaning in it? Is it a joke, a mocking joke, on the part of God? And the cruel light that will not let me sleep.

19.7

I am no more.

24.8.1897

Towards morning he sank exhaustedly into a light slumber. Voices, faces faded away. Life stood still, held its breath. In the silence he thought he heard footsteps. He raised himself from his bed, sat in his nightshirt and looked towards the window. There was a narrow streak of light between the curtains. They were moving, imperceptibly. He waited. It was so light in the room, as in some quiet absence. He could see that the trees were still, the birds lingering with their song, the room expanding. On the chair his clothes were folded like a child's. He was alone and his loneliness weighed on his shoulders. He listened. There was faint music, like the prelude to music. A cock crowed, someone was knocking at the door, so cautiously that only he was aware of it. He got up and went to the door. He heard the faint knocking and opened up at once. She slipped inside, stood there: her narrow wrists pressed together, her eyes pursuing and fettering him, her headscarf as white as his nightshirt: how pure everything about her was! She went over to the bed, looked around her, sat down. He came across and sat down beside her, took her hand, it rested there, motionless. 'I've come because Axel has always been kind to me', she said. 'I didn't manage to say that, last time. Father has been cruel. He believed the people who told those lies. And I didn't manage to say goodbye, either. So I've come in order to say it now. I'm going away. No, you mustn't say anything. That's simply the way it is.'

'But dearest child, have you any money? How will you manage? You know that you are my closest companion, my friend. I haven't been able to live without you this summer. But I knew you would come, I heard your footsteps in my dreams – do you believe me? I don't know whether I'm dreaming or waking. I could come with you.'

'No, Axel. I'm taking a situation as a maid in the town. The doctor's wife helped me. Here's the address. You must understand that I'll manage all right. Axel's concern for me makes me strong,

I shall keep it with me, it makes me happy.'

He could only lift her hand, place it against his cheek, close his eyes. So cool it was, her whole person, he said: 'I'll come too, and we'll go there together, and talk together, I can only do that with Rakel. I meant no harm. That's just how it is among people, I attract ridicule, but usually have to suffer for it alone. Now Rakel's come in for it. Forgive me.'

'I've nothing to forgive, I'm not a child', she said, and he could see she was not, so strong had she become, it was as if he had suffered a slight breakdown, as though she had distanced herself from her; if they met again perhaps she would be even a shade more of a stranger. She got up, he held her hand, stood there in his nightshirt and saw her, her youth, her eyes, sensed the fragrance from the cleanly-ironed, washed, sun-bright creature that was she, so close and at the same time so unreal. She said: 'I must go. Promise me you will look after yourself. Promise? Axel has music, after all – isn't that a gift?'

She was looking at him so appealingly that he had to answer with a smile, had to embrace her, her cheek against his, her softness against his rough, hot chin, she did not pull herself back but did not reply either, was simply there, close, then drew herself away, took her bundle, went to the door, opened it, looked back for a moment, and was gone.

He had to sit down, his legs were trembling, sweat broke out, he heard the door softly close, the footsteps growing distant. Emptiness and sorrow; but this sorrow was like a calm, moved like a calm, like the morning breeze no one saw, like the room that was still here, still expanding before his closed eyes; from the silence rose a coil of sound, a melody, like the echo of a horn in a mythic forest, a lonely voice, a sign. The darkness was looking for its voice. White over dark water. He sat dangling his feet, shivered slightly. Farewell and homecoming, why had those words appeared before him, torn out of any context, so beautiful and lonely, as though they had given a glimpse of childhood, eternal maturity, concealed assurance through their very sorrow. Oh, death was there, it was looking at him from such a distance; he was ready, too, suitably dressed for the farewell party, he smiled: the darkness had never come this close before, poverty had never felt so rich before. He sat there, a part not merely of the unmade bed, but of the room, the house, the town and the heavens above it; and from the August sky he heard a faint, blue echo expanding, his eye was stabbed by a glittering score in the water, as of fish-scales, so sweet and full of pain, and the light that had once smitten him to the ground had now at last been transformed, at least for a moment when every thought had vanished, with only his senses open, receptive, at once childlike and grown-up; so what if nothing had become of his life? An echo, a horn in the mythic forest, a return, a homecoming after a farewell and thanks to that farewell. He sat trying to conjure forth her image, but it was so pale, so smiling and rich in distance. He went over to the window and drew the curtains. How quiet the greenery that welled over the fence opposite, as though he had never seen it before; and in the fence a door, half-open, and behind it a streak of garden, so mysterious: he had never been there, had never seen the flowers. Such sorrow and joy blended together! When he opened the window the warm fragrances of the summer morning came floating in, already with a heavy, immobile sweetness, of autumn and death. He knew it. Everything was there, in that moment, in that morning: death and longing, light and darkness, childhood and old age, silence and song and the song that is silence.

He took off his shirt, lay down naked on the bed, lay very still, felt the breeze touch him, sank slowly into sleep and slept without dreams, calm, set free, slept as the happy sleep, in a clean room with little furniture, with their simple clothes as a fortune, and with the scent of autumn, the clatter of carts, the crowing of a cockerel, the murmur of waves, wind in the leaves, the first voices from down in the kitchen, slept through them all, until Anna knocked on the door, opened it, cried out, and he got up instantly, looked at her: 'Did you think I was dead?' And she fled down the staircase, with the same noise as a runaway horse. He went over to the door, closed it, stood in front of the window and sluiced himself down with the room-tepid water from the blue water-jug while his thoughts followed Rakel and then said farewell to her and hurried along the roads to the manor, the house of his childhood. He could after all go there. He could see what it was like. The day warm, and high as the sky.

From The Diary

1897

3.9

Clear autumn day, the sun already lower, in the morning coolness through one's eyes, each smell and colour distinct. Foliage motionlessly overflowing, greenery likewise. The road white, the swish of sand and the landscape familiar in every movement of the body. Even at Niemenkulma violent motion of the heart, O-näs glowing yellow in the greenness, the fields golden, too, and the sky cloudless. Olga with the children in Åbo, Agda welcomed us, ran after us, same scent of wood and sun's warmth as before. Agda's face furrowed, wanted to offer us chanterelles, in the kitchen sweet smell of berries and mushrooms. Every room occupied and belonging to someone, mine quite alien, Bertel and Åke live there. Asked Agda to leave me, sat in the drawing-room and watched the General in his golden frame, he was smiling as always. The mirror between the windows split me in two, so that I saw myself cut off, something black that stooped. On the music-rest of the square piano Sylvia's songs, covered in dust. Heard voices, squeaking of cartwheels, ran down the kitchen staircase in order not to run into anyone, it was just the farm foreman. Naturally didn't know who I was. The initials still engraved on the rock, and the year – 1872; I was fourteen then. The coachman had coffee in the kitchen, we sat there, the flypaper on the ceiling nearly black, and Agda kept running to and fro. On the way home the sun went behind the clouds, it became even more still. Saw and did not think, and there was a great closeness to all things, as when one has seen enough and is greatly tired.

12.9

I write the word 'love', it is too great for my body, and she too distant. It doesn't matter. I am alone, that cannot be taken from me, that dignity. Even though my body is tormented, I see, I hear,

160

sometimes even at night when I can't sleep, the music of the spheres. Sometimes more piercing caterwaulings. That is the sound of my inner agony.

22.9
Everywhere there is talk about 'stocks and shares' and capital, it swims like gravy on the verandas; but the deepest and most lasting shares are those that are held in art.

24.10
Over a month, in dreams and wakefulness. They say I have been ill; I don't answer them. Anna gives me the essential things. Have taken short walks, everything is in its place.

27.10
As darkness falls over the country, our native country, thousands of thoughts rise up like tongues of flame. As tyranny is forced to show its strength so it reveals its weak, rotten core.

3.11
Sibelius concert, with *Lemminkäinen Legends*. Something new is growing up! Hurrah! *Nya Pressan*'s review by Flodin★ hard to digest: for here there is no crime against the intellect but organic growth from our people's mythic origins. 'The Lemminkäinen illustrations disappoint me!' Illustrations! Especially close: the cold look over the dark waters in 'Swan of Tuonela'. There was my home, and is – I had already seen it all, it was all familiar! Saw to the bottom, sank into it as into the embrace of my mother, was cradled there, wept and rose up. Homecoming. This evening moonlight, went for a stroll and saw far and wide over lake and hill, wanted to talk to you, to someone, someone.

5.11
Dreamed that I was walking in moonlight, it was dark and chilly but water glittered. Dreamed that I waded out into the water and the leaves of the alder gleamed. There was light mist over the surface of the water and in the wet a narrow streak of blood. It was trickling out of my arm. I looked at it, it was white apart from the wound. Then I waded back, ran up towards the dark shore, held my hand around my wrist to stop my life trickling away, but there was no one there, Mother who had just been standing with the bathing towel was gone, then I raised my arm,

161

bowed my head, an immeasurable expanse of space flowed through my eyes, so that I woke up seeing. It was morning and on the ceiling there was the familiar damp patch. Outside winter-cold. Indoors it is snug, with draperies and ferns; we have few insights into one another and write in albums the same greetings and the same poems.

16.12

Quiet snowfall with large flakes. If only the words would fall as naturally. It is myself I am talking to in this book; but I am not always there. It's the same with my feet. There's a sock on the one but not on the other; and I don't know whether to take off the sock, or put one on the other foot as well. Mother knew. Soon a year will have run to its end, and that is all that can be said about this year.

Christmas

was celebrated in quiet, but before it we went to have Christmas coffee with the Z. family. Everywhere garlands, decorations and three-legged tables with palms and Makart bouquets; so in future we may expect there to be two-legged tables, and then perhaps they will be in no way distinguishable from human beings.

1898

1.1

One page, at least one page! One note! So I don't go mad with despair! Heavy sense that the world is unreal, light and fragile, and may break apart at my slightest movement. So: immobility.

2.1

I am entering upon my fortieth decade, towards what? Dizziness, paralysis.

3.1

Read about Rydberg, who in his own darkness inspires courage. He saw that his suffering was justified. This childlike suffering! Through his poetry a great, strong music.

5.1

Watching the rain. The snow sinks into the earth, dirt remains.

14.1

Topelius 80. Mother read the *Fairytales*, and the star still shines. The sea's blue rim! And Sylvia's songs, sunbeams in the big drawing-room long ago.

15.1

Forbidden all social visits. When I look back I don't see much. The few achievements I regard as my own have become alien to me. I was seized with terror over my responsibility, for they could no longer be concealed, as they lay outside me. That which comes to nothing must have its origin in nothing. My will spiritually paralysed early on, my life has been nothing but listening, immobility. It's a question of making myself invisible, of acting in the brief moments when I see myself, in all my stuntedness. The powerful eye. To listen – to the future! The swan's eye, and the turning of its neck!

18.1

Reading *Laureatus*⋆ in the chill of winter in a dead silent, forgotten town in a country with rigor mortis. The sonnet from the other side of the Styx: 'Say, do you know the danger of awakening death? / The passion of the dead is no mere play, / who fall asleep amidst kisses and caresses. / The feelings of the dead run bloody red, / and if their lips still tremble, pale with pain, / then it is only because their hearts want to bleed to death.' Also the hearts of the living dead.

25.2

Première yesterday of Adolf Paul's *King Christian II* with music by J. Sibelius. In the music in spite of everything an individual, personal quality, also expressed in the work's light dimensions. But the deep waters! Where are they? Are they not thundering beneath each one of us?

27.2

With my gaze turned down towards the worker, up towards the employer; to neither of them do I have anything to say, so: I talk to myself. Have a quartet in my brain, it is tormenting the life out of me; so I must let someone else create it.

4.3

Mother came to me in a dream and said: 'Poor Axel, how small you've grown!' And I saw she was speaking the truth, and was ashamed. And my sailor's suit was burning like a tunic of Nessus, the patch on the back cut off my shoulderblades, and so I was unable to fly. Must talk to Branders about a new mattress.

23.3

Topelius dead, Tavaststjerna dead; and the springtime streams are purling and out in the bay light is scattered that stabs the eye, the sun is already beginning to give warmth, and the birdsong.

25.3

In-sanity: something repetitive, monotonous, fossilized. Emotion consumed until it has lost its meaning. And yet I went on clinging to that in-sane hope that J.D. had understood my despair and the genuineness of my emotion, the pride – yes – in my humility! In vain! But Rakel saw it. Is she still alive?

28.3

R. has moved from Åbo to H:fors. What if I were to go and find her there? Would it only cause her suffering? Perhaps she is married and starting a family. Lay all night with staring eyes. Headache.

29.3

Would *The Magic Flute* sound as clearly without the occult over-tones of the freemasons? Is there concealed at the bottom of every source of clarity a secret which gives the water its character, its cool, vibrant and individual savour? What shadow of death is contained in joy so that it may feel deep enough? And in sorrow? I believe not in Satan, but in Emptiness – that is perhaps the same thing; Music saves, the song of Heaven brings remedy.

5.4

Intruders and usurpers with tar in their veins instead of blood. The boot-flaps on the tensed calves could be cut away with a razor or sliced off with a fencing foil; perhaps then blood would take their place, which would be something to show off both on the Esplanade at Helsingfors and on the promenade at Nådendal. Two flaps on each thigh, like whip-lashes. All this military brilliance, all these epaulettes and ribbons are decorations on corpses, and the army a mirror of the age's brutality and double standards. To love and to kill, truly to kill, with grunts and the jingle of spurs, while the country sinks in the swamp of its own making, and lonely wildfowl cry. I myself stand in black overcoat and bowler hat, as smartly turned-out as the man who cannot hide himself with ruble notes. And now further language battles, as though everyone were not sinking fast enough already.

13.4

Reading Tolstoy. This observing and synoptic eye! The still-white legs of the peasant girls in the mud of the field, Madame Frou-frou's stony gaze, the rhythm of the seasons – what power, what flowing life! From the deepest sources flows the richest unrest; wish the epilogue to *Anna Karenina* had not been included, though; but how many people would like not to have their epilogue included. And for how many is life not for the most part nothing but a continuous epilogue to a few hours of spring?

'Floradagen', 13 May*

Old Estlander spoke in H:fors about a future for youth in which no one will ask about language but only about ability. Yet: there is a kind of ability which cannot be measured in terms of action. I cannot share the kind of harmony E. is in favour of. One thing is necessary: look outwards!

12.6

Anna gone to the town; tried to do some washing while there was no one in the kitchen. Can, when it really comes to the point. As I was hanging up my shirts (three) old woman on the other side of the fence asked why there were so many clothespegs on the line – a brainless observation. Replied that all great music demands many notes on the staves, and that I wished, in spite of only having one line at my disposal, to demonstrate my own prowess as a composer. Her gaze went vacant, the yellow teeth were bared, and she fell back into her bushes as though she had received a slap in the face.

4.6

Discussed Ernst Ahlgren* with Anna. As we were talking, she began more and more to resemble the person we were talking about – long, thin, tense and unredeemed; how we get to know people most intimately through the images of them we create and how these images begin to live. A. sees me – though not so strongly as Olga – as a sheep, a marmot, something lost and bizarre, sick, a complete failure.

23.6
At midsummer I remember the big drawing-room at O-näs, which for the most part lay silent amidst soft sunlight and white curtains, Father stiff and stern, addressing his dependants in it, Mother pouring out grape-juice, and the smell of its fragrance, dark and sour-sweet as she did so. Did not know then that the Bøyg* had overshadowed my cradle and would soon turn my radiant memories of joy into a poisonous negation, into experiences of dizziness and terror.

1.7
Understand those who, richly endowed, are drawn in despair upwards or downwards, vertically; those less well endowed suffer horizontally, as in a desert. Floor, bed, street, open sea –: there also there is a view.

13.7
The difference between performing and reading (listening) from score and parts. Is it the same landscape that appears in Beethoven's *Serioso* Quartet, last movement, when I read the score as when I used to play it? In any case I play better when I just follow the part. The music in my head an imagined music, and therefore ideal. The violinist, too, must have this image before the performance itself? Or does it emerge during the performance? My hands still feel the strings, the bow, the movements of my arm, as though one day when I am dead all this will be put to use and I will at last be happy.

20.7
Ought I to say something about my closest relatives when I am lonely none the less?

22.7
To bathe is to seek to conceal the shameful body; so there hangs over Nådendal's bathing beach a peculiar feverish brilliance, a tang of forbidden fruit, half-rotten. Above this a merciful, all-reconciling sun, the water plashing, and the beaches of my childhood not so many kilometres to the north, seen no more, each stone intimate and vanished for ever.

September

The country harnessed between darkness and light. The traces are creaking and breaking, the coachman of Russification* is brandishing his whip and yelling like a chorus of gnomes.

23.9

'On the wanderer's way there often surged the waves of the cornfields, which must have belonged to someone, fences surrounded them, which someone must have put up, and the birds flew in one direction or the other, as to various home terrains.' And this clear, wondering gaze of Stifter's is also that of the child and the clairvoyant; he has seen that he is cut off, a stranger, an old bachelor, walking towards his death. In the year I was ten, S. committed suicide.

13.10

Bobrikov's speech yesterday,* a funeral speech over a nation not yet dead. The Holy Russian Empire is now emerging in all its naked and overbearing might, enlisting God in the service of its thirst for blood.

2.11

David against Goliath; from the depths a new and powerful music is emerging to be thrown, from the knowledge of Tuonela's realm.

23.12

While carving the Christmas ham thought of the necessity of paring all the fat away from music.

1899

1.1

The last year of the old century, all those hundred years whirling away like a snow-devil in a provincial town, a little one that creeps along the street, watched by the small faces of children and by the son of a Referring Clerk, and is then swiftly gone, the years, the children, myself, the town, all are purest white; and where is the family, the one of a thousand heads, where are my brothers and sisters, where are the old folk, my friends? In my dream they are all here, their faces alternating as in a panopticon, and are inflamed like these last few years; a New Year's sermon, of a kind! Then read some more of *The Magic Flute*, and see: the snow is falling more lightly, more radiantly, each flake like a token of joy. Lightness, bliss –: perhaps only a heavy, ill-conceived, misshapen body can comprehend the wonder of a magic flute which transforms that which is darkest into light. Perhaps not even beauty itself understands the dream of transformation from the most melancholy poverty to sparing and therefore all-fulfilling joy?

15.1

An attempt at recapitulation.

Early on I thought I would be able to do away with the friction between ideal and reality and live the life of the ideal. But poverty and the everyday dragged me down, and I had not the strength to put up a fight. I understand now that I will have to live with this adversity for the rest of my life, and from it derive the compressed diamond of strength which no one can see and no one is allowed to see. That is my pride. Between the ages of twenty and forty: nothing but confusion, crazy childish plans, failures, deeper and deeper loneliness, ever more parodic imitations of a splenetic mood – *fin de siècle*! Album thoughts in a time of sunsets that savour of death; and close to me my *semblable*, my friend: Fröding, with his dejection, his pessimism close beside that which is tenderest in human nature. All the brokenness, the suffering, the dearly-bought, the crown of thorns on the man crucified in solitude, for whom life became ever more unreal, mysterious, dark and unattainable.

My outward poverty is not accompanied by an inward one. Had I the inward one, I should not be hurled like this between despair and joy. But I would never exchange this for a degradation into stupidity. Ridiculed, I go around with an invisible longing, and burning dreams about a world of *spirit*, that which will subjugate the evil, the inhuman. Without the strength to break out of my shell I go around – a marmot, as Olga calls me! – with this adversity like a block of stone on the crooked body of a hunchback – stagger, rather than go, and the only consolation I am offered is that of sound, of music, its home-longing and home-coming, its light notes of death, the dark, quiet water of Tuonela. There is my fate. There an invisible water-lily grows, and the fewer who know of it, the more beautifully does it flower there, in darkness and solitude. There there is no time, only depth.

Perhaps it is the case that the less eventful a life, the more complex it is, the more difficult for an outsider to survey. And how, in this tangle of rules, imaginings, fears, insomnia, weakness of will could I ever find a single person who might help me to live a 'normal' life? The more inwardly-turned a life is, the more it repels any healthy person.

As for love, it has been – in the brief moments I experienced it – mostly burning discomfort, a compulsion, toned down and stunted into ideality, the kernel of which was lust; it was the confirmation of my loneliness. All that was there from the beginning, only love did not know it, and raged against a stranger, an enemy! Yet my senses were sharpened by that, too, so that even lifeless objects struck against me and hurt me. The manor house, the journey there! This pain is important to me, for it teaches me the healing power of distance and that the other person in me is watching me, seriously and critically, and smiling all the while; and that I have learned that nothing around me is empty of life *as long as I myself do not refuse to give it life.*

Thus I live as though I were dead, and see visions. I hear a new music, but am unable to write it down. My self-contempt meets a worthy adversary in my longing to discover the spiritual, from no other motive than my loathing reluctance to create. Thus I despair, but am not indifferent. I also discover a partial freedom in listening to great music, when I leave my human haven for another more universal, bound by no torments. For forty-one years I have gone to school, and have learnt something: how to take a step backwards and see myself, as in a flash of lightning, as then, thirty-one years ago. Is that not enough?

I have written all that I have to say.

18.2
The February Decree.* Finland trampled beneath the feet of barbarians. Only a unified national enthusiasm can now save whatever can be saved, now that the Senate, too, has passed it. Bitterness. Where is the fighting spirit? It is there, it is streaming forth, a song in the mountain! The great Bøyg wins everything with caution –: but this is no longer caution!

23.2
Never look at someone laughing. You will see his predatory teeth.

19.3
The People's Petition* sent to St Petersburg, the deputation not

received, insult! But unity, floral tribute at the statue of Alexander, enthusiasm compelled by means of threat, heightened will to struggle in face of death!

28.4
Two days ago Sibelius's First Symphony and *Song of the Athenians.* Viktor Rydberg may lie proudly in his grave! This people that is rising up. The symphony is a world, from a brighter Tuonela, for death and life have grown together and are begetting a new future.

29.4
From *Kullervo* to the First Symphony; one step from nationalism to a more profound sense of *nationality* in the universally valid meaning. Yet a danger in distancing oneself too much from the most deeply personal. To reach home again! To me it is closed, in spite of all spring's breezes. So may he succeed, find the way, the stature.

4.5
Anna took me to the photographer's. I was immortalized. Can one capture something in immobility which has perhaps died? A mixture of shop assistant, accountant, cad and buffoon, child and old man; and yet there is there something that is – dignity. What is this? A mirror-image of whom? Must see to it that this is not repeated, that the trap does not snap shut another time, that my death is not anticipated. Know I was posing, don't know whether this was me or that pug-dog posing and pretending to be A.C. But I had been expecting something worse.

18.5
Terrible pain and insomnia.

4.7
The Tsar has said no again. Contempt for all that is independent. Pestilence, smell of corpses in this Colossus. The brutality continues.

13.7.1899

He slept fitfully all night. Fragments of streets, faces, events, meaningless pieces of conversation from the days in Helsingfors floated up beneath his convulsively closed eyelids. Was someone shouting? He suddenly sat up, in the mirror a white figure sitting motionless in the half-dark, in the damp, dusty smell, with pale summer light filtering in between the drawn curtains, heavy and dirty brown. He tried to conjure this raging accumulation of remembered flotsam and jetsam, to make his mind free and clear, breathed slowly, walked with stiff feet over to the water-jug, sluiced himself down, sat motionless again. Silence. And in the silence the wasted years, the loneliness, and faintly, like an inhalation, music: a simple melody, a song, almost, just one lonely voice, all his longing in five notes, his own melody. Oh, he could develop this, weave it together into an ever tighter and at the same time ever more weightless web, bright, soaring, strings only –; and then, an infernal racket, metal striking sparks against stone, hooves, voices like barrels, the morning milk being rolled in stoops down into the shop beneath his feet, and he, in his nightshirt, with trailing wings, dragged himself over to the hard bed, pulled the bedcover over his head like a child, lay and did not know what to do: whether to go on lying there or to get up, whether to find his way back to his dreams or to endure the daylight. But the room had been invaded, he could feel it, heavy figures that moved between the stained walls, treating him as though he were not there, perhaps he was invisible? Perhaps they were not after all going to pull the blanket off him, mercilessly exposing him, but would leave him in peace; in Helsingfors, had he not succeeded in moving about unnoticed, almost unnoticed, had only met cousin Tor and Kajanus, with all due respect, with all due esteem, no, this he was not going to put up with, this humiliation! He opened his eyes, he sat up violently: there was no one there. Snuff-brown, smell of dust: one table, two chairs, the embroidered maxim in the beam of light from the window: 'The best things

are attained by toil and effort.' With roses. As though his whole
life had been directed towards this meaningless day, in a hotel in
Åbo. This is where I have reached. This is the goal of my longing.
Over forty, and at my destination.

When he opened the door on to Aningaisgatan the sky was
July-warm, the town was fragrant and the wind stroked his
forehead. He strolled down to the river, the bag that had followed
him around all these years suddenly felt light and easy to carry,
the cobbles were glistening as though rain had fallen overnight –:
he had lain and listened to it, lain and dreamt he was conducting
a gigantic orchestra –; he stumbled on a pavement-edge and went
on, his heart pounding. Security and insecurity, like ill-assorted
feet and legs on the same heavy body, delicate and yet heavy, and
the radiant summer around him! The tang of mud from the Aura,
the familiar streets, the school, the dark, bitter winter months:
had he not grown, grown in spite of everything, matured, grown
older – he sat for a while on a bench, listening to the birds, watched
the fishing-boats finding their way up towards the Cathedral
Bridge and putting in below Pinellan, then as always. He had sat
like this twenty-five years ago, hadn't he, and what had happened
thereafter? The wasted years, the smooth water, the violin he had
cast to its grave, the thoughts, the ambitions, the notebooks, the
yellowed papers, the notes of music like flyspecks he had tried to
wash himself clean of. Wasted. He looked at the clock, he would
have to hurry, the boat was leaving in half an hour, he wanted to
get on board in good time, find a comfortable seat in the after-
salon, protected, in a corner, with the sunlight streaming in
through the narrow windows, with the aroma of coffee, with the
brass gleaming, the mahogany, with the sleepy sound of the ship's
engine –

As they put off he stood on the after-deck, watching the town
slowly slide away, and the Castle move solemnly past, saw the
villas of Runsala peeping through the trees here and there, everything was still morning-quiet, no one was about on the passages,
the deckhouses empty, the long, narrow sailing-boats gleaming
with dew. In the after-salon only two people: the sculptor Sellén
whom he did not know, and the wife of Engineer Dahlman, a
woman to whom he had been introduced at one of Anna's damned
coffee mornings, he inclined his head and received a quick smile
in reply. The sculptor was reading the *Åbo Times*. He reminded
Axel of a boulder ridge with dwarf pines blasted into it, a dark
shadow in the July sunshine, a mighty black beard, a stubborn and

172

wearisome wrath: he had heard him sing, drunken and sour-tempered, at the Phoenix, he recognized that loneliness. How had Oehlenschlæger* put it, again? 'The Nordic figures move slowly and gravely with their broad Shadows' – slowly and gravely? Sellén moved quickly and astonishingly. Now he lowered his newspaper and stared at Axel, so that Axel had to hide behind his; there was a rustling from three sides, umbrageous shores slid by, the bays grew wider and the water glittered as far as the eye could see.

Someone walked past the saloon windows, paused, continued; Axel half-rose from his seat, it went dark before his eyes, he had recognized something, was it Rakel, was it her, here? So painfully and violently did his heart beat that he had to sit down again for a moment, he had to support his hand as it sought the water-glass, Mrs Dahlman lowered her newspaper and looked at him: 'What's the matter? Are you unwell? Can I –?' But he shook his head: 'I'm sorry, it's nothing, I assure you;' and behind his newspaper Sellén gave a snort: the sunlight was displaced, the boat turned north-wards and Axel got up on feeble legs, walked as steadily as he could, opened the door, picked his way over the raised threshold, and was suddenly outside in the summer wind and the glitter of waves. The railing still morning-cool and damp. He could not see her, went up towards the smoking saloon and the upper deck, surely she would not be here? The beautiful wide expanses of water, the wind that was getting up now so that he had to pull his hat down lower over his forehead, she was standing out on the forepeak, it could only be her, he wanted to call to her, he called, so softly that he himself could hardly hear it: 'Rakel!' How could she have heard it? She stood not moving, perhaps he was mistaken? Had he not fancied that he had seen her, now in the streets of Åbo, now in the alleys of Nådendal, and recently, when the journey to Tammerfors lay ahead, that he would never see her again?... He found his way down past wooden crates, chain cables, ropes, country-dwellers in kerchiefs and sombre town clothes, barrels, bales, past some people who greeted him shyly, who were they? He returned their greeting, made his way stubbornly onwards, the wind so full of summer and sea-tang, it was pulling at her headscarf, he touched her shoulder, it was her, Rakel, the beloved, the missed, and he noticed that his eyes were filling with tears.

But how carefully she looked at him, in order then to turn her gaze away! 'I've searched for you everywhere, Rakel – and now at last – how are you? Tell me! I've thought about you so much –

you must have felt that – didn't you? Are you coming back? Are you?'

Now she turned her face towards him so quietly, her eyes the same and yet unfamiliar, they looked past him and she answered: 'Father has died, I'm going to his funeral.'

Axel mumbled something, expressing his condolences, perhaps, she said quietly: 'He was a blackguard all his life, he ruined mother's life and mine – not totally, but enough. Axel asked a lot of questions so I'll answer them: I'm married to a respectable gentleman now and have children, we live in Helsingfors, and the past's forgotten. Has Axel found peace?'

They slid into a dark sound and the air became chilly. He said: 'Are you happy?' 'Yes,' she answered, 'I've found happiness in God. He demands of us all or nothing. I was in the power of the Devil, unclean and sinful, and God has saved me.'

She looked at him sharply: 'It's not I who needs care, but Axel. You don't do any work, you're in the claws of Satan, and if I'd known that then and been saved, I'd have been able to help you. But it's still not too late. Come to our temple, and you will find peace. There's good in you in spite of everything, I remember. Here!'

She stuck a ticket, an exhortation, a poor scrap of paper into his hands. There was something hard about the young features, and her gaze measured him, the stranger: 'Now you must leave me and go back where you belong, and remember that it is never too late for the sinner to find mercy. Will Axel remember that?'

He looked at her and said goodbye. He opened the door of the after-saloon, it was quiet in there, the water in the carafe quivered, the tables had been set for coffee, mechanically he poured himself a cup, there was no one there but him, he could sit in solitude, with his head in his hands, and there were only the sleepy thudding of the engine and glimpses of islands and water, of shores that vanished, all the closeness that vanished, with the winds and the years. He felt sorrow, deep sorrow, but it had always been there, had followed him all the way, in order to receive final confirmation. He sat and looked at himself. There was the scream of gulls, and silence. When they put in at the landing-stage at Nådendal he lingered for a while and was one of the last to go ashore. He caught a glimpse of her as she turned quickly off and made her way uphill. To Anna he said, when she met him in the hallway: 'I've been thinking things over, as you said I should. We're going to go away. It's time to make a move.'

To what, he did not know.

From The Diary

1899

14.7

When she saw me she had such cold eyes. In what way am I guilty?
In order not to fail I have to find a meaning. I drift along alleys,
I hide from people's eyes, I am an outcast and I seek, listen and
see only the hot summer. In the evening, when it grows cooler,
I sit writing, and sometimes jot down a simple melody on five
staves: quickly departing swallows, but the echo of their song
lingers. Through words and tones I live, and were they to find a
companion, a friend, I could perhaps not only live but also work.
'You don't do any work, do you?': those burning, smarting words,
this paralysing movement of my soul, as though some malignant
elf were tightly clinging to it and the curtains over the window
were aglow without there being any trace of fire, objects stand
motionless, the air is heavy with the scents of summer. It is like
a creaking wheel-hub, this town, this flyspeck on an old map, and
nailed to the wheel I am hurled ever faster out along the endless
dried-up roads. When I dreamed this I lay back on my bed, closed
my eyes, and with an extreme effort of willpower managed to
shut out the voices, the clatter, the waves, the soughing in the
melancholy birch-trees, shut out every sound in exchange for a
single, pure, growing song, which was like a memory of mother's
singing.

3.8

Letter from Axel T. The big stone house with the big carriages
outside is sure to be breathing coolness and darkness in the summer
heat; he is sitting in there shut away in his loneliness. He wants
to send me money, but I shall refuse: I am not worth it. Were I
to accept his gift I would go shooting up on one end of the balance,
while greed and avarice weighed me down to earth on the other.
How near and yet how far away he is. If only I could find a goal

for him, too, but I can't even find one for myself. Yet: if I am slowly to be drained, so that nothing is left, might not new, fresh water come trickling forth from a secret source? My faith is the faith of the hopeless. Who was it who spoke of the colourful, life-loving 'nineties? This shadow-play, this age of hunger and poverty, of rapture ground down in the cruel treadmill. The soul shivers in the warm bower where the aroma of coffee mingles with the odour of sweat. There is a dying-out and an ever more powerful confusion, a taste of blood in the face of the new century. Is my life merely a reflection of something more profoundly unfit to live in time and history, something which must be effaced and trampled down so that something new and healthy may grow? Medals, titles, pride in one's birth, outward ostentation are expanding like a wave of filth over this poor, muddy potato-patch of a homeland; from this there *must* spring a will to break the curse, the decline, the humiliation and the oppression. Something must grow in silence, and I must flee, not from life, but to it. The secret source: perhaps it is close, outside me, as yet concealed.

17.8

Sat in the Beach Restaurant and there met the sculptor P. who was reminiscent of an early November twilight, illuminated now and then by sparkling sunlight. He sat down abruptly at my table and I looked at his face, scored by wrinkles, like a sample selection of suffering. Broad and bony, with thick lips, it fought an unequal battle with some unknown enemy within itself. P. looked down into himself as into an astonishing precipice he had to throw himself across with the strength of a man mortally wounded who does not know where the blow has come from; he must constantly turn around violently, sprinkle some trivial remarks about, suddenly lean back again and whisper, then suddenly slam the door on any intruder. I didn't say much, which he explained he found threatening. He brought his bearded face up against mine and said: 'Axel, my friend, if I don't say anything to you, don't take it any further, but learn how to keep quiet about it!' Then he laughed loudly and heartily, so that Miss Selma had to put her hand on his shoulder, whereupon he calmed down. Even he possesses a sufficiency of artistic temperament: something hard, inaccessible, a mockery that contains a most vulnerable imagination. I looked at the bay, which was lying quiet, and thought of how distant Rakel was, and that it was all over, and that something new must come. Am now sitting in my room, a melody has come to me, a nocturnal adagio which when I wrote it down proved to be merely dust and ashes. I have destroyed it, like so much else, amateurish, helpless, well-conceived but subsequently, in the working-out, just shadow-pictures. All the same, I did have a short spell of happiness and enthusiasm. Perhaps even moments like that are capable of transforming me.

25.8

Another letter from Axel T. saying that he has been finding his life 'unnecessary' and has been accused because of it. That I have defended the necessity of the concealed life, and that each person has his own dignity and his own if-ever-so-impossible and fragile striving – that he does not forget (I had almost forgotten it myself, it's an echo from conversations which now really move me) and is grateful for my help. This exaggeration makes me ashamed. Self-contempt and pride, what a lonely and painful alloy.

3.9

From suffocating August with its motionless greenery we have now stepped into September with higher and cooler sky. There is leavetaking in the air, and the people are fleeing to the town. I am starting to be increasingly alone on the restaurant veranda, but today bumped into Architect D. In his narrow face, small, sharp blue eyes, almost forget-me-not blue. His voice distinct, looks for words, listens attentively and has a suspiciousness that is quickly exchanged for interest and warmth. It struck me that we could have become friends. Under the elegance I found suffering, little inclination towards sentimentality, and deep sense for music. He has no time for music-hall stuff and is against all sentimentality, therefore critical of much in contemporary musical life, an egocentricity I know well. Yet there is a *schmaltz* that is genuine, a stirring of emotion – e.g. Tchaikovsky's *Serenade for Strings*. He doesn't deny it, either; where then draw the boundary between genuine and false? Took up the subject of Sibelius. D. talks quickly with inner necessity, distrustful of S., he 'doesn't develop any of his themes, just blows them up and minimizes them again'; can't stand Mahler either, but finds Bruckner truly great. When I attempted to prove the contrary tears suddenly came into my eyes and I suffered a violent surge of emotion, a sign of old age. Tried to talk about a movement towards the inner, about fruitful uncertainty, the darkness of myth, the visionary, about the white swan on the dark waters and a music that does not divide but joins together, organically. He looked at me with sympathy. When I had pulled myself together he asked me if I thought there was such a thing as a naturalistic music; the quintessential is after all invariably a deep emotion, the most powerful element in the mind and the imagination, the most inwardly subjective, i.e. the romantic; for it is posterity that has stuck the epithet 'classical' on once-violent life experiences (take Mozart's G minor, for example), and Viennese classicism is merely an attribute of time and space. We imagine that strict form is equivalent to objectivity. But all true art originates in the individual's creativity and vision and can never be hemmed in by social, economic or political limitations. At that point D. replied that without intellect there would be no true feeling! I replied that without true feeling there can be no intellect! We parted on friendly terms after walk round the harbour which stank of fish and tar.

12.9
Recapitulation of summer, 1899: grey spritsails and white summer dresses, herring barrels and language wars*, Russians and budding hatred, and the scent of apples behind the house-fronts, in the leafy gardens. Little men in straw hats and large women in big hats, screaming children on the bathing beach and the old women with their gout-ridden hands down at the fish-stalls. Watery consommé on Socis' peeling veranda, Jean and Julie in disguise. The whole town with its board-scented alleys quivers in the twilight. From the muddy bottom rise bubbles of gas, and the town's swan looks balefully around for more food, but the fat female thighs have flown, and on the water sway fish-bladders and bits of rubbish. Reserved for the new century: blood and champagne.

15.9
We are moving at the end of the year, Anna and I. Tammerfors: I know nothing about the town, nothing about myself, and the days come and go and don't concern themselves with my agony. So why suffer? Aren't the drifting clouds enough?

16.9
Law-speaker D. during a conversation about birds, their migrations and songs: 'the swallow has the song that is intended for it'.

19.9
When I read scores I am all attention, when I listen to music my

thoughts begin to wander over the widest fields, and my memory comes up with people long since dead or long since passed from my acquaintance.

22.9

Stopped by the church, looked at my turnip watch: it was time to go back, lie on my bed, look at the ceiling. Then I looked at the watch more closely: it was the one Father gave me the week before he died. He was giving me his time, and only now do I understand that. My thoughts moved to the graves behind the church and the circle of those who sat in the library of an evening, sat there like small stones. Went to my room, fell asleep and had a peculiar dream: that I slid from the attic of an unfamiliar house down to a dark room in which Father and Mother had just left a table that was ready spread. There were the abandoned plates, the glasses, and two flickering candles, as though a draught were coming from somewhere. They were there with their absence. Looked for them, then slid down into the next room, brightly illuminated by a great number of windows, and there again sitting opposite each other were silent old men and women, the way there usually are at festivities in the country, but Father and Mother weren't there. Then I stepped out into an overgrown garden, and there was my old class-mate R. dragging a sledge-load of scrap metal, iron beds, sledges and springs down to a marshy creek. As I was about to go and help him, I woke up. Had a strong sense of loss and sadness; at the same time it was as if I had reached the insight that I myself was alive, that I was invulnerable and full of something new, as though I could now at last continue my way. This evening have taken a longish stroll around the town as a kind of farewell, and haven't had many thoughts. Autumn is approaching and is, I suppose, the same as ever, whether in Nådendal or Tammerfors. Surprised at my curiosity with regard to small changes and sounds, the creaking of landing-stages, the colour of the water, trees that have been growing since I first came here, as a boy, and went up to the headland where I met Rakel. A few lonely sailboats were resting on the water, their shadows black on silver-white, and the stays were flapping. Did not see many walkers, the town is drawing in its head and preparing itself for its long winter sleep, and I strolled on my way without any thoughts and almost happy!

28.9

Over two months left until the move. Anna said it's the only 'realistic' solution. People employ so many explanations when silence would be enough. Realism – it's what's accustomed, habitual, habit. But to find one's way to that which is central, to the nerve-paths, the ground-water, the light, the breathing, the skin and the dreams – is that not the true realism which can move mountains? It's as if I was carrying a dream around with me, but I don't know what it represents, what its meaning is – yet.

4.10

In front of a dark, heavy, motionless spruce-tree a trembling poplar in yellow attire reminiscent of a flock of birds: it violently moves thousands of wings, but doesn't get anywhere. It murmurs exclusively to itself. Two contrasts – which one should I choose? I shall choose the poplar, but my longing matches the spruce-tree. I wish I could compose a song about this, so simple that spruce and poplar would stand there as they are, darkness and light close to each other.

7.10

Autumn rain, and my soul acquires peace in this calm, and my eye rests, and I listen to the rain. Soon it will become cool, and then colder, and then winter will be here.

9.10

Writing in a new blue notebook, in the afternoon went to the shop, didn't have enough money, on the way back I tripped on the cobblestones, tried to tidy up and stood in the kitchen, ironed my trousers and nearly burned one of the legs, but got help from the housemaid. In new pair of trousers found a banknote I had forgotten about, went back to the shop with my heart in my mouth, made them open up and got my notebook, there was still one blue one left.

12.10

One of the lodgers, well-known as a joker and wisecracker, came up to me in the street and asked me, probably aware of my interest in strategy: 'Which flank ('Flügel') did the Baron employ at Lützen?' I quickly forestalled him, saying that I hadn't used any of them, as I had a square piano of my own. Confusion and hesitant laughter, like a lapdog yelping.

15.10

It's not Beethoven's demonism that disturbs me, but his turgidity.

For Tolstoy B. is lean and passionate, for me fat and choleric. Yet not always (the sonatas, the quartets). But doesn't Sibelius knead his material? Know too little of him, but there is something powerfully light-seeking, a necessity and intensity that borders on the objective. Wagner is Beethoven's successor, not Sibelius. Isn't he casting his pearls before swine?

22.10

In autumn there is nothing challenging, nothing to attach oneself to, for it abandons everything and everything says farewell, which is – or ought to be – consolation enough for me. Even my insomnia becomes endurable, and questions that worry me have no answers, life simply is that way.

28.10

What are we to embark on with our new century? What is the masterly plan which is going to create a world better than any previous one? What are we taking with us into our new century? That we are descended from the apes, that poverty is not inherited (many still believe it), that we are the cogwheels of history, that money rules supreme and that we – like Poe – seek vainly to soothe our fever 'by impotent attempts at creation' (this last applies in a more private sense to myself). But perhaps the fairytales will stride forth from the forests and demand a new language!

2.11

Today the sky was springlike blue and above the trees a light shadow, and between autumn and spring the iron-hard parenthesis of winter, two claws holding nothing together.

4.11

In Helsingfors they are celebrating Press Week and displaying tableaux of our history with music by Sibelius, and the salon is like a witches' cauldron, dully seething. It struck me that the time is beginning to ripen even where I am concerned; I have found a goal for Axel Tamm's seeking. Shall I dare the leap, hurl myself over the abyss, and how will S. react? Like a white flash of lightning in the darkness, but this time perhaps lifegiving, rousing, so that dead trees begin to live and blossom again, and so that I may find someone, someone. Presumptuous, perhaps. Yet I have nothing, nothing to lose.

3.12

Anna has started to pack our poor bric-à-brac and stuff wicker trunks. A lot of the things we could do without, but for Anna it is a question of preserving that which has not changed, as though it had not already faded and been cast to the winds. We have visited Tammerfors, where there were chimneys and sleet. The Tammerfors was yellow water and black people. The Misses Rosengren of Östra Esplanadgatan put a room at my disposal while Anna travels on to the Färlings in Suoro, Tavastkyro. The last bonds that unite us with our home are being severed. Stayed a day and a night in Åbo, spent some time in Phoenix, slurp of punch and talk of women. Most of it was like thumbed leaves from some decadent novelette. Incredible when something hardly 'charmant' erupts like lava from a volcano. This cosy hypocrisy, these snuff-brown waistcoats like cushions ready to burst, from which the entrails could come flowing at any moment; from this chatter about 'devilettes' I fled, and will now stay in the tranquillity of Nådendal for another few meagrely doled-out weeks. For a long time I have been homeless, and the place in which I live is therefore without meaning.

31.12

On the last day of the century I am sitting in my rented room in the home of Miss Rosengren, who invited me to New Year's Eve coffee, there were also other lodgers there. There was much bow-ing, introducing, and eating of biscuits, together with nibbles about the future of our country, the future of the language question, the triumphant progress of industry and the latest news from Helsingfors and St Petersburg. I am now happily alone, outside in the streets where the people are drifting around waiting for the fireworks display. Ought to try to recapitulate, but there isn't much to be said, only one thing: that the stove is cold and needs more logs, and that I must go the way I have laid out for myself, whether I sink or swim. Have put on my overcoat and hat. Sound of bells ringing out an old, used-up life.

1.1.1900

Demons led Axel across to a new century. They were invisible, concentrations of darkness in rooms that were like those of his childhood but were now disintegrating around him; cool, white curtains began to burn and shrivelled up glowing, wallpaper peeled, faces whirled in the hot air and dissolved, and all the time the demons were there, stood pressed against the walls, opening and closing doors, opening and closing their mouths, and Axel stood shivering in the hail of sparks. Snow and flames, snow that fell into a black mouth and again went whirling up, as though they were the dead woman's breathing. Were the demons there, hidden behind the stripped trees, were they wearing double-breasted jackets like the one the Cathedral School's headmaster used to wear, were their white teeth flashing? He only saw them for a few fear-filled moments and tried to pull off the bows of his spectacles which were burning the bridge of his nose, but he couldn't do it, he had to see everything, he had no eyelids now, after all, he could see straight up into infinity, he was a child and unable to move, to cry out, he was just as immobile as the child-bundles in the sleigh, they looked like morels, their faces were covered by pieces of cloth, woven shawls, bandages, but between them their eyes gleamed, they were looking at him. He had to take a few steps back, there was the trunk of the memorial tree, but it was bleeding. He half-sat up in bed and did not know where he was, a red sock was glowing on his foot. If only his mother didn't come and pull it off! She was kneeling in front of him, her head was leaning against his bare knees, there was so much tenderness that he was able to sink back in the darkness which was full of murmuring, the murmur of water or people's voices, he lay in the secure and familiar envelope of anxiety. But the sound of bells was there like a booming reminder of his guilt: 'Coward! Coward!' he heard them scream, the tormenting spirits that surrounded him, with outstretched arms preventing him from fleeing, forcing him in against the wall. 'Say it again! Say it again!' they shouted, and

183

he held up his violin, his toy violin towards them like a magic wand, a magic sign, and they withdrew, suddenly turned their backs, their white caps on him, and he stood before a laughing woman, she had Olga's features, she had Hjalmar on her knees, she was laughing, a red stain was spreading out along the sleeve of her dress, but only he could see it, Hjalmar laughed and said: 'It's only wine! Wine! Did you think it was blood?' But he knew it was blood, that he had deserted her, that her face kept constantly changing in the same way that the sounds and scents kept changing, so that what had been shouted was now whispers, and a scent of lilac surrounded him: there she sat, Greta, in a white dress, there was not a stain on it, a dress so white that it dazzled him, and she was looking at him, looking at him so provocatively that he had to take out the violin, but the demons were there, forcing him to play faster and faster. It sounded out of tune and it spread fear in the little family, there was the room with plush velvet, glowing punch, and chairs as high as sword-backs, immobile sharp-edged palms, he ran through the room. A door stood open on a light veranda and there sat the aunts, his mother and father, all leaning forward over something they had in their hands: needlework, books, they did not even look up. He was invisible. It was a warm, clear July morning. He stood by the shore and turned round: they were still sitting there, in their white world, immobile. But over dark blue water a swan drew near, it looked so coldly and contemptuously at him and turned away, and he knew that he had been rejected, that he was not one of the chosen, that he was doing nothing. He raised his arm, straightened his cuff, now they would see! He was immaculate! He turned round: children were whirling there like dandelion puffs, the low, crumbling shanties were sinking into the mud, a door was violently opened, shrill female laughter was heard, he began to run down towards the harbour, away from Skatudden, he heard music from Kapellet and sank panting onto a bench, he could hardly breathe. Doctors stood around him, they were talking softly to one another, he could hardly hear what they were saying, a burning sense of shame washed over him, he could make out snatches – 'mental invalid' – 'vestigia terrent' – 'tremolo' – 'madness' – and he opened his eyes, lay like that, closed them again, there was Doctor Wargentin with his large, white teeth, as big as piano keys, and the black ones were there, too. Doctor Wargentin was standing in front of a fish-tank, with a swift gesture he caught a wriggling fish and threw it on the table, it twitched in its struggle with death, but Doctor Wargentin passed

184

his large, bony hand across it and it lay still, completely still, and from the adjoining room music was heard – Bach? Now a narrow rivulet of dark water was beginning to find its way under the door, sleety water which was finding its way towards his bed: this was their ultimate attempt at forcing him into flight, but they were unable to succeed: he had the secret music which was flowing in from the window, he opened it and sunlight came flowing in! And there was Rakel sitting at the kitchen table and she looked at him with her gentle eyes, it was still with the quiet of Sunday. He placed his cheek against hers, she had a fragrance of snow and spring-water and said to him so softly: 'You don't do any work, do you?' He looked at her, this was another face, old, furrowed, that of a witch or a demon, he had been duped, he backed away. She leaned forward, her face altered and was again almost that of a child, he wanted to reply to her but could not, she slipped away as snow whirls away, disappearing through an open window that bangs and bangs in the night. He had to sit up in bed, he sat like that, his eyes open, his nightshirt cold and wet around the shoulders, tore off his sock, pressed his feet against the cold floor, stood up and walked over to the window, pulled the curtains apart. There was a dark street, voices shouting, then silence again. He could sense a dawn. It was his life. He saw it.

II

From The Diary

1.1

Brought in the new century in grand style, with a nightmare.
Only one way out of this: out of myself. Outside the most finely
glimmering snow and black human figures, and neither the age
nor its expression have changed: everything trundles on as before.
There is a peculiar silence, as before a catastrophe, or is it – before
a miracle? Went for a long walk and let the wind slap me in the
face and blow right through my soul, so that only the most essential
was left: dreams, action, that which must be done. Stood among
bare trees and tried to give myself up to seeing and listening. Only
in the forest is there this calm, and the silence between the trunks
of the trees. Here solitude has no bitter, burdensome role, as I
share it with the trees and the twilight that there is in the forest
and is always there, even on a day of high summer. In the forest
the cold is less severe than it is across whistling fields, and in
summer the forest is cool in spite of the fields' heat. In a forest
people move in self-evident solitude, even though they are talking
to one another. Recalled how in childhood the forest was something to remember and also to fear: when some woodfowl suddenly
flew up with a tumult and disappeared – black grouse or capercail-
zie – and afterwards the commotion quickly died away. In the
forest there are the most delicate sounds: the wind through the
boughs, clearer now that the leaves have gone, people's voices
like the buzzing of flies, a branch breaking – who was that, what
was that, how did it come about? I listen, but all is silent once
more. And the muted voice of the town. From the forest arises
all our solitary music, purifying eye and ear. All this I thought
without thinking, on the first day of the century.

28.1

The shanties up and along the ridge cling to it as tightly as chunks of rock, their wood and tiles notwithstanding. Here life lives out its poverty and its strength, even at night, and the town becomes a beast of prey with the same glimmering sky as over Odensaari (yes, let it be called that) or Nådendal or Åbo, and the Great Bear holds its scoop above me, showering me with eternity. In the mornings I wash in cold water, as though I were preparing to fight a pitched battle, eat what is essential, as much from compulsion as from desire: I stick to vegetables, even though the Misses are forever pressing their meats and sauces on me. Have sold some stuff I don't need, some books, among other things, which I shall never read again, and thus have managed to gather together some extra *den'gi*. Have not written to anyone, and no one has written to me. The cold of the interior sparkles here, and the air is dry and easy to breathe. Try to sleep with the window open. This is a way of talking to myself, sometimes I mumble. Sink into scores as into a glowing cave in which I discover my own voice. Have written to Robert Kajanus about Sibelius's K II Suite about the point in the Minuet where there ought to be a diversion in B major. Ending of same bizarre. Also took up the subject of the Paris visit, its importance and significance. Now music's language is speaking in me and with me, and at nights I dream in a half-waking state that everyone is listening to these words which are simply the purest song and music, my words which belong to everyone.

22.2
Received a reply from Kajanus and wrote back in turn. It's precisely the *melodies* that the foreign orchestras make the heaviest weather of – e.g. the French orchestra that attempted to play Scandinavian music at the 1899 World Exhibition in Paris. We are now assured that this will not be repeated, and the Philharmonic's visit will be a watershed in the understanding of that which is at once Nordic and universal. The title of the commissioned overture which Sibelius is composing ought in my opinion to be called 'Finlandia', the way Rubinstein calls his 'Rossiya' and Liszt his 'Hungaria'. Also reminded Kajanus about Mielck's pearl of a symphony.* Brooded about how many craftsmen there must be before the Genius can appear. For the Genius is the great Gatherer, and, through the act of drawing together, also a Precursor. He is the finest of craftsmen, works hard, leaves the cheap to one side, is ridden by demons but can extract victory from that: his dreams are fertile and hard as stone, from them cathedrals are built. If he is not driven by this frenzy the result will be triviality. But I believe

in S. In spite of everything! In spite of his café-elegance. Wrote to Axel Tamm about the transfer of funds in a dignified and correct manner.

10.3

Now I have written to Jean Sibelius, using the original signature 'X'. Have exhorted him to muster his energies for an introductory overture to the Paris visit, which could be like a storm-wind blowing through the French spring. It must have something demonic about it! Mentioned that I have not heard the First Symphony – in the next one I hear fir-trees singing, the forest approaching with darkness and light. Recipe *ad libitum*: Allegro (sylvan mysticism, the sound of the herdsman's horn, atmosphere of the wilds), Adagio (magic of a summer's night by the shore of an inland lake), Scherzo (spookery) and Finale (storm and roaring forest, daybreak with birdsong, sunrise). After he has completed this Finnish *Waldsymphonie* he should return to the love of his youth: chamber music. Thus have I, with feverish agility, determined. At the deepest level my advice is a hope, a dream in which a renewal is taking place, both for him, for myself and for all who will listen: so that a new freedom may pass like a breeze over the nations. Finlandia! Walk restlessly along the streets, stop, look for signs of spring but there are few of them, yet morning was brighter, as though it were flowing from some secret source. The nights filled with dreams and fantasies, as though I were certain that they were going to force their way in: that he will reply! That once I have gathered myself for something even more constructive, he will reply! But it is not yet time to unveil the name. Last night I wrote down a short piano piece in deep happiness, in the morning it was dead and had to be thrown away. What is an 'X'? The great unknown.

27.4

Tammerfors is coming to life with the spring, the water is flowing under the bridges, there is an energy that is also making a narrow, silvery river-branch, a stream perhaps, a narrow, pulsing vein, flow through me. The shift work gives the town its specific rhythm, and I who am used to waking up at nights feel both alienated and in agreement with the constant activity. In Nådendal my insomnia was soundless, so that I could hear my own breathing. Here dogs bark, rough voices rise like sparks towards the heavens, and the Misses Rosengren are like two innocent lilies in a jungle of stone and smoke. The bays are opening up, the ice is drifting slowly away, the light is playing among the tree-trunks, the sun-spotted pine trees are breathing summer, and from everything an intense, rebellious music is arising. Am now weighing my words for my next letter to J.S. It is like taking a deep breath, holding it, and letting it out again.

4.5

Have slept peacefully for several nights in a row, with no dreams. As though I were growing into a completely new landscape, as though a dead tree were coming to life, as though music were no longer the only way out but in harmony with others on a map as yet obscure. Remember how I sat close against the window at Odensaari and let the light play on an old atlas in which strange countries stretched out with cities and rivers. Under the coarse rafters the heat was motionless and filled with the scent of wood, as from great, foreign jungles where unfamiliar birds suddenly screamed, challengingly. As though they were now screaming inside me.

14.5

I have never even asked myself whether I am doing the right thing with all my advice and exhortations, my anonymous outpourings. If I want to transform, I must myself be transformed. That is how simple it is, a constant shifting of waves; no wonder that I feel like a rolling deck and sometimes suffer from on-shore seasickness. I go walking a lot, it's a fever that makes the trees burst into bud, the waters flow, the people love or hate, a country free itself from its fetters and a middle-aged man dream crazy dreams with his eyes open. When I am not reading scores I read books, most recently Tolstoy. Natasha in *War and Peace* merely a dream of eternal youth; when the dream is shattered she is soon transformed into a coarse, middle-aged lady. Must it be like that? Can I not preserve Rakel's image unaltered in my memory? But perhaps Natasha went through the hell of *The Kreutzer Sonata* – the sexual, which for Tolstoy is shameful and dirty? In spite of feelings of shame I have – strangely enough – preserved a childish innocence in these matters. So Rakel continues to live, as though I had never said goodbye to her, and she had never said the words I heard on the way from Åbo to Nådendal, for it was not she who spoke them, but a caricature. What energy we put into transforming and distorting our own images, from purity to filth, through our own filth. In general we have to make ugly those who have deceived us, or whom we have deceived. In the presence of the ideal dream, can I forget the cold gaze? Are not both necessary in this duet of despair that is each day repeated on the stage? As a matter of fact, Tolstoy is probably too healthy to understand that which is weakest and most fragile –; or else suffers because he destroys it. Hence the hatred, the puritanism, the mortifications. Self-flagellation *à la Russe*! God knows, one sees enough of that every day throughout our unfree land.

13.6

Wrote two letters to Sibelius. Added to the list of requests a violin concerto or phantasy for orchestra. I have urged him to travel to Italy, the land where one learns *cantabile*, moderation and harmony, plasticity and linear symmetry, where everything is beautiful – even the ugly. Just as in my imagination I see the Canale Grande opening out towards the sea, San Marco shimmering in calm, harmonious beauty, so ought new visions to open up to him, who can unite forest with colonnade, darkness with light. When music is truly great, it is characterized by a personal comprehensiveness of vision which looks outwards and imbues every phrase: Mozart, Chopin; and the source-stream of a country – Austria, Poland – rises in their music; then why not in that of Jean Sibelius? Now that he has penetrated to the country's deepest level, the bedrock, the primary rock, he can go further and from that material build something that is not bound to the nationalistic. Through love for Finlandia the great perspective! But sometimes only distance can give one a perspective on what one has left behind: therefore Italy!

17.6

There is the quiet of a Sunday, and the exhausted people are asleep. For me Sundays have always been empty hours of oppressive silence. They are the time when one lets one's thoughts aimlessly wander. We demand explanations for everything, even music, and are unable to accept that something *is*. Even composers occasionally supply explanations – afterwards. They don't give an inch to what is, its growth. That is why opera is such a fatal art form, which easily passes over into the comical; fortunately the words can seldom be heard. Myself weighed down by the most sentimental images, I require of music spring-water, vision and intensity, ambiguity and clarity! My wandering thoughts cease their movement: from the room next door I can hear the horrible strumming of a piano, scales over and over again, and some prosaically faltering study by Czerny. Must escape outside, like a swallow from an attic that is too confined.

26.6

When tonality is shattered, so is the vegetative capacity of life and music. The damage that is done when the natural aspiration towards melody is distorted into 'originality' is irreparable, for 'originality' is the enemy of art. One must be original, not 'original' in the peculiar sense.

27.6

Advertisement for the Philharmonic's Paris Concerts on Sunday and Monday in Helsingfors Fire Station. Can I afford to go to them? The unreserved seats in the gallery cost 2 marks. To these practical problems I must find a solution, am constantly forced up against the wall in order to preserve the interests of music, it's like being slapped in the face. But this is music which can be preserved, concealed. There are two *Kalevala* Legends; the deepest, darkest, most translucent – has he found it? Dreamt about Mother, she was walking ahead of me but didn't see me, I ran after her but she turned away and vanished.

2.7

Arrived in Helsingfors yesterday evening at 7.08 pm, the train a quarter of an hour late. I had not told anyone, not even Tor, that I was coming, put up at the Hospitz.* The Sunday-quiet streets gave off a dull warmth. Strolled down to the market, there was the cry of seagulls and the tang of salt sea, and fortunately met no one I know. I am wandering, but in towards the centre, and no one can see the infinite spaces that gleam within me. Just as well. From Observatory Hill the city opened out, and I sat on a bench like an empty vessel that must be filled. Went back, lay on my bed sleepless, got up early this morning, bought tickets at Hagelstam's bookshop. The Fire Station hall half empty, somewhat more people in the gallery. Weakness came over me, and prickly heat. Counted the orchestra: 66 players, Kajanus conducted: *Finlandia*, Kajanus's own *Summer Memories*, Järnefelt's *Korsholm*, J.S.'s *Spring Song*, Kajanus's *Finnish Rhapsody No. 1*, then –: 'Swan of Tuonela' and 'Lemminkäinen's Homeward Journey'. It was noticeable that there hadn't been much time for rehearsal. Yet: jubilation, enthusiasm, especially for *La Patrie*, *Suomi* or *Finlandia*, that is, which was encored, and Kajanus presented with a laurel lyre. Looked around for J.S., but did not see him until he was standing there, and his shadow fell over me, and shall remain.

Now to the works, the two Legends – for *Finlandia* was like a meeting after a long absence, so familiar that I wept. There was in 'Lemminkäinen's Homeward Journey' something strange, an uneasiness, a sense of departure when the themes were trumpeted out with vigour but somewhat superficially, too heroically after 'Swan of Tuonela'. Here was the song of my sorrow, as gentle as though it were autumn and death not yet here. Life was now so still that it reflected shores, starry skies and coolest longing, and there was a sorrow as eternal as solitude, as silence without people. The Nordic element – my thoughts turned to Grieg on occasion – is here conscious of darkness, the repressed and never concluded insight that our traces are merely accidental, while forest and lake will live on, indifferently, as though we had never existed. But how can words describe the landscape of a soul? Jean Sibelius, you have seen my darkness! My longing for home! In the end it was sheer happiness just to listen, without looking for meaning and intention. I am a child who has received a present. It is night, but I cannot sleep, and the light outside is as silent as before extinction – or birth.

3.7.1900

A tang of sea blew towards him while he was still on the rise of Nikolaigatan. He had dressed formally, his white double collar was chafing him but he hardly noticed it: it was the day of the orchestra's departure, and he was on his way to pay homage. The long night had left him empty; for the first time in his life he was adrift, as in growing fear, and the scents from the wooden houses, the dust that rose from carts that were trundling by on their way to the market, the clatter of hooves that struck sparks from the cobbles, drifting clouds, people black or white, children who ran out of gateways, barefoot, and disappeared again as though swallowed up by the earth, all of it paled before the stubborn thought: he was about to see them, these men who were to be sent out into the world in order to make the country known, to bring it honour: Finlandia! He still had plenty of time. He turned in along Elisabetsgatan, the school building was finished, rising above the wooden shanties, in Mariegatan a little flock of children was streaming out under supervision: frocks, white collars, children of summer in the city which was slowly awakening to a hot day. Preoccupied, Axel looked at Sundqvist's sign with its boots and shoes: there were five of them. They were severed from their legs, silhouettes, they were supposed to bring in customers, he looked at his feet: black, split, low-heeled shoes, had they ever been new? When?

He walked down the hill and turned along towards Ständerhuset*, it stood there glistening, a display, the friezes, the pillars, and a fountain on the other side of the street was murmuring. He was thirsty, but there was no soda-water kiosk in the vicinity, only heavy stones, glistening sunlight, the Senate Square empty apart from three carriages with tired, silent horses outside the City Hall. The hum of Salutorget was like a distant swarm of bees in the stony heat. He stopped, indecisively. Should he go down Unionsgatan or Katrinegatan? Was there anything he needed to buy at Stockmann's? The boat wasn't due to leave until eleven o'clock, he had more than an hour to spare. Someone came whistling

196

towards him swinging a stick, he hastily turned round and entered the dark, narrow ravine of Katrinegatan. Voices and water glittered towards him, a three-master had anchored outside Norrmén Palace, seagulls were screaming above the stalls, a laughing couple came out of Kleineh's Hotel and passed him without a glance. Foreigners. The bandstand was open, but the music had not yet begun. He sat down and ordered a glass of soda-water, the waiter dusted the table hastily, contemptuously. Faint murmur of water. No one he knew. He sat in the shadow. An old man with a basket in front of him was selling oranges and cigarettes, his beard was catching the sunlight, Axel looked away, made a negative gesture. The old man was stubborn, Axel quickly stood up, walked towards the market, there was the scent of wood like a greeting from something childhood-warm, remote: deep forests, echoes, silence. With this was mingled the smell of hundreds of horses' dung and urine, of the salt-barrels' silvery fish, the tarred barges' sea-tang of wind and hot wood. Fish-scales on sun-refracted arms, yelling and laughter, kerchieves, long, wide skirts, men with a sharp streak on their foreheads when they took off their peaked caps and smoothed their hair, and everywhere the children, children like the sky, with movements like those of the frightened pigeons, everything in swift motion, unintelligible, pale with light, and there, ready to sail, the vessel. The pennants were fluttering in the wind, there was a sound in the air that made people, buildings, masts, rigging, clouds and breezes quiver before Axel's gaze.

He looked around him. He would have to get hold of a basket, he wouldn't be able to hold that many bunches of violets in his hands, he had made inquiries the day before, had worked it out, he had the money, he had the agreement, there she was, in the peasant stalls, smiling at him, everything was ready, everything clear, sunnily, fragrantly clear. He was so short that he had to look up to her, or was she so tall, he didn't remember. Proud, and at the same time as though he had made a laughing-stock of himself. The basket, he hadn't reckoned on that, did he have the money? He began to rummage in his pockets, had he left his purse at home, had he lost it, he grew dizzy, he had to seek support, she drew him in under the coarse grey roof, he was given a stool to sit on, legs walked by, perhaps they were looking at him, sweat trickled down his back. This was his punishment for having come in the first place. The comic, the clown. He breathed slowly, heavily, and things began to resume the places in which he was accustomed to see them, encounter them. He was doing the right thing, after all. Albeit on a restricted scale. The money was where it should be, he would have to be careful how much he paid, but she was leaning over him and he smelt her fragrance, her pure fragrance: he could have an old basket for nothing, she didn't need it, and he had after all ordered and paid for a lot of bunches at once. She placed it in his arms. He looked up at the broad, smiling face, the hare-lip did not disturb him at all, he also had his deformity, his loneliness, he hid himself in the correct, in the reduced, in bunches of violets. He sat with his face inclined over their fragrance, it surrounded him as once his mother's had done, he sat with his eyes closed, and the bustle and immense life of the market became unreal, powerless. 'I want the great and hide myself in the small, in order to survive': the thought was familiar but only now there, close to him. My heart, he thought, is none the less of the same shape and size as those of others. And even if he had made a laughing-stock of himself, was it not important for many people to have this to entertain themselves with? The earnestness of suffering that entertains. The comedy of the deformed for those without feeling. Perhaps to provoke laughter is a shield against stronger, more violent forms of aggression? Even in myself? Shall I hail a cab, he wondered, but he shook his head: all is well. I shall just walk.

He looked at his watch: it was twenty past ten. He got up hurriedly, the basket in his right hand, the stick in his left, he strolled on his way, people were already standing on the quay, cabs were pulling up, five double-bass cases stood propped against the wall of the packing-warehouse, the *Wellamo* already had her steam up, he hurried towards the gangway, he must get this done, now. He felt so oddly light, outside himself. But had it not always been like this? With clouds flying, birds screaming, people moving in their unintelligible orbits like strange planets, and he ran after them, or pressed against the walls; now, in this place, there was no protection, the packing warehouses glowed flaming red, cabs smacked screeching by, bowlers and top-hats, flower-baskets on the swaying heads of women, the gaping children, the embraces, the ceremonies, the heat that was rising in the harbour basin, the pigeons like market madams waddling jerkily amidst thrown-out remains, the Russian with his ice-cream box, and the steam from the vessel that was now sweeping over them –: what was he doing here? Against a hovel sat a man tanned almost black, asleep with a bottle of Fennia in his hand, had perhaps seen better days, dressed in black as in eternal mourning, everyone dressed in black, or white, and Axel had to force his way through the mass of people, stationed himself beside the gangway. There they came with their violin cases, their violas and cellos, their oboes and cor anglais, their flutes and clarinets, their bassoons and trumpets, their French horns and trombones, all like his music, his dreams, shut up in black cases, but not yet put to sea, not yet sunk to the bottom, not yet doomed, lost, the memories, shiny black waters of long ago; here there was still life, music, the future –: he pressed bunch after bunch of violets into astonished hands, felt the interested or quickly indifferent gazes, how many did he have, how many were left, like pieces of his own flesh, like pieces of his childhood, all his hopes, and the scent of violets that cut against the smell of salt, sea, and soot; and the light that flamed!

He could see barely anything except his hand, it held out the violets, drew itself back, there was water on the quay, the light was mirrored there, the light stabbed his eyes so violently, 'Triumphant journey!' he whispered, but hardly anyone could hear him in the babble of voices. There was one man, a cellist, he had seen him yesterday from the gallery, huge and fat, who waved his pale, meaty hand, would not accept his mite, his young, glowing spring hopes, the lightest and best of his youth, waddled up the gangway, breathing like a bellows, where was the music? The profundity? The burning faith in the future? Sixty-six players, and he only had twenty-five bunches, it was just as well that not all of them had taken one, now they were finished, now he could withdraw, no one had driven him away.

He straightened himself up, the two blue eyes behind the glass lenses gazed suddenly calmly and clearly, the face ageless, the childish look about chin and mouth, the gaze intense and at the same time absent –: he stood with a ring of loneliness about him, without thinking, the people turned aside. Now came the cab bearing Kajanus and Sibelius, he saw him at a distance, the heavy but at the same time agile form, the impatience, Kajanus there beside him, more acute, with a soft linen hat pulled down over his forehead, because of his excitement he did not get a proper look at them as they were saying goodbye to the crowd of people, he needed to clear his throat, he wanted to shout but could not, he could not go forward, they would meet in good time, not now, he couldn't have given them flowers, they would probably have laughed, he would not have been able to take that, would have veered away like a flapping seagull, a drunkard, an outcast. From the gathering on the quay there were no songs, no shouts of hurrah, nearby two gentlemen dressed in tophats and frock coats were talking about the closure of *Nya Pressen*, about Axel Lille★, who was supposed to be arriving at Helsingfors that same day, there was a ferment, it was all happening now and in eternity, only he was not changing, was merely sinking the way old houses sink, or the way shouts and voices sink in the summer verdure so that only sea and wind are visible, sea and wind. Naturally, in his half-waking state during the nights he had gone up to him, or at least to Kajanus, had stopped, asked about the journey, how they could cope with such burdens, Stockholm, Kristiania, Göteborg, Malmö, Copenhagen, Lybeck, Hamburg, Berlin, Amsterdam, Rotterdam, The Hague, finally Paris – he had made that journey a thousand times, always in sleepless ardour and sweat-dripping agitation – and seen the dawn palely filtering between the curtains, nothing out of nothing, but his task was fulfilled; he left the basket on a cart there, and wandered completely empty and open, nothing but eyes and receptive senses, up towards Observatory Hill and on down in the direction of Brunnsparken.

The *Wellamo* was late in leaving, not until half past eleven did he see it put off, saw the town, the small, fresh-planted trees, the ship decorated with pennants, it slid away so silently, as though an invisible hand had pushed it out, the smoke from its funnel now white against the sky. He sat in the outdoor restaurant at Brunnshuset for a while, someone was singing there, someone who had been watching from the veranda, between the trees a wooden barge with grey sails slid slowly by, in the grass here and there groups of camping families could be seen, children for the most part, a boy in a dark blue peaked cap passed between the tables, shouting '*Hufvudstadsbladet!*', and he bought one, saw that Lille was arriving by train from Åbo, in Åbo he had received a laurel garland from the Nådendal Bathing Society, Lektor Cygnaeus had made a speech at the festive supper.

He remembered Cygnaeus. He saw the room with the writing desk, what had he said? Something about him that made him go down to the river, moved to tears. What? He had to order a light punch with ice, it was against his custom, but he felt as though he himself had put to sea, as though he were gliding out into unknown waters, above a deep he was only now able to measure. Here it was cool in the shadows, here he was more alone than in Nådendal, only Tammerfors would be awake now, dark, almost threatening, above his life. What if he were to move? But he was imprisoned, this had been arranged for him, his brothers and sisters had placed him where he was, Anna was near and could hurry to the rescue if necessary, Elin – all these dwarf-like machinations when the country's future hung in the balance, when the power of a superior nation moved smilingly among the trees, spurs, white uniforms, ladies' parasols, society with blood-taste, he had had enough of that, he was lonely, unknown and invisible. He could wait.

He left the bottle of Palmros punch half-empty in its cooler, paid and wandered slowly down past the bath-house, looked out across the expanse of sea, a narrow streak of smoke from those who were now setting off to conquer the world dissolved on the horizon. One of the sloops from the Nyland Yacht Club glided by and went about, white-clad gentlemen moved quickly, winching the sail, it was all a summer idyll, as though nothing were happening. But everything was new. He wandered and looked, hardly thinking, deep inside him there was a happiness that followed him step by step. He had seen him! They would meet, he would tell Jean what his music had given him, how an empty vessel had been filled, how a glass of water reflected the streak of light there, on the table, in the dark room, he had lain and watched that light grow.

His shoes were pinching him. He sat down on a bench, looked vaguely at the trees, the villas amidst the greenery, got up again. Parkgatan was midday-quiet, about half an hour later he was standing on Sandsvikstorget, the wind whirling sand in his eyes. From the Sinebrychoff* barges the stink of the town's manure drifted up towards the centre. Axel wandered slowly up Vladimirsgatan, in towards the town: knobs of rock, shrunken wooden houses, children who suddenly rushed out screaming from behind some fence, flocking around the confused figure in the dark overcoat. Children, always children, town children who could not go to the country, snotty-nosed, barefoot, hard as stones, suddenly gone like flower-seeds with cries like those of the swallows. At last, with aching feet, he reached Östra Henriksgatan and the University Pharmacy, was nearly run over by a cab, the driver swore and the hooves flashed their sparks against the cobbles. He went inside to get in off the street, sat down on a chair, drank a glass of water. He closed his eyes. There was the Swan of Tuonela gliding on the dark waters, the *Wellamo* steaming out towards an open sea, darkness and light mingling before his eyes, each sound was strange and distinct: the screeching of carriages, the shouts of the newspaper boys, the door that opened and closed, muffled voices. No one could see it, no one could hear it, only him: the deep singing of the future, the sound of deliverance within him, unheard, invisible.

From The Diary

1900

5.7

In *Hufvudstadsbladet* screaming white censored spaces in the account of the ovations on Myntgatan. Reading this as at a distance, am living in the music. Something great, dark and powerful is about to rise from hills and forests, from seas and human souls. This is the classical that is eternal, for this is not romanticism, not demonism, but – myth. In order to refresh myself I read Haydn's Op. 76. In the Fifths Quartet there is the alternation of major and minor, yet with a constant germinating background of D minor, throughout all the movements: there, too, a unity, an organic structure. Thus: rootedness in spite of changes in mood. The fifths! They descend like birds on whose wings the last rays of the sun are falling, against the background of a dark sky. I found even more sunlight in the fourth quartet. There there is also passion in the light, for all passion is not born of night and darkness. There there were those sudden outbursts which I imagine to be characteristic of J.S. Perhaps the keenest form of understanding is a bright and life-affirming one, which does not obstruct its depth. The way the sunlight reflects itself on the sea-bed, playing with its own life. There are shadows there, just as there is always death in a human life right from the beginning, no matter how happy it may be later on. It must have existed in Jean S.'s life, too. It is there, in his music. And at the same time the power, the light! Walked across Pyynikki, in under the great, airy mass of leaves, then climbed higher again, and looked out over the summer-quiet villas and Pyhäjärvi lying there with motionless waves, and in the distance could be heard the roar of the town, subdued as its inhabitants.

12.7

Received short letter from Axel Tamm in which he tells me among other things about the scandalous venue arranged for our orchestra in Stockholm: the Olympia Circus Hall! But then, after continuous rain, came Hasselbacken, where *Finlandia* was played and the cry went up: 'Long live our brothers, the Finns!' A large garland of white and blue flowers was presented: 'The same flowers grow in Finland as in Sweden'. T. says he caught a distant view of Jean Sibelius: an aristocrat. It's just as well that S. was at least outwardly satisfactory, and that *Finlandia* aroused enthusiasm; I am reckoning coldly: it means money for S. T. has promised to send something. As soon as the money arrives I shall forward it with a letter, something cheerful, not too obtrusive, to give him a push! *L'art prétend!* Already have the wording in my head – how art demands the utmost, how it must grow, expand towards new horizons: the Italian ones!

18.7

Axel Tamm has promised to send 3000 marks. The summer is going by and I am letting it go, have remained in the town. Days of expectancy, fever, a wonderful, almost hallucinatory dreaminess. Childhood landscape and always S.'s presence. The letter containing the summons to a journey to Italy almost finished, during hours of sleeplessness torn up, rewritten. My movements are confused. The ants run too, but find their way through the labyrinth of the anthill in the dark. But I – a rambling, a rage, a self-control in a dark overcoat, with a stick, a body that is now foreign to me, an image in the mirror: is that me? Ever more remote, my needs. Sometimes write letters to aunts, relatives, but am hidden in my dream. Shall I sign it 'X' or...

16.8

Caterwauling, the strumming of a piano, the heat of the sun, nights without sleep, coughing from the neighbours' rooms, dogs barking far into the night, what do I care about it? Miss Rosengren has bronchitis. My letter to Jean Sibelius is posted, and I signed it with my own name. Necessarily painful, painfully necessary, as it is someone else's money that is involved. And also some of my own – not pride, but ambition, secret and iconoclastic!

25.8

Reply from Jean Sibelius: views the demands of art as 'a terrifying truth, but one which occasionally – as now – awakens joy. I think I ought with gratitude to accept the generous offer, and shall, if

I encounter no unforeseen obstacles – of which the Herr Baron will be informed – follow your advice and embark on my journey in November or at the latest in December. May I never unintentionally offend the unknown benefactor or stand in a false light before him.' These words have I weighed, this attitude enclosed in my inner being. From this point of departure there is one way to go – where, the future must show. In the honourable, in the moral, music seeks its germinating soil; if it is there, the atmosphere is elevated and free. – Was overcome towards evening by a limpness that made me incapable of thought and feeling, as though all the blood had been drained out of me. I was seized by a great fear: lest I myself should emerge in a false light, lest my intentions were not pure, lest I remain anonymous, invisible, as always before in my dreams and striving. The irresolution, the lack of will-power which must be overcome.

18.9

Days of sunlight and days of rain and grey weather, unease and indecision, as though the most dissimilar people were living within me, shoving and squabbling for room, tossing one another out of bed until one of them in the dream gets up and shouts in order to still the cacophony, and I wake up, wet with sweat. Then it is sometimes a blessing to go in to the Misses, listen to gossip, drink coffee, function the way people function in the great monotonous everyday when they talk to one another about trivial things and sleep like logs.

20.9

On my usual walk met a young boy from Finlayson's*, one of the many under 15 who only have an eight-hour workday. He spat snuff from his pale features and shouted 'Look, a sparrow!', whereupon I turned round violently, thinking that he was being rude to me, but he was already on the run with his companions. There was a little hunchbacked old man dressed in grey homespun there who really did look like a sparrow. Somewhat later I was witness to a violent battle between children from Pispala and children from Amuri; they threw stones, and will themselves become stones in the factories if they are not ground to gravel or wasted away with TB. Strolled around on Pispala Heights, something draws me there, to the bare-legged, cold-ridden, flaxen-fringed, yelling children with their ragged braces, scurvy, screaming like birds. There was a smell of outdoor lavatories, phlox, food, and voice seized at voice with fangs, carrying out over the heights. From the roads direct entrances to second- or third-storey apartments in wooden houses which are most frequently surrounded by overgrown verdure. Pyhäjärvi gleamed in autumn clarity, there were waves, but they were standing still. A young ragamuffin threw stones after me, but when I quickly turned round with a 'Pax Vobiscum!' he fled with ferret-like swiftness. A tall woman who was beating a feather-bed with malicious frenzy – perhaps in her mind she was thrashing her husband – turned round and smiled at me. I said hello, took off my hat and walked onwards. If I had grown up as a working-class boy, what would have happened? Would I have become healthily hardened, or would I have quickly gone under? Thought of Mother, her softness and cheerful spirits, her radiant eyes, and suddenly mourned deeply all that has gone and cannot be restored.

27.9
In a letter to Sibelius have warned him about the southerners, who are not to be trusted. The bacilli in the Italian food and drink are lively ones, and their idea of music different from ours. During his visit he ought therefore to observe the greatest caution, so that his nerves are not affected; no doubt he has a fondness for dissipation. By all accounts the ice-cream in Rome is treacherous. Cleanliness, circumspection, carefulness should be observed in foreign countries which do not hesitate to profit by the innocence of northerners. In their music something airy, swift and superficial, but the landscape wonderful, I am told, and I have seen from pictures and in art and photographs that they are not lying. What does he think of me? That I'm just an eccentric benefactor? Yet he ought to see that in all this there is concealed the deepest seriousness; my nights are filled with the rushing of wings, like Prince Myshkin I have ideas but am unable to talk freely, as the words remain in my heart. That is a humiliation which must be overcome.

6.10
Am suffering from musical scales which in the hours of the night seek their way upwards and never seem to have any ending, they alternate and continue to the point of madness, of deepest pain, like an inhuman voice that is trying to break through the bone of my skull. There is a fruitless, helpless fumbling with the outermost extremities of the nerves, and in my case the consequence of this is photophobia, sensitivity to sounds, difficulties in communicating

and even opening the door when people knock; then I get blind-spots, losses of memory which can never be restored, are simply there, and the only thing that brings relief is to go over in my memory some of the most consoling compositions which I have hidden away inside myself. This does not mean the brightest and most radiant ones, it often means darkness, or twilight, a music which – like that of J.S. Bach – creates landscapes, space and distance in the timeless. Yet how light-toned the death-theme in 'Swan of Tuonela' is, how in the music light and darkness alternate, but both are from the same sea, and the wave only seems to move, a part of the great breathing. It gives rest.

12.10

The days go by in reading, walks, waiting, the study of scores. Have returned to the *Snöfrid* of my youth, to Viktor Rydberg. J.S. has composed an improvisation on this work, there I shall meet him, in the world of the storm! In the world of courage! Of loneliness! To be faithful to one's dreams is to return to 'the flower-ing yards of childhood memories'! But then the journey must lie through storm and struggle, that of the individual as much as that of the nation. To fight a hopeless fight and, nameless, die: the words are those of Rydberg, the companion. But as a sentence on my threatened land they are not suitable. To fight a hopeful fight and find the name, freedom!

20.10

Attended soirée for collection of funds as the Philharmonic's Paris trip made a loss. Listened to *Snöfrid*. J.S. came over to me, we grasped each other's hands, I saw his form, like a firm chunk of rock, the heavy face, stern and yet smiling, the hair somewhat dishevelled, the first signs of baldness. Is he conscious of his headstrong energy? At the heart of his manner of speaking – quickly, the thoughts flowing out with the animation of a river – something restless and easily vulnerable, a mistrust, even, which at the next second is capable of changing into the most cordial warmth and then back into absent-mindedness again. He treated me with the utmost attention, which was noticed by the assembled gathering, felt proud and at the same time wanted to sink through the floor, make myself invisible. He introduced me to his wife Aino, who gave an impression of the greatest refinement. There was something birdlike, something nervous and sensitive, and a sorrow in her gaze that gripped me, and she seemed to observe that and gave me a smile, as though we had something in common that he knew nothing of! In him there is so much health and absent-mindedness, the only thing that unites us, mine shrunken and sterile, his open, fertile, a spring storm. As in the music to *Snöfrid*. I spoke about the bond I felt with Rydberg, about what he meant to me, and how I had received his photograph; he replied that he too considered Rydberg important because of his moral strength. He gave me an account of the Paris trip, spoke of his feeling for nature. I told him about what his scores had given me, about the clarity, the alternation of light and darkness, inner vision and outer form. He listened. Was able to inform him that a Finnish patron had also thrown his hat in the ring, and that the journey was now insured for 5,000 marks, and that I hoped he could now venture out into the storm, into the Mediterranean wind in fresh spirits, whereupon he embraced me, moved. I do not remember how I found my way to the T-fors train, fell there into a strange, deep, dreamless torpor and awoke with a sense of happiness and peace, so that even the most menacing aspects of the town began to shimmer like snow-crystals.

15.11

Have been in bed ill, days of mist and undefined sounds, that this should happen now, just when life seemed so radiant! But this process of being hurled between health and sickness is an instructive one, and quickly cuts everything down to its true proportions. The Misses Rosengren visited me, shook the blankets, walked clacking their heels about the floors, and Anna was here with helpless eyes, she has aged. Doors slam, dogs howl, children shout far away, and when I feel my face I sense that it has shrunk, do not dare to look at myself in the mirror. Am sitting up today for the first time, the pen feels strange in my hand and my hand feels stiff, but it's as if deep inside all this had nothing to do with me. Have had a picture postcard from J.S. in Berlin, where he is still staying. There is a lot to do now, as soon as my strength has returned: write letters to my aunts, to my sisters, give back borrowed books, go through available sheet-music and scores for J.S. and decide what he should send me, resume my walks again. It is November, and dark, and I am going back to my bed.

12.12

Wrote to J.S. about my sorrow at not having made his acquaintance earlier. How my life would have changed. Perhaps the desert would have begun to flower and would now be a garden containing the strangest blooms. Yet even in my early childhood music was there, it was there in Mother's singing in the evenings, by my bedside, so gentle that I fell asleep. There was also music – if ever so halting – in my aunts' strumming on the piano, it was there in the most inaudible sounds, in the wind, the birds, the cook's humming, the sound of an accordion: it created a house, a garden, indeed the whole neighbourhood was created by these sounds which formed a music I could not yet understand but to which I listened as though spellbound. That music is consolation I had an inkling of even then. Of what significance then are the simple conditions in which I now live compared to this, the eternally repeated memory in which light leaps forth from the darkness and the darkness gives the light its meaning and even the most insignificant has its pride? I have promised J.S. to stand fast in all life's ups and downs, as I live my truest life in music. I have discovered – and regret it – how I have experienced within myself the terrible struggle of two wills, the most horrible tragedy of life, its night-black woe that weaves my soul around; too late, all over, all lost! And yet! This yearning for deepest understanding, for beauty that is consolation and ennobling strength, to freedom. Finished by pointing out my difficult position between two patrons. I am after all making it possible for him to visit Italy, not beer-cellars in Berlin! Confessions and threats – a fine pedagogue I make!

18.12

Jean Sibelius has replied, works of his are being performed in Berlin. Nikisch and 'Swan of Tuonela', a great success. S. has not touched the 5,000 marks and will leave as soon as he can. In sleepless nights I travel with him, towards the great freedom, through the Swiss tunnels into the sunlight and the light, free air.

24.12

It is Christmas, the snow in the streets muffles noise, the horses' hooves move so lightly over the ground and bells jingle. There is light, and people gather together. The Misses Rosengren flutter around, throwing gentle and sympathetic glances at me; J.S. is still in Berlin. Taken out on Lake Lucerne – will J.S. pass it? – Prince Myshkin says: 'I noticed how beautiful it was but at the same time felt terribly sad.' It is from this sadness that the work of the creative, gifted person grows, whereas in me it merely gives rise to self-abuse and loneliness.

31.12

On the last day of the year have been turning over the leaves of old photographic albums, one of them mine, the others borrowed from the Misses Rosengren who wanted to provide a commentary, but I declined the offer, wanted to see the past without commentary, and they reluctantly gave in: 'the mad Baron'. The fear that then slowly gripped me at the sight of these faded pictures, these strangers who are gone, these clothes that have mouldered away, these tailor's dummies that would be comical did they not express the whole of a lost world's twisted view of things. I observe these figures, individuals in the room, tree-branches, houses, verandas, objects on tables and chairs, as though I were observing a mould-grown miracle. What were they listening to, how did they live, and do they remember me somewhere or am I dead? There are shadows over the sandbeds at Odensaari, there is a voice calling, the scent of sunlight in a house full of people asleep or dead, and it is as though I were experiencing it for the first time only now, when it is too late. 'Too late!' the pictures call, 'too late!' A Requiem for the Forgotten. Too late the arm over the friend's shoulder, the sudden fright in the rye-field, the fishing on the landing-stage, the rendezvous for coffee in the arbour, the cycle runs and the evening rocking on the glass veranda. Too late the music, and therefore painfully familiar: I have already heard it, it was there before anyone created it, it is the roads that glow in the darkness for someone else to walk on, not for me: too late. If only a slight turning of the arm had occurred, the billiard ball would have been cued in another direction, the branch of the tree been pruned and found its way out into harmonious growth towards a clear sky, if only the fear had been transformed into activity – but has it not, in fact? Pictures, pictures, dead pictures. If I had received the right impetus at the right time – would now be standing in the concert arena, raising my violin to my chin, creating music of which during the bitter years I had only dreamt of, dispelling the darkness? Too late. Something was lost without my noticing it, a bolt of lightning struck me, too soon; after that everything was too late. At times, for the space of a moment, all the possibilities, all the dreams, all the hopes, all the decisions were there. How could I have known it? Then everything grew dark. The roads were blocked with snow, trees fell under the snow's weight, space shrivelled like rotten mushrooms. In the forest the rain trickled like tar over trunks and down on to the ground that opened like a grave into which one after the other were hurled: Mother and Father, brother, uncle, the aunts, as though they had never possessed life, were mere rag-dolls: pictures. Faces pressed against the windowpanes that are steaming up. Trees that fall in a rain of sparks and are swallowed up by the snow. The silence and the wind's organ that swells asthmatically: too late. This is my New Year's sermon on the theme: 'Too Late'.

1901

15.1

Visit from Anna, who travelled down for my forty-third birthday. The Misses Rosengren are buzzing like winter bees around cakes and basins. Had put on my dark suit, we talked about the necessity of the Market Hall and my soul cried out for music. After the coffee-orgies and worried farewell from Anna, whose face had gradually been growing longer and whose eyes had been growing larger and more watery, strolled down to Trädgårdsgatan, sat in the periodicals' room and read. It was already dark, and I saw myself in the black mirror of the window, and there was no one else there. At the age of forty-three I am making an attempt to abandon myself and rediscover myself in another, I, the self-appointed life-architect to a Genius, marmot searching around for light, I who know that the picture, the music does not exist until it has been created, and that it is not reality that builds music, but music that builds reality, builds every leaf in the forest, every silence among the trees, every wave on the sea, every night in the valley, and the sunlight that dawns like a fanfare!

7.2

J. Sibelius has left Berlin now. According to Adolf Paul, at Lessman's home in Berlin Ida Ekman sang *Flickan kom ifrån sin älsklings möte* ('The maiden came from her lover's tryst'), a setting of one of Runeberg's most beautiful poems, where in 22 lines he gives an account of a whole lifetime, the contrast between the white that is innocence and the red that is passion, between the white that is death and the red that is suffering, between trust and abandonment, faith and faithlessness. Abandoned, lonely, yearning for the grave – the most dispassionate insight is needed in order for this not to become sentimental.

28.2

I have written to J.S., proposing that we drop titles in our letters to each other. Anguish about the letter which has already been posted and in which my thoughts are uncouthly disconnected. I have felt close to Shakespeare of late, and have called J.S.'s attention to some of the later plays: *Cymbeline, A Winter's Tale*, above all *The Tempest*, are worthy objects of composition. Suddenly I saw him with my letter in his hands, the Italian landscape, the broad views, the air, the fragrance of spring, all from my own icy burrow. Every ugly strip of wallpaper, every wretched chair in my room, every graceless voice on the other side of the wall and out on the street cried its need for beauty; but was he not listening to deeper voices, as Shakespeare did, and would he not turn his back, deaf-eared, on all suggestions and exhortations arising from obscure and impoverished life-situations in order to be able to steer a course, a straight course under the stars?

12.3

Jean has replied, feels in his own words doubly enriched 'when a soul like yours wishes to come close to me...' Flattery? Don't want to believe that. It's obvious that J. isn't yet willing to initiate me into his work, he quotes Rydberg's *Autumn Evening*, where the clouds wander heavy with woe across a *Nordic* landscape and where the wanderer listens to the empty wilderness: 'Does his soul feel a harmony with / the song that is raised by starless night? / Does his woe die like a quiet tone in / the autumn's mighty poem of grief?' There, in Italy, he has these thoughts about Nordic autumn, the eternal, inner companion! Whoever yearns from the South, his yearning seeks a heaven.

13.3

Have been seized by a restlessness unknown in many years, so that illness and insomnia become insignificant by comparison: as though I were feverishly waiting to create, through him. It strikes me that he too in his young years dreamt of becoming a violin virtuoso. That romantic desire – to play to the birds, to experience jubilation, to dream of greatness, also existed in me – alone I danced in the attic at Odensaari, conducting Beethoven, soaring and losing my foothold, in contrast to S. He did not, as I did, inherit the curse of nervous debility, it took his sister instead. He can create the 'Swan of Tuonela', while I am able merely to listen to it. There is much openness in him, but his innermost, darkest, loneliest being is concealed, or so I believe. He is creating a free country while we are still suffering the ukases of the oppressor. I perceive signs of spring, hence the restlessness.

22.3
The ice is breaking up with fearful energy, the restlessness is increasing, so that I am unable to do anything. Between clouds of mist a low-gazing sun.

27.3
I hope the Italian saccharine will leave no traces in Jean's music!

6.4
At last, another letter from Jean. He writes of the work he is undertaking: 'Rather this great, tragic fate than the everyday jog-trot of life. Actually, it's my belief that one does not suffer in vain.' Perhaps not – if one's fate is great and tragic. But does he – can he – take into account a small, petty-tragic fate? A black, threadbare overcoat creeping out in order to look at the spring and dream great and impossible dreams?

18.4
What is genuine in music, and what is false? That which is borne forth from a deep inner spontaneity, built up in a completely personal manner: is that a criterion of genuineness? Is it possible to moralize about music? A cheerful polka at a funeral, a funeral march at a ball – both funeral and ball would profit thereby. Music creates – as Schopenhauer pointed out – a world of its own. This world, I would add, is real in a rather profound way. Even when it is tragic it gives consolation and ennoblement. For the practising artist music also has a tactile significance: the bow against the strings, the fingers against the keys or the valves, the mouth against the mouthpiece, the legs enclosing the violoncello, the body stooped over the double-bass – can these things be compared to the passage of the pen over the lines of music, with the process of composition, the indescribable leap in the consciousness between tone and tone-series, the rhythm inside me, and the musical note? I am sitting at my piano, a monstrously ugly upright wolf's maw that makes a sound like that of hollow ice, and dreaming about Fanny's square piano, Engelbrecht Norberg, whose sound was fragile but originated in beauty.

11.6

The long intervals between writing filled with – what? In the monotony the letters from Jean like sunlight. Wrote in response to his thoughts about Verdi, Dvořák and Grieg, about nationalism in music. In that domain too there are exclusive varieties and narrow-minded chauvinism. Jean had enough of it in connection with his First Symphony. He now sees – or so I hope – that the way to a deeper nationalism is the way of internationalism; what we need are not tasseled stockings but primary rock. His idea of writing music for Dante's *Divine Comedy* strangely exalting, see myself as a pocket-sized Virgil dressed in a white toga shambling along leading Jean by the hand towards the Gate, if I don't trip up before I get there.

13.7

Have written appeals to various persons, wasted a lot of time, and managed to scrape together quarterly allowance for Jean. Tormented by spells of amnesia again, and I am endeavouring to turn my back on ailments and insomnia in order to concentrate upon that which is power and genius and which has so often had to live on alms. How many gilders did Mozart receive? Beggardom! I am the begging arm, the errand-boy, The Great Messenger, and am not ashamed of it. Take my regular walks – trait inherited from Father – and avoid presenting my hideous physiognomy to the eyes of the two-legged beasts of prey that are called human beings.

20.7

Sitting here in the bathhouse at Elin and Fredrik Färling's house in Siuro, Jaskari, Jumesniemi, am called 'the old baron' by the servants, and that is how they see me: age-stricken, on the brink of the grave. Light fires with old newspapers and sketches for compositions without form or content, hence a mighty cantata becomes the birth of Fire. Last night it was so cold that I had to wear all my clothes, even my overcoat, and I had trouble keeping my hat on, found a coffee-cosy on the shelf. Around the bath-house wild chervil grows to head-height, and my thoughts pass to Odensaari and my childhood. For some reason Father's image came before me with especial clarity, as though the wild chervil had prompted it. When Mother died, Father became homeless, as I am now. He used to wander through the upstairs rooms, stand still, when he tried to take a drink his hand would quiver so that he spilt it on himself. I remember that now. Things must have seemed dead to him, they had died with Mother. We children would keep quiet. Children! We were grown up, Fanny and Elin had gone, we ought to have been able to have our own life. But everything bound us to our home. Perhaps our being thrown out was in the end the only solution; but by then the damage had already been done. Well, these are marginal notes to a cold summer whose chill finds its way into one's soul. Warmer weather is promised.

7.8

Letter of thanks for the 500 marks from 'your Jean Sibelius who finds it so hard to really live life, even though he really loves it.' Can he not see that he is creating reality and life, that his lack is his strength? Why should he? Too much insight into the question of one's own ego has the effect of dividing and crippling one. I am a good example. Do I really live life? Sometimes when I am sitting motionless as now and not even writing, have no outlet, it is as though I were slowly fading away and only a few things were left: an unseeing eye, a silent conch, a shell inside which a faint voice somewhere tried to listen, to answer: no answer. It is not a question of calm, but of absence. I am absent, I don't live, I exist, but everything, dreams and hopes, thoughts and feelings, past and future, even the present moment, has gone. My spells of amnesia are an active form of this absence; they are more like bouts of illness, and in them something I want to hold on to is mercilessly erased. Of course I know what Jean means: that so-called reality often feels unreal and work, creation are the only real, obvious things. This painful conflict is surely that of all artists, when they are conscious of it. In creation it does not exist.

13.9

Now the autumn has come and my thoughts are growing cooler, my insomnia is easier to bear and trees burn quietly. I am alive, in spite of everything. I lack hope, therefore I hope. In the end I will lack a name – will become nameless and immortal. This I can imagine after my more severe bouts of sluggish memory, headache, malaise and exhaustion. I have observed that when a torment is very bad it sooner or later provokes relief. As in music that which is darkest and most despairing enlarges, makes us see. Brilliant letter from Jean who seems to be sailing out into open waters, his work on the Second Symphony is making progress. Like an apothecary I weigh out my words to him, in the hope that he will swallow the things I concoct in my steaming retorts, that he will find some of them bitter but most of them lifegiving.

2.10

I had a strange dream. I saw Rakel in a vineyard, far away, and she was young as when I first met her. She was leading a child by the hand, a girl in a blue dress, she herself was dressed in white. I knew that the girl was my daughter. They were surrounded by such radiant light, as though it had risen out of the earth. I woke up with the tears streaming down my cheeks, whether from sorrow or joy I don't know. I have no children. If I had had one, how could it have avoided being weighed down from the cradle by my restlessness, my lack of willpower, my clumsiness and incompetence? Would Rakel and I have had any future together? No. I would not even have been able to earn the most elementary form of living. But children are drawn to me, as though they knew that deep inside I understand their mockery and laughter, and that there is something helpless, not yet fully-grown there, and that it never will be.

12.11

Jean is afraid he will not live long enough in order to be able to complete the Second Symphony! Is he trying to console me for my darkness, my suffering? He is after all the supporting strength around which we who dream of a future in freedom from the Russian yoke could gather.

1902

2.1

A new year is coming in, full of threat, with a taste of blood in its mouth. Jean is working hard, he has written a few lines to me: 'Keep well, glorious heart!' But this glorious heart is beating wildly like a mad prisoner, or else is as if it had fallen silent and existed no more, and I am hurled like a spark between the poles of life and death. He thanks me, but the one who creates has no one to thank, only his Genius.

25.2

Jean has sent the score of his Second Symphony to me with a moving,

magnificent dedication. The whole symphony is dedicated to me!
Even if the whole of my life had been lived in emptiness, this
would have been worth it, this music that speaks of new life out
of darkness; have not had time to study the details. Now my
insomnia will be easy to bear. Here in my(!) symphony there is a
message, a freedom like a tree stretching its roots deep into the
soil of our land and even deeper, to the all-embracing, the limitless!
Cannot sleep.

28.2
Today received advisory note from the good Axel Tamm, went
to the bank, they looked at me suspiciously as I had a scarf tied
around my face under my hat: the cold is crackling at the doors.
Made the withdrawal, went to the post-office, forwarded the
money to Jean. Then went to the tailor's and bought a new shirt,
as my old one is falling apart *molto vivace*. The town smells of
bitter smoke, sunlight and ice, and the voices sound like clear
metal staves, fixed by invisible threads to the sky. Am taking
warm drinks with quinine, as I must keep well for the première
of my symphony. The Andante, an insight into death with which
we must live.

6.3
Appearance today of the advertisement for the concert by the
Orchestra of the Philharmonic Society and Female Voice Choir
in the University's Hall of Solemnity.

Programme:
1. Overture.
2. Impromptu for Female Chorus and Orchestra.
3. Symphony No. 2 in D major.

Tickets price 4 marks, unreserved 3 marks, student 1 mark from
Head Porter Gillberg. I don't need to call on him, have a ticket in
my pocket! The advertisement might at least have said that the
choir is to sing a text by Victor Rydberg. Wander up and down
the room reading the score, this is a high point in my life, and
only *I* know it. I am merging with music, and that is consolation
enough. Now I lay it all aside, all the mocking and whispering,
the looks and threats, all that is shabby around me, all that is frayed
and worn in objects and ideas: there is a music, almost abstract,
which yields nothing but experiences of space and dilation, as in

the field and forest of childhood... Pure happiness on a summer morning when the child doesn't know where its happiness comes from, it is simply there, like the most radiant grass, the purest water, like reflections of rock and beach-shadows when no one is awake yet and I possess the morning and see birds resting on upward-climbing currents of air. At last I am set free.

9.3

Total triumph! Ovations. A.U., writing in *Hufvudstadsbladet*, calls the symphony, my symphony, a masterpiece, but the idiot adds bits about 'charming melodic episodes resembling calmly-flowing crystal-clear brooks between sky-high mountains'. But the Second Symphony is not a photograph album! In it Nature speaks directly, darkly and powerfully of the eternal things, of death and reconciliation. Immediately after the concert, sneaked away through the standing members of the audience and their thunderous applause, it was like rain in the desert, got back to my hotel room and am now sitting looking out into the dark, radiant February night.

12.3

Dead days aren't worth writing about. Kajanus, writing in yesterday's *Hufvudstadsbladet*, sees the 2nd Symphony as a struggle for freedom against tyranny. That is a grand thought, but one that is also dangerous – for the symphony: the truest and deepest music stands above the movements of current politics and aims at a brotherhood that is greater than the national one. The D major Symphony is a European work! Must write to Jean when I have sufficiently gathered my thoughts about the stellar world of the folksong. More and more he is emerging as the gathering force in a time when the usurper is seeking to throttle us.

16.3

Relapse, and I'm used to it, lie in bed mostly. Have sent Kajanus article for Axel T. in Stockholm. No more for now.

1.4

Axel T. has replied, with deepest insight: 'that which springs from a genuine feeling for life draws its strength from a wider sphere than that which already stands finished in the consciousness of the creator.'

26.4

In the street met nephew Bertel who stopped, told me that he has refused to obey the illegal military call-up. Saw him in Nådendal four years ago when he was a newly-fledged student, now a technologist. He told me that the conscientious objectors in Åbo are still few in number. Not 'Finland Proper', after all? Olga and the other children were in good health; then he rushed on his way. Back in T-fors I crept into my burrow, back to staleness, dusty silence, papers.

13.5

At least one entry per month, so I can see that something has happened, that I am alive. In this wonderfully beautiful month of May I suddenly remember my mother's fear that she would have to go before Father. The light of dawn was filtering in through the curtains, and in the silence I could feel her gaze. Father stood in the doorway, speechless; perhaps he couldn't say anything to her because his throat was too constricted? He had entrusted everything to her, and now she was abandoning him. I was 34 then and had shown the essentials of warmth, now I sat beside her bed and held her hand, and her eyes sought mine as though they were asking for forgiveness. For what? For what? For the fact that she was leaving us? Lonelier than ever I went out of the room and left them to each other. About an hour later she was dead.

29.5

Balmashov has assassinated Sipyagin*, displaying great courage: 'My only collaborators are the Russian Government.' Where tyranny grows, resistance grows, also. Have received the 5000 marks and sent the warriors on to Generalissimus Sibelius on the battlefield, and the generalissimus has replied: 'If you knew the place that you occupy in my Lady Musica's heart you would lower your eyes in shame.' He also entreats me: 'You must not die before I do.' That is a moving and impossible appeal, and he knows it. But it all gives me the deepest consolation.

13.6

Janne has gone to Berlin again, urging Aino, who told me this when I met her in the street, to be 'cheerful, courageous and healthy.' She smiled, but there was pain and concern in her eyes. Deep inside, Aino is a person who lives on her nerves, one who grieves and makes desperate sacrifices in silence, and Janne takes advantage of this or does not see it, does not want to see it, goes abroad because he must go abroad, entrusting everything – finances, housekeeping – to her. We only talked for a short time, both of us shy, but there are unspoken things about which we are of the same opinion, and we both have Janne in our thoughts and – hearts.

1.7

The summer is passing, and Janne has returned from the beer-fumes of Berlin. He is now fleeing towards clarity, solitude and self-confrontation(?), to the pilot's cottage at Tvärminne. I have been invited to visit Elin and Fredrik in Siuro, but am hesitating: when I'm there I am like a tortoise on its back, a curiosity, a relic, and I would rather try to stay here in T-fors, even though the Misses would like me to go so they could casually rent out my room. As usual go for walks on the ridge, sit looking out at the wide expanse of water. Try to make myself aware that this is reality, but it tends to dissolve in front of me. The things around me, the window, the very daylight, the streets, the trees, it all feels so incidental, even – and not least – the people. What is this reality? Painful meetings and partings, mostly, and indeed it is more real than the watery gruel offered up by everyday life. To live a real life, that is to live on a knife-edge between fear and happiness, to listen to the music behind the music, to see in the eyes of the living the long-ago dead, see them mirrored there, see how in the dead man's gaze the living man can no longer see himself, and therefore loses himself, is gone, and the bedroom is silent, the curtains drawn, the door locked, the voices hushed, the objects motionless and the fragrance of the flowers heady. Each sound then seems to come from another world or is like the waves of Näsijärvi which cannot be heard at all up here, and everything is dreamlike and painfully obvious. For sorrow is the most real and most obvious thing of all.

22.7.1902

Axel caught sight of the pilot's cottage among the pine-trees, stopped and put down his travelling bag. He had inherited it from his father, it was worn with age. His shirt-collar was rubbing him and his linen hat felt tight: it was a hot day. The sand began where he stood, stretching right down to the water which moved indolently, barely audibly. The sky was pale with heat. Like snow the drift-sand lay amidst the rough grass. The air was full of the pine-trees' hot, dry scent. It was like something from his childhood, but purer and more clear. Here there were no reeds, none of the things that were found in the skerries, no mud – just trees, shore and sky in quiet harmony, and the wind that could merely be sensed as a coolness against his forehead.

Axel took off his hat and narrowed his eyes at the cottage that stood black in the heat-haze. Not a movement, no one outside, not a sound. He felt slightly giddy and had to sit down on a stone. He felt like an intruder. Had Janne been serious in issuing his invitation? Slowly he leaned forward, undid his shoes and emptied them of sand, looked at his feet for a while, then quickly pulled off his socks and burrowed his toes into the already warm sand. He stayed sitting there, looking at the heather and the lyme-grass, listening to the cry of the birds. Then he rolled up his trouser-ends, took his shoes in one hand and the travelling bag in the other and began to stroll towards the cottage. Out towards the horizon a few islands floated like thin, lancet-shaped clouds. From the open window the piano could now be heard: yes, he was there, sitting with his back to him as he silently reached the open door and stood there, not daring to move. Everywhere on tables lay books and papers, and the sunlight streamed in across the rag-rugs on the floor. An exclamation of 'Damn it!' gave emphasis to the repeated chords, then Janne banged the lid down and swung violently round: 'Ah, there you are! Someone sensible at last! Welcome to the demons!' Janne gave a short laugh, looked at him first with a sharp, tormented gaze that quickly changed, grew smiling and

radiant, and he came over to him, embraced him: 'Barefoot Lasse!'
And he added: 'Come on – I want to show you my music.'

As they stood there in the doorway that looked out on the sea
they could hear the silence breathing. Axel put down the bag he
was still carrying, took off his jacket and they both stood in their
shirtsleeves squinting at the sun. 'Do you bathe?' asked Janne. 'I
bathe every morning, early, go out fishing at sundown, the rest
is music, you'll see soon enough. Four men dragged that piano
here across the sand, you can see the marks, there's gravel getting
into the songs, but it's doing them good, I think. Songs – that's
what I'm working on just now. Runeberg, Wecksell – 'Was it a
dream – that sweetly once – I was your heart's companion – I
remember it like a vanished song – as the string still quivers.' He
quoted the words more loudly, stamping his foot on the ground:
'Listen! It's quivering. The overtones – you know? When I'm lying
on the shore resting I hear them, the songs that rise out of the
earth. Do you believe me?'

Axel nodded. The swift changes of mood, the silent, muted
pauses, he recognized them, the intensity, the violent concentration, the difficulty of speaking when one has lived alone, and the
abrupt joy of breaking through it, he replied: 'Here the sky and
the sea have no limit.'

'As in childhood,' Janne said. 'Come on.' He began to stroll
down the beach, and Axel followed, both men in dark, rolled-up
trousers, one large, one small, one gesticulating, one still. They
let the waves wash over their feet. Axel leaned forward and rubbed
his face with a wet hand. But Janne tore off his clothes, waded
out, threw himself shouting and snorting into the sea, it was as
though it had risen, as though notes of music were gleaming and
whirling about, Janne's voice rose out of the sea, a happy voice,
it sang: 'Hold deep this memory within thy breast, it was thy
finest dre-e-eam!' Axel stood with his hand before his eyes, he
had to smile, Janne strode wet and powerful, like some prehistoric
creature, from the sea, shouting 'Finest! Got it? Finest!' He waded
ashore, ran past Axel and pulled on his shirt and trousers. 'And
now to the look-out rock. Can you manage?' And without waiting
for a reply he set off. Axel followed at a half-run, panting. From
the rock they could see Storlandsstrittan, up there there was a
slight breeze and he thought he could hear the sound of the sea.
'Listen – the pedal of the deep!' Janne said, extending one arm.
'Have I not always said that the orchestra must have a pedal!'
Above them terns screamed, rising, falling. Axel sat down and

wiped his forehead with a handkerchief. Janne looked at him: 'You're pale. And I was the one who forced you up here. Come on, you must get some rest. We can talk later, all night if you want.'

Half an hour later Axel was lying on the sofa bed listening to Janne play. The day had turned and the sun was slowly beginning its descent. The folk-tale's theme rose and fell like the sense and the sight of the sea and waves. He listened, dreamed, it was like travelling and yet standing still. Janne had stopped playing, sat quiet for a while, then turned round and looked at him absent-mindedly: 'Everything here is pure, you know – like Mozart, or Mendelssohn, or Weber. There you have a triad that meets the sky.'

He listened and let Janne talk. Later on Janne disappeared and came back with smoked fish and a salad, ceremonially he mixed the salad dressing and poured it on, tossed the salad, went down to the cellar to fetch a misted bottle of *brännvin*, and they drank, toasted each other. 'You have put narrow-minded national roman-ticism on the spot – that's my opinion, at least', Axel said. 'There's no point in trying to draw a line between classical and romantic – in you they come together.' Janne nodded, chewed his food reflectively, washed it down with the *brännvin*. 'Our reality is far too rational,' he added. 'What we need are visions, dreams, folk-tales – do you remember them, the folk-tales of your childhood? Mmm.' A little later Janne added: 'I used to dream of being a virtuoso violinist, you know. I still do, sometimes.' 'That was my dream, too, but it came to nothing', Axel replied. 'One can't have everything in this world', said Janne, his face gleamed, was he making fun of him? For a moment his heart skipped a beat, then Axel replied: 'No, you're right, one can't have everything.' He suddenly felt almost exhilarated. Janne looked up, and said: 'Here's the pilot; we're going out fishing now, you'll come with us, won't you?' Axel shook his head: 'You go. I'll stay here and rest, I'd just be in the way.' Janne made no reply, they sat in silence, then footsteps were heard and a knocking at the door.

When they had gone it became echoingly quiet. Axel lay in the small guest chamber, looking at the ceiling. The sun was sinking like a ball of fire, he could see it through the narrow window, the room was gathering twilight. One night, half a day, and then he must leave. He turned to the wall but there was a glimmering stream of pictures that gave him no rest. He was like a mirror, he tried to breathe slowly, to banish all thoughts, he was here, now, he listened. There was a faint murmuring. His task was to listen.

He must not reel off his litany, amass his warning like a crow in winter when the summer was at its most beautiful. 'Am I sponging?'

He sat up violently, looked out into the dim room with unseeing eyes, then stood up, put on his shoes, his jacket and his linen hat and opened the door. The evening was cool and immense. The wind had freshened, the waves were roaring and a few lonely stars were glowing in the sky which was still shot with blue deep in the west, where the sun had gone down. Axel pulled out his spectacles and polished them, then attentively studied the dark rocks and the boat that was being rowed towards the shore out there. He felt a great sense of relief: nothing had happened, Janne had come back and was safe. Axel sat with the collar of his jacket turned up, his hands in its pockets, his shoulders hunched. Then he quickly stood up, went inside and began to make a fire in the hearth, and when Janne came in the blaze was already aflame. 'Ah, that's a good idea, it gets colder at night.' He lit the oil-lamp and they sat opposite each other at the table, Janne had made coffee and they carefully poured some of the *brännvin* into it. Axel warmed his hands on the cup. A northerly wind had begun to blow. They talked, hesitantly at first, and then ever more eagerly, about things that affected them. They talked about the fishing-trips of their childhoods, about the importance of living in harmony with nature, and about the need for solitude which could fulfil and often too much so, so that it overflowed and turned to dread; then music could be a source of freedom. They saw the pine-tree in the west holding the stars in its top. From the infinite universe they moved to the difference between intellect and feeling, and from the role of feeling to Schopenhauer's ideas about music as the most universal of languages. Axel told of his dream of a musical language that existed beyond systems of notation and five black lines. He had laid out his violin the way once upon a time sick children and old people were laid out to die, and the violin had sunk in its black coffin, he had buried that dream, the dream of the violin virtuoso, but another dream always remained. What was it? The dream of attaining music's innermost kernel, of understanding its essence. He had such crazy dreams that they often frightened him.

For a while they sat quiet. Then Janne told him about his journeys to Italy and Germany, about the homesickness that had seized him, about the fear he had always experienced whenever he had had to mount the conductor's rostrum, how tense he felt, that was a purgatory he wished upon no one. Composing, that was something else, it was the loneliest, happiest, most difficult thing, it was – dreams. Dreams made things real, Axel said, dreams produced forms, metamorphoses, unique ones – 'play for me, Janne!' And Janne sat down at the piano, there was a music that was seeking its way towards something ever clearer, was this not classical music, the music of eternity which one could not label? Then Janne said he had two bottles of champagne at his disposal, and that he wanted to share them with his friend and also deliver a talk about music, the demonic and the cold, and about life's heaven and hell, its magic and all the inexplicable things it contained: its secret was our longing for it, our pleasure in it – it was this sense of wonder that made us create. Us! Axel felt himself being drawn into a gigantic magnetic field in which musical themes were attracted to one another and then broke apart again. They sat in the lamp's soft circle of light, and the silence outside was immense. They found their way out, stood and breathed deeply, gazing upwards: stars had come out in the sky, the birds had grown silent and the wind moved homeless in the trees.

'This is my world,' Janne said, 'and it isn't a limitless one, there's logic in it, the fixed logic of the constellations.' They considered the fixed logic, then walked in among the trees, went back inside for a while, and Janne talked about instinct as a guiding star, how it led him into the wolf-grin of the piano, how it and memory worked together. Axel talked about his spells of amnesia, about the pedantry that gave his life its logic, and about music that gave it its meaning. If Janne was hurled between pessimism and joy in life, he probably had these struggles too, but more muted, as it were, almost invisible, indeed. Pocket-sized poltergeists, he was familiar with them, they were built into his rooms, his possessions, into his very self and were there, behind his eyes, under his skin, when he lost himself and was one of many flying thoughts, one of many shadows.

'Away with the shadows, forward to a new sunrise!' shouted Janne, and he opened the door on the quiet summer night; away in the east a faint streak of pink was visible. For a while the silence made them reticent with words. 'The powers – when one listens to the great calm one might think they didn't exist', said Axel. 'And does not all great art strive for harmony, calm and balance? Is it not timelessness that you're in quest of? The vanquishing of death? Those conflicting powers, those colliding energies, that play of demons – does not your music exist in order to vanquish them, in order to create harmony, forgiveness, peace, consolation

225

and oblivion?' With each word he spoke Axel stretched out an arm, as though he were conducting a gigantic invisible world orchestra, and Janne could not help laughing. The powers, he said, the powers were inexorable and sometimes impossible to vanquish: gnats, gulls, gannets, bank managers, loans and promissory notes! And then Axel intoned in hymn-like fashion: 'Harmony, Forgiveness, Peace, Consolation and Oblivion', and Janne responded in an antiphon with 'Gnats, Gulls, Gannets, Bank Managers and Promissory Notes!' There was a recklessness in it all that made them dance, the sand was so cool, the water so warm. They ran, Janne in front, Axel panting after, until they had to fling themselves down in the coarse sand-grass and, with their hands behind their necks look straight up into the giddying, luminous heavens. 'It makes you feel dizzy', Axel said, and Janne repeated: 'It makes you feel dizzy!' 'Can you express this in music?' Axel asked. 'Just wait,' Janne replied, 'you're going to hear a lot more from me, for I can work here, in the solitude. If I could create a music that was one great silence –'

He stood up and stretched his hand out to Axel, pulled him to his feet. 'You're beginning to get cold, let's go in to the warm.'

Before they went to bed Axel said: 'You seem to be on your way towards something completely new again. I envy you. You have a pact with your Genius. I have none.' Janne replied: 'You have the Genius of understanding and friendship.' Axel sat in silence. Janne said: 'I have to pay a heavy price for the powers that dwell within me, or my Genius – my work is the loneliest work of all. Sometimes I feel as though I were merely a catalyst, for what? To be hurled between heaven and hell, to be misinterpreted and acclaimed for something other than what one really intends – if I even know what it is – that is unimaginable, beyond explanation –'

'And that's why music exists,' Axel answered him. Now they were talking softly, the silence was flowing in, and the tiredness. They went to lie down, Axel in the little guest chamber, Janne in his bedroom. For a while Axel lay still, listening to the morning, the birds were waking up and it was light, he looked at the window and the dawn, then lay without thoughts and at last fell happily asleep, to sleep without dreams, as after a long, productive day's work.

From The Diary

1902

13.8

Tvärminne with its conversations, deepest silence and great closeness still moves within me. It now occurs to me that Janne did
not mention Aino, and I didn't want to pursue the matter, either.
She is to have a child in January. There is, on her part, an understanding and a loyalty which he cannot live up to, and he knows
it; but that is the creator's dilemma: the frequently reckless egoism,
the great loneliness, the durable structure into which no one can
have a complete insight. The unanswered question is like a beacon
and theory an autumn leaf that, like other autumn leaves, is whirled
away by time.

12.9

Staying with the Färlings. Tavastkyro a region of melancholy and
twilight. I go walking in it and am moved to morbid ecstasy when
I listen to the slow movement of Tchaikovsky's second string
quartet. I have written to Janne asking him if he knows of some
suitable piano, cannot endure the jangly old thing I have at present.
Has Axel T. grown tired of me, as there is no word yet of the
'apanage' from Stockholm? Seek consolation in Vitalis Norström's
Religious Knowledge.* The word 'sin' ought not to exist in any
dictionary.

4.10

The linen-weaving factory at Tampereen Koski is spewing out a
terrible smell and the wind is blowing it over the town. On the
way to Västra Esplanadgatan I met F., a member of the industrial
aristocracy. Friendly and well-mannered, he asked for news of
Janne, 'the maestro of us all'. He did not display the usual façade
of boasting and condescension typical of these *nouveau-riche* par-
venus, but seems to possess a natural interest in art, more than

227

there ever was in my family, where military and civil service interests dominated. If I hadn't had music, what would have become of me? But nothing has become of me, anyway.

10.10

For Janne the Second Symphony was a confrontation with youth. Now will come manhood, the Third Symphony.

29.10

Robert Kajanus has conducted Janne's Second Symphony in Stockholm, and for once PB did not indulge in outright abuse but actually acclaimed it! Otherwise the days sink one after the other into an unnoticed oblivion, the autumn sky has been high and the chimney-smoke pink in the increasing cold. But the people move about like insects.

2.11

The new version of *En Saga* has been performed, and my thoughts go to Rydberg's *Singoalla* and my youth. In the good folk-tale there is something that has no beginning and no end, it is an eternal lullaby, often cruel but more frequently a healing poultice for tired eyes, or a fear responded to and overcome. The folk-tales mother read to me were magic runes with which to fight reality. Janne's *Saga* doesn't narrate, it is. Simplicity and directness – but perhaps it is resplendent with too much melody: perhaps when all is said and done Janne's innermost essence lies in the ascetic. I do not mean the way he lives his life. There the money vanishes like smoke, and he does things 'in grand style', for 'that's how it must be.' Does he feel more secure in the world of society that way?

3.11

Brooding over where forty years of life have led me. They have led nowhere, merely lie like dead ballast in my leaky body.

5.12

The great critic Lagus has attacked Kajanus's concert programmes in *Hufvudstadsbladet*, not finding in them his household gods Mahler, R. Strauss and Weingartner. It is an indirect attack on Janne who is upset and has turned to me. Am trying to formulate a riposte.

27.12

The most difficult time, from a psychological point of view, is now at hand, like being locked up in a dark box-room without any air to breathe. Always like this, from December to February: inability to sleep, irritability, confusion, choking sensations, hallucinations, ever since I was 15. Dragged myself to Tavastkyro and Anna, the spruce trees nearly disappeared among the palms there. I felt as though I had run into a wall, got up and run into another wall, and now it surprises me when on looking in the mirror I don't see any bloodstains, just the usual paper-whiteness.

1903

15.1

On my forty-fifth birthday Elin and Fredrik Färling came down and invited me out to a tavern, but I suddenly felt so weak that I had to leave. Can no longer cope with fat, vinegary wine, cigar-smoke, cognac, coffee, people, conversation. Snow is falling, and is covering everything, all the old footprints and memories, most of which have lapsed from recollection.

3.3

All I need is one quiver of a hand, one bloodshot eye, cigar-ash spilt on the arm of a jacket, sweat on a temple, and all the signs are there – the dissipations, the degeneration, and the swelling upwards and yearning downwards that can smother the imagination. I watched Janne carefully and decided that he must get away from that restaurant existence of his. Even his moustache looks as though it's drooping. He gazed past me as though I were not there, then suddenly this smile: 'I say! Do you remember Tvärminne? You simply don't know how I long to go back there!' Aino sat in silence as she listened to this, there was tension in the air. In the hallway, while Janne was pottering in the living-room she suddenly took my hand and held it and said: 'I'm afraid for Janne! Does Axel understand?' I nodded, kissed her hand. On returning to my exile I consider that the only solution for Janne is for him to get away from the whole of this shabby city and tavern existence. I am going to write to Aino and ask her to inform Janne's drinking companions, who are no companions at all but rather spongers – even the ones with fat pocket-books. They are a half-educated rabble whom it will be difficult to awaken to their responsibilities, and Janne himself is one of them. Will Aino's faith and loyalty be enough?

8.3
Reading Nietzsche during sleepless nights, he too a crucified one and a fool. There is in him a purity of mind so violent that it burns the slag away. I am discovering that the vulgar image of him as a megalomaniac has nothing to do with his – classical! – striving for clarity, and that he saw more deeply into the problem of the Apollonian versus the Dionysian than most. Then he went insane through stretching the bow too hard – he dared to! Like Kivi, Wecksell in our own country. I remember the village idiots of my childhood, always on the run or hiding in thickets and behind the corners of houses, or sitting heavily and motionlessly on the cottage steps looking in front of them with unseeing eyes. Mankind has an infinite gamut of dissonances, which come to the surface in some unfortunate people.

15.3
I have received an affectionate letter from Aino, who writes that my letter 'will be for me a source from which I can draw the best advice a friend can give.' She forced Kajanus to fetch Janne from the tavern – just like that! – while she sat in the cab and waited. I can hear Janne's angry silence.

3.4
Anna was here and we talked haltingly about trivial matters. Does my association with Janne simply not interest her, or is it that it irritates her? What does she suspect? It has been cold, and I have been from my bed to the stove and back. From Janne not a word.

10.4
Bobrikov's dictatorial decree* the final death-blow to freedom. I lie and listen and hear, far away in the night, the most loathsome barking of dogs.

20.4
Out for the first time in weeks. The town strange, or is it me? The water flows under the bridges as before. Long for Helsingfors and its expanses of sea.

30.4

Helsingfors in its most translucent spring attire, Kapellet has opened, this morning the Academic Choir gave a concert at Brunn and the Esplanade was filled with confetti. I feel as though I were invisible. Hesitate to make contact with Janne and Aino. Strolled in Kronohagen with Cousin Tor, we talked about the country's future and dreamt dreams of freedom; beneath the surface there is a lot of activity. Janne's role as a uniting force important. Is it too much for him?

4.5

Talked for a short time to Aino out in the town, she gets no help from Janne and the violin concerto is still not making any progress. I remembered Janne's words: 'The ground is being pulled away from under me...' It is not the alcohol that is causing this paralysis, but the difficulty of creating the flight he requires, the most childish oblivion.

18.5

Anna had asked me to come and I went to Tavastkyro a few days ago. There all was as before, floors and tables overflowing with bric-à-brac and the piano out of tune, like everything else. While there I had an outburst of anger which I regret, shouted at Anna that not only my life but all our lives had been destroyed, were meaningless, as empty as a wilderness, but that at least I had realized that a long time ago. I discovered that in myself, too, most things are out of tune.

15.7

Here people bow and scrape before the Russian peacock uniforms, the ladies prance about and all is unchanged – the fish, the peasant carts (discovered Leevi from Osaari, he didn't recognize me, was selling potatoes, had to turn away as my heart was beating so). For these people in white clothes nature is 'exquisite', but the stink is as before. Examined by B. who seemed concerned, recommended 'healthy living habits, a lot of fresh air and salubrious sleep', and gave me a prescription. General lack of misgivings, or do people look convulsively away? Sent the 500 to Janne in Lojo after much trouble with patrons, received thanks: the violin concerto is on its way. *Finlandia* may no longer be called *Finlandia* in Reval, the programme in Estonia only in Russian and German. Janne conducted his 'Impromptu'. How long before prohibitions affect us, too? Strolled to the outlook tower, the church bell sounded as before, the water glittered as before, the sun shone. A profound nationalism that is the opposite of cheap chauvinism is the salvation for an age that does not know where it is going and is gripped by fear. That is why it enacts its rituals, its summer balls, its mud-and-massage baths, its double standards, its gallantry with a lecherous wolf-grin behind the punch and the joviality, so that there may be no goal, no clear struggle. But not all who scent blood are noble warriors. Meanwhile the sun of Nådendal shines on rich and poor alike with the same warmth. In Mann's *Tristan* it is said of the useless that 'we abhor the useful because it is vulgar and unlovely – and yet we are eaten away by bad conscience... The whole of our inner life has an unhealthy, undermining and disturbing effect.' There is plenty of work here for all kinds of layers-on-of-hands – priests, doctors, masseurs and *bon-vivants*. And the artist? He registers the first symptoms of earthquakes. He descends into the depths in order to see if there is light there. He rises in darkness and interprets the starry heavens. He goes disguised, and alone.

12.8
Drove past the manor of my childhood, people were moving about there, presumably Olga and her children, it was a splendid day, there was a scent of summer, and at Masku Cemetery the dead had the cooling shadow of the church. Put flowers on Father's, Mother's and Hjalmar's graves. Ten years, an eternity ago, and I'm still alive.

30.8
Here at Sunnanberg in Sagu complete stillness in woods and over meadows, as though all wounds could be healed. Have received the score of the 2nd Symphony with printed dedication! Even the 'cursed' violin concerto is nearing completion. The first movement of the 2nd waves, as in Tvärminne, and starlight, birdsong; the wind instruments' thoughtfulness in a constantly moving drama, wings over dark waters, a surge of new life towards passion. What is the colour of yearning? Every growing question has its own gentle echo. In the Andante we are on the way, in a fascinating structure of forms – must write to Janne about this. From thoughts of death a way towards reconciliation and back to shadows again, lonely struggle that is the struggle of all. Sorrow that must be borne. After the tympani in the scherzo the beautiful oboe theme

rising out of the stillness, an accidental peace. Yet, finally, the D major of the finale! Triumphant, a world of passion and beauty. And still – I long to get away from this pathos, this Beethoven-like atmosphere, to – Mozart. This eternal sea, this eternal wave-motion in the soul – does it not contain clarity, reconciliation, the coolest silence?

12.9

The first two movements of the violin concerto finished, with piano accompaniment. Aino and Janne have decided to move, Järvenpää, Tusby! Thus my most cherished thought has been realized!

15.9

This is the age of spies and informers, and brother stands against brother in this divided land. Here we receive daily injections of hatred and lawlessness. I feel as though all the melancholy symptoms which winter usually brings with it for me were already beating at the door; I am sick in a sick time and a sick society.

18.10

Janne has asked me for a list of conductors and editors of music journals who might be sent copies of the Second Symphony, and also of the *Saga*. I am collecting addresses to the best of my ability, but my eyes keep failing me.

30.10

I have studied the Second Symphony anew and in depth and have written to Janne about the mythic and visionary element in his art. One can see it clearly in the songs, where the mysterious and the fantastic are close to him but are counterbalanced by something soft and gentle, as though the whole of his creation were constantly swinging between two poles. I have requested a Christmas carol from him! A choral work! A string quartet! I have also asked him if the passages for woodwinds in the first movement of the Second a few bars before letter F can be interpreted as youthful excitement, later mounting to recklessness, until the second subject, now transformed into despair, breaks through 'poco largamente'. Is there really development and counterpoint here? It seems to me that the section from the oboe's first announcement of the second subject, followed by the bassoon (and the transformation of this dark passage into sunlight by the brass), all the way up to the 'poco largamente' is the key to the whole symphony. In the Andante, wonderfully deep tragedy. Is there development in the true sense there, or merely imitation?

19.12

Janne has informed me that the violin concerto was completed at 5 a.m. Rejoicing and daybreak.

1904

18.1

I have received a letter from Aino about Janne's work on the violin concerto, in which a wealth of thoughts pours forth. 'But even though I revelled in it all, I suffered as well; you know, Axel, a woman's brain cannot endure the surges of an artist – of such a creative one – which now and then move so wildly – so wildly that one grows afraid...' Aino had thought of coming up here when she was so depressed: 'Sometimes he says he has taken me as a companion, and then I am proud.' Poor Aino, to be hurled around like that! Does he see her at all clearly, her restlessness and deep spiritual energy, does he think what he would be without her? I read the following lines over and over again: 'If I had had someone to talk to it would not have been so hard, but Axel is the only person who is close enough to Janne for me to do so freely. I think that an artist's inner being is the finest and most sensitive thing that can possibly exist – don't you agree? Axel's friendship is of immense value to Janne. Remain forever the friend you have been to him up till now!' These words move me to my core, and I am torn between concern about Aino's loneliness and the heavy burden she has to bear, and joy at being a confidant – perhaps more of a confidant to Aino than to Janne, as the life of a true artist always demands an extreme coldness and distance, a *noli me tangere* in which the innermost secret of creation is inquired after.

18.2

Janne is thinking of me and cursing my fate, he writes. I am trying to lie still and accept everything, good and bad alike.

10.3

I have sent the quarterly sum from Stockholm to Ainola. Janne says he is confronting something new – 'death is approaching', but in reality it seems to be an exacting, life-giving power that is able to produce 'many new ideas' which I merely note down in amazement. There is a purposefulness and hardness that rejects all interference, and this hardness is vital and essential. Only from it comes the sound of metal. When I read Aino's and Janne's letters I long violently for home, wife and children. Elin has been here, helping me. She possesses a kindly silence.

16.6.1904

Axel had fallen asleep towards morning and had dreamt about a funeral cortège. The grotesquely adorned catafalque floated forward on upward-stretched, blood-stained hands. Axel himself was floating above this loutish procession of people that sooner resembled a migration of lemmings, heaving their way forward like whirlpools pressed together by walls. He awoke to a furious barking of dogs. The water in the jug was lukewarm, he rinsed himself and stood before the half-open window: it was going to be a warm day. There were bright leaves and misty sunlight, the thermometer read 12°C. The Referring Clerk had been in the habit of writing down the day's temperature in his almanac. The hot summers. In those days his face – if he had ever noticed it – had been smooth, innocent. Now – something gripped his kidneys, or was it his liver, Axel stood leaning forward, then slowly straightened himself up. Better to think of external things. Where was Janne now? In Estonia? The Russian fleet was steaming its way to Japan. Who was laying siege to whom in Port Arthur? Pyhäjärvi and Näsijärvi would never be able to receive such enormous vessels. Dazzling white uniforms, black funnel-smoke – Axel sniffed the air. There was a smell of coffee.

The two engineers who had moved into the double room for a month were already sitting at coffee when he came in. Anna Rosengren was serving, and gave him a nod as he stood in the doorway. His chair was occupied. He did not know what to do. A hot wave flooded over him. The two young men looked up. He performed an uncertain bow, and they nodded. The elder of them noticed the short man's neat appearance, but also his shabbiness: old shoes that glistened, all of his clothes black, even though the day promised to be warm, his high collar, his face pale, almost grey, and his spectacles. There was something comical about him and at the same time something that did not invite conversation.

The table was large, and Axel was able to sit down at a reassuring distance. One of the men – the younger one – leaned forward: 'It's a nice day!' Did he expect any answer other than a nod? Axel replied that he preferred the cool, beautiful autumn. On the white table-cloth stood bread, jam, the sour milk which he drank regularly for his stomach's sake, it was important to make it function per-fectly. Lydia swept through the room and Axel asked her to close the window: there was a draught. From the street an untrained voice could be heard singing something incomprehensible. One of the young men whispered something in the other man's ear. They did not look in Axel's direction. They promptly got up and vanished in their white linen clothes, leaving a trail of cigar-smoke behind them. He remained sitting where he was. Now Berg, the commercial traveller, came in, they knew each other from earlier, Berg played the violin in the solitude of his room. His tone was as thin as he himself, his hair sparse, his Adam's apple moved up and down, up and down, his brown eyes searched carefully among the delicacies of the table. An early food symphony – what key would Axel suggest? Berg smiled, showing yellow teeth. Bacon minor. Something had stuck in Berg's throat, he coughed and coughed. He pulled out the large, white table napkin, held it in front of his face. Axel considered him, then looked down at his plate, it contained the remains of a cheese sandwich. He pushed it away. Lydia sat down abruptly beside him: did he not feel well today? Had he slept badly? Would he like another cup of coffee? The large, coarse face was gentle, there was a warmth there that he could not deny, her eyes were sometimes as sharp as her tongue: they knew each other.

He got up, he did not want to eat any more, he gave Berg and Lydia Rosengren a nod and went back to his room. It was quiet, the papers on his desk lay where they were. Axel had nothing to do. He took the letters he had written the previous evening, his coat and his hat, and walked towards the door. Clattering could be heard coming from the kitchen. He hurriedly locked his door and went downstairs quickly so as not to meet anyone. Out in the street, he looked along the bright row of trees that lined Västra Trädgårdsgatan, breathing in the light, dry summer air. There was a peculiar smell, he had begun to get used to it, but Janne had remarked on it immediately. Cellulose, fabric, wood, soot, metal – the plaster and wooden walls were impregnated with it. But there was also the smell of water, lakes and inlets that reflected the sky. Should he walk to the bridge or the hill? He chose the hill. It was still morning-cool. He took off his hat. He wiped his forehead. He sat and looked at the trunks of the trees. How each tree was differently clad. In what freedom they grew.

A man came walking along, whistling Offenbach. They greeted each other. Alfred Schrader, the orchestra's conductor, asked if he might sit down. Axel made inquiries about his work, and Alfred Schrader about Axel's contacts with Sibelius – where was he just now? In Estonia. Reval. And the new compositions – was there a third symphony in the offing? Probably. The second had been – quite something. Yes. Without doubt. And now the summer had come and was playing its music for bumblebees and gnats. And harps.

They got up and strolled towards the lookout tower at Pyyniki, then Alfred Schrader turned back, he had a rehearsal – a simple summer concert of Strauss & Co. *Geschichten aus dem Wiener Wald.* He disappeared among the tall, cool trees, with his chubby, ever-smiling face, a picture of health. Axel remained standing there, watching the light glitter between the tree-trunks. It almost hurt his eyes. There were not many people about, he had the woods to himself. Should he go on, or turn back too? He studied the lookout tower, it was tall, taller than the one at Nådendal. A hot wave flooded over him, he had to sit down in the grass, it was cool there, almost cold. He lay down cautiously and looked up at the sky between the treetops. Birds flew by. There was no depth there, only pale emptiness, and he had not a thought in his head, only a peculiar, grinding fear.

Axel lay there until it passed. With an effort he got to his feet, brushed himself down and began to stroll back towards the town. If he had been afraid they would watch him, scrutinize him, he had been wrong. He strolled towards the bridge, encountering more and more people, carriages, and horses, they stood in rows on the market square with their bags of oats. There were the peasant carts, farmers in slouch-hats and black-clad women in kerchieves, and the air quivered with the smell of hay and horse-dung, smoked ham and factory fumes, water and metal. Under the bridge the water flowed, as always. There had been a small notice in yesterday's newspaper about a man who had fallen in, been swept away. How many corpses passed through the mighty river-system each year and were washed out into the great lakes? The ferry-boats moved doggedly hither and thither. There were the *Sotka* and the *Jyry*, the *Sampo* and the *Tiira*, and the *Mänttä* leaving a pennant of smoke after it. He usually took the boat to the Färlings', but now he balked at it. The horses tossed their heads patiently, it was all the same to them who came and went. Pails were being emptied over the cobblestones, and from the

Palander site rose a cloud of smoke. They were blasting.

Axel wandered slowly across the bridge to the railway station. There he bought a copy of *Hufvudstadsbladet* and sat down on a bench to read it. At Klippan, he observed, *Dirigent* Josef Silberman's Ladies' Orchestra was giving both midday and evening concerts, the editorial leader was about woodfelling and floods, everything was the same as usual. From Berlin there was a feature article about the Women's International Council. The siege of Port Arthur, Russian heroes – and then something worth closer attention: that Janne had received a complimentary gift in Reval, six silver goblets, had thought someone had stolen them from him, but had found them again, having left them at his hotel. Axel sat with a far-seeing look in his eyes. He could hear Janne raging and then – perhaps he could act as his Sancho Panza? Or better, as his Virgil. Or his Odysseus... Axel's thoughts wandered far and wide. A train snorted into the station, and children and old people, townsfolk and country folk came rushing over to gape at the gas-smelling, smoke-spewing miracle from far away. Was there nothing else to see...

Axel got up and wandered slowly home across the bridge. The square had emptied, there were only leavings, old women sweeping up, shiny cobblestones. And there at the head of the bridge he heard the newspaper-boy shouting, bought the flysheet and read it. 'At 11 a.m. this morning on the landing of the second floor of the Senate an attempt was made to assassinate the Governor General of Finland and General Adjutant of the Armed Forces N.L. Bobrikov, as a result of which General Adjutant Bobrikov was wounded by three revolver shots. The culprit, Eugen Schauman, shot himself instantly. Kaigorodov, Major-General of the General Staff.'

The text was in Finnish, and he spelt it out slowly to himself. With blind eyes he looked out across the rapids. He was gripped by fear: the bloodbath might begin at any moment. The town went black, he must get in touch with someone, Janne was far away, something must be done, what was happening in Helsingfors? He began to go home, practically half-running, the people rushed palely by, at the same time he felt a sense of jubilation: Bobrikov gone! And the war with Japan – that could not be going well, something was constantly working away underground, it was not only the earth of the Palander site that was shaking. At the house of the Misses everything was summer-still, the window-sashes were lowering their cross over the carpets. He shouted, but no one answered.

He went into his room, his heart was beating violently, he must lie down, he had left the door open in case anyone came. He swallowed. He was always prepared for small changes: for a chair to have been moved, a document mislaid, they gave him the illusion of being present at some concealed, mysterious, obscure event. But this! Would Janne have heard the news? How would *Finlandia* be interpreted, listened to now? He turned round, groaning, and looked out into the room, there was his jacket hanging on a chair, with helpless arms. He could not lie still, he sat up, got to his feet, went over to the window, listened for screams and cries, but all was deadly silent. This must be the silence before the storm. Could he not hear the clatter of hooves, was not the militia on its way?

The door to the staircase banged shut, and he glimpsed Anna and Lydia, they were talking excitedly, he went into where they were, in the drawing-room, for a moment they all looked at one another like three white screens. Then they pounced on him: had he heard? Yes, he had heard! But they had been on the telephone to Helsingfors! The line had crackled horribly, but they had still been able to hear. Three shots, one in an epaulette, one in the throat, one in the stomach. Schauman from a good family and a school-board official. His poor mother and father! The capital was in a ferment! Both Anna and Lydia were in a ferment, too, Anna paler and more resigned, Lydia nourished by the catastrophe like a cuckoo-chick in its nest, the whole room with sofa and table, palms and draperies, was filled with rumours of threats and fires, spies and murderers, the crash and collapse of morality and the law trampled underfoot, and no one would be able to go in safety any more – no woman would be safe now, not after dark!

They were beside themselves, he looked at them. Headless. He tried to bring order and discipline to his thoughts, but all he could come up with was: 'Silence! In God's name silence!' In amazement they looked at him and fell silent, and in the silence he said: 'This is the beginning of our freedom!' *They* had nothing to fear, not even in the dark. But this was the crowning blow. A tool of the powers-that-be was gone. Now it was important to keep one's presence of mind!

Axel straightened himself up, looked at the Misses, turned and went back to his room. He closed the door, all was quiet. He sank down at his writing-desk and hid his face in his hands.

From The Diary

1904

18.6

Bobrikov died at 1.10 a.m. A service of mourning was held in Helsingfors yesterday. *Hufvudstadsbladet* has reprinted *N. Vremya*'s lamentations*, in which attention is drawn, among other things, to the good results achieved by 'Bobban' in the field of Russification since 1898, together with an interview B. gave to a certain Mr Belyayev, in which B.'s loathing for the intrigues of the Suecomanes* is made clear – for him they and the young Finns are one and the same. 'My personal sympathies are on the side of the Old Fennomanes', who according to B. represent 7/8ths of Finland! A new, clear morning must sooner or later dawn as long as the Russian militia do not stain it with blood.

2.7

I received a letter from Janne in which he writes briefly about 'inner change': seems depressed about increasing cold, probably feeling of emptiness after 2nd Symphony. The building of the family home at Järvenpää is now in full swing, and one might have thought that Janne would have enough to keep him busy there, but he seems to spend a great deal of time travelling, and leaves all his burdens at home for Aino to carry. Has she enough strength? In addition to all this the darkening mood in the wake of the assassination, in part irresolution and indifference that must be cured!

15.7

I have been trying to read scores but am not getting anywhere with them. The summer hot and stinking of the smoke from fires. In the cemetery this smell has a peculiar effect, as though it were rising out of the graves. I observe that this communion with the dead has its risks, one's soul is infected with rigor mortis, and in this context music could be a liberator. But sometimes the ear listens without hearing anything and the eye cannot read.

25.8

Instead of devoting himself to his violin concerto, Janne is occupying himself with songs and snippets. I have no objection to the songs, since it is Rydberg, the great master of my youth, he is setting: 'Autumn Evening', 'On a Balcony by the Sea', 'In the Night', 'The Harpist and his Son'. 'Autumn Evening' is classically limpid and melancholy, full of solitude and melting into the eternal starry heavens. It has a grandeur of tone that suits Janne. So, too, in 'On a Balcony by the Sea': the longing for eternity, the silence. 'In the Night' takes up a related theme, that of the 'stillness, dreaming, stillness', which our longing, all the world's longing reaches out towards, far from 'woe and pain'. The Harpist from *The Armourer* speaks of sorrow's source, of 'mighty growth and noble death'. What they all have in common is a classicism, a grandeur of tone, a sense of things happening under the vault of heaven, and they show Janne's dreams: classical form, eternal subjects… Janne complains of pains in his ears – 'yet my inner hearing is intact'. And in that inner hearing speak wingbeats and stars, silence and closeness, and from the abstract is born the concrete, the song.

24.9

Janne's most recent letter radiates optimism. He has fresh plans: a Third Symphony, incidental music, the major chord of life. He has invited me to Villa Ainola! Aino and Janne have promised to help me when they themselves have free hand. The new symphony is to be in C major. I shall go!

27.9

The new villa, smelling of fresh wood, comfortable and stately but not too big, not an ostentatious structure. Aino and Janne showed me the greatest solicitude and joy at my presence. In the evening long conversation, reminded me of Tvärminne. I told Janne that when I am seized by thoughts that are too gloomy I consciously divert them along channels that bring consolation: with the reflection that life is full of chance, man is a speck of dust (in Janne's case a rather large one, it must be admitted) and yet as eternal as the atom. Perhaps death is not so dreadful, after all? Will not my dead body be just as near the sun as my living one? Janne did not want to talk about this, moved the discussion on to the subject of music. I spoke warmly of Rydberg's poetry and brought up the question of Janne's leaning towards the classical, which he confirmed. The Third Symphony ought to lead out across clear waters with lofty space above it. Lay in the guest bedroom, listening to the soughing of the wind in the trees, and there was a great sense of calm there.

22.10

There is around the artist a solitude that is vitally essential and is very often considered reckless egoism, which from the point of view of the outsider it undeniably is. In Janne's case two moods, the 'frightening' and the 'naïve', exist in a constant, unique and most intimate cohabitation. When he is at the piano he is deep inside himself and neither hears nor sees anything else. Beside this primordial energy Aino represents culture and modesty. The whole of Ainola smelt of forest, Janne must be taking it with him into the Third Symphony.

26.10

Late in the evening stood on the square and reflected that this was my place: empty, deserted, and the wind whistled and the torrent roared, and in all this there was a consolation that I cannot explain.

29.10

Janne has been going round the banks in a hunt for money – the sad and gloomy trotting-course of the Finnish promissory note brigade. To think that great art must live by alms and begging, and this in 1904!

22.11

On this gentle November day I ventured out among yapping dogs and met Death on Trädgårdsgatan; he was dressed in the shabby overcoat of a petty artisan, which he had stolen from me, distorting my mirror image, moreover. His face looked as though it had been scratched by a knife in pumice stone, and he smelled fusty. He followed me along the road, now we walked in step, now out of step, but then he would accommodate himself to my gait. When I stopped, he stopped, mumbled something I could not catch at first. I began to think of a quotation from Marcus Aurelius that was grinding away in my head and seemed to suit the occasion: 'To be separated from human beings is not so dreadful – as long as there are gods.' This shadow of mine appeared to exclude the gods, he himself was a minor Satan, in a very human and impoverished form. I, who in general am hypochondriacal to the point of cowardice, it must be admitted, observed him: small, pale, surprisingly well-cared-for hands with dirty fingernails, his gaze at once wandering and sharp in his bloated face, the stubble of his beard shot with red, his bowler hat worn and shabby like his velvet collar, and ratty hair that stuck out at the sides. When I asked him what he wanted – my voice easily passes into a falsetto when I am upset, but I whispered instead – he wiped his nose with his fingers and looked at me without saying a word, and was then obliterated. As soon as I reached home I had to lie down, felt powerless, as if drained of all my blood. Was he an omen?

10.12

Janne suspects he may have diabetes. Believes that the illness will help his music, then he will be able to immerse himself more deeply in himself and write more: the healthy man's superficial view of illness – or the hypochondriac's. The word 'hypochondriac' suggests to me a great, mighty bird of prey, like a condor, but its cry surprisingly soft and squeaky. It builds its nest in closed-up rooms, with suspicions and whispers. Its hearing very well-developed, like that of a composer.

1905

15.1

Have completed forty-seven years of this slow downhill journey, and had the usual cake at the Rosengrens'. I often repay their concern far too meagrely. Tried to listen attentively to the gossip of the town. This time none of my sisters came here, perhaps I have frightened them away? But they did send cards, Fanny one with a musical theme, but then she is also the one who is closest to music: she has the Norberg piano. So beautiful it was, with its lid up, in the big hall at Odensnäs, and the sunshine was in harmony with the music's brittle sound. As though it were an eternity ago, and when I was a child. In reality I was over thirty at the time.

23.1

Dr Klemperer in Berlin has prescribed lemonade for Janne in place of wine. *That* beverage can hardly be strengthened by seasoning from R. Strauss, Busoni, Pfitzner, Magnard and other notabilities! Compared to Janne they are mostly dwarfs – only Debussy, to some extent Strauss, who is rather the sorcerer of the superficies. The Second Symphony has been successful. The future will wash out the gold, free it from the naturalistic attributes that have stuck to it, not to speak of the programmatic ones, and the music's visionary individuality will be restored.

7.2

Lennart Hohenthal has shot Procurator Johnson, styled Soisalon-Soininen* and I have bought a new shirt as my old one was worn out. There has been sparkling sunshine over pure, white snow, and it is only the people who make things dirty. I have given up coffee, which has not been agreeing with me, in favour of tea.

18.2

Janne is still being examined for diabetes in Berlin, the doctor has discovered hypochondria, in him it takes bottle-form. Janne is working on *Pelléas and Mélisande*. He must have a strange ability to divide up his time between recreation, *Bierstube* and composing. A single task is enough to undo me, the work expands like bread-dough, filling up the whole room, often with horrible results. Was, for example, sewing a button on to my jacket – had lost it originally (the button) and borrowed one from Anna R., somewhat feminine in appearance (the button), and managed after various difficulties (threading the needle, knotting the thread, etc.) to sew it carefully and firmly in place (more or less), but then found when I had to go out that I had sewed up the breast-pocket and couldn't get my wallet out without unpicking the whole wretched mess. Fate, life, existence, call it what one will, is *against* me, and it is clear that no creative work can be carried out and sustained under such circumstances. Yet it was an ugly button (velvet-covered with a brass rim), so the loss was not as great as it might have been.

28.2

Janne receives an annual payment of 8000 marks from Liemann for four works a year. Is that not a slave contract? Will it not drive him to desperate measures, cheap art, hasty, slipshod work, and distract him from what ought to be closest to him: symphonic music and chamber music?

11.3

After days of lying in bed I dragged myself to the bookcase and unloaded all my exercise books full of diary notes on to the table. Is this my life? Or is it being enacted outside this heap of paper, the first pages of which are already beginning to turn yellow like the first trees in autumn? There was a smell of something tragic and forever lost about this bundle in which all my thoughts, dreams, hopes and failures are being pressed together like the plants in a herbarium and like them are turning pale, withering, falling to dust... Carried the whole lot back to the bookcase. Had a glass of brandy and smoked a cigar, which gave me such a fit of coughing that Lydia R. came in, afraid that something had happened to me again. She saw the bottle and glass, and stood as though petrified. Have I made too good an impression on her? Does she have certain ideas? I am still sitting in my nightshirt and my handwriting is uncertain.

13.3

Politics and strategy are like moving quickly over the ice of one night's frost, in case one falls through. Decisions must be taken, even if they are wrong, and where there is hesitation blood oozes forth and the occasion is lost. Tsarist Russia is like a great whirlpool, too large for the separate particles to grasp which way the suction is pulling. Desperate ukases are thrown out with increasing desperation around a confused, weak centre: the Tsar. Strategy is being able to move the point of gravity quickly or divide it into several. The really important actors are waiting in the wings while Holy Russia tears itself into shreds, the chimneys smoke, the anarchists sharpen their weapons, the ice breaks up and hidden corpses are brought to light.

24.3

Rhythm is sensually and sexually determined. Who dares to see Janne's music from this point of view? The slowly intensified rhythm leading to eruptions, and then subsiding again. This can hardly be described as respectable musicology.

10.4

To be noted: my daily routine consists of getting up, washing myself, eating breakfast, practising the piano, my daily walk to the hill or the railway station over the bridge, then home, study of scores, meal, reading, rest, immobility, insomnia. And in all of this something I cannot explain, which prevents it all from seeming meaningless. That is my daily routine. I omitted: writing of letters, my diary.

27.4

It is spring on Pispala Square. From the hill Pyhäjarvi is glittering as never before. Again the same kerchieves, bowler hats, slouch hats, black waistcoats, white aprons, children's screams, horse-dung, sour and fresh cream, butter that sparkles with salt, leavened bread, eggs, smoked ham, black pudding, the smell of leather, and from Santalahti saw the fragrance rising from the timber deposits like a hot forest that reminded me of Ainola... The train stops there, whistling and spewing out smoke.

22.5

The month's note: when I remarked on the absence of vegetables the housemaid grew insolent and shouted that a lot of people had to make do with herring and bread soaked in milk. When that day comes, I replied, I shall move. Whither, I do not know.

23.5

Janne has invited me to Helsingfors for a personal meeting! In a week's time. Conflicts at home? In order to be able to help I ought to know myself completely. 'Know thyself!' cries he who thinks he knows himself, and goes on his way like a hare-brained nincompoop. Is it not more fruitful to get to know someone else thoroughly? 'Know thyself!' But what if what is there is really something rather uninteresting – why spend so much effort on it? But to get to know a genius – that is an entire university with all its faculties, and a living one, at that.

1.6.1905

According to the timetable, the mail train from Tammerfors to Helsingfors was supposed to leave at 1.28. The clock already said half-past one. Axel was getting impatient. If he was late, what would Janne say? When schedules were broken, the world tottered. People were scrambling to and fro in complete disorder. There were bundles and barrows, smoke and dust, and there was a smell of gas. The day promised to be a hot one, the snuff-brown curtains at the carriage window hung resignedly. The seat already felt hard, and people were jostling, children crying, hard-board suitcases bulging on the racks. The train was due to arrive in Helsingfors at 6.35. That made five hours' journey, five hours spent opposite a crafty-looking peasant with a bundle in his lap.

Axel had put his doctor's bag under the seat, he dug out the day's newspaper. But he was unable to concentrate. There was moisture on the window, the station was shrouded in mist. Now there was a jerking, followed by a squealing and shaking. Slowly the platform, the people and the station slid away. There were low wooden hovels which Axel had never seen before. The city meandered down into thickets and up again, ditches of brown water, young verdure, little patches of field in which ill-defined clusters of humanity dug and hoed. The train passed a bridge, people and carriages were moving across it. It felt strange, as though he were cut off from everything. The man opposite him had a broad, greedy face, the sweatband on his hat was soaked, his grey jacket of thick homespun, his leather boots smelt new, and had pointed toes. Axel huddled himself up, tried to arrange his legs so that they were not touching anything, and sat squeezed. To his left a woman was swaying, her eyes closed, her skin like parchment, her hand resting on a covered basket. He ought really to have bought a second-class ticket, but had carefully counted his resources. They did not permit it. He felt with his hand: his wallet and purse were still there.

The man opposite took out a knife, undid the wrapper, and cut himself a thick slice of the dark ryemeal bread, propping the loaf against his stomach. He did not look up. On the wall the water carafe shook and shook, the water in it was slightly yellow. Low forests and fields, here and there a grey house slid by. The fact that they never cut their entrails out in the event that the knife slipped was probably due to habit, Axel reflected. He closed his eyes. Vague fragments of newspaper headlines glimmered before his eyes. Svinhufvud* defended Hohenthal. The ladies' orchestra played on, chalk-white arms swung bows up and down. The music drowned in the rhythmical thud of the rail-joints. Beautiful June forests, shanties on tall stone foundations, a white manor house among the trees, the cowshed, pastures, fields, flocks of crows that flew up out of the ditch-coppices. Would Janne be waiting for him on the platform when he got to Helsingfors? Hardly. Axel took a deep breath and leaned his head against the curtains at the window. They smelt of snuff. He tried to find a melody to go with the rhythm of the rail-joints, it turned into a homespun waltz. His heart thumped, there were the faces being shuffled the way cards are shuffled, the Misses Rosengren, his sisters, Hjalmar's face was there, he was asleep or dead.

Axel was unable to sleep. He looked at a young girl in a striped headscarf across the aisle. She reminded him of Rakel. She had a child in her arms, swaddled and asleep. She herself was a child, perhaps it was her little sister. The child's eyelids were completely blue. Sleep surrounded it like a cocoon. Everyone he saw was enclosed in the carriage's rhythm, each one of them alone in their sleep. The dead woman had looked at him with half-closed eyes, her children merely dark bundles in the snow. Axel looked tensely at the landscape slipping by, there was nothing to see. In the window's dirty mirror he thought he saw Julia Döhr, someone laughed, he felt the sweat standing out on his forehead. The man opposite produced a bottle of milk from a creel and drank, with a slurping sound. The enormous might of the people that could break down doors and iron gates, they were welling forth, all on their way to the same city, the same goal. Axel turned his newspaper and folded it together. The Straits of Korea had swallowed the Russian fleet, from a strategic point of view the operation had been a crazy one, the ships tin cans that could be opened. The water lapping in. The train passed vibrating into a dark forest, the trees were so close to the track that it was almost dark. The theatre was giving performances of Hedberg's comedy *The Captain of the Frigate*, it remained afloat week after week, gliding across a sea of applause. The thud of the rail-joints was quite clearly in 3/4 time, regular and no good for use at concerts. But all right for society life.

Axel closed his eyes and tried to imagine society life. The artists in Tusby, Janne and Aino among laughing people, what did he know of their lives? The Järnefelts were very particular about the company they kept, not everyone was allowed in. Just as long as he didn't drag his footsteps there. Hardly. He looked at his trousers and shoes, they were worn but presentable. The train was slowing down, was this Tavastehus, or had they already passed it? Axel took out his watch. Heavy and solid it lay in his hand, leading his life onwards. The man opposite threw him a crooked glance and produced his own turnip. A conductor, as thin as a pole, stumbled past, Axel hailed him and asked the time of their arrival in Helsing-fors. The man thumbed through a timetable in irritation. The cap of his uniform was too large for him, his ears stuck out. Axel could have answered the question himself. Six thirty-five p.m. But he wanted certainty, the knowledge that he had got it right. He had. The conductor gave an uncertain salute and disappeared. He was probably not used to people asking questions in third class.

Slowly he sank into the monotony, he was used to repetition. The girl diagonally opposite cast a shy glance at him. He didn't belong here, she could see that, but his shoes were worn, his wrists protruded, narrow and white, from his cuffs. Smoke drifted past the window, and Axel slept. He did not wake up until the train was passing Dickursby. It was not far now. Near the city there was a flash of water, that was Tölöviken, there was Kajsaniemi, Axel felt strangely agitated. On trembling legs he climbed down onto the platform. He followed the human flood. Everywhere people, long dresses, soldiers, Finnish and Russian words being hurled around like confetti, but he could see no sign of Janne. What should he do now? Go to the travellers' hostel, deposit his suitcase, then what? Could he not take his suitcase with him? Janne was bound to be at Kämp, had he not spoken in his letter of inviting him to supper there? What if he had misunderstood, and they were supposed to meet each other there?

Axel crossed over to the other side of Station Square with its horse-carts and pigeons, on Mikalesgatan there hung a large ther-mometer, it read 20°C, it was five to seven and the train had been late, perhaps Janne had been standing there but had got tired of waiting? There was König. Might he be in there? Axel went slowly down the staircase, the head waiter was standing there, a babble of voices rose like smoke from the rooms. There was a smell of cabbage. Professor Sibelius had not been seen, not today. The head waiter gave Axel a look. It was inscrutable. Further up the street the kinema was showing moving pictures, a handwritten scrap of paper gave information about the reign of Louis XIV, who had been the Sun King. On the Esplanade strolled those who wanted to be seen.

Axel stopped at the corner, he hesitated. There were voices and the play of light and shadow, Axel felt strange, uninhabited, he crossed the street, sat on a bench for a while. He had experienced it all before, but he had been younger. All his companions had had student caps then. Someone said hullo to him, and Axel quickly said hullo back, it was a stranger who stopped, bowed, extended his hand, sat down, pulled up the ends of his trousers, asked how he was, had he visited the dear old school of late, he lived in Åbo, didn't he? No, Axel was unable to place the features, the beard, the moustache, the narrow eyes, the pouting mouth, but he answered politely. It grew quiet. The man in the white summer suit hummed a tune from some operetta, tapped his stick gently on the ground, what was there to say? Perhaps this man had been one of the tormenting spirits? Axel got up, made a quick bow, and found his way across the street between the carriages. Music in the air, gentleman and hats on the Esplanade, the limes in bright-green flower. He opened the door, glass and glitter, and in the hallway with the staircase leading up, the pillars and the chandelier, the leather sofa, the soft carpet, they looked at him suspiciously. Was Professor Sibelius there? Most likely in a private room, on the first floor; but no, they shook their heads, he was in the restaurant. He asked them to let him know he was there, in a tone of voice that made them answer and obey. Something, or nothing, still remained. He discarded his thin overcoat, his suit was quite presentable, he straightened himself in front of the mirror.

There was Janne, he came and embraced him. Couldn't manage to meet him, business conference, but now everything was in order, just a small gathering, he would introduce him to the people he didn't know, Kajanus was there, how was his health, we've just been discussing the world situation. Inside the restaurant the company looked up, Axel stood embarrassed but collected, a trio was playing in a corner, Russian officers at the next table, the whole place fully occupied, everyone looking at him; he bowed in silence. A mixed bunch, a few 'vons' and 'afs', Kajanus cordial. And how were things in Tammerfors, was it seething, the water, the bloodstained water? That he was unable to say, all he knew was

251

that there was hatred. Against whom? But immediately backs were turned, Axel who was sitting next to Janne was pressed to accept a glass and a bottle of Carlshamn punch, ice-cold from the cellar, white napkins with stains on them, he could see them, the men red, blustery and excited, and one of them stood up, proposed a toast to the Russian fleet – may it flourish upside-down! That calmed them down, and they were silent for a moment, that was daring, soon voices were raised, then shouts that drowned them, but one of the Russian officers got up and came over, clicked his heels: were the gentlemen insulting the Russian fleet –? Not at all, they had just drunk a toast in its honour! And to the Grand Duchy of Finland, someone added. 'Things are going to be rather different around here soon,' the man in epaulettes retorted, turned and went back to his table, the conversation grew muted, perhaps they ought to move to one of the newly renovated private rooms, someone was sent to reconnoitre, more punch arrived, the waitress flushed with the heat, black dress and white apron, the head waiter silent in the background. Hohenthal's trial, and did anyone feel like going to take a look at Tolstoy's *The Power of Darkness*... and Aino Ackté had signed a contract with the Opéra Comique. Had anyone seen the news that poor Fröding had now discharged himself from hospital in Uppsala and was going to travel abroad with his sister? Janne and Axel sat in silence for a while; how those who are most fragile and see most profoundly are broken and driven into illness – Kajanus proposed a toast in honour of Fröding, and it was adopted with acclaim. The conversation moved to the subject of eccentrics, and Janne had a titbit in reserve, about how – 'Do you remember, Kajanus – how on the quayside in July, when we were about to sail for Paris, there was that little man in a bowler handing out bunches of violets – that was a truly faithful flowergirl – faithful to music at least –'

They smiled, they laughed, the conversation flowed on; a gentle mist formed before Axel's eyes, he could hardly breathe, he stood up, they looked at him, he mumbled something. Janne turned to him, 'Mind you come back, now!', and turned away again, he walked out, tottering slightly, through the hallway, straight outside. Cool air, people, he stood still for a moment, had to support himself against the wall, some passers-by turned their faces towards him, he began to walk, down to the harbour, they laughed and stared after him as he went, a whole horde, a threat.

He broke into a run, then slowed down again. Panting, he sat down on a bench beside Kapellet, Apostol's★ brass band struck up a bold march and a flock of pigeons flew up, there was a gentle twilight and lamps were glimmering. He sat bowed forward, he was invisible, he had been born defenceless, they could treat him any way they wanted to, did not even recognize him, could insult him and wound him, he was bleeding to death, he leaned back, closed his eyes, there were only voices, the gleaming brass of the band's instruments, the mild June air, and like a sense of burning shame the laughter, the teeth, the flowergirl: this from Janne! Over and over again the humiliations, and the days that went on. With effort he got up, his demonstrations of protest would make the situation no better, the most sensible thing was not to show that anything was wrong, and he went heavily back. Not that they had noticed anything. 'You were away a long time – constipation?' 'Yes – something of that kind.' His opinion of Wagner? Too much beer and bacon for his taste – and they laughed, someone called 'Bravo.' Janne put his arm around his shoulders, he sat, his forehead white and damp, his hands knotted together, a tense smile, quietly he said to Janne: 'Did you want to see me about anything in particular?' 'I just wanted to see you, my good friend! My noble soul! I'm a little worried about Aino – but we can talk about that tomorrow.'

He filled Axel's glass. Axel drained it, quickly, to the bottom.

From The Diary

4.8
Sent money to J. Have also received few pennies myself which will no doubt come in handy.

23.8
Albert Edelfelt has died. Janne is upset.

3.9
Am trying to write in an unheated bath-house in Siuro Jaskara. It is horribly cold, and I have gone to bed every night with my clothes on. I have been unable to sleep, and am threatened by financial ruin. J. is ashamed about not having written all summer, and I am ashamed about *receiving* letters. What is the point of remembering someone who has been dead for 20 years? But it's not worth struggling against fate. Every lamp has its measured gauge of oil, right from the beginning. Am unable to write as my hands are getting stiff.

22.9
People talk behind my back, I can scarcely hear it, it is spoken yet unspoken. It comes up from behind, there are mocking ripostes, 'meaningful' glances, arms that impede me and force me in against a wall. There are white shirt-fronts, booming bursts of laughter, bared teeth, raised eyebrows, a man leaning against a woman and whispering in her ear, they are looking at me. There is orgiastic, pus-coloured music and grotesque footsteps, couples stumbling over a bloodred carpet. In the darkness glow cigars, the smoke rises with the voices and I who stand hidden drag myself out onto the floor, am almost carried forward, for I am paralysed and they put me on a sofa and lean over me, all the dead faces. Strange that I am able to look at them so calmly, watch their grimaces and

feigned sympathy, tenderness, interest. They are made-up like dolls, clowns or dead people. That is their shame, my own is indifferent to me.

23.10
After some difficult weeks I have now picked myself up again. Janne's violin concerto has been performed by Halik in Berlin. So it wasn't Burmester, after all. I don't have the strength to get inside that darkly flowing and in part death-lamenting work again.

3.11
General strike broke out on the 30th, was on the train from Helsingfors where I had been visiting Tor, could only get to T-fors with great difficulty. Manifesto read out to cheering crowd of people. Yrjö Mäkelin★ pleaded the cause of the people. Uproar.

6.11
The November Decree★, law and order restored, it is said. All this a sign of continued unrest and fear. It interferes everywhere, spreads like the plague, into my dreams. There people shout with severed throats, and I pass through them in a body that is not my own. When I wake up I am in another dream.

10.11
The Senate has resigned.

7.12
Janne is in London, Bantock is introducing him to the homes of the aristocracy but has asked him to be 'as he is'. The bear is showing its true character. Naïveté and worldliness, within the same fur coat. Under the fur – angels and demons, swans and birds of prey, and – silence.

12.12
Janne has now reached Paris, that haughty woman who is cold to all foreign music. Janne is now 40 and is seized with melancholy. But there is a much darker undercurrent that passes through a person's life, it can well forth at his birth and colour everything, and slowly the person's insight into this circumstance grows.

15.1

This past year has been dreadful and only a change for the better ought to be possible. On this, my 48th birthday, have resolved to live in the everyday without making major demands, to listen, receive and learn. To live according to life's conditions. That is not easy, as my dreams get in the way, and I am trying to free myself from them. I had one of them last night. Dreamed that some stranger had taken over my body, was dreaming my dreams and thinking my thoughts, and I awoke to a dream I could not free myself from. Like someone who, blind with terror, rushes out of a burning house in order the next moment to rush back into a thundering inferno, I rushed back into my dream, into a complete absence, almost abstract, with the most desolate remoteness. Was the appealing gaze from a peculiarly pale, flabby face my own? I ran and saw myself running, there were a lot of people called Axel running beside me or at my back, and they were laughing in common understanding or pursuing me with cries the meaning of which I could not catch. I crept under fences, ran over muddy fields, stumbled, fell, got up again, and high in the sky I saw a white kite merrily dancing, and a child who was holding its line gave me a look as I rushed by and, in exhaustion, reached the veranda where all the old people were sitting, and they went on drinking from their cups and didn't see my despair, and when I turned round a white road stretched away there, everything, treetops and fields, was black, but a peculiar brilliance lit the horizon, as though some alien power were coming to destroy me, and I woke up and saw the dawn, and sat up with pounding heart. Could not go down to breakfast, tried to read score (Second Symphony) but suddenly it didn't say anything to me any more, was merely incomprehensible marks on paper, and I fled outside into the cold and a bitter wind, and forgot that Anna was coming to visit me. When I came back they were all sitting round the birthday cake, waiting. The coffee was heated up again and I heard myself answer on being spoken to.

8.2

Janne has returned from his journey. A few days ago he and Aino visited Eero Järnefelt in Träskända in the company of Maxim Gorky, Gallén and Saarinen.★ What could that group have had to say to one another? Sigurd Frosterus★ is prophesying the end of the national culture. No – not the national, but the nationalistic one! The national culture extends its roots down to the bedrock, the universal. That is how I interpret it, that is how I hear it, in Janne's music.

3.3
Janne writes that the Third Symphony is nearing completion, and has asked me to come.

26.3
Janne preoccupied with intense work, and was unable to receive me. I am sitting in my room and am a part of the shabby furniture.

10.4
There is in Janne's music a form of impersonality, in the best sense of the word. Not that one does not immediately recognize his language, his intonation, but what his music speaks of are the most universal things – loneliness, happiness, pain, the sense of eternity, the ascendancy of nature, ecstasy and silence. And is this not a characteristic of true art when it is at its most personal, this universally humanizing instinct, this impersonal and eternal striving towards that which is hidden, unsaid, that which has not yet found expression?

13.4
Scandal when I refused to eat the liver loaf with large fat sweet raisins. Have now locked myself in. My room full of frightening sounds, as when swans rise, thundering like heartbeats.

18.4
'When you die the grass will grow over you and that is all', Tolstoy says through the mouth of Uncle Yeroshka. I took a good look at the grass at Masku Cemetery the last time I was there, it's grass just like any other. But it's true that the wind passes through it and the silence there is of a different kind from the silence than e.g. the one in my room just now, it's eternal but is perhaps also an interlude, or so I would like to imagine. This is one of the quieter days, some of them blaze up and burn themselves out in feverish fantasies, as though someone was trying to torture me.

23.4
As I was going home in the twilight heard someone call my name.

It was a frightening experience, for there was no one there, but I had been called and my time has been measured out. It was like a bolt of lightning from a clear sky. Afterwards there is always a sense of emptiness, as after the evening at Kämp, or other experiences. As though I had been branded.

7.5
Difficulty in breathing, but *Ich will das Unbekannte*, I too!

1.7
It is summer and I happen to be here in N-dal. The money from Axel T. in Stockholm has dried up, and I am now worth even less than before, if such a thing is possible. Here Rakel walks invisibly towards me during moments of dizziness, I see her then, as she was before she had rejected me, her gentleness was like the scent of lilacs that flows to greet me everywhere. I have made inquiries before about her life, but it's hard to get hold of the address. One or two old friends are left, and we exchange a few words about trivial matters, complain that time is passing too slowly, or too fast. But at night strange sounds are heard. Someone gives a sudden scream, a rough male voice replies, someone is running and the air is full of tension and the expectation that something terrible or fantastic is about to take place. Towards morning the pressure slackens, a cock crows, a sheep bleats, the town begins to wake up and I go to bed. Sometimes I try to read my notes from years gone by and see my life as in a steamed-up mirror, by glimpses, enlarged or alien, and yet familiar. The unknown! Which Busoni – and with him all great artists – strives towards. What unknown is it that I dream of? I dream of what was once familiar and a riddle, about my childhood, and about Rakel.

3.7
Sveaborg is now in revolt, and on Hagnäs Square Red Guards and military volunteers have opened fire on one another. Fear is taking over.

15.7
At last a sign of life from Janne, who has had his mentally ill sister Linda visiting him, but in order to protect his work he cuts her off. That is the hard and only way, but how does Aino view it? That which is healthy has its opposite pole in that which is sick. Janne overcomes his fear of death and all that is connected with

illness and death in a music which derives its darkness from the sense of death. What deep wounds our sorrow at life's brevity inflicts upon us, and what vital energy it gives him. He overcomes the most vulnerable loneliness, he is the Advocate of sorrow but also of the Will to Life. There was in our meeting in Tvärminne a peculiar sense – never expressed – that we shared the same loneliness – or, rather, were lonely in the same way, deeply and irreparably. Janne overcomes it in his music, in his man-of-the-world lifestyle, but it hurls him swiftly from light to darkness. I grow petrified. When I would like to be as open as possible I become a frustrated and petrified rustling.

13.8
Anna Rosengren usually looks after me when I'm ill, I try to return her friendliness but am unable to touch her. At nights there is a recurrent musical theme, like a boulder hovering above me, and if the meagre thread that suspends the boulder is cut, it will fall and crush me, and I lie with my eyes open and watch it hovering, a boulder in G minor with streaks of silver, as though water were flowing through it, giving it its clear echo. If it falls, perhaps it will open the heavens?

12.9
In Niemann's book *Die Musik Skandinaviens*, Janne represents *die Heimatkunst*! This brandmark will haunt him for a long time, and even our own countrymen will apply it to him. I have written to him about this: saying that his *Heimat* is the world, the seasons, nature and its powers which are audible everywhere.

20.9
Had a fearful dream in which I was embracing a woman's legs but she kept pushing me away from her over and over again in loathing, until I woke up in fury. Red marks on my skin where I had scratched myself.

24.9
Suddenly I have to grope my way out of bed in order to make sure that my jacket is there, my possessions, my spectacles, that I haven't forgotten anything or been deprived, robbed of anything, that I haven't lost anything. The whole of my life has been permeated by a fear of the inexplicable in small objects and caused by small alterations. The cane and top hat of my mathematics

teacher on the hall table at home when I was a child: he had come
to talk with Father and Mother about me. I was doomed. The
dirty apron flung on the chair in the kitchen. The man who stood
at the edge of the forest and suddenly disappeared. The drawer of
my writing-desk half-open when I came back from my walk:
someone had been into my room. Lydia R's hair-slide left behind
on the drawing-room table. A branch knocking against my window in Nådendal one moonlit night. Bared teeth. Rakel's gaze.
A door being shut with a bang. The hand that is raised, for a blow
or a caress? The mouse that scurried across the floor and under
my bed, the terrible fear of being bitten. The fear that makes me
start at a fancy, a shadow, a movement, a gust of wind... At such
moments everything is exposed and vulnerable, and may die at
the slightest touch. Houses and streets hurry away like shadows,
the ravens rise cawing from the trees and the darkness floods in
behind me, and everything is inexplicable and frightening, both
the living and the dead are parts of the same mighty conspiracy,
and the only way to overcome this greedy horde is to sit up in
bed, fumble for one's slippers, walk slowly through the room,
open the window, stand in the cold for a moment and see trees,
streets and houses, and here and there a gleaming streak of light
that says there is life, that someone else is awake as I am, that
something exists.

13.10
Not a line from Janne. The hollow silence, when he turns away
from everything.

1.12
Children are so alien to me that they become strangely close. Now
that the snow has fallen they are playing in great joy, running
around and climbing hills and tumbling down, muffled up in long
scarves and with knitted woollen hats pulled down to their tender
eyebrows. Their shrill voices so loud that I can't hear what they
are saying. They take no notice of me, which gives me a certain
freedom. I stand, myself a bundle, and stamp my feet, and the
snow goes on falling and falling, and suddenly they are gone. I
stand alone, there is a big tree, I hurry in, away from the play-
ground, and hide as once I did forty years ago, when my bark
was seared by fire and touched by God's hand.

10.12

Janne has been invited to conduct in seething Russia. I have warned him not only of the harsh climate, but also of the Black Hundreds, Stolypin, the terror and the violence. St Petersburg is no city for Janne's music! After Bobrikov one should observe the greatest caution. Hope Aino can talk him out of this. *Tschuchonica sunt, non placet – tschinownikis!* * No, they won't appreciate him.

31.12

On the last day of the year I can confirm that the world is in its proper place, that it has trees with no leaves, that it is winter, that the sky is pale and clear, and that all this gave me very great happiness when I was a child. To grow old is to lose reality bit by bit, and to try to discover it again within oneself. It is to mature, to remember, to forget, above all to forget.

1907

15.1

Today I am forty-nine. I have now known Janne for seven years, that's one seventh of my life. I have heard nothing from him, his visit to St Petersburg must have been a success. Did I annoy him with my warnings?

22.2

Janne has again been drawn into the beer-hall life of the would-be-gentlemen, I see him gesticulating, red in the face, his hair ruffled up, the cigar-smoke like a cloud around grubby, sweaty cuffs and collars, half-empty glasses, and I remember the evening of my humiliation and how fragile seemed thread of my life. How hard it must be for Aino to sit alone with the girls in Ainola once more. The grand piano is silent. Is it possible that a new symphony will be born from this, is all this sinking necessary in order that something may rise?

4.3

A big, burly fellow was whipping his horse which, whinnying and snorting steam from its nostrils was trying to get away, jerking, the cart half buried in snowdrifts, and the oaths were flying. I saw that the driver was drunk and desperate, that something was compelling him to strike, something that had no connection at all with the horse, and that both had those wild eyes in common. There was obstinacy, craziness, loneliness, despair, cruelty there, all of which daily live their more or less hidden lives around us. May God preserve this people of mutes and fanatics. Darkness rules over them for the greater part of the year, and a vague longing for something wholly other, something warmer and more full of love, which they are unable to express. The longing for words! That is why they hurl themselves into choral societies and amateur theatre groups where the words are all ready-provided; the rest is oaths and swearing. How could I persuade him? 'Dear sir, please stop whipping your jade of a horse, you're not making the situation any better?' But with a fearful jerk of its muzzle he got the horse moving, threw himself into his cart and trundled off into the slush with his whip at the ready. No one cared about the situation, everyone hurried on as though they hadn't seen anything. It's not enough that we're deprived of speech – we are also deaf and blind.

3.4

Have been up and about for a few days now and am able to read again. Have been studying Beethoven's later sonatas, the inward-directed strength that opens up universes – is Janne on his way here? I am waiting for a letter for him, or at least a line or two, the way a thirsty man waits to find water in the desert. He must understand that I am always at his side.

4.4

Tolstoy hates music because it encroaches upon his life, threatens his moral empire with its richness. He is frightened by its ability to speak to the emotions and to the irrational in us, and he is not entirely wrong in this. There is in music a power which can be abused, something that moves towards the desperate, the broken, the nocturnal, towards hell. But did he not see music's harmony, light and exaltation? He had a distorted view of it, it was his own features in the mirror he saw, and he confused them with those of music. His anguish is tangible, just like his rage and his fear, of music, of sex, of the spontaneous.

6.4

If I had a right of primogeniture I would, like Kierkegaard, gladly give it up for the porridge-with-butter of my childhood. Yes, in my thoughts I am still sitting there at the table with Father and

Mother, my sisters, my aunts, Uncle Fredrik, as though I were unaware that I sit there alone.

8.4

Still not a word from Janne. The pigeons on the window-sill toss their heads and turn their blind eyes on me, extend their necks and defecate. In the past there are several white spots, and I find I can in part fill them up with these notes. What is not here is gone.

18.4

That male friendship has an erotic character I cannot deny. It has to do with the enjoyment of the eye and also of other senses. The ugly dilettante need not bother! Symposia of manly strength, dubious memories, overflowing friendship and salvoes of noisy laughter as a shield against loneliness and failure, the sunning of oneself in the glow of epaulettes and grand stars, wealth and power, rituals and saunas make me sick. So my contacts have been restricted to associations with men of ideal character, such as a warm correspondence can give. Just as Viktor Rydberg and Axel Tamm were close to me once upon a time, so Cousin Tor and Janne are close to me now. With little faith I allow my meagre ideal striving to direct itself towards genius, towards Janne, in order to try to counteract an outer and inner poverty. The church mouse as patron! But it is at an end. What remains? A bed, a writing-desk, a bookcase, a few bundles of papers, a few chairs, a bag in a cupboard, faded photographs, two of them taken recently, of Tor and Janne, with greetings. Not to forget the piano. And these bundles of notebooks, my only outlet apart from letters and music. Is that not enough?

20.4

Have now obtained Rakel's present address. But what gives me the right to enter into her life and that of her family? I do it with the right of dreams. I lie awake, burning. It is the most beautiful of my illnesses that now demands relief – or at any rate a name, a name! Going there tomorrow.

21.4.1907

He had worked out the way to Berghäll in exact detail. Directly upon leaving the train he crossed over to the other side of Station Square in the direction of Regeringsgatan. There was a pawnshop in a back yard there. The day was sunny and warm, and from the horse-drawn carts a warm odour of manure was rising. He emerged through a dark gateway into a built-up courtyard with scrubby arbours and two garden swings with flaking paintwork. A few steps down, and he was in the familiar, dust-smelling, over-crowded cavern, where watches and jewels, clothes and furniture jostled for space, lit by a few cold, naked lamps on the ceiling. The man who scrutinized Axel was the same, two blinking eyes in a face that was criss-crossed with furrows. He named the price. For a moment Axel hesitated, then accepted. He fanned himself with his bowler as he waited for the hand-worn notes. Hurriedly he stuffed them in the pocket of his waistcoat. As he came out he heard the bells of St Nicholas's ringing, or was it his imagination? The city lay in a gentle mist. He walked towards the church. Some professors were coming out of the University, he crossed to the other side of the street. Ought he to turn in along Fabiansgatan or continue on until Unionsgatan? And if she wasn't at home – what should he do then? Wait till tomorrow? Did he have enough money? He stood uncertainly on the corner of Unionsgatan and saw Senate Square awash with sunlight, the sky and the birds that circled crying above the roofs. Then with the sun on his back he began to walk quickly up towards Kaisaniemiviken and Långa Bron. He passed the University Library and felt a violent yearning to go in, sit down in one of the reading rooms, sense the tranquillity of the past. He had sat like that in his youth when he had dreamed of taking the university examination. That had lasted for a few weeks. He passed the Russian Hospital. The old Russian church stood yellow in its silence, he had never been inside it. He passed Kronohagen and Kaisaniemi Park, the trees still had no buds as yet, here and there lay dirty snow. He saw just a few people and carts trickling southwards.

On the bridge he stopped and took a deep breath. People were moving about outside Kaisaniemi Boathouse, the boats were already lying part-way in the water, the smell of mud and tar reached him, and a few violently gesticulating firemen passed without giving him a glance. Eastwards, towards Brobergskajen, lay the smacks with furled sails, smoke was rising from the chimneys of Stenberg's Mechanical Workshop and Foundry. That was where she worked, on the evening shift, as a cleaner and cook in the canteen. 'J.D. Stenberg & Sons, Ltd' it said on the hoarding. Small boats, a few yachts lay at anchor out towards Pannkakan. In front of him two women were walking arm in arm, their grey skirts whirling up dust, their hats tilted forward on their foreheads, flowers uppermost, large black envelopes moving along on feet that protruded from under the coats and the skirts. It was as though he were seeing it all through a magnifying lens. He felt slightly dizzy. When he reached Cirkusgatan he found his way to a bench in the little park and sat there for a while, listening. From Hagnäs Square rose a gentle hubbub. He must keep going. He drove himself onwards.

Railway carriages screeched as they braked on the square, the shops formed themselves into a cluster, and the horse-drawn carts struck sparks from the cobbles along Broholmsgatan. There were clothes, root vegetables, leather goods, he walked past them towards Tavastgatan and the Lines. Between the pinnacles of rock lay the fire-gables of houses he had never seen, now and then a cluster of wooden houses, then open gaps in the land again, and a broad view out over Djurgårdsviken and eastwards, over the hills. Here and there in the verdure down the bay lay the villas, there a spire stuck up, a balcony could be glimpsed, there were flags. He had been there once, with his aunts, he could no longer remember whom they had visited, the children had been served fruit-juice. After they had rowed across the bay to the skittle-alley at Kaisaniemi.

He stopped, panting, and took out the piece of paper that had the address on it. A cart stopped in front of him and a man in a leather apron dragged out some milk-churns, rolled them quickly over to the steps of a small shop, carried them down, grunting as he went. There was a clang of metal, the chains of the lids jangled, he felt thirsty and squeezed his way down into the sweet-smelling, cream-soft-twilit room that was filled with the fragrance of newly baked bread. The white-clad woman whose red arms were glowing carried on a conversation with the milkman, two children in straw hats and Axel, all at the same time, her clear voice rose above the shoulders of her waiting customers like the cry of a bird, she laughed: 'Just a glass of milk?' And she picked up the half-litre measure on its long shaft, conjured a glass into his hand, lowered the measure into the churn, raised it and let the milk pour down into the glass from a height, it foamed and was filled to the brim, but not one drop spilled over the edge. She laughed towards him, and he drank. It was lukewarm, creamy, it took his thoughts back to his childhood. From the security it afforded he found his way out to the restless street. Everything there was life and never-ceasing movement, children with hoops, straw hats and shrill voices, men laying paving-stones, dust that whirled about, and pigeons, dirt-grey, eagerly in search of food. He looked at his piece of paper, before him stood a row of wooden houses on a flaking cement foundation, a gateway, and inside the courtyard another wooden house with a great many stairs and doors; an acrid smell was coming from the outside lavatory, wrapping itself around the large quantity of washing that was fluttering in the wind on the long clothesline that filled up nearly the whole of the courtyard. There was a laundry there, women with baskets were moving about, but he didn't dare to speak to them. His heart beat as though someone were beating a carpet, it was like going deaf.

He found the door, knocked on it. It opened hesitantly. A pale, small boy stood there, his head shaved completely bald, his eyes large and brown, they looked at him with fear, he was dressed in a blouse and short trousers that covered his chapped knees, he was barefoot. Those were Rakel's eyes, Axel could see that. His mother was in the laundry, the boy got the words out with difficulty, then turned quickly away and sat himself down at the far end of the room, watching the strange, dark-clad man who was standing hesitantly in the doorway. In the room there was a table and two chairs, a three-legged kettle could be glimpsed in the stove. Suddenly the boy ran out of the room, scampering past Axel as though he were being pursued, as though he had only been waiting for Axel to take a few steps into the room, and before Axel had even had time to ask his name. He heard the boy's swift footsteps on the staircase and his shrill voice: '*Äiti! Äiti!*'* He looked round. Everything was clean and quiet, on the table a coffee-cup, in the corner a cupboard, along the wall a sofa bed, and the boy's bed in the corner. The sun fell silently in, throwing the window-frame's cruciform shadow over the wooden floor. It was so quiet.

He could hear his own breathing.

The door opened, and he turned round. She stood there, white-clad, her face dark against the light, slowly she put down her laundry basket and took a few steps towards him. She smiled hesitantly at him – 'Axel?' He could only nod. He looked into her eyes, it was her, she had hardly changed, a few of the lines around her mouth had deepened, he stretched out his hands and she put hers in his. The boy peeped furtively from behind her, and was then gone again. 'I've been looking for you', he said. She did not reply. 'I just wanted to know – how you were getting on, see that everything was all right.' Rakel drew her hands away, made a gesture towards the chair: 'For goodness' sake sit down, Axel.' Mechanically she dried her hands on the apron, drew up a chair for herself, sat down. 'I'm glad that you've come. You don't know what suffering I've been through since we last saw each other – does Axel remember? Oh, the things I said to you! But I'd – I'd taken the faith – and that sometimes makes people cruel...'

He leaned forward, touched her hair, it was like stretching across eternities of time and yet as though nothing had changed, he fondled her hair, she let him do it, then leaned back and said: 'My husband died a few years ago. But how are you? You look tired. I'll put on some water for coffee – I can at least spare the time for that. Now that Axel is finally here.'

He wanted to say: 'I came because I can't forget you. But he did not say it, merely sat in silence and watched her, her movements, the way she spoke. She told him about her job, which was hard, but she was glad that she had one. She asked about Miss Anna and Mrs Elin and Mrs Fanny, asked if Axel had been in Nådendal – she herself had not seen the town for many years. When he came to tell her about his life there was not much to say. Loneliness and despair were transformed into foreign words on his tongue: neurasthenia, hypochondria, he tried to explain, it came out stammered, vague and childish. They sat in silence. She poured the coffee, told him about the boy, her son, he asked what his name was, and she looked at him and said she had named him after Axel, that he was called Akseli. 'If only he were mine,' escaped from him, 'if only I had something of my own, something, something' – and he leaned forward, it stabbed him, the pain in his middle. 'Don't, don't,' she said, appealingly, put her hands round his head, 'Axel must have known that nothing could ever come of that, we were friends, weren't we, aren't we, friends...?' He leaned back, took out his handkerchief and blew his nose, oh yes, they were friends, they would always be friends. His feelings took him back to the old days, sometimes without warning he would get violently moved, tears and wretchedness...he smiled hesitantly at her. Someone called her name shrilly out in the courtyard – 'Raaakel!' The door opened, the boy came in. 'He's seven', she said, drew the boy towards her, hugged his strangely large, fragile head, looked at Axel. 'He's such a lonely one. But nice. And it was nice of Axel to come. Now I must go back to the laundry. Will Axel come again? Where do you live?'

He told her he lived in Tammerfors, but that he often visited his Cousin Tor in Kronohagen. Could he help her? If she were ever in difficulty she knew where to find him. He had written down his Tammerfors address, he gave her it. It didn't take long to get there nowadays. He also wanted to...he had wondered... if she would accept, as a present, something to spend on Akseli and the others...

Axel was interrupted by the door being opened; a large, thickset man stood in the doorway, watching them. The boy twisted himself out of Rakel's embrace and hid behind the man. Rakel got up – 'This is Reino, he takes such good care of Akseli...' And she turned to the man and said something quietly in Finnish which Axel did not understand, he felt as though he were falling into silence and loneliness, and everything froze in its place and listened, he sat there on his chair and grew smaller.

Reino took a few steps into the room and looked at Axel. His completely green eyes swiftly scrutinized him, his voice was unusually soft when he said: 'We don't need any money. The gentleman can go.' He made an elegantly deep, mocking, bow, gestured with his arm towards the door, Axel got up, but Rakel said sharply to Reino: 'Don't make a fool of yourself! The money's for Akseli! Thank you, Axel.'

He got up. He could not touch her. Would it be all right for him to take her by the hand? She stretched it towards him and he held it for a moment. He could feel Reino's silence at his back. He went out, stumbled down the staircase without seeing, the sun was still shining, it stabbed his eyes. He walked quickly across the courtyard, did not look round, in the gateway he heard her footsteps, she was running, she seized him by the arm, she whispered: 'Thank you! Live well!'

She held him for a moment, he felt her breathing, he managed to force out: 'Come to me, don't forsake me' – but she was gone, had scarcely heard his last words, heaven and earth collapsed around him, and he had to support himself against the wall as he heard her running footsteps die away. He stood with his face against his sleeve. The sounds sank away and it grew quiet.

He straightened up and went out into the street and down the hill towards Tavastgatan. He could still feel her lips against his cheek. There was a café there, he stepped inside, sat down and looked at the traffic and the people through the window. Spring was coming, he could see. It was like something slowly filling an empty place with life. He had seen her, spoken to her. He had completed his task. He could go back. He walked through the streets, and everywhere he saw people coming and going, trees with their scarce-suspected leaf-buds, everything felt strange, as though someone had followed him with his gaze all the way to the station, had sat with him throughout the whole of the journey and was even with him still as he lay in his room on Västra Trädgårdsgatan, listening to the rain that the evening had brought with it and that was now falling, silently and soporifically, outside the window. Was she also lying as he was, remembering?

In the darkness he passed his hand across his face. So calm it was, the life that was flowing by, with dashes of raindrops on the windows. 'Live well,' she had whispered, 'live well.' But that, too, was far away, like the rain.

From The Diary

1907

3.9

The dark summer went and all the flowers and trees died, and came to visit me where I lay. I saw myself there, and wept. Now Dr Wargentin is forcing me to write, but I am disguising my handwriting so he won't be able to read it. Elin is sitting on a chair, watching me, I see. There is Neckan* with dead open mouth, and he that was Axel but now is dead.

12.9

Have been very ill, but am now able to sit up. Reading Janne with difficulty. Dizziness and sense that something dreadful has taken place. Confused images of faces. Elin is coming to take me to Jaskara.

3.10

In Jumesniemi again. Janne has sent the music of the Third Symphony, the second movement is like a 'God who loves His children dear'. It is comparable to the Allegretto in Beethoven's Seventh, but even richer. Regarding the allegro development in *Pohjola's Daughter*: the allegro tempo should not be observed too strictly: much of the polyphony is then lost, *allegro ma non troppo* would be nearer the mark. Dreamed that I visited Wecksell's grave, he came towards me with pale features and a streak of blood at his temple, woke up and remembered what he looked like, how almost every day he came to see my parents at no. 16 Södra Esplanadgatan, the Röö House, the house in which I was born, in order to call for his friend Valfrid Alftan, who lived as a lodger with us. He was even then marked by loneliness and illness, neurasthenic nervousness, restlessness and sudden, feverishly blazing joy. He suffered from insomnia and his face ran down the mirror as when strangers look at me.

17.11

Clear-headed but weak. My strength is ebbing. I have written a farewell letter to Aino and have asked her to show it to Janne only when I have departed. I can do no more. They have shown me great patience in my outbursts of moodiness and my nervous illness. Life is mystical and dreamlike, death an unfathomed mystery. The new visionary symphony will remain unheard by me.

24.12

By the burning candles in the darkness Rakel beloved the despair leave me I want to rest

1908

15.1

The Misses have been nursing me and have given me a religious book as a present, I have been weak and can't remember the summer or the autumn.

13.2

The first letter from Janne in many years. He is worried about his throat, he has been suffering from influenza and sleeplessness and is trying to continue his work on *Svanevit*, he is to visit London, my letter is hardly mentioned, Aino the finely-sensitive soul has perhaps only hinted at its contents. Tormented by remorse about my letter.

3.3

For all that, I was once a child who yearned, and Mother understood me.

12.3

As I sit motionless on a chair by the window I am like a potted palm, one of the household effects. Then comes the tranquillity that reigned back at home. It's a long time ago, but I remember it, then it disappears again, and I am seized with violent agitation and then the feeling that nothing concerns me. It is like being hurled from wall to wall by the wind.

19.3

Took a walk to Tammer Rapids, but I became so tired by the crowd that I had to seek refuge in the nearest spot to hand, which was an automat*, where there was a smell of bouillon, cabbage soup and Russian pastries. People bolting, gulping and swallowing with open mouths and unseeing eyes, with sweaty foreheads and white cheekbones. Jaws grinding and throats stretching while faces redden with the effort, are soiled and creased. Unsteady hands with stabbing and cutting weapons attacking the dead creatures, the limp vegetables, the fish torn from the water; lips bulging, glasses and cutlery knocking against each other, trouser waistbands loosened for bellies that swell more and more, mouths ringed with grease emit porridgy sounds, the whole company is slowly sinking in a sea of food and *brännvin*, to an accompaniment of yells and groans, strainings and belches. Fled, and am belching this up in my turn, in my silent room. Am unable to listen to music, the contrast is too great – it is unendurable, the beautiful sound but also this slurping and gorging, and these the poorest people, scraping their plates with their knives so that the screech passes through marrow and bone. That is music 'with a vengeance'. It wears me down.

23.4

I have heard it said that when Janne conducted his Third Symphony in St Petersburg last January, a certain Dr Botin came up to Aino's and Madame Siloti's box and let off a mighty stream of invective against the work, unaware that Aino knew Russian. In the face of anything new people are for the most part stupid ignoramuses, and most of what is great in art has at some time been mocked, unrecognized, betrayed or misunderstood.

13.5

Janne has asked me for the score of his Second String Quartet, I assume he means the one in B major. I have never had it, remember its bright tone, its quality of restraint, and recall that I must have seen it in Kajanus's home some time around 1902. How can Janne be so careless? It's not as if it were a matter of some old box of cigars, after all.

14.5

The fearful cold weather has continued, and Näsijärvi and Pyhäjärvi are still covered in ice. The house I am living in is to be demolished and a move to Jaskara awaits. How I will manage to endure the cold I do not know.

20.5

Aino and Janne have been forced to resort to beggary along Henriksgatan in Helsingfors, going from bench to bench in order to raise the money for Janne's throat operation. In the end the friendly director of an insurance company took pity on them. It is a disgrace for the country and a humiliation for Aino and Janne.

26.5

The expression of pain and despair in music demands a total mastery of form if it is not to become turgid. The pain and despair must be there at a distance, viewed dispassionately. Many a composer founders on this paradox, in despair and pain.

29.5

Even through my window I can smell the fragrance of spring.

3.6

I have joined the other human relics which, with due observance of all the rules of propriety, seek oblivion in Miss Rosendahl's rest-home at Sonabacka, Skuru. A much-savoured diversion is to stroll down and watch the train pass.

12.6

Reading Vitalis Norström's *Lines of Thought*. A letter from Janne has arrived: 'I don't know why I should have thought about you practically every moment today, unless it is because you might possibly be interested to hear about my illness. It isn't cancer, as the doctors believed. They sent me to Geheimrat Fränkel in Berlin, he's the best man around in these matters. Have now been to see him 9 times. But not even he has succeeded in removing the scourge that plagues me. It would be strange, though perfectly possible, if you were to live longer than I.' Yes, it certainly would be strange, and quite impossible! But there is in his thoughts a warmth that does me more good than weeks of egg gruel.

17.6

I took part in a violent debate about the extent to which art ought to reflect its own time. If music were to do it – what would it be but a cacophony of broken melodies? But music imparts wholeness, beauty, seriousness, and is a solitary quest that always moves ahead of (or rather above or underneath) the swiftly–changing 'currents' or 'topical' ideas. They smell stale after a few years and are replaced by something 'new'. But the new is the wind moving in the forest glade, the hidden waterfall, the silently lamenting person, a gaze, a touch, a farewell. It is the pain of living, eternal and ever new. It is the blessedness of hope, the silence in that which has been determined by fate. Music always reflects its own time when it is at its most momentous: the passage of the seasons, the alternations of the landscape, the new forms of the clouds, the echo of the swans in flight: it is the eternally new, it is *experimentum* = experience', in the sense that the Ancient Romans meant it. Forest, sea and sky, and strangers roaming about or sitting motionless on a silent veranda, is that not new, drenched in time? Must music reflect women's fashions? Men's fashions? The state of the parties in Parliament? Oh no, Axel is having his little joke! What do they want, then? A debate!

20.6
After thirteen unsuccessful attempts the tumour has finally been removed from Janne's throat. Now he is forbidden both tobacco and alcohol. Ah well!

28.6
Helsingfors in summer: the dream of my childhood. Windows open on Esplanadgatan, the echo of hooves and wheels, low houses outside around the square, I remember the wooden scaffolding around the Uspensky Cathedral. Still the same fishing-boat sea of masts and grey sails, cliffs, but the paths across the rocks out at Skatudden have now gone. Gone: the small, dirty wooden cross-gates spread out like frightened vermin in the crevices, hilltops with lonely bath-houses, and stone villas in Brunnsparken. Potato patches and back yards, torchlight processions in winter along the Esplanade and the skaters on the ice at Södra Hamnen, there I flew onwards, alone. The air in the shops charged with leather and lamp-oil, excursions to the customs-posts out past the Karamzin House★; I remember the shanties behind the wooden bridge over to Hagnäs and the balls at the City Hotel, all gone.

5.7
Slow walk on Pyynikki, overcast and oppressive. Sometimes nature fills me with terror: will my remains decompose in the earth

in order to produce flowers and trees whose roots will stretch through ribs and eyesockets?

13.8

The summer is going past my window. Heard from Janne about his meeting with Mahler last year; how during it Janne laid emphasis on the symphony's strictness and gravity, its deep logic that unites all the elements into one. Mahler replied that he was not of the same opinion: the symphony ought to be a world, embracing everything; apparently the composition of Janne's that Mahler listened to was the eternal *Valse Triste*. Could Janne not have showed him the score of the C major symphony? Heat: it is cold that is the friend of lively activity, not heat. Now for the second week running. Trying to rest, lying motionless, and know the damp patches on the ceiling off by heart. Sound now painful with its dull, shapeless moistness. From this a vindication of cold, of control, action, strategy. Even the military kind: ditto. The most extreme precision will be the saving of this country.

3.9

The firewood-man struck up a conversation with me. 'The way the axe splits the wood, that's how they'll split up there one day' – a gesture towards his head – 'the gentry.' Merry, blinking eyes, then turned his back to me.

22.9

Peter Altenberg: 'My compassion was always greatest when I saw life wanting to rest from life (in the presence of my dead mother).'

26.9

Saw in a dream Aino bent over as if in pain, completely alone, and then she faded away.

2.10

The trees are burning. To attain detachment; to see the traces of autumn in the spring soil and its omens as early as July. To perceive what unites us and what divides us, and not to be blocked in this perception by details. To see and feel life's undular motion and to realize that it is no more than this motion, this recurring breeze. The meaning of life? To have lived as a part of the wave, oneself a wave, soon obliterated.

2.11

Since Seyn* arrived our shortlived freedom has begun to be stifled. And yet: this country exists as a whole, and will continue to do so, in spite of xenophobia, self-contempt, melancholy, unruliness, silence, hunched over a dark sea, listening... For there is a riddle concealed there which no one can answer, but through listening may approach. Then death's power is cancelled.

6.11

Suddenly occurring and painful intensifications of light and sound, so that I am unable to move, can only lie motionless. This is my fate and my destiny. Tried to compose, and burned again. One Axel in the desk drawer, another in the stove, yet another, the most silent and ugliest one, in the daylight. After severe pain a great calm. Dreamed of a music, and it coincided with Janne's; I knew it, saw it. Like a musical score in a dark room, lit by lightning. It had always been there, and was timeless.

10.11

For four days total peace. My body is shrivelling like paper in fire, the skin is drawing itself tight across my face, as on the face of a dying man, but my cool faith continues. I dream of an ordered, rational world, with regard not to content, but to form. If God had thought more about this when he created the world a great deal of confusion could have been avoided. More form is what every true artist has tried to give it. The form of longing is for Janne the wingbeat of swans and cranes: how eternal, and outside the everyday human context, a dream of the formless format. It is perhaps understandable that Janne is not interested in Leitmotifs: the forming process must follow its own laws which are not, and can never be, laid down in advance. But what do these birds see with their cold eyes? Do they see the lakes, the trees, and Janne rushing down to the shore in order to listen for their signs? Signs of what? Of the fact that life contains the seeds of death, and death those of life? Is that the source of Janne's fear of death? Is that the source of the weight of death in his music, a weight which he tries to overcome, like a man balancing a rock on his fingertips? The inhuman oppresses me, and yet: there it possesses a light that need no longer be dreaded. Time stands still as in dreams and describes what we experienced back in our childhood: the eternal recurrence, the seasons, and how all things flow towards silence, and attain it. Musical outbursts for Janne merely gates that open on to eternal existence. When we are dead the birds will descend on to the dark water of Träskända as before, like us, leaving no traces, but existing as names – swan and crane, duck and swallow – when our names have been forgotten.

11.11

Dreamed about Janne. He walked in front of me and into a dark forest, as into a wall, and turned round, waved, dressed in a smart dark suit, his shirt collar gleaming, turned up towards his chin, on his head he had a black top-hat, as though for mourning. I hesitated but followed, the darkness closed around me and I couldn't see him any more, shouted, but no one heard me, snow was falling over a mirror-calm bay, he stood on the opposite shore looking at me, intently, then disappeared. I awoke in tears.

14.11

Janne's affairs in a dreadful mess. Urged him to go and see Rettig in Åbo. He has 'great plans': a symphonic poem. He is living without nicotine and alcohol – at last! Pater Familias! Aino gave birth to a child in September. Dreamed about Mother. Her sitting beside me and us looking at my feet and the hole in the toe, and it spread and expanded like an enormous lake, and that was all there was.

18.11

What remains in my memory of Mother and Father? There are memories which have become so strangely clear. Father shading his eyes with his hand as he took his afternoon nap. There was something emaciated, bitter and withered-away about his voice and his manner. He was a champion of justice who was shipwrecked on it, an orator who heard his own voice go silent. His orderliness became a straitjacket, the gentleness that broke forth in his old age was there but often received no expression. A watch-chain, a thin frame, a waistcoat, a perpetually stiff collar, a gaze that would lose itself in the twilight, an utterly dry and cold hand that seldom touched me, something about him from the very beginning alone, upright and isolated. And how he lived with Mother who was overflowing with joyfulness, life and – naïveté, how he became helpless in the last year after Mother's death. It feels as though they remembered me better than I remember them. I remember the sunlit floors, the long, white carpets of the big drawing-room, but Father and Mother, moving from room to room, are so pale. No, it is only Mother who moves, comes running while Father stands like a dark shadow in the background, and she enfolds me, enfolds my face in her small, narrow hands that are warm with excitement, with joy in life. She sits on the edge of my bed, but Father stands at the writing-desk in the library, looking out of the window. As though he were waiting for something, an instruction from the Ministry he left, a redress for some hidden wrong?

Am I increasingly living their lives? Because I can't live my own? There is a hunger, a burning sense that they could give me something other than these memories and dreams in which doors are closed, voices are muffled, and each sound is almost painfully clear for me. Mother taught me the names of the stars, she is the evening star. I am standing on the roof balcony, a fragrance of lilacs is borne up by the warm breeze, the window of Father and Mother's bedroom is gleaming, shadows are moving there, and it is as though I knew what the future is going to bring with it: the window will grow dark, I will go down the staircase, open the door and close it, and I will be alone and forgotten.

26.11

I have again had a letter from Janne. He writes that he can see from my letters how I live in the past and in my childhood, adding: 'In fact I believe that spiritual baths of this kind are a vital necessity for the soul. It is as if one perceived the guiding principles of one's life, and understood them better. Now that I have come to rest I am able to obtain a true insight into my life and my art, and think I can achieve a constant forward development – the only thing that will satisfy me. The unmusical Goethe uttered what is perhaps the greatest musical truth in his *Sprüche*. And he has of late given me backbone.' Yes, this bears evidence of calm and detachment, and augurs well for the Fourth Symphony.

17.12

The second desperate letter from Janne, his financial affairs are in total disorder, the spells of hypochondria come and go, he suffers from depression and despair, and loans fall due. It doesn't make my physical condition of exhaustion and respiratory trouble any better. This accursed winter the darkness is like a wall, and at night I beat against it until my hands bleed. But about pecuniary misery something ought to be done, he is after all the gathering force. I have written to Cousin Tor, perhaps it might be possible to organize a national appeal. There must be enough citizens who are sufficiently far-sighted in order for this to be put through.

24.12

Another Christmas Eve has gone and the light is flickering like a vital flame. I remember the big drawing-room at Odensaari, the servants, and Mother full of joy and devotion embracing us all.

1909

10.1

Janne has asked me to find out how long the best-known string quartets are!

18.1

I am not content with poverty and do not get used to it either, but put up a secret fight, have recourse to my pen, write to right and to left, that is my way of speaking, and when I must speak I grow silent.

23.1

Both Aino and I are trying to protect Janne, but he is often his own worst enemy, and I suppose it must be that way, so that he can overcome him (himself) and attain clarity. Aino can remember how her father, too, used to wander to and fro in the hall of her childhood home, how rigid he was and how lively her mother. There is much that was the same, and which does not need to be clothed in words. Even the closed, the pessimistic, the life-melancholy is familiar to her. Hostile criticism strikes at her very roots, far more deeply than Janne who is essentially healthy, merely grumbles and goes on his way.

28.1

Review in *Hufvudstadsbladet* of Siloti's performance of *Night Ride and Sunrise* shows that he has ruined Janne's composition. *Novoye Vremya* is ironic, *Novaya Rus'* somewhat better. So: a fiasco in St Petersburg, and it doesn't surprise me. What effect will this have on the already tormented Janne? His throat, his financial affairs... He has also had a murderous review from Krehbiel in New York. How could they possibly understand Janne's inner landscape, in which he is most alone and most intimate?

4.2

Have been studying Haydn. There is music that dances, hops, leaps and runs, music that sits still and watches. Haydn's music is a naturally walking music, to the accompaniment of quiet breathing I see in it towns, landscapes, people in contact and closeness, in a single shared space. That is the human.

20.2

Two items of news ought to be noted down: that Janne has had great success in London, and that in front of Parliament Svinhufvud has refused to bow to the Tsar's demand for obedience.

2.3

Days somewhat lighter. Have been taking the usual walks, new houses are sprouting up and old ones are sinking into the ground. Aino had had word from London about Janne, he had been to a ball, met Debussy who apparently suffers as much on the rostrum as Janne. These suffering, dancing artists, these creators of that which is most fleeting and most durable, do they see us at all as we wander about with our collars turned up and our trouser-legs too short in the cold, preoccupied with the thought of how we are going to manage the following day, and of whether there's fuel in the primus stove?

25.3

It is milder, and my strolls have lengthened. Look in on people at their tables, families who invariably *'sont dans le vrai'*, as Flaubert says. But in my feeling of exclusion there is one great advantage: as a rule I can harm only myself.

3.4

I have all the time in the world in which to philosophize. I wonder if anyone is really interested in what a person really is, as long as he is active. His actions can be a mirror of what he is. But a person is many people, and behind an action of seeming refinement there can hide a brutal liar. Don't be too sure of yourself! Perhaps it wasn't you who performed those actions. I want to see what you are like when you're alone.

8.4

The ice has broken up with a rumble, and it is spring.

25.4.1909

There is a long corridor and rooms in a row; white curtains lead moonlight in across the dizzying floor, and Axel sees Doctor Wargentin standing over by a black window. So many hangings, so much silence. People near doors are talking softly to one another and turn away when he approaches. But the walls, too, approach, there is something like cobwebs and a faint murmur of water that is getting louder. Is that not Janne there in a Panama hat and white suit? He is looking at him with amusement, puffing away at a reeking Sibelius cigar, and rings of smoke are drifting out through the open window where black trees move in lamentation. Axel sees himself standing there, the wind is great and thundering like sails.

Now Doctor Wargentin is coming closer, he is talking incessantly, but Axel is unable to hear what he is saying. He is pointing to a picture, surely it is Josephson's* *Neckan*, the mouth wide-open and black like all death's mouths, the suffering penetrates the body in music, in shrill tones which the water in vain seeks to drown. And yet it is silent, is it at a gesture from Doctor Wargentin that all life ceases? There is something like a contour of fire and unbearable light around him, and Axel sees his own mirror-image. Under each picture another one! So heavy, cold and dark in the corners, above the oak floor, over towards the panelled walls, where an old woman sits on a chair, weeping. It is Mother, she is dressed in white, but she doesn't want to look at him, just sits there wringing her hands, and a path of light falls over her so that she is almost obliterated.

Now he can hear what Doctor Wargentin is saying: 'Total inept idiocy!' He can read his lips. It is what he has always known. It is lightning-like, and sweeps away tables, chairs and walls, and there are wintry roads and trees in a violent gale. A clamour in the air, as though someone were weeping. There is the murmur of oar-strokes across water, the tinkling sound of water, calm and healing. The stroke of bows from an invisible orchestra. And Axel

281

in his shabby clothes, why hasn't he smartened himself up, he runs through the streets like a clown, trousers, jacket, trailing coat – he who is normally so tidy! He stops, there is a shadowing hat, a horse-face, someone taking him by the arm, it is his lady piano teacher: he is doomed. His heart beats so loudly that he wakes up.

Dawn and the faint singing of birds. He tries to recall, yet doesn't want to, the sheet is twisted, he is wet with sweat. Her face, but it drifts into the face of the other woman, she caresses him absent-mindedly, she despises him. Despised him. In the corner the simple iron stove glows white. From Estnäsgatan not a sound. As though he had drowned but by his own effort had struggled to the surface and was now resting there, exhausted. The whimpering of heart-beats against the sprung base of the mattress. The tenacious life of the body. And he knows that this is one of those days when everything will affect him. As in his childhood, when Mother leaned over him, so that he lay in shadow.

This is Axel, this and the fear that his face is the face of everyone, and no one. He sits up, birdneck under a face that is sagging in folds, so that his cranium is slowly being exposed. In this well this dark water, and nowhere a lasting abode. His gaze rigid, his forehead wet with sweat, and behind the wall noise, voices, the day getting screechingly underway, the quick, vicious barking of a dog, the cross of the window-frame black against the white dawn light. Had he been dreaming, or were these hallucinations? They disappear into oblivion, and he clings fast to the memory of yesterday, his conversation with Tor, the quiet, green lamp, their friendship's odour of security. A spasm of fear that he has lost his wallet: no, it's there, in his jacket's inside pocket. He must get out of here, of the boarding-house, he is to meet his sister Elin in only half an hour's time, he must collect himself, get dressed, he has a thousand things to think of, he must unravel all this, master the orchestra, drive off the wild music, the dawning panic, raise his arms: silence, and the gentlest, softest upbeat. Axel stands on the floor in his nightshirt with his eyes closed, lets his arms sink down.

On his way to Elin's he stumbles in the gateway over a man asleep, the whites of his eyes visible under half-closed lids, a gaping mouth – is he dying? But the smell of *brännvin* slams into him as from human excrement, and he hurries out into the April gale and up the hill of Estnäsgatan. Wooden houses and newly-erected stones, the bumpy landscape of Kronohagen, intimate and compact. There is a street-mirror, as tall as a man and adorned with gold lettering, he catches a glimpse of himself, a stranger, and stops. This exhausted face above the velvet collar and those sloping shoulders, the cane – unpleasant and unfamiliar. He hurries on, towards Konstantinsgatan. Scurrying April clouds, and on the corner of Mariegatan the smell of fresh horse dung; *izvozchiki* are already rolling down towards Salutorget, and a seagull is scream-ing derisively. On the corner of Konstantinsgatan two Russian soldiers are standing, he makes a detour, there's a smell there too, boot-grease, and the voices, scorn and saliva. A city of raw winds, rawer than the ones in Tammerfors, but also freer: the sea. Inside the gateway he has to stop and lean against the wall, only a swiftly-passing indisposition. He tries to remember a musical theme, any one at all will do, a melody, a song, a consolation; but even in the gateway the wind is blowing, and a sun-reflection from a window being closed is hurled like a token of spring across the courtyard. On the staircase a woman is scrubbing. In a window-niche stands a flowerpot with no flowers in it. Things to which no one pays any attention have a great consoling power. Axel goes mumbling up the staircase amidst the smell of soap. He is trying to breathe slowly: that is how one prolongs one's life and cheats death, by preserving one's calm in all situations. For a few minutes he stands still outside the door, its nameplate elegant with 'Elin Färling' in cursive script.

Over coffee the terrible secret comes out, the moment has come, the disgrace is complete. Calmly, as it were in passing, as she nibbles at a biscuit, Elin relates that Margit has become engaged to a Russian officer. Axel gets up from the table, his hands grip its edge, Margit is in an adjacent room, he tries to keep his voice low, but it is forced up by his larynx – 'A disgrace! For the whole family, a disgrace! All right, so perhaps he's a Polish officer by birth, but his soul is in Tashkent – and this at a time when the country is being strangled – do you think I'm mad? Are you mad?'

His spectacles become steamed up, he takes them off, looks around him as though he might discover a way out, but they have captured him, set a trap for him, attacked him where he is most painfully vulnerable: in his honour. Elin's expression is quite inscrutable, her lips move but he is unable to hear what she is saying, cake-crumbs have become lodged in the corners of her mouth, her eyes are watery, they have the same eyes, all the brothers and sisters, her chin quivers. For the sake of a pair of deceiving eyes and a uniform that belongs to the enemy, the brutal extortionist – the uniform of the executioner – the family's honour has been sold. 'It's a disgrace,' he repeats, 'a disgrace to the whole family! How can you allow this to happen?' 'And who's a disgrace to the family, I'd like to know!' Elin shrieks. 'Who? Take a look at yourself in the mirror!'

Elin bursts into tears and Axel moves back, trembling, towards the door. 'Not another word!' he manages to get out, 'Not another word! I shall go mad!' And Elin raises her wet features and looks at him: 'You're mad already! Don't you understand?' Then, as though realizing what she has said, her eyes widen, her mouth hangs half-open, the room becomes quiet, completely quiet, and the only sound that can be heard is Margit's whimpering behind the closed door. Axel turns and practically runs out into the hallway, gets his coat and hat on and rushes outside. There is a thundering between the old ceiling vaults, the wooden staircase snakes towards him, he hurls himself out into the street, doesn't know which way to go. Almost blindly, he knocks into dresses, hairstyles, clouds of perfume, has to make his excuses, bow, take off his hat, he is streaming with sweat. His legs carry him down a hill, it is Konstantinsgatan, and he reaches Kanaltorget where the Uspensky Cathedral towers up before him on its treeless clump of rock. Sand blows in his eyes, and the water slaps against the landing-stages with its 'clip-clap' sound, utterly indifferent and mechanical. He tries to remember Fredrik, Elin's husband, what would he have said? Four Russian officers are coming towards him, laughing loudly, as though they wanted to mock him, they don't see him, but he sees them, their epaulettes, their boot-flaps, their strutting: just wait! One day their happiness, their success with women and their mockery will come to an end, and a bloody end, too! In spite of everything, in spite of all the humiliations he has suffered he still retains – his honour!

He turns up his collar, a cold and cutting wind is blowing on Salutorget and he makes his way up the leeward side of Riddar-huset, stand in the park for a while. He is totally alone now, he can no longer go to Elin's home, the thought of suicide enters his mind. He could throw himself off one of the landing-stages, but the water would surely be cold. He knows he would start shouting and be rescued, an absurd figure, and his action, too, absurd. He has no guns, he abominates them. Sleeping pills – yes! To finally get all the sleep he wants. He begins walking back to Estnäsgatan. He slackens his pace, then moves more quickly. Each sound is a pain in his head. At last he reaches Estnäsgatan, the silent staircase, his room. Cousin Tor lives quite near, should he ring him? But he is not used to using the telephone. He must stand fast.

Slowly he takes off his coat and jacket, puts his hat on the table, starts to look in his bag. There are no sleeping pills there, he has left them all in Tammerfors, he is extremely careful with medicines, they can be habit-forming. He sits down on the edge of the bed. He brings his clenched hand to his mouth, bites it, there is blood. He wants to get up and scream, but is paralysed. It is growing dark outside, the sun is going behind the clouds. He lies down prostrate on his bed. Somewhere a baby is crying, and somewhere someone is beating a carpet in fury. It is as though he were finally being borne away, completely empty. He is destitute. There are no more images, and nothing to say.

From The Diary

26.4

Terrible dream about Engelbrecht Norberg's yellow row of teeth
and the lid being slowly raised, and a bestial mouth that was going
to swallow me up as I lay there with severed eyelids; all this like
a hallucination, with phosphorescent light. As I tumbled down I
had Julia D.'s horse-face close to me, and could not distinguish
one abyss from the other; then I sat up in bed, ran to the window,
pulled at it, but heavy beating at the door froze me into immobility.
Bertel came in with the cane I had left at Elin's, we were both
embarrassed to the point of speechlessness, but he gave off a great
deal of warmth, said he was a great admirer of Janne's. After he
had gone I lay exhausted, and Janne bent over me, dressed in a
white linen suit, in order to find out if there was still any material
for songs in me. Now it is time to walk to the Station; H-fors
unreal, as though T-fors had now become my home town, against
my will and like a hard, alien, cutting body in my own, truly a
town, living in every limb, with blood of bricks and smoke of
breath and the percussion of hatred against a mirroring sky! There,
too, from Pyynikki a view over the lakes, and not this cruel blast
that leaves the soul naked and screaming. Shabby notebook, to
you do I cry my need. Not to be loved is the most difficult thing
to overcome; it is a question then of living entirely in the external.
It is the most merciless light that illuminates each crevice of my
body, so that everything lies exposed, empty and scraped bare.
Total emptiness, total fullness of objects, remnants, sounds,
closets, beds, thin, threadbare clothes.

29.4

At home. Spring light. The human person a faint musical notation,
barely decipherable. But who has composed it? Someone who sat
in the darkness, furiously scribbling on the scarcely visible white

paper. The result uninterpreted.

3.5
Trees moving in the wind remind me of my childhood, as though they were touching me, or reaching out towards me as I lie in my bed.

10.6
Living a little less each day. What bungler was it who said that suffering ennobles? Myself? Suffering makes one bitter, crushes the will to happiness, succeeds in bringing about a state of indifference and turns its back on one, merely checking now and then that one is 'alive', it is the cuckoo chick that throws one out of the nest, south-cuckoo, death-cuckoo, and I hear it, but how many years it is measuring out I cannot tell; they cannot be all that many. Janne has returned from Berlin in a whirlwind of debts. Dogs barking. J: 'One of the few who understand my music and myself' – me!

3.7
Back in Siuro, Jaskara. In a meadow I see a cow: it inspires calm, whereas horses always seem to gallop towards the horizon. The cow creates an intelligent silence, a not insignificant contribution. Place a group of people on a meadow, and they will seem like walkers-on in a peasant drama; but the cows are at home in their own masticatory symphony. Swallows wait on telegraph wires like people about to migrate, cows wait for sleep and are rest in themselves; I envy them, and try to chew my daily bread more slowly. If life contained more rest and music were to follow life, slowly grazing and looking out over the meadows, some truth might be attained. Quiet happiness in cool air and evening mist.

10.7
Received the score of *Night Ride and Sunrise*, a present. Strange, ghostlike, visionary, journey through horrors to triumph, not defeat; far more effective than Liszt's *Mazeppa*. Finland lives. This music is my nourishment, my life.

23.7
Janne complains in a letter about his 'cycle of debts'. Elin visited me yesterday evening, we talked about Margit, and while she understood my point of view, she felt she could not interfere with

the girl's freedom in these matters. We made it up, but it left a bitter taste. It struck me that all my life I have lived for the most part among women. Father and Hjalmar were, after all, in many ways absent during my youth. Hence my attempts to come close to men: my correspondence with Viktor Rydberg, my friendship with Axel Tamm which I ruined with my selfish complaints, and now Janne. This female protectiveness and walking-about-on-tiptoe is paralysing me, making me ill-disposed towards those nearest me. I know for example that Lydia Rosengren takes the most sympathetic view of my debilities, it feels like a terrible burden. Under my clothes I burn for tenderness, it is my most secret dream: to be loved and to love in return. This constantly being driven to gratitude will destroy me. I am becoming ever more forgetful and slow-witted, my spontaneous feelings are being stifled, my eternal sense of guilt clings like a shirt of Nessus to my flesh, and I can only break free in my thoughts, in letters and diary notes, in reading and daydreams. But even in letters the invisible cruelty compels me to something false. That I find hard to endure. There is something about the feminine that stifles me, something about the masculine that repels me. A mental invalid, I live alone in my room and inhabit it with ghosts and Samaritans. 'I, glorious Ego!' to use Janne's words.

20.9

Letter from Janne about *Night Ride and Sunrise*, a title that always comes before me with graphic sharpness, in triumphant light. The trumpets at the end sound loudest (*fff*) when they are on their own.

15.10

I have written to Atterbom in Göteborg about the origins of *En Saga*. Janne has been to Koli, which was a great experience for him. I have read through the score of *Voces Intimae*, it is a quartet full of humour and generosity and reminds me of Beethoven. It is the coming triumph of idealism, but lasts not 25 minutes, as Janne claims, but 29–30. I have only found one mistake, at the bottom of p.16 where the first violin repeats the same figure alone (*'allargando'*) for three bars in succession, and then for a fourth bar when the cello comes in. The next quartet ought to be something in the style of Beethoven's C major op. 59 no.3, the slow movement of which has the character of a ballade, or even the F minor, op.95.

22.11

Seyn is now Governor General of the country and Markov is head of the Senate's financial department, things are looking black. Aino and Janne have invited me to Ainola to get a picture of their desperate financial plight. Slight dizziness and lapses of memory, small and insignificant. Janne has been complaining of a cold, and I have attributed it to the draughty position of the piano by the veranda door: perhaps it will have been moved by the time I get there.

30.11

There were the two worlds which Janne has to live with and which clash with each other. The debts now amount to 100,000, and Janne has not received an increase in his pension for 13 years. Aino was pale and under strain, and her anxiety could even be felt in the pressure of her hand. Janne improvised at the piano for a while, played *The Rock* and *The Wanderer's Thoughts*, everything centred on the coming Fourth Symphony. Hardly slept at all, travelled back early, Aino was asleep, Janne silent and reserved, then launched into a violent outburst about his financial plight and how degrading it was for him to have to beg year after year, and how Aino's strength had practically been exhausted by this. At the same time he spoke, with a characteristically swift change of subject, of the strength of the visionary, and of how the Fourth Symphony was going to be the innermost landscape of his soul. I am going to talk to Cousin Tor and Magnus Dahlström★.

6.12

We sat in a private room at the Catani Restaurant, Werner Söderhjelm★, Ernst Lindelöf★, Tor and I. I had a draft of the petition with me and maintained that it was in the interest of the whole nation that Janne be rescued, that he was in the process of creating his own Mont Blanc, *Voces Intimae* and the Fourth Symphony, and that I was convinced of their greatness. In order to complete this edifice he needed complete peace in which to work. Söderhjelm undertook to polish up the wording of my text here and there and to send it on to Leo Mechelin★. If we get the signatures of L.M. and Walter Runberg★, we shan't need any more (?). Our next port of call is Consul Ek★. Magnus Dahlström is a key figure here if the great lottery is to fall in our favour. Finally I told them that I did not want my name to appear on the petition. This must be respected! In this context, my name is insignificant. But it must be done, and done quickly! After the gentlemen had left I had a conversation with my close friend Tor. I told him about my amnesia and about Ainola, how absent I had been there, about my intermittent awareness as a result of insomnia and thoughts of death, told him about Elin's daughter's engagement. Since the age of seven I have been deeply damaged. No one has yet looked into my soul – I would like to but *cannot* explain what lies in anxiety on the bottom there, like a leaden weight. Tor grasped my hand, we didn't need words. Told him how on my way to Ernst Lindelöf's on Tuesday I fell headlong in the street, knocked my head on the pavement and got a burning headache. As I was, after all, in Helsingfors, I went to the opera and saw *Madame Butterfly*. If this is the apogee of *verismo*, then *verismo* isn't doing very well. The whole of the second act is a musical fiasco, the greater part of the third act likewise. Ida Ekman was terrible – no, the opera is quite categorically an abomination, a devaluation of music and also of drama. 'It was what I said' sung *forte*! What I heard of the Fourth Symphony made a tremendous impression on me when Janne played it to me. But he ought to get out and shovel some snow, otherwise he'll get too *fat*! I accompanied Tor to Kronohagen, the Senate Square lay empty and serene, and there was a strong, wintry blast from the sea. Life surrounded me on every side, I felt a new strength, and when I reached my room I fell asleep instantly, as though I had been clubbed!

27.12

Janne has thanked me, but I told him that I had already conveyed his thanks to Magnus Dahlström. Read Merezhkovsky's *Gogol And His Devil*, in which I discovered the following: 'The whole of his life was one slow, continuous process of dying – his face was inscrutable, and there was nothing to betray the fact that the most terrible thoughts and visions passed through his soul, as his features bore the imprint of the greatest calm.' These words feel at once so familiar and so alien, as though with all the strength at my disposal I were trying to rise up against a truth.

31.12

The housemaid is clattering about, tidying up like a madwoman, it is freezing cold everywhere.

15.1

To be noted: I am fifty-two. On this same day, but somewhat earlier, were born Moliére and Grillparzer, the authors of *Le Malade Imaginaire* and *Weh dem, der lügt*. This as a curiosity.

3.3

These have been difficult weeks, but a break in the clouds is visible. Have written letters to Tor, Werner Söderhjelm, Yrjö Hirn*, Guss Mattsson* and Sigurd Frosterus in order to save Janne from ruin, and have got writer's cramp, on top of all my other cramps.

7.3

Went to consult Christian Sibelius about the ailments that torment me, he accepted a poor man's fee, and showed the most sensitive cordiality and insight. Here in Tammerfors the mood is heavy, and the Inland Revenue are harassing me even though I own nothing.

27.3

I must go to Helsingfors, the rescue project is now underway, and Tor has put rooms at my disposal.

5.4

Janne has written to thank me with all his heart, and my own is full of joy: the situation has been saved on this occasion and thereby also the Fourth Symphony. But otherwise the thumbscrews are still being tightened, in Helsingfors I saw militia everywhere, and the Imperial decree is leading towards an impossible situation.

18.4

The spirit stove in my room exploded and I was nearly blinded. There was no one in the house at the time and some potted plants and the small curtains at the window caught fire. I didn't dare open the window to shout for help, as the fire would then have spread rapidly, so the only thing for it was to put it out myself. I got a burn on my left hand and now my arthritis has joined in, too. It seemed quite natural to me that this should happen.

20.4

Voces intimae moves me deeply. The first movement expresses something of a longing for eternity, the second is full of fantasy and humour, the third movement is a reply to the second, and a new world is glimpsed. The cello replies in C minor to the question of questions – behind the veil there is an eternal reality, that which we most desire. The movement's Faust-yearning subsides and dies away peacefully, mysteriously. The fourth movement is a religious dance, it is innocence and melancholy. The final movement alternates humour with country fiddler's tunes. The whole quartet displays a total fusion of form and content.

27.4

Voces Intimae had its first performance in Helsingfors two days ago. I couldn't go, am completely besieged in T-fors by the Inland Revenue's demands for 320 marks, and I have nothing. The house is also to be repaired, and then I shall have to leave, but where will I go? I have sent Janne Ture Rangström's music criticism. Something is happening in Sweden, a change for the better, there are new critics who appreciate Janne.

23.5

I am back in Nådendal in the beautiful, green-speckled spring, as though I were back in my childhood again. Am staying in Gerda Rancken's house, and almost everything I see reminds me of Rakel. It is completely light and quiet by the window at night, and all that is heard is the scrape of my pen on the paper. Have not written to Rakel, but am certain I will still meet her. In the silence I often have the most violent dreams, between sleeping and waking, they are drying me up. Have been forced to go to a few coffee mornings, sit on the edge of my chair and make conversation, and then a smothered cry rises up inside me, it is as if I were betraying myself.

25.5

Father stood living before me again, pointed at me, and I obeyed. The relationship between Mother and him was not without conflict, I remember her tearful silence and his rigidity. Where he would refuse, she would secretly permit, and I would struggle between saying nothing and being honest with my ever-righteous father. When I was caught with a piece of cake I had to confess I had stolen it, and Mother did not dare to say she had given her permission: she drew the line at that. As though I only saw that now, in all its clarity. I remember sitting locked in the dark cupboard, my head pressed to the door, in thunderous silence; that must have been before my tenth birthday. Mother came and unlocked the door, but I didn't dare to leave the cupboard, I backed and backed away, there was a wall I couldn't back through, the darkness was full of old clothes, of dead things and the smell of sawdust and summer-warm paper. In the end she had to give up, whispering, left the door open and I closed it, closed it for ever, didn't cry, didn't shout, sat there until Father came, whereupon I immediately crept off to bed. There I lay completely alone, and it is true that the lightning strikes me and marks me with the brand of uselessness.

28.5
Woken by someone screaming. Saw the window-sash snap, the curtain blow like a banner, the darkness surge in and defile the springtime, flowers screamed and I was buried by this suffocating, incomprehensible thing, and was unable to breathe.

3.6
Did the dead ever take their leave of me? I can't remember it. Did they think they were going to live for all eternity, or were they already so far away that they did not know what was happening? I was not present at Hjalmar's deathbed, but saw the aunts quickly burn up and be extinguished by their pneumonia, just a fire taking the short, easy leap from one withered tree to another. But I remember the deaths of Mother and Father. There was in the bedroom a silence deeper than loss, and Mother's half-closed eyes; everything was changing, and she had finally abandoned me. After that, Father soon faded away, and I was gripped by a strange sense of compassion, which I had never felt earlier, but which ever since has haunted me in the presence of man's loneliness. Does my turning back to childhood mean that something unchangeable has sneaked its way in, like a premonition of autumn on the most beautiful day in June? The bird-cherry is in blossom, the lilacs are coming out, the bustle of the harbour sounds as it has always done, and in the kitchen there is singing, making my heart suddenly beat faster, in confusion, until I see that it's not Rakel.

8.6
In a small town most conversations turn into gossip. I am only a few bays south of my childhood haunts. If one listens to the wind it is obvious that it isn't even, but rises and falls away again differently in different places, makes its leaps from tree to tree, storms about

293

in the summit of the birch but scarcely breathes in the tree next to it, until suddenly the whole chorus breaks forth with rustling, quivering foliage. That sound is a lonely one, and was already there when I was a child and could not sleep. It is completely natural that composers should have keen senses, in the way that tightrope-walkers have a keen sense of balance. And I? A keen self-criticism that affects all my senses to the point where I become incapable of action.

11.7
Back in Siuro, Jaskara again. Janne has sent me Ekelund's *The Classical Ideal*★, a purifying bath and an exhortation to responsibility in life and action. 'This healthy longing for Apollo's hyperborean land of miracles on the other side of joy and woe, on the other side of twilight and melancholy and cloudy passion.' Perhaps that healthy longing can be understood at its deepest level only by those who are familiar with grave illness?

15.7
The daily rituals, the observation of time and space, protect me from further torments. Habit maintains order over that which threatens to disintegrate into fragments and may even be capable of summoning up a pattern if it really tries. Were it not for habit we would change fashions like women who refuse to grow old and who plaster themselves with make-up. Habit is in league not with time that counts minutes or seconds, but with the seasons. It is a refuge that can turn into a prison.

8.8
When I am sitting still first one knee begins suddenly to quiver, then the whole of my body, and I am unable to stop it. This is followed by an intense feeling of cold and emptiness, followed in turn by loss of memory. At such times my bed often seems to be on the glide, and I have to lie down in order not to be hurled out into space. I get up again in fear and dizziness. Did Father suffer from this? After all, he did use to lie in a dark room and we were not allowed to disturb him.

18.8
Janne has composed some new songs, is going to Norway in October, and is to conduct his Fourth Symphony in Helsingfors in November – four is, according to him, 'a proud number for a

symphony, and I am only 44'. What kind of a number mysticism is this? He has sent me Goethe's works and confesses that he is not a mite interested in politics – I had written to him about my fears concerning the situation in the country. He says he works solely 'for king and country'. What king? He works for his Muse.

12.10

Aino's arthritis is now so bad that she has had to go to hospital, while Janne's life is entirely absorbed in the Fourth Symphony, though that is taking its time. So far as I can see, it is not just simply worries about money that are to blame – fading creative powers, bad conscience and uncertainty are also playing a role. Wrote immediately; he must believe in his ability, it is great, formidable and vitally important for us all.

24.11

Janne has sent me 'The Dryad' and 'Impromptu' – the latter with a strange breath of late antiquity. As I know that Janne is interested in Tavaststjerna, I have now reread his poetry – it is high-school stuff with unintentional humour, a mish-mash of unmeaning and platitudes. Between T. and Wecksell there is the same difference as between a bit of glass and a precious stone.

1911

1.1

A new year is coming in with great anxiety, resignation and indifference. I am reading Bergson and brooding about the nature of music; the difficulty about seeing it as a language is that it has no object, it does nothing but simply is, and this 'is' is in a certain sense opaque. It is the listener who 'does' something, who acts and recreates it as images, memories, emotions. Music in itself is none of this or all of it, gathered into an 'is', a *now*, an eternal moment.

26.1.1911

He saw the blood that was flowing from the wrist, and the fear in the man's eyes. He also saw the shame, as though it had stuck to him. He had heard him calling in a feeble voice for help. Fortunately the door was unlocked, he had hurried in and seen him lying on the sofa, a trail of blood on the floor from the wash-stand over to where he lay whimpering softly, as though someone had wronged him. He had clumsily tried to slash the artery in one of his wrists. Axel jerked a towel towards him and tied it hard around the man's arm, but the blood continued to flow. On the table lay the flute that had caused him such torment during the weeks gone by, he had not heard it these last few days, now he remembered it, he had marvelled at how sad it was.

He knew him slightly. He was a shy and reticent man, always friendly and correct. His wife and children lived in Helsingfors during the autumn semester. The man was alone, an insurance inspector with a Russian-sounding name, but Swedish through and through, and his Finnish was rather halting. The family was from Vyborg – Axel had asked in what language he had his roots, and for a moment a hesitation had slipped across the man's features. Without answering, he had suddenly withdrawn inside his shell.

He now looked intently at Axel, whispered that he had not wanted to be a nuisance, that he knew that Axel suffered from insomnia, but that he felt remorse. There was in the room a great, lonely silence, and Axel hurried out to ask for help. Again and again the man kept saying that he could not take any more, and that he was not the only one. He said he was being persecuted. Axel appealed to him to be quiet, saying that help was on its way. 'I'm a coward, a coward', the man kept saying. Then he lay in silence, his face pale and the towel soaked through, black in the half-light. He saw the blood flowing from his wrist and the objects that stood expectantly in the room. 'You're going to be all right,' Axel said, 'you're going to find life worth living again, everyone has their measure, and life is a gift, a hard gift, but a gift nevertheless –; he heard his voice, hoarse and fragile, just a single sound in the soundlessness, and the face that did not answer, the footsteps approaching up the staircase, the man catching hold of him, Axel standing motionless against the wall and suddenly alone, the room like his, simple things that kept quiet, observing: table, chair, bookcase, clothes neatly folded over the back of the chair, and the sounds from Västra Trädgårdsgatan through the half-open window, muffled by the snow.

He saw the blood and remembered the man's expression of shame and fear, as though he had not planned this, as though this was the ultimate degradation, and that he had whispered to him that he had not wanted to be a nuisance, and that he was not the only one. Not the only one? To suffer, bleed, want to take his own life? A correct life, a tidy room, family and children, a profession, a future, a perplexity, a loneliness, a deep despair – Axel stood against the wall, looked at the light falling in and the day that was running its course out there, and through the doorway came Mrs Kähölä with cloth and pail and began to clean up, began to pull at the sheets, drew the curtains, lowered past him like a thundercloud, swept him aside, muttering and fuming, fell to her knees and began to wipe the floor, as though something must be erased, as though she, too, saw it as a shame, a disgrace to the house, to humanity, that bright red face, those thick knees, that massive, groaning and living flesh and blood, skin and secretions, pink and flowery, purposeful and grotesque – was that life?

Axel withdrew from the room, opened the door to his own, everything was as before but something had changed, there was a silence that was too great, an atmosphere that was too heavy. He opened the window and let the raw, snow-smelling grey daylight force its way in. He remembered how the man had complained that everyone thought he was a Russian, because of his name: he remembered how he had said that he was alone in the town and knew practically no one, he had said it in a gentle tone of voice, and Axel had not gripped the outstretched hand, he had gone back to his room. He had heard the man tentatively playing the flute, a minuet he could not place, there was a sense of rhythm, a purity that had made him pay attention, but the music had suddenly broken off and he had strained his ears, but nothing had been audible. As though the man had been listening to him. He had sat motionless.

Axel looked at his hands, writer's hands, pale and covered in veins, they had once held a violin and a bow, those fingers had run across the strings, then later the same hands had pushed away all hope, a small, black coffin on shiny water, that had been long ago. It was cold in the room. There were chance occurrences like blocks of stone and impassable walls. Even in his despair the man had at least done something about it. His gaze displayed helplessness and shame, but also something else; he had finally turned to Axel because he knew that Axel understood, and more than understood. Had he himself never thought of suicide? A thousand times; but there was something that stopped him – cowardice, or a feeling that he did not matter enough to himself for it to be worth it. When he had run in to the Misses he had noticed that he was alive, was engaged in action. So too when the rescue operation to save Janne got underway. Was his life so grey that only catastrophes could make it live? A row of jars and bottles stood on his bedside table. Surely they could cause enough of a catastrophe?

He went over to the window and looked at the snow, the cold, the town where people were moving, all towards the same goal, not giving it a thought. So grey and black they were, as though they all worked in some mine or other. In the room next door all had now been cleared up. Lydia had promised Axel that the man would be allowed to come back, and that his things would not be touched. He still had a vague feeling that everything would have been better if they had been able to talk, there, as he had sat on the edge of the bed, if they had been able to talk freely, touch each other, share life's burden. But the man would come back, sit in a chair, look at the window, smell the fragrance of the snow, perhaps open a book, perhaps try to live for another few years, perhaps look at the photograph of his wife and son. Or perhaps there was no consolation at all, only the fear of being a nuisance, and the razor.

From The Diary

1911

28.1

H. has been the universal topic of conversation ever since the 'event'. I have not been able to endure it, took myself off. Today he came back and went quietly to his room. I hesitated, then knocked on the door. He asked me in a friendly fashion to come in and thanked me for my help. I had saved a life on which he did not set much value, but perhaps this was none the less the right solution, he had after all asked for help. He had brooded about what would have happened if I hadn't heard. He would have died. Was that what he had wanted? As he had fallen silent, I looked for something to say. Then I declared that life has its riches to give even to the lonely, that life is so many-faceted, so full of contrasts, and that the only way is to try to remain open and accept everything, suffering and happiness, loathing and despair. 'Happiness?' he replied, and sat silent again. I exhorted him to continue with his music, told him I had listened to his flute-playing and that there really was talent in it. H. said it was too late, he had his work and family responsibilities. Yet hadn't he tried to free himself from those –? He said he was going to change his name – even though he couldn't change his character, worse luck. At that point he gave a short laugh. He had done the deed out of necessity and great fear, yes, fear. I asked him what he was afraid of. 'Everything', he replied. I said that unlike myself he had a family and children waiting for him. 'Waiting?' he said. After that we sat in silence again. Then he got up, gave me his hand and said he would go home that very evening, that that was the best thing to do. He looked at his bandaged wrists and then followed me to the door. When I closed it I was overcome by a sense of depression, I knew I would never see him again, and that one day he would succeed.

In my room I listen now, but not a sound can be heard, no gentle flute-playing, nothing. There is a taste of blood in my mouth.

I look at the snuff-brown curtain, the silent door, the indifferent silence is everywhere, eats its way in everywhere, not even in fire does it burn, it is the indestructible insect that burrows its way into the bone of cold-blazing life. I have this insect in my flesh and my blood. We walk among the living and are unable to tell ourselves apart from them. We live our lives, and they burn with invisible longing. We want to be builders of cathedrals, but can't scrape together enough for an outhouse. We view the living with amazement: how is it they know nothing? We listen, but there is for the most part silence. Sometimes a shout penetrates the wall, and we rally quickly to the call, but are unable to offer help, not the kind we have dreamt of at unprecedented, crazy, unreal, tormenting, ecstatic moments – love. No flute-playing in the world can give us that, no music in the world can replace it. The loftiest music, the music heaviest to bear, is silence.

10.2

Janne really is a perfect example of Goethe's characterization of the natural genius as someone who undergoes 'a repeated adolescence, while other people are young only once' – if they are ever young, that is. Wasn't I an old man even at the age of ten? Janne is of course aware of this feature – at moments of clarity. Hence his shyness, his attraction to brilliance, his rejection of people, his longing for them, his 'gripes', his warmth of heart, his aloofness, his swift repartee, his great silence. Increasingly I experience the great silence. He has apparently been visiting Stenhammar in Göteborg, and is now on his way to Riga.

12.2

Must do something, and am working on an article about *Night Ride and Sunrise*, it is weighing me down to earth.

22.3

To be noted: *Göteborgs Handelstidning* has asked me for an article about Janne's Fourth Symphony. Strange when voices from outside reach a world of daydreams, perplexities and extreme fatigue after an endlessly dark winter. The symphony is to have its première in April. If only I had the strength to travel!

6.4

The audience failed to perceive the Fourth Symphony's greatness. There was coolness and hesitation in the auditorium. Aino and

Janne greeted me, I expressed my joy, indeed rapture at Janne's most profound work, and he thanked me with stiff features. Aino invited me to Ackté's matinée. In *Hufvudstadsbladet* Bis has written an unconsciously parodic review of the Fourth Symphony as a story about a journey to Koli! But the symphony is no tourist attraction, but *weltentrückt*, spiritualized. Its treatment of form is wholly original, superimposed fourths in the harmony, e.g. in the finale, where some of the woodwinds play in A major, others apparently in E flat. There is an unmistakably classical aim and direction, and the orchestral texture is reduced to 23 voices. All modern cosmetic devices à la Strauss and Mahler have been banished, all the movements end in a *piano* and are organically linked to each other. The entire symphony is a protest against the stylistic direction that is now the dominant one, especially in Germany, the symphony's true homeland, where instrumental music is in the process of degenerating into an art of timbres from which the life has gone, into a kind of musical engineering which attempts, by means of an immense mechanical apparatus, to conceal its own inner emptiness. It is only to be expected, then, that a stupid music criticism should try to criticize a work like this to death. The Fourth Symphony is an aristocratic work. But the truly high-born has a wonderful way of sooner or later becoming the property of the many. The symphony was applauded most warmly by the young – and the oldest. Professor Rickard Faltin called out after the concert: 'This is a revelation!' No, this is not Koli, this is the rock of the spirit.

9.4

This Sunday my life was despised once again. I turned up at Hotel Fennia but could not get in to see Ackté's *Duke Magnus* as I did not have the ticket which Aino had promised me. Would they have dared to treat a person of wealth or social standing with such nonchalance? Attacks of nerves, difficulty in breathing. This is the end.

13.4

Janne has apologized in flattering language, and I have replied. One ought to keep one's word, always. If promises are broken on the heights, what can one then expect of the people, or of Stolypin & Co? Faithfulness to one's word, punctuality, tact and courtesy were given me as rules to be kept even as a child. This the second time that Janne has given me a beastly mule-kick – the incident over the bunches of violets ('the silly clown can go to hell with his flowers') was a sore test of my self-control. A lot of things depended on it, including the question of whether Janne's family was to be left high and dry. The fragile thread that binds me to existence became thinner then, and so it has done again on this occasion. Don't want to hear any more excuses. This summer, too, the mice of Jaskara await me.

16.4
The letter I sent to Janne cannot be recalled. All has been destroyed.

18.4
I have written to Janne. I have always been a psychopath. With fear I began this life which ought never to have come into being. The fear has grown with the years. I am forever ready to be met with cruelty, hardness and mental torture. First laughed to scorn by some of my brothers and sisters, then mocked by my companions as a coward and an imaginary invalid I have seen ridicule and pity in everyone's attitude towards me. I really have been treated hard and unjustly – and have ended up believing myself to be exactly as other people consider me to be. Someone once said: 'Pretend to believe your fellow human beings, but secretly call into question everything they say consciously; as for what they say unconsciously about you, however, that you should believe!' These words fell upon fruitful soil, and within my soul developed a poisonous tree which I have never succeeded in cutting down. I have not slept for 30 years. I have been viewed as a parasite, my cowardice has led to malice, and I now know little about moral tact and finesse. How childish then to reproach others! I who all my life have lived off others' mercy and favour – without me Janne would still have found his way forward because of his genius. My own appearance on the stage is a pure riddle to me. Vanity of vanities! Will Janne understand and forgive?

24.4
Sulphonal. *Göteborgs Handelstidning* has sent a clipping of my article published on 21.4. Janne has written to thank me. I am beside myself.

18.5
Sulphonal. We live among great mysteries, I have mortally wounded my only friend.

23.7
Miss Cajander is trying to cheer me up, N-dal is gathering outside the window, mocking.

September
Against the evening sky a pine forest so dark that it was a wall but with its trunks differentiated, the sun could do nothing against that, it is icy cold.

13.10
Card from Janne who is travelling from ugly Berlin to Paris, says he believes that 'things are best when we are at our most human, when we hate, love, fight and caress' – the vanquisher.

1912

15.1
I am 54.

13.2
Up after a long nightmare. I received a ticket for Friedmann's recital, he was so subjective that large sections of the Chopin became unpalatable, though he gave an excellent performance of the C sharp minor Scherzo and the Etudes. I have been studying Napoleon's campaign of 1812 from a strategic point of view. Nothing is certain on this earthly ball, the whole of whose surface is charged with electricity. One slip can cause a violent shock!

14.3
Janne has written, he is uneasy because according to him each time he produces a new work his debts increase. But I am beside myself with powers that have dried up.

12.5
Saw this much-praised young violinist leer at the audience as, like some prelate, he put his violin to his chin. His tone pure and thin, his playing characterless and without depth, ensemble with the gesticulating conductor non-existent, ovations from the invited audience (representatives of the worlds of politics and business) even between movements, whereupon the soloist bowed! A scandal.

It struck me that if an artist lacks the basic seriousness that is not the product of education but is there already, like a birth-mark, a stigma, then he lacks everything, and no pretended empathy will later be able to save him from the mediocre, unless he experiences great suffering. In my case it did not save me.

14.5
Rakel came to me in a dream, greeted me in a friendly way and disappeared among other people, and I ran to look for her, as though the end of the world were near, and wept.

16.8
Lying here, it is August in Siuro, Jaskara, and a few empty weeks in Nådendal are over. There a vessel is as empty as I am, it can only be slowly filled. Resignation as strength – does it exist? Have I ever really been completely resigned – was there not, even in my greatest poverty, a kind of – pride? Is that so very presumptuous? When I see the meaninglessness of it all I am sooner or later prepared to contradict myself. I may lie still on my bed, but I do not resign myself. Never finally. I have my dreams, they are like a stone in my hand. I throw it. Let's see if it will turn into a star!

4.9.1912

Axel came to Ainola one grey day in September. Even in the hallway he encountered the special fragrance of wood and silence, in spite of the romping girls. They were dressed in white, pigtails were tossed, they opened the door, laughing. Margareta and Heidi looked up at him expectantly, while Kaisa stayed in the background. Behind them stood Aino, unsmiling. She was looking at him intently. He suddenly felt embarrassed and put his travelling bag down. Janne had met him, was standing out in the garden listening, looking up at the sky.

Axel felt in his jacket pocket and took out the three cotton-reels he had carefully wrapped in paper. He was no handyman, but this he could do: make notches in the sides, put paraffin on them, cut wooden sticks, being careful not to wind the rubber-bands too tight. He got down on his knees with the girls around him. Jerkily but surely the little waggons rolled forward. Aino, too, knelt down to look at the waggons and the girls, but avoided his gaze. Janne stepped past them with his best shoes on: a gentleman. The girls planted wet kisses on Axel's cheek, then disappeared. A clatter could be heard from the kitchen. Janne was calling for him.

In the drawing-room everything was as before. The Gustavian seated group, the white curtains, the crock in the opening of the hearth, the beams, the tapestry, the wreaths – 'Yes, there are more wreaths now,' Janne said, following his gaze. 'People usually lay them on a shovelled grave-mound, but in this house they hang on the wall.' Janne's voice was harsh, there was a tension in the air which Axel experienced physically, he felt hot. He looked at Janne. There was something about him that was cold, absent, turned-away. Suddenly Janne altered, took him out to the balcony, smiling and close: 'My friend! You know how welcome you are. Come and take a look at my landscape!'

They stood looking out towards the fields. The pine trees stood in a faint haze, there was no wind. They stood for a moment in silence, then Janne said: 'Aino's upset about Favén's portrait*, she

305

thinks it makes me look like a butcher – a drunken butcher. Perhaps she's right. Perhaps that picture will kill her love for me...' He drummed his fingers on the wooden railing, it was the first movement of the Third Symphony, fast; suddenly it broke off: 'I can't create! I've got stuck! Everyone – everyone makes demands on me! Except you!'

Axel looked at him, and he at Axel. Axel said: 'The true likeness can't be effaced by a false one.' 'How do you know it's a false one?' Janne replied. 'Perhaps it's a true one! I'm no Sunday-school teacher, after all. You know that as well as Aino does. Heaven and hell – I strive towards both! And am – lonely. Do you understand?' He turned away and pointed up at the gentle sky: 'Look, it's almost empty. No birds – I haven't heard the sound of wings for an eternity. Am I beginning to go deaf? Like Beethoven? What do you think?

Axel replied: 'I think that if you're worried you ought to see a doctor. As for Favén's portrait, I'll have a word with Aino. The fact that you can't work is just a coincidence, you know that. The only demands you should listen to are the ones you make on yourself.'

A gentle breeze stirred, and the clouds began to lift. Axel felt slightly dizzy, and put his hand to his forehead. He had an admission to make to Janne, too: that he had been very ill, that he had lived in impotence and self-contempt, and that he had discovered that long sequences of his life no longer had any chronology. He forgot things, coming events which he experienced with painful intensity were displaced into the past, and more and more often he stood outside himself and felt guilt – that word which ought to be banished, from the Bible, from the creed, from people's lives. Guilt – ever since childhood: guilt.

They stood silently for a while, listening to the wind in the trees. 'Yes, I also feel guilt', he said. 'Towards Aino, the children, about my trips to town...' With the years he had developed an ever-increasing need for solitude, and it was as though many things nowadays were a matter of indifference to him... All that was left was music. Creation. To be an interpreter – that was what sometimes gave the greatest happiness, the greatest pain.

'I've listened to it,' Axel said, 'it's there, in everything you create, that longing. Look – the sun's breaking through, like in *Lemminkäinen in Tuonela*! Have you ever thought about the similarity between the words *ensam* (lonely, solitary) and *gemensam* (shared)? Perhaps loneliness is the most shared thing we possess – not just you and I. Everyone.'

'We're getting damned philosophical,' Janne said. 'Listen to the wild ducks – they always fly for their lives! There they are!'

Their eyes followed the flock of wild ducks in its panic-stricken flight above the treetops. Aino came out to them and told them about the garden, what she had been doing, Aino asked the questions and Janne joined in with grunts. They went in and sat down in the library. Janne had put on weight, even more weight, his chin glistened above the spotless white collar, his hair was carefully combed – not at all as in the portrait by Gallén which hung in the drawing-room, no more the wild revolutionary – he had filled out. The wrinkles between his eyebrows like rolls of fat, the eyes that would suddenly lose themselves in the distance.

Axel felt strangely worried, as though he were imposing himself. He changed the subject to music, how few concerts he had been to, the simplicity it was so difficult to achieve, and in contrast to that the mechanical Teutonic apparatus that Wagner had done his best to construct – 'that brawling gnome from Saxony with his thunderous talent and inferior character.' Axel was quoting Thomas Mann. Janne laughed, then grew serious: 'That bit about inferior character could apply to anyone, you know.' He gave Axel a quick look. Axel nodded: the money that was never sufficient! 'You're in the trouble you're in now because you've lived in grand style a little too often', Aino said. Yes – he admitted it. And how much of Axel's money had he not squandered – simply because he wanted to please others – and enjoy himself! A petty bourgeois trait which Axel possibly did not understand.

Axel understood. But it was not his money that Janne had squandered – if that was the right word. He himself had no money, that had been his situation for a long time, and he was used to it. He often felt socially humiliated. The only thing that mattered was not to humiliate oneself, at the innermost level. If he had understood Janne correctly, the innermost level was the Fourth Symphony and *Voces*. The room was getting dark, Aino sat silent, her face pale against the window. 'Take the inner road and how much thanks does one get for it?' asked Janne. 'Do I even know myself? Perhaps I am a butcher, the way Favén has painted me, I shall drink, live and get as old as that rug on the wall there.'

Aino got up and went out. Axel looked at the rug: it bore the words 'Lemo W.1841'. 'It's from my neck of the woods', said Axel. 'Masku, Lemu, Askais, Merimasku – those are familiar sounds to me. It's only 71 years' old.' He heard his own voice, he listened for Aino, but there was silence. 'It's old and shabby, like me,' said Janne. 'You're a fine one to talk about being old and shabby', Axel replied. 'I'm so tired after my journey that I'll have to go and lie down for a while – we can talk business later. And if you'd play for me – I'd be grateful'.

Janne followed him to the stairs. The room was cold, the window was ajar, they had remembered it, his habit. He lay down and closed his eyes. He wished he were away from here. Happy children's voices could be heard, and someone hushing them. He tried to summon up Rakel's features, there in the far-off room, in the gateway, he tried to hear her voice. Her face kept changing, it was Aino's face, he wanted to run to her but was a child, there was a scent of phlox, there were women dressed in white vanishing into the mist.

Axel woke up when Aino opened the door. She said: 'Dinner's ready. If Axel would like to wash his hands and face the water-jug is there.' She took a few steps into the room. 'Axel is Janne's best friend, and mine, we are so glad that Axel's here, but things have been very difficult just lately – Axel must surely have noticed it. And Favén's portrait – I detest it! It isn't the proper Janne. It's the other one – the one I don't want to admit exists.'

'We're often two different people, like night and day, and perhaps they need each other', Axel said. 'But I also – don't like the portrait – it's just the surface, the most superficial surface . . .'

He had wanted to say so much more, but was unable to. He had wanted to take her hand. But she simply nodded, gave him such a serious look in the eye, there was gentleness and melancholy there, and he felt inadequate. She turned and went down the stairs, he quickly washed his hands and face, dried himself on the towel, saw with unseeing eyes the stranger with his rigid face, closed the door carefully and listened: from the dining-room happy voices could be heard. He went downstairs.

He sat on Aino's left, then came the girls and Janne who was tossing the salad himself and pouring on the dressing. This was one of his rituals, he performed it with the gestures of a head waiter. When Janne sat down, Axel saw how big he had become, the napkin under his chin glowed, the complexion red, the beads of sweat standing out on Janne's forehead. They ate long and intimately. Janne told stories, the wine went to Axel's head. He sat there as though he were among his own family, as though he had had one, he fielded his replies. Was it here it came from, that ability, that swiftness? September light and the aromas of food, the cook who came in and withdrew again, knives and forks being raised and lowered, glasses gleaming, the dark walls, Aino serious and Janne hunched over his plate – did he see him at all? There was something silent, something squandered about him, there were stains on his cuffs, there was a veil of wine, of fat over him, his lips were wet, his belly bulged against the table-edge. This was Favén's model, all right.

Something stuck in his throat, he heard an indistinct murmur rising up, he leapt to his feet, there was Janne's wrist with raised fork, he seized it: 'Not one more potato! Do you understand? You've become fat! Fat!' He looked into Janne's eyes, there was a glint there, something quite alien, mocking, Janne got up quickly and shook himself free of Axel's hand: 'No one says such things to me in my own house! No one!'

Axel took a few stumbling steps backwards, a chair fell over, the table had become gapingly silent. He saw the whole monument, the layers of fat, the music hidden somewhere far within, the face florid and vulgar, he himself burning or frozen to ice, he hurled down his napkin and began to walk towards the hallway, began to run, almost, rushed out half-blind, his heart beating like the blows of a fist against his meagre ribs. He was dying! He knew it. He began to move forward without plan or purpose, into the woods, there were streaks of sunlight, birds flew up, people came running, Aino and the girls, they seized his arms, he stopped, exhausted. Aino held him by the arms, spoke appealingly, quickly, stumblingly, saying that he must not simply go his own way like this, that he must not abandon them, that they needed him, that she didn't know what she would do if it came to a break with Janne, that Janne was overstrained, desperate – Axel mustn't be that way, too! He must come back, Janne had not meant any harm...! Axel raised his eyes, saw her suffering: it was he who had been at fault, he realized that now, he had had no right to talk like that in Janne's house, but he had not been able to endure the sight of him – even when he had first arrived – there was something he could not cope with...

Aino took his arm, the girls followed in mournful procession, there was the Master standing dark, as in a gateway, stretching out his arms, and they embraced each other, they had no words, they stood there, swaying, Axel almost disappeared in Janne's embrace, he was agitated and half in tears, he sank down on to his chair and wiped his face with his napkin. He didn't know what had got into him, what it was that had made him do it. The table, the people. The light was unreal and tormenting, and yet he felt a strange sense of relief. That it had come to that, that something of what had been weighing him down had achieved expression. They crowded and murmured around him, they wished him well. Janne laughed and wondered if he dared to have any dessert in Axel's presence. 'I've often told you that you ought to live a rather more ascetic existence in many respects', said Aino. 'Wasn't the Fourth Symphony ascetic enough?' Janne replied. Wasn't it possible that he might feel a voracious hunger after that meagre repast? He had something to show Axel: the Fifth.

They got from the table, he followed Janne to the piano, and Janne sat down, his face became stern and closed. Out of his body, out of his fingers, out of his closed eyes, out of the unknown it came, flowed over him, the new, expansive sound, there was yet again something new, a greater freedom, a richness, a – joy. There was the sculptural element – yes, it was not images, but blocks that Janne worked on, they hovered around between the log walls, they found their way out through the open door to the balcony, it was starting to be twilight. A late sun glowed like honey on the walls, it was like resin, or amber, there was a soft, dry fragrance of eternity.

The landscape outside was growing still. Janne stopped playing and walked with his arms around Aino and Axel into the library. Aino excused herself and disappeared, walking slightly stooped forward, a bird. The two who remained sat in silence. They listened to the silence that was never truly silent, there were voices, the wind stirring, the singing of birds. But here was the calm, the centre that Janne needed – Axel himself had nothing, he said. A rented room. Did Janne know how lucky he was? And whom he had at his side?

Of course he did. Soon he would be ready to embrace everything – soon, but not yet. There was so much unrest, not merely in the age, but also inside him, and there was a pain he could not express, a sorrow he was trying to overcome... 'Yes, sooner or later there's always a lake between the shores,' said Axel, 'there's the Swan of Tuonela and the sorrow we feel at our footsteps being erased so swiftly and that so much is idle chance. "Dark is the heart of the black bird – even darker than my own", as it says in the song. But Janne, you're going towards your Fifth Symphony! Your dark moments will soon be alternating with bright ones, and from the darkness you will derive strength. Longing and departure – and longing for home – that's what you always seem to be talking about.'

Janne sat silent. Axel saw before him the morning mist over the silent lake in Lemminkäinen's Tuonela. A wind got up, and the lake gleamed like melted tin, but when he looked towards the window there were only dark treetops there. The music was somewhere else, it was not here, not in the things he was saying, not in the silence, it was Janne's property, and everything else was feeble explanations. There was something he had forgotten. He gripped the chairback convulsively, and hoped that Janne wouldn't notice anything. Didn't everything conspire to hide the loneliness, the poverty of creative lives – to hide his intermittent attacks of amnesia, his mental invalidity, his fear...? Even now, when he wanted to come close to Janne, be open with him, something false crept in. He was silent. Janne got up and stood by the window. Axel took his watch from his waistcoat pocket and turned it towards the light from the window, it said midnight. It was time to go to bed. 'I'm going to turn in now, I've been talking too much', he said. 'Good night.'

He walked towards the staircase, turned round, could scarcely make out the dark figure. 'I'm glad you came', Janne said. 'Your friendship means a great deal to both Aino and myself. And to my music. You hear what I hear... That's more than enough.'

On his way upstairs Axel kept stumbling, his heart beat violently, wet with sweat he went into his room, sat down on the edge of the bed and closed his eyes. Vague images glimmered by, fragments of speech. 'All is not music', 'mentally retarded', 'the biped creatures', words without meaning. The gale roared in the birches outside, it was autumn. What was he doing here? Sitting alone on the edge of a bed, a speck of dust. People were breathing all round. He lay down slowly with his clothes on, the quilt felt cool. Were they lying like him, listening? To what? There was nothing, nothing to listen to. He turned slowly on his side and closed his eyes. Was he asleep or awake? Like a child he lay, with his legs drawn up, or an insect.

From The Diary

1912

7.9

When I came back to my room in Tammerfors I noticed that it had become even more hostile. The furniture turned its back to me and the wallpaper had grown dingier in defiance. The more closely I looked at table and chair, bed and cupboard, the more loathsome they seemed to me. When I am writing their silence is almost menacing, and is only made tolerable by the reading–lamp and its gentle circle of light. God knows what is going on in the gloom, and what opposition the bookshelf and the bedside table are planning. The longer I live with them, the more foreign the room and its objects become. In the end everything will be equally cold.

2.10

The dogs are barking in the streets again, as though they know that I am lying awake, listening. There is something demonic about their echoing bark, even though nowadays the whole of my reason rebels against 'the demonic'. That there is darkness – yes! That there is sorrow, desperation and evil – yes! But the demonic is a construction which a dying age resorts to in order to excuse itself, it is the construction of someone who has never, in his innermost being, experienced loss. It's the demonic that prevents me from appreciating Wagner. All that ecstatic roaring: by comparison with the *Ring* the *Kalevala* is a miracle of clarity, pellucid wisdom, lyrical imagination. If the intensity of the life-sense is forced to stand on one leg and crow from early morning until late at night, it will totter, grow hoarse and end by wringing its own throat. But the intensity that creates comes from deep purity, and – everydayness. Thus spake Axel.

8.10

Autumn, and high sky. Long walk to the hill. The trees in flame. Sat on a bench and furnished my ideal home. It had blue shutters and was Danish in style, low roofed, with rafters and small, gentle windows. There was a hall, a sitting-room, a library, a bedroom, a spacious kitchen, and a guest-room. There were flowers in the deep window-bays, everything breathed inner peace and purity, and in the dim light of the sitting-room stood a grand piano. In the library a log-fire blazed, and there was my comfortable reading-chair with its adjustable music stand, and around me stood my library, in scrupulous order. If I wandered up to the attic there were darting swallows and a little window open on the garden, and down towards the shore stood three old oak-trees. On the landing-stage, out towards the moon's trail on the water, a white-clad figure turned round and came strolling towards me, and I was filled with such a great sense of happiness that my eyes filled with tears. There were only pine-trunks there, and Näsijärvi gleaming far away.

23.10

I had such a peculiar dream. I was walking over the long bridge, and at the other end of it, looking towards Berghäll, was a wooden house with a dark gateway, and in the gateway a little boy with a large, pale head, when I held it in my hands it was so thin, the back of it was like an eggshell, the veins finely visible as a river-system, there was not a hair on it, it was clean shaven, as the heads of poor children usually are in the summer, and its eyes were big, looked only at me, and though I was holding his head so gently he faded away, and I searched for his name so as to be able to call him back, but I could not remember it. I ran through the streets and alleys of the unfamiliar town looking for him, and everything was glowing, everything was strangely alive precisely because it was unfamiliar, the way it is in reality when one arrives in a town one has never seen before, and I suddenly noticed that I was running along Södra Esplanadgatan on my way home, I could not have been more than three or four years old, and as I was going down Högbergsgatan I met Wecksell, he had a big peaked cap that hid his face, and he pressed himself against the stone wall and said: 'I don't exist! I'm dead!' And I knew it was true, I tried to touch him in order to console him, but woke up.

3.11

I have succeeded in getting myself to a concert. Busoni playing the *Hammerklavier*. A great silence expanded, walls and ceiling blew away, space grew deeper, and I had to grip Tor's arm. There are moments of happiness in life, but I forget even them, and so write this instead.

14.11

Lions and dogs surround me, they show their fangs and leap at me and are held back only by rough chains. They have already seen that I am scratched, and have got my scent. Psalm 22, verses 15-23, also the magnificent Psalm 90 about God's everlastingness and the vanity of man: 'Thou carriest them away as with a flood; they are as a sleep...' To me, who suffer from sleeplessness, those are strangely consoling words, and when I wash myself at the wash-basin I feel like offering up a song of praise, like the one in Psalm 104. The rich landscape of a life is depicted there. In general the Psalms are now a consolation to me. There is a music in them that fills me with purity, and it seems to me that I was not dark and full of doubt from birth, but only became so through my sorrows and unrequited longing. And my thoughts go to Rakel, to how she said goodbye, and how no letter has come, and I have not written either.

15.12

Where has a month of autumn rain and darkness gone? It has blown the days away like leaves. Janne has written to tell me that Copenhagen understood nothing of his Fourth Symphony. The Danish smile very ironic, and Janne's inward-turning asceticism is too much for them. According to *Berlingske Tidende* he is 'alien to reality' (cheese and sausage), and 'moves on the periphery where music ceases to be music' (the champagne galop). It is a question in music as in other arts of distinguishing between the eccentric and the original, or, to use another set of terms, between the eccentric and the personal. The Fourth Symphony is a touchstone which many will stumble over. It is always hard to understand other people's loneliness and painful but also liberating to see the features they have in common with others. '*Ensam – gemensam*', alone and shared.

15.1

summons me to the usual note about my birthday (my 55th). It is twenty years since Father and Mother and Hjalmar died. Now, as then, the snow is drifting over the ground. Remember that spring (1893) when summer came each flower glowed with extra colour, as though life were particularly full of enjoyment for me, who had survived. I saw things I had not seen when my nearest and dearest were alive. In spite of the emptiness and the pain the dead give us they also give us things we did not see when they were alive: they kept them hidden. But this is only momentary, soon everything fades again, and we ourselves stand there, hiding something from those who are to come.

14.2

When Janne's Fourth Symphony was being played in Göteborg with Stenhammar conducting, officers and bourgeois philistines shouted abuse, and a scandal developed. That is how it should be: that which is difficult has never been accepted at once, and the philistines have always thrown stones – in order to exult and applaud a few decades later. What foolishness, constantly recurring.

17.2

I could not endure myself any longer, but dragged myself out, and found in the raw weather a refreshing emptiness. A freezing wind blew the last sluggish warmth from my body, and the town appeared as what it is: a place of work. Snow-mist was drifting over the ground, making the road indistinct. And the man who notices he has chosen the wrong road continues to walk on and shows no signs of despair.

15.3

Our country is darkening towards spring. It is said that Tsar Nicholas II told our own Langhoff*, when he resigned and at the same time had the courage to direct some criticism at the Emperor's policy on Finland: 'I hope everything may yet be all right!' All right – oh, holy stupidity! Nothing is going to be all right. A storm is approaching and it will raise roofs and piano lids!

23.4

Janne has sent me a letter which in its bitterness demands instant cremation. He sees the campaign to help Kajanus as directed personally against himself. I have replied that it is an axiom for everyone that Janne is the creator of Finnish music, not K. Janne's is the only great name that has a world-historic ring – and it will not be robbed of that because he has put his name to the document in support of Kajanus. Strange, this despair and pride about not being perceived in his true greatness. Can one imagine anything similar concerning the pride at not being seen for one's littleness? Our land is stones, and it will last, for him who asks for warmth.

29.4

Janne's composition *The Bard* points in formal terms to something new – Runeberg's poem is after all just as hypnotizingly free, and gives a striking portrait in the third stanza: 'And unknown, closed off in himself, / but to a giant nearest, / he learned strength's tongue from country elf / and loss's tongue from beck and forest.' The unknownness, the reticence ('your flowering *closed off* still in bud'), the nearness to nature, the strength, the sense of loss – from these elements Janne himself is, after all, constituted. *The Bard* is a portrait of most delicate shadows and rays of light, a chamber work. New York called Janne a cubist and futurist after the Fourth Symphony's début in the New World, and did not mean it in a flattering sense.

4.5

After the long, always difficult winter period I have been brooding about my illness. If it's not in my blood, where is it, then? Has it to do with the vague, tormenting memories of my childhood and schooldays? With this age that honours outward success (that is something that began back in the 1870s) and strikes down those who are weak, that laughs at the sick person or treats him – above all the neurasthenic – with contempt, but does not see its own heartlessness, how could such an age not reject someone like myself? The bipeds are creatures that have weapons stronger than teeth: they can put the evil eye on one, strike with derisive words or social morality. Yet even so I believe that deep inside man wants to strive for the good, it is just that he is forced too early to be someone else. He has to swallow the morality and prejudices of his time, and is constantly set about by words like 'sin', 'shame' and 'guilt'. He that is sufficiently strong and upright has, however, his own morality, that is something that Father taught me. For him life was painfully clear, for Mother it was vague, full of warmth – a sometimes suffocating warmth. I was unable to choose between these two attitudes, I sat as if paralysed with a sock on my left foot and the right one bare, and when Mother pulled the sock away she laughed as at some huge joke, and put her arms round me. I sat there, without a will or a thought of my own. I lay down and saw myself from a great height, dead, with a few people whom I did not know leaning over me, and felt a great sorrow that Mother and Father were not there.

12.5

Now May has come with 'joy and beauty great'. The gentle sunshine is wakening publicans and murderers, market women and soldiers, farmhands and servant girls, street singers and piano-strummers. Anna and Elin were here, nibbling at the Rosengren cookies, and the goodwill was great and enfolded me. We spoke of bygone days and shed a few tears over them. I am planning to go to Åbo in a few weeks time, if my strength holds out, and will then seek myself out, incognito, like all princes.

23.5

I made the driver wait and strolled in the sunny spring breeze down towards the shore and the landing-stage out on the point, but had to turn back halfway – it was less a physical tiredness than a sense that I was trespassing and an anger about wanting to make myself invisible. The water was glittering in the distance, so that I had to shield my eyes with my hand. What does nature care that people move among the trees for a moment and are then gone forever? I glimpsed Odensaari, yellow on the hills among spreading trees, the sun-blinds were drawn and the lilac shrubs around little Odensaari were in sweetest bloom. Asked the driver to pass the manor quickly and take me to Masku. The graves were in good condition, I placed my usual flowers. When I got back to Nådendal I managed to scrape together the money for the fare. Since then I have been sitting down here at the harbour bay, watching the boats and the first tourists. The bathing season is slowly coming to life, shame and suffering are cured with mud-baths and massage.

28.6

I had asked to be present at Ainola when Eva married A. Paloheimo*, but could not manage the journey. I have been feeling so deeply alone, but it doesn't torment me the way it used to. Things are not meant to fall into our hands without our paying for them.

16.7

It is high summer, and the swallows are hurrying by like the days. I strolled down to the lookout tower, then to the church, lay down in the grass above the bathing beach, there were happy voices, striped bathing-suits and frocks, hoops, straw hats. Children's feet in grass or sand remind me of little fists. Then I suddenly remembered Rakel and Akseli, how could I have forgotten them, felt their presence as though they could have stepped out between the trees, but they didn't, they're long since gone, how are they now? Everything flows over me and I ought to accept everything. Perhaps my losses of memory are acts of mercy and spring from a deeply-felt need to forget and have peace. 'Thou carriest them away as with a flood; they are as a sleep...'

25.8

Here in Siuro Jaskara the nettles are growing to head-height around the cottage walls and form an excellent screen. I have lived without music for a few weeks, have felt that necessary, but on sleepless night themes appear like ghosts and disappear again. Gentle ghosts, and courteous ones. It would seem that the sense of hearing is more conservative than that of sight. If music's form could be made visible as architecture, Janne's Fourth Symphony would be accepted as a masterpiece of modern architecture – an architecture beyond all *Jugendstil*. Every man his own cathedral-builder! Shingled rooftops smoke, the starry heavens open and the Great Bear enfolds me in his embrace.

3.10

The bonds that tie me to people are breaking, or rather: I am quietly removing these threads which often bind me and cut my skin. It is autumn, and I strolled out towards the hill yesterday. In the moonlight the trees seemed to be gathering themselves into a dark wall. The murmur of water floated like brackish light between the leaves, and the deadly-pale light from the great, heavy moon with its spotted face made my footsteps silent and hesitant. The shadows hid sinkings and risings, and still I strolled, with a strange feeling of insecurity, myself a shadow. Now and then the moon scurried through the clouds, or was it smoke – everything became ill-defined, and when I stood still the world stood still. Away among the trees a fire was visible, some men were moving around it, and I felt as though I had been spying on them and they had discovered me. I went away in silence. It was strange, the fire, the shadows, the pale, clear moonlight. The night was a cool one, with not a breath of wind.

1914

4.1

I have finally had a letter from Janne, he knows what suffering is, reaches out to me and sends me the scores of *The Bard* and *Luonnotar*, the Two Serenades for violin and orchestra, and *Scaramouche*. So I can follow him again, at a distance, in thought and feeling.

11.1

I have written to Janne about suffering as a purifying purgatory, without it there can be no proper life for the human self. Janne's greatest works must see the light of day during his seventh decade. I was here in Åbo when a twelve-year-old boy played the harp part (on the piano) in Bruckner's 4th Symphony, I saw his eyes and gaze and will never forget them. Janne is now in Berlin, I have written to him about his natural disposition for composing, his idealism, straightforwardness, originality, seriousness, all the things that make him relatively uncomprehended in our mechanistic, naturalistic and pompous times. The natural sciences are riding our generation like a nightmare and they believe that if one searches for examples one will attain individuality. But it is not so: the personality is the diamond-hard, the irreducible; the environment that which flows. The artist creates his environment, not the environment the artist. He plays a part in a greater whole – even if he is born on Kamchatka.

22.1

Letter from Janne in Berlin, saying he finds his own influence in the music of the young. He was carried away by Bruckner's B major, and has written a setting of Rydberg's 'We Shall Meet Again' (*Vi ses igen*) – that bitter-sweet poem about eternal love, perhaps not one of Rydberg's greatest, but it moves me: will I never see Rakel again? It is seven years now. Akseli must be nearly fifteen, Rakel herself – thirty-four. Is Reino still in the picture? I see them in my dreams, they approach me, but don't see me. My dream-life upon earth, and a religious longing is growing stronger.

23.1

Anna R. came in in her dressing-gown and said I had been shouting in my sleep, could only remember fragments, sat down on the edge of my bed and I, old man though I am, leaned against her, and she held me for a moment in the deepest understanding. She asked me about the dream I had had, but it was gone, only a vague, sickening sense of catastrophe remained. The room in which I am living is becoming more and more alien to me.

6.3

Janne is welding together *The Oceanides* – will he have it ready for his trip to America? If only he could give the world another symphony, a fantasy with the motto 'festivitas' or 'gaudemus'! I thirst for joy and melody – and the Finnish nature ought to invite to that, to divination and intuition, to invisible poetry, to sweetest song. Janne has the kind of recklessness that leads to visions transposed into sounds.

14.4

Went to the market after weeks of illness, there was a stall selling second-hand clothes, and the very air was saturated with cloth, fibres, the smell of homespun, the sky was a blue sheet, the town a rag-and-bone shop, the rapids an eternal handloom, and I myself wandered like a shabby overcoat with nothing under my shell except perhaps for a ragged shred of worry, fear, humiliation, a few scraps here and there to cover the most naked parts of me. And if my thoughts, my self-scrutiny could, like a garment that has been worn too often, be turned outwards in the clear spring light and the ugly, ill-humoured surface be turned inwards – how would I be then? Even more disguised? Alas, there are garments which are equally wearable or unwearable however much they are turned inside out. I shall vanish to my grave like a hopping magpie, with a black coat-tail.

16.4

Janne has now completed *The Oceanides*, which is a suitable composition for a long boat journey. Meanwhile Aino has had to bear the heavy burden of practical cares. Janne is shaken by Viktor

Nováček's* suicide; he was only 41, gifted and well-liked. There is always something moving beneath our feet, the earth's crust splits, fissures open and close above our heads, and I remember and hear a cry through the wall, but if it were Rakel I should not reach her.

22.5

I have been having trouble with my heart, and have been to consult a doctor in Helsingfors. The city breathed freshly around me, there was a smell of spring and sea, and on Sunday housemaids and soldiers strolled along the Esplanade, and from Bröndum's café came the strains of *Valse Triste*. I went there, there the Great Artists sat in a cloud of smoke, elevated above mere mortals, but with frayed cuffs. I took the tram from Boulevardsgatan to Skatudden, got off and strolled among the tall stone houses, and the wind blew. Here many years ago I used to walk among low wooden shanties, the church was the only tall building then, and I would usually end up with some friend in Kapellet. Then I heard a woman singing. This pale memory, why has it remained in my mind – the water in the ditches, the roar from the seamen's inn, windows like swollen eyes, the sky yellow above torn sails and black masts – a forest of masts and rigging. Strolled slowly back into town, arrived at Salutorget, and there were the women selling fish, with scales on their red hands, and out over the sea the gulls plunged screaming. I looked at the lovely *Havis Amanda* which has borne her six water-gleaming years well. Took a cab – 1 mark – to Brunnsparken and got out at Ulrikasborg bath-house – there once were health and youth, singing and happiness! Now my flesh is decaying, my bones are being hollowed out by years of monotony, and my heart is jerking. I sat on a bench and looked at the sea and thought of Janne swaying across the Atlantic in a rondeau of the waves. Wondered if I should look up Rakel, I felt such an intense longing that I decided not to, sat in the train like a blind man on the way up here, and am now sitting in my room with my sole partner in conversation, a cheap notebook with ruled lines, and a pen. It is completely light outside, and early morning.

13.6

I have received two letters from Janne in America, he is to have an honorary doctorate conferred on him at Yale on 19th June, and feels like 'a fish in water'. Even the Fourth Symphony has received appreciation, it feels almost painful, as though I wanted to keep it for myself. Do they really hear the inner voices? Those who talk of inner integrity, of following one's *own* way – *odi profanum vulgus . . .* The orchestras in the USA are magnificent, the woodwind chords in Janne's words such that 'you have to put your hand to your ear to hear them in the *ppp* passages, even though the cor anglais and bass clarinets are playing. And double basses that sing.' I am seized with great joy, wander vehemently around the well-known paths of Siuro, look at the sheep and experience their bleating as a song of praise to the countryside and its quiet melancholy and its coffee-mornings of gossip choked by greenery. This, too, is life, over-flowing music and trivialities in a beautiful mixture. And here there are women who don't make fools of themselves and pity me and play protectresses but who wash out the bath-house as though they wanted to clean my inner self as well, and I sit on the bench and smell the scent of hay and the swallow cry high to the sky: perhaps I have changed, or grown tired of seeing the contrasts around me. Perhaps everything has a hidden meaning, evil as well as good, and solitariness is not the worst of attributes.

25.6
Aino has written me a letter about Janne's adventures in America. At the degree ceremony he wore a gold sash, a gown and ceremonial collar, a biretta, and the Cross of the Legion of Honour, and *Finlandia* was played. I got up from my Windsor chair in excitement. I was wearing a white shirt with no collar, braces and linen trous-ers, I had my spectacles on and my own home-made crucifix, and a blackbird formed the orchestra.

18.7
Janne's Malmö concert has been cancelled; the reason was, of course, bowing to the Russians. Cousin Tor who travelled down there says that the concerts in Sweden and Denmark were extremely weak. Here we are experiencing a heatwave, and I am wandering around practically naked: Axel Degeneratius! Aino and Janne are back in their own country again.

30.7
Janne has informed me of a large number of new compositions: *King Fjalar, Sandels, Ahos Juha* as an opera, a ballet about the bear's death-feast in the *Kalevala*, songs and piano pieces, a heatwave as good as any, but too lofty, too great. He ought to give up writing operas, the symphony is the eternally valid form. For the rest, I can

see that old Europe's hour of destiny is approaching. In Russia there is crop failure, revolutionary propaganda is flourishing, the universities are opening themselves and the workers are already in total revolt. It is no wonder that the war-party is winning and making an appeal for external war in order to avoid an internal one. France is, of course, playing timidly along, weighed down by debts: soon Europe will be in fire and flames. Our sufferings will be terrible. We are in a state of readiness for war.

7.8

I am completely exhausted, and have sent Janne a long letter about the treachery of England and Italy. Things have not been so hard for me since Father and Mother died – Germany's ruin cuts my nerves to shreds, the country lacks bread! This is the triumph of the East! Janne should go into the wilderness and listen to his inner voices there, and forget about his debts. Everything has once again acquired sharp outlines and is glowing faintly in the dark, and at nights I have strange visions. Nebulae are born and destroyed in fire, but Rakel's face gazes gently, as though she were saying something, and I follow the movement of her lips, but hear nothing.

29.8

Janne echoes my sentiments in a postcard, where he says: 'We are approaching the prophesied age of religion. But a religion impossible to define – in words, at least, but perhaps music is a mirror.' Yes! A mirror to the starry sky, serene and infinite, arching on an August evening above a dark earth.

24.9

'God opens his door for a moment and *his* orchestra plays the Fifth Symphony,' Janne writes; then the door is closed and it is dark and silent in the world again.

3.10.1914

On his last day in Åbo he went to the Cathedral. It was quiet under the high vaults. He sat down on one of the chairs right at the back and listened. Someone coughed, muffled voices could be heard from the crypt, but the silence lasted. He sat in grey twilight and tried to draw his wandering thoughts together, he longed for a sign, a peace, something that could give him lasting security as nourishment for the journey back. He closed his eyes. There was a fear and a joy he associated with Mozart's *Requiem*. An echoing door, a fumbling note on the organ – they paled before his listening for the voice, the word, the sign. He longed for purity, from the Dies Irae to the Day of Lamentation; in between there was The King, four times repeated, Rex Tremendae Majestatis, a tremendous chorus that changed into a single, heavy figure, a Prince – of darkness or light?

He opened his eyes and looked into the heights and the daylight filtering down. *Sanfte soll mein Todeskummer* – where had all these fragments arisen from? Was there an invisible choir singing there, or was it inside him – *sanfte, sanfte* – and did not this aria resemble 'I Will Pluck The Forest Violets'?...'*sanfte soll mein Todeskummer*'... So gentle, this conviction that his days were numbered. An old woman wandered down along the centre aisle, looked at him for a moment, then greeted him, as though they were privy to some common experience, he greeted her back, he did not know her. He froze. What if now she were to appear, sit down beside him, give him of her warmth, Rakel, the longed-for? He drew his head inside his overcoat, like a tortoise, stuck his hands in his pockets, he was cold. In the gloom the dead lay on their catafalques, only sleeping, clad in armour or ankle-length costumes. He had walked here as a child, in the same gloom, holding his mother's hand.

No, there was no rest. He got up and found his way to the entrance, stood for a while on the steps, listening to the town, to the autumn wind, then walked carefully towards the Cathedral Bridge and down along the river. On the opposite bank he saw his old school, it was here and yet far away, as through the wrong end of a telescope. The trees were yellow or ablaze, and the new Library gleamed like a palace. The river slid by with yellow water, a man came rowing a skiff, Axel followed him with his gaze until he disappeared. There was the bench, there were the steps and the water, there he had stooped down, laid the black case with its intimate music on the surface of the sky and pushed it out, out of his life.

He stood up. Perhaps he had acted wrongly, what meaning did it have any more? He felt no loss. He lifted his gaze. There was a woman walking on the other side of the river, dressed in dark clothes. Something in the way she moved, in the way she inclined her head, made his heart beat violently. She stopped, looked over in his direction. He raised his arm, were his eyes playing him true or was he making himself ridiculous, should he run across the bridge, would he be able to make it, was it her? His overwrought mind – what signs did it demand, what was he looking for, what hallucinations must he suffer until he attained peace? The woman had continued her walk, and was now vanishing among the trees. Carriages rolled silently over the bridges. It was getting dusk. He shivered, turned and went back to his room. He took his travelling bag from the cupboard and began to pack.

From The Diary

16.11

The insignificant is so insignificant that whoever sees it smiles. The insignificant has a tough life-energy, is always there, always signifies something and is a significant warning. It warns the significant against always believing that it is significant. The insignificant displays itself in the cracks between the stones, or is it perhaps the mortar? Why am I interested in the insignificant? Because the insignificant does not simply draw nourishment from the significant; the significant is also dependent on the insignificant, as the landscape is dependent on its sometimes almost invisible shadows.

22.11

Days of quiet. The streetlamps are being painted black, the windows are being covered over and I am sinking deeper into my burrow.

1915

1.1

I strolled round the block in the mist, it is strangely mild and wet wool is wrapping Tammerfors in its silence. The ugliest buildings become resigned and tolerable. Janne has written, he seems both fascinated and repelled by Schoenberg and the dialogue between the tonal and the atonal, as all the while he attempts to build his symphonic world, completely alone. Will my dream of 1) a classical and 2) an expressive symphony be fulfilled? Janne has begun his Fifth and Sixth symphonies in parallel fashion, at the same time.

15.1
My 57th birthday, card from my brothers and sisters, but too tired to join in the Misses' kind coffee-party.

7.3
For weeks now my hearing has picked up nothing but a thin murmuring sound, as though all music had ceased and been replaced by this sound which is nothing, not silence, just a thin murmur as from a distant crowd of people, or a far-off waterfall – I prefer the waterfall.

18.3
I have been studying the Fourth Symphony, the asceticism of which is manifest even in the orchestration – this is symphonic chamber music, or a chamber symphony, a room, a conversation about unknown things, about sensations of distance in chords that hint at new horizons to be conquered (the scherzo). But nowadays music is strangely distant from me and leaves me in peace.

2.4
I dreamed that I saw Dr Wargentin lean over me and say with an expression of distaste: 'He's all stained and dark!' And I succeeded in getting out: 'From unrequited longing!' But he did not hear me, it was the girl selling violets on Salutorget with her hare-lip who was looking at me, she knelt down in front of a fireplace – the one at Siuro – and shoved into it music and papers, they began to burn and I screamed and woke up to Father's determined voice saying: 'Sit straight!' And I sat straight up in my bed, and did not know if I was still dreaming or not.

16.4
Janne has written about the disposition of the themes in his Fifth Symphony: 'as though God the Father had hurled down bits of mosaic from the floor of heaven and asked me to work out what the pattern looked like.' God the Father is becoming Janne's best friend.

24.4
Janne has reported seeing 16 swans – they make the same sound as the woodwinds, like cranes but without their tremolo, the swan's tone being closer to that of the trumpet. I listen to this inside me, and there is a landscape with bays and forests and dark

water, but when I turn my gaze there is a room with stained wallpaper and worn-out furniture. When I move out the window will be opened and sunlight will stream in, and a fresh spring breeze will sweep the dust from the wash-basin and clear the marks off the mirror, and there will be a scent of lilacs and a taste of wild berries and springwater, I can already feel it on my tongue, and there will be birdsong and a great emptiness and liberation.

13.5

The time of our departure is at hand. Together with the Misses I am leaving Tammerfors for ever and moving to Åbo. But just as the moss clings to the raw boulder I suppose I have a few invisible roots here – a closeness to that which is poor. Here the strangest figures move about: beaten, wiped out, never adapted to the town, a brown-black, sweaty-grey horde of woodlice. Turn over a stone and they come scurrying out with spirits and oaths as though they had something to reveal. Then there are the factory workers, they go in seething silence. Outside it all, I have stood and observed.

27.5

I have been brooding on one of my hobby-horses: military strategy. On the continent there is a catastrophic case of closed strategy. Where there are no opportunities for swift, direct attacks, there is gangrene. On the eve of Austerlitz Kutuzov went to bed and left the generals to their theorizing. His strategy was the right one: wait patiently, and then strike. But one cannot strike in a charnel-house. In classical strategy the rituals were there in order to conceal death. In modern strategy there is an element of the incalculable, and death becomes invisible. In our country everything depends on small operative units. Our geography demands it. A stench of corpses is floating across the world, people are being brutalized without noticing it, and their fear permeates their sleep. Feel the traces of fear, and you will master your own.

2.7

Looked at myself in the mirror of my provincial room. What did it reveal? That if I look closely enough, a stranger is standing there.

13.7

I get up, I exist, I go to bed, and the days vanish with their own scarcely audible music which grows louder at nights, a summer requiem for midges, flies, sheep and cows, with solos for stable-boys and innkeepers' wives, masters and maids, but most of all for the local priest and police superintendent. Janne has not written.

20.8

Janne has sent a postcard – he is the object of intrigues, and Aino has insomnia – 'things are going downhill for everyone.' The children talk about '*Akseli setä*'★ – and my thoughts go to a fragile head, a silent gaze in a room long ago, far away. Akseli, Rakel, and the unknown Reino – are they alive? If one has no children something is finally cut off. Best that way.

4.9

It is a part of 'good manners' not to display spontaneous emotion. But I perceive that these manners, the good ones, are not those of music or art. In them all depends on the spontaneous and the intuitive, the seeking, the passionate, just as long as it is given form and made visible to our senses. 'Good manners' are society's bad ways, which hinder, make silent, destroy.

16.10

After a dreadful train journey from Tammerfors I am now installed in Åbo at '3 Russian Church Street', 1 Aningaisgatan, in other words – two small rooms and a kitchen. I eat at the Misses', and follow Åbo's rich cultural life as best I can. Food and fuel are expensive in times like these, and I save. Åbo Cathedral, however, stands firm as ever, it is a guiding landmark. The people are surprisingly friendly, and I feel at home.

23.10

I wandered with difficulty up the hill to the Art Museum and saw my beloved Westerholms★ again, and the water flowed darkly as before, and silence reigned. There was a strange sense of presence. In general I noticed that people in museums stand and look as if they had happened there by chance and were face to face with a surprise: 'Just fancy – that picture's here, too!' They walk past W.'s Kymmendedal and I feel both offended and relieved, offended because they didn't stop, and relieved at having it all to myself.

8.11

For the first time I heard Janne's violin concerto, played by Burgin. It was an unexpectedly good performance; strange trying to adapt it to what I had created in my head, like trying to superimpose two pictures on top of each other, there will always be a remnant of indistinctness.

24.11

Aino has invited me to Janne's 50th birthday party, but I don't know if my strength is up to it. If Dr Stadius gives his permission I shall go. I am deeply touched by this undeserved goodwill. Looked out my dark suit and sewed on two buttons. Elin came to visit me, she has gone completely grey. The people in our family have the faces either of pug-dogs or of horses.

6.12

I have been given permission to travel, as long as I am careful. I have also sent Janne a few simple lines of thanks: he is our uniting force. Where other men experience their fifties as a time of petrifaction, he shall make them years of ascent and harmony. The signs are there: his attraction to the Eternal, his will towards God, his best friend. And at his side stands, as ever, Aino.

9.12

I am trying to sum up the overwhelming impressions I have received. Yesterday Eino Leino* led the way with a magnificent poem of homage in *Helsingin Sanomat*. Janne's portrait adorned many of Helsingfors' windows, there was a reception for him at the hotel and I, too, was there, my morning-coat was too tight and stuck up at the back. Janne and I talked – about cranes and swans, about wings and the flight of the years – strange and unreal! He looked pale but collected, there were the familiar lurches between gravity and lightness. In the Hall of Solemnity Janne conducted *The Oceanides*, then Kajanus made a speech, Burgin played the two violin serenades, and during the interval the citizens' petition with its 15,000 signatures was presented. After that the Fifth Symphony was played for the first time. My first reaction was: Mozart! Janne was pale and trembling as he merged completely in the conducting. After the concert, ovations, then a festive banquet in Börsen, on either side of Janne, Aino Ackté and Ida Ekman, had occasion to exchange a few words with Aino who held my hand in both of hers. Werner Söderhjelm gave an inspired speech in which he successfully employed the metaphor of Janne as a tree with roots in the concealed – the tree of independence in a country that lacks independence. Can the tree's summit create a storm? The *Kalevala*, Runeberg, Sibelius: our future. Wept a little into my table-napkin and hoped that none of the ladies at table, whom I didn't know, observed it. Finally Kajanus spoke of Janne as the great pioneer, and a sea opened up – I remembered Tvär-minne! No one can take this away from me. Now back to Åbo, worn-out and rich: I possess Janne's and Aino's friendship.

12.12

While lying in bed I have read *Voces* and the *Third Symphony*. *Voces* is not at all pessimistic: the first movement speaks of melancholy and demoralization, but not of *Weltschmerz*, the second is a visionary piece of spookery, the third contains a lofty pining with tones from a world above. Our birthday conversation about cranes and swans led me to the Third Symphony and confirmed what I fancied I noticed on a first reading: that in the trio of the second movement (the woodwinds) the rhythm is derived from the twittering of *swallows*... So this cold, wintry day is filled with the birds of springtime, and summer, and autumn.

15.12

I have been continuing my study of the symphonies. The poly-phonic structure of the Fifth leads one's thoughts to Mozart in his outer movements, e.g. the G minor and C major: the simplicity, the plasticity. At the concert the first movement did not come across in a truly artistic fashion. Erik Furuhjelm's* article in *Ord och Bild* correct on many points, but too intellectual and abstract. He sets Janne in the right historical perspective, but spends too little time on the individual and unique aspects. I am suspicious of divisions into periods, they do violence to life and reality. There are only two periods: one of technical learning (*Sturm und Drang*) and the other of development. Often the artist takes up themes from earlier in his career and turns the chronology upside down. The comparisons with Tchaikovsky, Grieg and Strauss do not please me (and neither do they please Janne). But E.F. knows what he wants and has courage. Gunnar Hauch is better at thinking with his heart and feelings. Janne proposes to go to Stockholm, a town of musical philistines. He is wasting his time. He ought to be warned.

24.12

I have celebrated Christmas Eve with three candles and two Miss Rosengrens, a dried stockfish and no spirits. I have been reading Otto Andersson's* extraordinary article in *Tidskrift för Musik* and have underlined his assertion that Janne 'never as completely and unconditionally as has been suggested, belongs to the nationalist tendency in music.' Nature and literature (Swedish and Finnish) are his principal sources of inspiration. 'Properly speaking, Sibelius is classical in the broadest sense.' Bravo! Werner Söderström's★ words are memorable, too, but Gripenberg's★ poem is mere empty rhetoric. I also remember what Mikael Lybeck said, that Janne didn't approach his ideal humbly – 'you were never made like that.' But in true defiance there is a humility that demands just that – truth, defiance. NOW the populace is ready to applaud the Master and give him support when not so long ago (the Fourth Symphony) it was rolling its eyes and greeting him with derision or silence. The society of the plebs is always true to form, inclined towards the most dismal kind of nagging; and the artist who is willing to sell himself to those salons must be genuinely split in two in order to be able to work his way out of that rubbish; the pseudo-artists strut about for a time, cut their laurels and are then forgotten – the same is true of the snobbish know-alls.

1916

23.1
I have had pneumonia and have seen strange visions. Very weak.

14.2
Letter from Janne, fearful about my health, 'the sun went down for my music.' That is consoling.

23.2
It's not *He that Yearns For the North* but *He that Yearns from the South*, but I yearn in the North – have not much time left – suffering not worth much, but life a great deal.

12.5
I am writing merely in order to tell myself that it's spring – haven't the strength to do anything.

20.5
Elin has had an attack of apoplexy, Lydia has broken her arm after slipping, and I have palpitations. The Sick Menagerie is playing to an empty house.

15.6

There is nothing left for me but to go to Nådendal – Anna has moved there from Jaskara.

22.6

I have had a letter from Janne – 'especially when I have finished a composition – then one of my first thoughts is: "I wonder if Axel will like it."' Janne's words better than mud and water cures, but not even they can rescue the man who is sinking and sees in his dreams the realms of his childhood.

26.6

Strange peace and strength, as though Rakel had whispered in my ear: 'Get up! I'm here!'

5.7.1916

Axel was woken by the sounds of the early morning: a cockerel crowing, an early cart squeaking against the gravel on its way down to the harbour. He stuck his feet outside the blanket, moved his toes, he was still functioning. His heart, his lungs – he felt well and strangely happy. Somewhere in his midriff there was his constant sensation of hunger, but that too was a challenge. He looked at his emaciated features in the mirror, they were not an attractive sight but not an interesting one either. He turned away.

It was going to be a warm day, the sky was already high and the warmth from outside was flowing into the room with a smell of foliage. He chose the linen suit. He had cleaned away the stains, it was passable. He bathed his neck and forehead with eau-de-cologne. Olga was in Stockholm, the children had spread their wings and flown. Odensaari lay empty. He had heard it from one of the stable-boys the day before, and had hired him for the drive. He had borrowed the money from Miss Cajander. He felt a great expectancy, as before a fateful journey. Silently he stole downstairs to the kitchen.

Selma was already in there, clattering the stove-rings, a sour-tempered woman. She kept sternly silent, merely nodded to him. The coffee was on the table, but he asked for tea. She ought to have learned long ago that his stomach would not tolerate coffee. She served him in silence, then turned her back on him. He stirred his cup absent-mindedly. How does one avoid excitement? By foreseeing it? The doctor had warned him against excitement. It affects big men in a big way, small men less so. Afflictions like shoe-sizes.

He got up from the table, took his linen hat and his cane and closed the door silently after him. The morning was fresh and the sun already had warmth in it. He walked down to the harbour. There were carts, boats, grey sails, men and women, the tang of the sea, the clouds of summer. He sat on the steamer landing-stage for a while, thinking of nothing, observing, simply. He felt at peace.

Pentti was waiting with the horse and cart outside Badhusparken, the horse tossed its head, the driver took off his hat, and Axel climbed in. The town went swaying, shaking past, the streets were still empty and trafficable, and Axel paid his compliments to passers-by he knew. They took the road to the north and then turned off in the direction of Masku. Fields and forests, always the edge of some forest closing off wider views, a bend in the road that wound between grey cottages, then opened on to fields again. Axel took off his hat and let the wind cool his forehead. The horse's behind was jolting from side to side, its tail was swinging, and now and then he and Pentti exchanged a few words: he pointed, asked for names, nodded affirmatively, the road was endless and the same, he remembered it. They turned off towards Niemenkulma and now the farms and forests lay closer together, for a moment there was a glimpse of Nådendal's church-tower, then it was onwards again, uphill, through forest, downhill. He took it all in, and everything was morning-clear and close to him. He knew when the manor would come into sight, there was a glimpse of it, yellow with white sun-blinds behind the maples. Little Odensaari lay bedded in greenery, could hardly be seen. He asked Pentti to drive up the avenue and hoped that none of the children were there, but if they were, they were asleep, all was silent. The clip-clop of hooves and the scrunch of the wheels on the gravel, the smell of leather and horse-dung, the shadows of the lilac bushes that surrounded them on their way up to the house of his childhood, he had seen it all before, the larch tree, the oaks on the slope, the bath-house peeping out from the opening in the woods, the leaning apple-tree – his heart beat violently. Everything was summer-quiet and morning-clear, not a breath of wind stirred in the leafy crests of the trees as they stood gainst the blue sky. The horse ambled slowly up the hill, the cart swayed. They stopped at the entrance to the kitchen. On stiff legs he got out and asked Pentti to come back, he only wanted to have a quick look at the house, it would not take more than an hour. Pentti had an errand with the farm foreman, he turned and drove away. Axel walked slowly across the sandy courtyard, everything looked closed, locked-up, the house was as tall as he had imagined it, the potted palms stood on the banisters. The kitchen staircase grey and unpainted, slowly he made his way up, the door was open, the hallway with buzzing flies. He knocked on the inner door, an old woman came and opened it, her jaws moved, her eyes intensely blue. When she saw Axel she dried her hands on her apron, took a step back: it was him! He had come! Did he remember her? How could he fail to remember – after all, it was only a little over twenty years since he and Anna had moved – but Hanne had recognized him! Yet he had really changed, had he not? No, she remembered him, she could not have mistaken him for anyone else, she thought of him so often – but the lady of the house was not at home just now, no one was, she was alone, had hardly anything to offer him. He stopped her: he had come to see the house again, the rooms, she didn't need to put herself to any bother. But perhaps she could serve him coffee? Here, in the kitchen. While he went his rounds. Yes, of course – and could she accompany him, help in any way? No, he wanted to be alone.

He walked through the office and into the lower drawing-room. The furniture stood there, waiting. The dining-table in the centre, the serving-hatch, the palm. The coat of arms on the wall: post-horn and star. So strange, and perhaps a little – vulgar? He felt restless. The stairs to the upper storey echoed. They had always done that, and they smelt of clothes, fabrics, hidden stores. In the upstairs hallway hung the Swedish kings and queens in their oval frames, the whole series of copper engravings, it had hung here before – but where? In Father's and Mother's bedroom? He opened the door and peeped in. Drawn curtains, dim light, the old, heavy mahogany bed, this was Olga's room. Opposite him was the door to the small bedroom which had been his. He hesitated. First he went out on to the balcony, looked across the fields, phlox was growing in the garden, ths wild vine was flourishing, clinging along the high walls, what if someone saw him and wondered what he was doing? He turned and went quickly back inside, opened the door and saw his room: so narrow. Two new beds, a white table by the window: unfamiliar. In the boxroom the smell of wood and paper, the old newspapers from the 1700s still stuck like wallpaper along the walls, clothes hung in there, there was an old table, yes, it was familiar. In someone else's house.

In the upper drawing-room hung the general, Lovisa Ulrika and Kristina, and the Chinese urns stood on their table. There was a new piano, it was painted white. Narrow white rugs on the gleaming floor, white curtains and sunlight outside: only towards evening did it fall in through the windows here, and people sat in the library and drank coffee, the aunts, the parents, the children, Uncle Fredrik – and on the lectern lay an open copy of Dante's *Divine Comedy* with Doré's illustrations. He walked quickly through the room, there was the upper hallway, he heard Hanna rattling the stove downstairs, the door to the attic stood half-open, was there someone up there? He had to sit down on the old clothes-chest and get his breath back. Before the steep staircase to the attic. They had played there. He had had his hideout up there, he had sat there alone, in peace, it had been his place of refuge in the summers, until they had been driven out, how old had he been then – thirty-five? They had used to call for him, but he had not answered. He had used to creep down in stealth, so that they would not find his hideout. Even then he had hidden himself, had always hidden himself. How hot it was. He took off his jacket, laid it on the chest beside him. The chest had been painted an ugly blue colour.

Axel climbed laboriously up, had to put his hands on the stairs above him. Beams, air, rafters, sawdust between the great oak timbers, narrow attic windows looking out on a pale blue sky, a couple of them broken. Swallows flew twittering in the big room, arrow-swift wingbeats, and were gone again. Behind the heavy, brick chimney he had had his room, had dragged a few old shelves together as a screen, and he had been able to look down at the courtyard and the garden: strange figures moved there, parents and brothers and sisters. He sat down with effort on one of the beams. He looked out into the emptiness. An old perambulator, old iron bed-ends, bundles of newspapers, all old. Like himself. And the sunny cries of the swallows which did not allow them-selves to be impeded by him as he sat there, one object among others. Something that was simply there, a consoling moment, shot through with the shooting-swift flight of the swallows, the flutter of wings up towards the nest, and the quiet, wood-warm air. The attic – his cathedral. The narrow windows, so safe for the eye. Had Father ever been up here? But Mother had come up to get him, had called softly, sat by his side, he remembered it now. What if his loneliness had been different from the outset, sought voluntarily, warming and secure – but it was something to be borne, a fear, a bolt of lightning, an eternal mark. Such cruel light: how could a life of insecurity cope with it? Here there was twilight, sunlight that forever seemed to be declining towards evening, sinking, quiet as a Sunday.

There was an old scythe there, and Axel got up, took hold of it, held it in his hand. The worn, shiny shaft, the poise, the move-ment – he had never experienced it, never experienced the joy of the hand. What he had learned was learning itself, the letters of the alphabet, the facts, music as a pastime, merely, the music of aunts, songs he had been compelled to sing, psalms on solemn occasions. How he must have starved! Had he listened to the swallows, their swift flight, their song, the swift whirring – just as Janne had listened to the swans, the cranes? What if Janne had sat here? He would have filled up the whole attic, or stood there like a stranger: he needed wide open spaces, forests, oceans. And Axel: closed-in walls, silence, and the dust suspended in the narrow beams of sunlight that came through the windows. Something gripped his heart, carefully pierced it through, he straightened up, held his breath: it was over, only a memory.

When he stood up he had to support himself against one of the crossbeams that ran along the ceiling. He grasped hold of one of the stairs, it was as though he were sinking back into the utterly strange world he had to live through, to rooms and people, and their demands. In the downstairs kitchen the table was laid, a cup, a saucer, a bun. He asked Hanna if she would not have something with him, but she turned shy, said she had had hers already. How pale he looked, how thin he had grown – was anyone looking after him over there in Tammerfors? Yes, thank you, he had all he required. His brother's children had all found jobs now? Could she go and fetch Pentti, he was hanging around with the farm foreman? He looked at her. We're drying up. Lines, furrows, wrinkles are tracing their paths over features that once were smooth and clear; hands are growing mottled, hair thin, heads shake as though they wanted to deny the ravages of time, sinews hold the ever more fragile limbs together, we move as though on thin ice, at any moment we will sink soundlessly, with black mouths, with throats that will swallow snowflakes, with eyes that will be lit by a lightning-like brilliance, only to grow dim again, with eyes that fill easily with tears but can still see, as Hanna's saw, with sudden keenness, like a suddenly keen brilliance over autumnal water, blue ice and diamond. She saw him and said nothing, touched his shoulder, understood that he wanted to be alone; surprisingly quickly she went down the kitchen staircase and disappeared along the road towards the farm foreman's cottage.

Axel quickly got to his feet and stood there, undecided. He had seen the rooms, they had said hardly anything to him. Silent, unreal and forsaken; or was it he that was forsaken? It was the same thing. He walked through the downstairs rooms, a brown photograph hung on the wall there, a group of people, Father and Mother, his brothers and sisters, he had to put on his spectacles, but he wasn't in the photograph, had he been ill in bed, or had he been in Stockholm? There was no indication of what year it had been, it must have been around 1890, before death had come and smitten them, mown them, dispersed them, covered them with earth, before everything had been dissolved and driven away – all long ago.

He hung the photograph back in its place, stood looking out of the window down at the courtyard, the garden, the hedge, the fields, the meagre edge of the woods. Liberation, relief – or indifference? When the manor came into view for the last time he asked the question again. Hanna had wanted to hold his hand, had looked tearfully into his eyes, they both knew that this was final; but he had cut off her words quickly, turned away, asked Pentti to hurry up, and off they had trundled, downhill, away. it was not a new one, this sense of bankruptcy. There really had been surprisingly few tormenting memories. Had he expected that everything would be as before? Everything had been – almost. But the people who had lived there were gone. Had he not seen that? The fresh wind, the squeaking wheels, the familiar farms, each bend in the road known to him: what message did it convey if not that time passes, that we live for a moment and die a thousand times and for ever? All was change and the unknown, and reality was not behind him but in front of him: the sleepless nights, the downhill journey, the din of the everyday, the intimate silence. Yes, those were the words he was looking for: silence, loneliness. The notebooks he wrote in, the letters to and from Janne, his one or two human contacts: were they not enough? No – they were there to replace something else – something he had no knowledge of yet and which, when he had found it, would be able to share with no one else.

This sense of calm and assurance followed him into his sleep. Yes, he slept, without dreams. He had not drawn the curtains, and the summer night stood, faintly glowing, in the room. How light was a person's breathing, as though the faintest breeze, the merest invisible current of air could extinguish it, leaving nothing behind but silence. On the writing table the notebook lay open, and on the bright page there was only one word: Sorrow.

From The Diary

1916

8.7

Sorrow. In the deepest recesses of life a sorrow, that everything is transient, and that our lives are so short. This sorrow has followed me since I was a child. And it is this sorrow that gives life its beauty in spite of everything, in spite of illness and failure, loneliness and confusion. It is this that gives the sky its depth and the trees their whispering, that gives me the silence in my room and the remoteness in the voices I hear and the remoteness in myself. I think of those who are dead and those who are still alive – somewhere (Rakel). And I think of myself: that life is forming me, still, and changing me, and that I will doubt and despair, and that I must accept all that. I think of the pure, strong voice I heard as I was walking across Miss Rancken's courtyard: it was that of a seven-year-old girl (Märta Armfelt), who looked and moved like a Jenny Lind. I thought of her future fate of which I know nothing and will never know; I think of the hours of happiness we forget and the bitterness we gather. I think of the changes wrought by time, of old shanties torn down and the lower-class children now become an upper class, of the assistant caretaker who is now an organist, of the fisherman who has become a civil servant, girls whose job was opening gates turned assize judges and cartographers; in every third farm a barefoot boy who is now a student. I think of the kindness I meet as thanks for a quarter of a century's kindness from myself... Life is dreamlike and incomprehensible. It contains Sorrow that is the neighbour of Joy.

20.7

Sent a telegram for Ruth's wedding; in thoughts of Ainola. So many faces here, and all remote. Sitting on the landing-stage, watching the gulls, they all scream in the same way, as though seized by great anger and exhilaration at the same time. I have tidied my room, now it contains only the most necessary items.

12.8

Letter from Janne. His mood is heavy – great loneliness. Listened as Ernst Lundquist, the friend of my schooldays and youth, improvised on the organ of Nådendal Church: fire and flames! And he's self-taught, too. His literary interests go in the same direction as Janne's: volumes of memoirs from the reign of Gustaf III. I saw him last in 1885 – we got our student caps on 20 May that year. Now out of 26 there remain only 12 from the Cathedral School days.

15.8

As I lay at death's door this winter I had a dream about Höffding and Grundtvig* pursuing a debate by the Aura River. Beethoven came in from the gardens of legend and all the people stretched out their arms to him, beseechingly. He made himself known and played his Tenth Symphony, which he wrote after crossing over into the other world. It was called 'Evening Voices', and he raised his baton towards the trees and flowers, and they were the orchestra. Then he turned towards the innermost of the gardens, and there was a rendering of 'The Bells of Creation', with Our Lord himself as performer. Bliss, and everyone wept, even I who (six inches long) lay in a cellar air-hole. Afterwards, Helmi Fager (the nurse) wiped my forehead. I then witnessed my own funeral, flew into the shape of a dragonfly on the almond bushes of Observatory Hill and saw the cortège moving over Nylandsbacken. I felt sorry for the people who were following it, troubled, I wanted to tell them that under one of my wings there was a golden key that opened the door to the unknown world. Life is more of a dream than people suspect, and death is a kind and glorious angel.

17.8

Yesterday saw Miss X – my *idée fixe*, did not manage to say hello and my heart beat with shame and agony. I can't leave Nådendal as my rooms in Åbo have been rented out until the fifth of September.

2.9

I have returned from Dr Stadius who confirmed what I have long suspected: I am suffering from pancreatitis (inflammation of the pancreas), an extremely rare disease with only one outcome:

dehydration and death from starvation. Uncle Otto died of the same illness. Hence the irritability, the surges of emotion, the depressions...I don't want Dr Stadius or anyone else to have responsibility for my life. I have come to the point where I can do without most people. I am not in despair and am not afraid. Now it is time to think through the greatest matters, on the wide arenas where I have moved along so many confused roads. Much is now empty noise, even certain aspects of music. But much in my life has also been unnecessary isolation. If I can reconcile myself with death, I will become in a certain sense invulnerable. Death has, after all, set its mark upon the whole of my life. I no longer demand answers to every question. Death, too, is a mystery, after all. Nowadays I often experience a great sense of calm in which time has no significance and I rest in something that is, perhaps, myself. Psalm 39: 5-14.

16.9

In my childhood we all gathered in the same room for reading aloud. In the summers the light in the library was gentle, but when autumn came the reading-lamp was lit. Even what was read became gentle and soporific. There were rooms for coming together and rooms for being alone. Now only the latter are left. Sometimes it seems to me as though the room I now live in is temporary and is already in the process of disintegration. The brown wallpaper is splitting and shrivelling, as if from fire. Black ants come crawling out and vanish into the cracks in the floor again. A photograph of Odensaari recently fell to the floor for some unknown reason, and the glass of its frame cracked.

26.9

Janne has written, he is struggling with his Fifth Symphony and, in between, with the music to *Everyman*. Autumn is here, and we are both glad.

2.12

R. Kajanus is fifty. His compositions stand in the shadow, but the man and conductor in controversial sunlight. I have a dim memory of the '90s. The universality in greatness we experienced then will never come again. Spring storm! *Kullervo*! Janne is on his way here for his 51st birthday celebrations. Tiredness.

10.2

Here in Åbo Janne conducted his Fifth Symphony in its new version which could still do with some revision. The Allegro molto a midsummer night's dream, the woodwinds are elemental beings, a swan-hymn! The violin pizzicati in the Andante strike me as monotonous, but the total effect is overwhelming. In future: nothing but first-rate works. Janne excited, eager, full of energy.

22.12

Janne has thanked me for unforgettable moments – makes mention of intrigues. It is quietly snowing. The river flows black past the banks where I saw Rakel.

27.12

Rasputin has been murdered by Prince Yusupov. But the evil has not been silenced by this. A new and terrible year is beginning. Strange cries were heard coming from Aningaisgatan last night. This morning Lydia asked me if I thought my bedroom was too cramped! I replied that I shall soon need a room made of wood, measuring 50 by 170 cms. She shrank back and fled.

1917

15.1

I am now 59 and am still alive.

22.1

What is important, what unimportant? What if there is no great difference? Janne has sent me Becker's biography of Beethoven, it is extraordinary. His opinion of, e.g., the Piano Sonata Op. 31, No. 3 and the little one in E minor (second movement) coincides with my own. Furuhjelm's book about Janne is excellent, particularly the things he says about *Kullervo*, which I have never heard. Am meditating, in a purely senile fashion.

14.3

Aino, the good creature, is badly ill with gout, Janne is suffering from loneliness and guilt feelings, I can sense them. In the silence distant voices are so near.

9.4

This country must suffer for its geopolitical location. I can see the dark clouds of Slavic nationalism amassing, who knows when they will send their lightnings down on us. If the people in Petrograd go on waging war it will mean the triumph of nationalism over socialism. Perhaps it will end in blood-red anarchy. Then the inevitable corollary will be reaction – and from it will come nothing but evil.

23.4

Does Tokoi's* speech in the *lantdag* portend an independent Finland? Is a monster to be born? I am withering away.

18.6

I am staying in Nådendal and went for a walk yesterday after a long spell in bed – don't want to go to hospital. Saw through a gateway a cool, closed garden with many flowers, they were glowing in the verdure, and a young girl sat there, sewing. At the harbour one hears Polish, Russian, French and English. I am reading a great deal, but am bothered by deafness and have poor vision in my right eye.

12.7

I strolled up to Tupavuori, had a wide view over Erstan and Luononmaa. In the summer of 1897 I stood here with Rakel.

18.8

I am as emaciated as a scarecrow, yet there is still calm, if not joy, between my shoulderblades and my sticking-out ribs.

28.8

Inns and bath-houses are being cleared out and scrubbed, the dirty water is running out. It has been quiet and it is time for me to go to Åbo. People have been avoiding me and I have been avoiding them – that is the best, and most honest way.

22.9.1917

In the evening twilight Axel strolled down to the river. His bench
awaited him. He often sat there. Everything around him was familiar, and he grieved no more. It was autumn, and the trees were
aflame. In the mist all sounds became muted and unimportant. He
fell to thinking of the old man in Tolstoy's *Resurrection*: 'I have
given up everything, I have no name, no place, no country,
nothing. I am simply myself.'

Myself? What was he? Had he no name, was he invisible? The
old theme – it felt strangely remote. In the dusk everyone was so
silent, they walked past and were gone. There was hardly any
traffic on Aura Bridge. In the mist the streetlamps spread their
faint circles of light, and from the trees the moisture fell in heavy,
silvery drops. Axel turned up his collar. He sat still and listened.
Footsteps were coming along the gravel path, a woman was walking with her head bowed. He recognized her immediately, but
before he had time to call to her, Rakel saw him and stopped. He
got up and they looked at each other, she took a few steps towards
him and stretched out her hands, he took them. He felt no surprise,
he had been waiting for her. How many years had it been? Ten.
Since they had parted in the gateway, since she had whispered:
'Live well!' and he had felt himself abandoned. He had so often
sensed her presence.

Yes, she lived here, in Åbo, she worked as a cleaner at the Art
Museum, Reino was no longer a part of her life, and Akseli – her
son – had joined the Reds, she hardly ever saw him, was anxious
about him, he wasn't very strong. Axel looked at her, her face,
her figure, her hands still on her lap, they had sat down on his
bench and were talking softly together, as though the years had
never passed. He saw her tiredness, her tensed features. She had
long been denied tenderness. He noticed that he was holding her
hand again, and that she had not pulled it away; cool and thin, it
rested in his. She told him that she was living alone, she had lost her
faith. Did Axel still have music as a consolation? He had to think.

Did he? Yes, it was there, but it wasn't everything. He said he thought he had too little time in which to listen to it.

Too little time? Yes, he too had been ill, but he was better now, he had come to an agreement with his body, he often sat here, listening, there was something peaceful about the place, and he had been waiting for her. Once he had seen her on the other side of the river, had it been her? It was possible – she did a lot of walking, he had eyes in his head. He could see the state she was in, the way life had dealt with her. She had to earn her living, Akseli sometimes turned up demanding money, but she had given up Reino completely, she didn't know whether he was alive or dead, he had started to beat her, and one day he had disappeared, and Akseli with him. The boy had turned up a few weeks later but had kept silent – he was good at that, keeping silent.

Axel felt a great sorrow, his eyes filled with tears, he took out his handkerchief and blew his nose, tried to conceal his emotion and said he was cold. Could she accompany him a short distance along the way? Yes she could, where did he live? Aningaisgatan. Did he remember the time she had accused him of sinfulness? Rakel laughed, briefly. Yes, he remembered, that had been in Nådendal, 1899, was it? Was he able to forget the ugly things remember the beautiful ones? He thought he could. Perhaps something good might even come of this, of being deprived and living alone. Being exploited but living a pure life – if Axel could understand what she meant.

He looked at her, listened to her, she was close. If he was cold, perhaps her arm could give him a little warmth? Did he live alone? Was Professor Sibelius still his friend? How was Mrs Färling? Miss Anna? She herself still lived with a female friend in Raunistula, they shared a room. She was glad she had met him. A lot of things here were foreign to her. She had nothing against the town, whether in mist or sunshine; but there was no sea.

There was something forced, tense about her now. She was talking too fast, as though each silence were something to be seized upon; he came to a standstill. If she found their meeting trying he did not want to prevent her from going. Almost ten years had passed, and so many things had changed. He was ill, but the Misses Rosengren were looking after him. He was so glad they had met. But if she had something else to do – she could come back, after all – they could meet, or she could come and visit him, if she wanted to talk – he felt as though he were hiding something – he didn't want to be an intruder, but he didn't want to listen to her fears either: she could come to where he lived and talk to him, if she wanted to, or she could go. He couldn't offer much in the way of help, only listen.

She put her hands on his eyes, and he remembered painfully how she had done the same thing, once, in a sun-filled room; her wrists were so thin, her figure almost bent forward, as though they were sharing a sorrow together, he held her by the arm, he took her hand, the fingernails bitten as then, it had not been in his room that she had done this, but up on the headland, that was where it had been; at any rate, she had been close. She stood with her face turned away, then said scarcely audibly that she wanted to talk, to come to where he lived. It was now almost dark, and the lamps of Auragatan stood forlorn. They walked to his room in silence. He took off her threadbare coat, she undid her headscarf. He felt an aching, burning pain in his midriff and said he was sorry, he would have to lie down on the bed, she could sit beside him, and could she please get a glass of water? She moved about silently in his room, as though she had always been there, she supported his head, gave him water to drink, looked at him attentively. Had he a good doctor? Yes – they were doing what they could, the doctors. Had he understood how she was managing in life, what she had been compelled to? Yes – he had understood, but was she really compelled to it? She – she had another child, out of wedlock, it was boarded out. And her son kept demanding his due, came on visits and threatened her, had already put himself outside the law – those were things she could not tell him about. But if he were now to try to help her, by no other means than the little money he had – would she promise to try to make a living by some honourable form of work?

She sat in silence. A bitter, almost mocking expression passed over her face. 'Honourable –? What's that?' No – she didn't want his money. She had to go. She got up, but he held her hand, she did not release it: he had expressed himself badly. He was the last person to judge. He had failed in everything, and yet he felt – happiness. Did she know that here by the river, where they had been sitting, he had buried all hope over thirty years ago? That he had always been one of life's outcasts, and that only in the last few years had he begun to realize that that was the way it was, that it was not worth struggling against it, except in his innermost being, in his dreams, his thoughts, his longings, did she understand that? That there was a value beyond all the failure, beyond all the filth? –: that was the striving that mattered. All the people he had been attached to had departed, his father and mother, his brother, his closest friends, he had only Janne left...and even he was often remote, and that was the way it had to be. And Rakel had always been there – in his dreams, and been close to him. Could she help him? Come now and then and talk to him, do a little tidying up, he would make no demands on her, he could give her so little, but she could give him – her trust. Did she want to? He surely didn't need to explain how things were for him? She had seen it, that shadow, that darkness, it comes to everyone – did she remember the bright headscarf she had used to wear, could she perhaps wear it when she came to see him, next time, if there was a next time...

Axel leaned back, exhausted, looked at her. She was sitting beside him on the edge of the bed, she leaned towards him, put her head gently on his breast, he stroked her hair, they rested in silence. Then she got up, tied the black headscarf: next time it would be a bright one. She smiled, turned round in the doorway, and then was gone. He closed his eyes. It was so silent that the room floated. For a moment he too smiled. After all, she had promised to come back. He was gripped by a sense of unease. What if she had been pretending? Ease and unease: how could they live so close together? He had come down to the kitchen at the Branders' house – there had been sunlight, and she had stood there, turned round and seen him. So many years so suddenly vanished. If he lay still, perhaps the pain would pass.

From The Diary

1917

28.9
Rakel was here for a short while, tidying my room. We did not talk much, she was reticent and worried about Akseli. Had she come out of a sense of duty? She said she hadn't, and I believed her, and she put my hand against her cheek when she was leaving. But that too was remote.

14.10
Dagö and Ösel have fallen, thanks to German strategy. Kordelin* has been shot by the Reds at Mommila, and Bergbom at Hertonäs Manor. Murderers sense the air of morning – or coming darkness. I am getting thinner.

2.11
The mob is moving past the windows on its way across the bridge. The Cathedral is striking its still, echoing chimes above screaming and shouting.

13.11
Rakel has not been here for a long time. The Red Guards are running riot, they have captured the Governor and the Chief of Police, and have demanded half a million from the town for the restoration of law and order! In St Petersburg the Bolsheviks are now in power. Terrible energies are moving blindly around. Have not the strength to write letters.

12.12
Finland declared itself independent on 6.12. The fulfilment of a dream. Here in Åbo rioting among the populace, shops are being looted by hordes that are driven away – by Russian soldiers! Janne has asked for a sign of life. Not a peep out of Rakel.

31.12

I have looked up Viktor Rydberg's *Prometheus and Ahasuerus*:

> Blood laves the earth in limitless cascades
> and it is thou, god of my heart, that bleed'st,
> and of the world the east, west, north and south,
> they are the poorer in the absence of thy cross.
> Art thou the weak one, ever suffering? –
> I am now him I was and not another,
> but on my head yet lay thy hand!
> It feels so cool, so cooling to my brow
> and in my soul so wonderful and warm –
> Day breaketh in the darkling valley now,
> and it may break upon the world e'er long.

'Day breaketh in the darkling valley now...' Had a strange dream about that valley, people clad in white were walking through it in summer light, and I saw it all but was not there. Now sitting with Viktor Rydberg's photograph, the one he sent me with a friendly greeting over thirty years ago. That happened in another world that is now being obliterated.

1918

8.1

Janne and his family must leave the country, it is the only solution. These people are full of bloodlust and rapacity. The ghastly logic of geography: Petrograd is three hours' journey from the border. Finland's destiny is sealed in the stars. 'A tide of philistinism is sweeping across the world', Janne writes.

12.1

I saw a man run in through a gateway with a rifle, two men were pursuing him and they also vanished, then a shot was heard and the two men came back out into the street again. The gateway was like a black, open mouth, and snow was falling.

16.1

Yesterday my 60th birthday was celebrated with formalities which I could not escape, fettered as I am to my chair and my bed. The other members of my family were here and Lydia Rosengren gave a speech: 'the story of your life has been a tragic one' – a funeral oration! I managed to get up out of my chair, asked for silence, and got it. I said I had been sent alone to judge my life, and that the tragic did not preclude the happiness of a great friendship – the one I have with Janne. Not everyone has such a friendship. Then in the afternoon his letter reached me, a letter I shall never forget. It said: 'I often feel as though the good God had given me a wonderful toy. Many of my friends pick and poke at it – blabber about the purpose of this or that wheel; but few take delight in the thing as a whole. You are one of those few, and have become so in the degree to which you have been able to teach the owner gratitude, something that seems to be the thing he finds hardest in life. In thanking you now, Axel, I do so with joy and pride. Joy at possessing your friendship and pride that such an uncommonly rich mind as your own should have accepted me.' Accepted him! How could my life have taken shape without him?

18.1

Rakel has been here, brought homemade bakeries with her, and we sat and talked about the years in Nådendal and about Akseli, about how she is trying to manage on her wages from the Museum, and there was peace and friendship, but also the warmth and intimacy that exists among people of sensuality, and I felt my age but was not bitter about it. I told her about the fifteen years I spent in Tammerfors, where have they gone? There is only the glitter from Pyhäjärvi, and the cruelty and poverty, and I mentioned my fear that blood will be spilt into gutters and sprayed against walls. Rakel looked at me and said it was the blood of brothers and comrades. We sat in lonely silence.

27.1

Rakel was here, in despair at the threats she has received from her son, he had found out about her visits to me. 'Axel is the only person I can talk to', but I can't protect her, only advise her not to come here...We parted, I saw her walk through the snow and across the street, she turned round but did not wave. Then I felt such great pain that I had to go to bed and hide. I thought I had achieved a lasting peace of mind, in the face of the inevitable, but this farewell was a hard one.

27.2

Janne has fled from Ainola with his family and moved in with Christian at the hospital. It is all so far away.

8.4

The Reds capitulated in Tammerfors to the Whites, who held a religious service. Can God give his blessing to this? There is blood everywhere, even on the streets of Åbo. Where is Rakel, where is Akseli now?

12.4

The revolutionaries have left Åbo since boats were blown up in the harbour. Lundberg who has had dictatorial powers maintained order and shot a rioter at the railway station in cold blood.

14.4

The *Åbo News* is appearing again, humane article by Elias Lodenius: 'The settlement of the conflict should not bear the hallmarks of revenge.' Helsingfors has been liberated with German help. Here in Åbo the Skerries Frikorps marched in, there was rejoicing that could be heard even in here. But there are those who turn away in the deepest bitterness.

26.4

Received short message from Rakel that Akseli has been killed.

16.5

The softening of my heart muscle is continuing. General Manner-heim* has marched into Helsingfors.

22.5

Janne is working on the five *Humoresques* for violin and orchestra, new songs, violin sonatas, *Oma Maa* to words by S.S. Berg; the Fifth Symphony has now been recomposed, the Sixth ought to be wild and impassioned, the Seventh full of vitality, expressing joy in life. And these strange words: 'As though I were in two minds about abandoning life and upon my descent into my grave shot an eagle in flight – aimed skilfully and well, without a thought for what may lie ahead.' No eagles for me.

5.6

The calcification in my heart and coronary arteries is forcing me to go to Nådendal, for my health's sake. Here ladies and gentlemen live as though nothing had happened. No word from Rakel. Sometimes, in my dreams, I see Akseli's pale features, he was a boy and I only ever saw him once, and he was named after me.

4.7
Slow walk to the steamboat landing-stage, sat and looked at the harbour and the church, and it struck me that I have heard no music in a long time, either within me or without me. The silence is deep, in spite of all the life there is about. So much forgotten.

23.8
Have now been transported to Åbo, oedema, legs swollen. My being able to write proves that I exist.

5.9
Words from Janne, are they consoling ones? 'You who are dear to me and are important to my art must not – indeed cannot – write the word down.' The word 'death' is hard for the living.

26.11
The secretary of Åbo Academy was here, talking about a commission for a cantata to accompany the inauguration ceremony in March. I promised to discuss it with Janne, but insisted that this time the honorarium ought to be increased 3 or 4 times, which was accepted. These practical realities are like open windows in a darkening room. Moments when everything is calm and unimportant.

28.12
Janne has sent *Jägarmarschen* and the wonderful songs, Op. 72. I have looked in Åbo for the Op. 80 Violin Sonata and *Luonnotar*, but they were not to be found. Dr Stadius has succeeded in curing my angina. Attacks of giddiness. Saw Rakel with her white headscarf on, it was like swan's wings the tips of which touched the black water. The enigmatic has no name.

31.12
My music: silence – Silence. Have accepted my destiny, with some pride, and joy.

8.1

Janne has sent *Luonnotar* as a New Year's present – it brings me consolation. Of the singer it demands, in addition to considerable vocal resources, a natural intuitiveness and a mystical imagination – Lilli Lehmann could have sung it. Wish that Janne could get *Kullervo* published. Have read a great deal in my impatience to know everything – unnatural in a 61-year-old, but it heralds death's imminent arrival. The broad wingspan of the coldly gazing swan. As though it gave strength.

23.1

There was a dog at Odensaari, if I told it to bark it did, it wasn't clever enough to refuse. There was sun every summer.

8.2.1919

Janne came to Åbo with his cantata *The Song of the Earth*, Op. 93, for mixed chorus and orchestra, to words by Jarl Hemmer*. He met the rector of the newly-formed Academy, Edward Westermarck, was fêted, feasted and felt a deep sense of unease. In the end he telephoned Lydia Rosengren and announced his arrival. Yes, Axel was somewhat better, he had been waiting, he was able to sit up and receive visitors.

Darkness and silence reigned in his room. A cold light pierced in between the drawn curtains, and the green lamp on the work table was on. As Janne stood in the doorway, Axel thought he looked like a giant, bringing with him a scent of after-shave lotion and cigar-smoke. Axel got up with effort, and they embraced each other without saying anything. Then Axel lay down on the sofa again, and Janne spread the blanket over his legs and inquired after his health. Axel was moved by this, and turned away. After a brief pause he said that his respiratory trouble was giving him pain. That was why he was speaking so slowly. Janne must excuse him. His visit made him feel indescribably happy. How had the cantata gone? Yes, Janne had received the fee that Axel had demanded of the Academy. He thanked Axel for his comments on *Luonnotar*. As for himself, he was unable to find the original score of the composition.

Then Axel got up, in spite of Janne's protests. After much mumbling and searching he found Norland's *Music Dictionary*, which contained the information that *Luonnotar* had been performed in Malmö on 25.6.1914. Janne must have had the score with him there. This ignorance disturbed Axel, he found it incomprehensible. Janne tried to put his mind at rest, saying that he would do all that he could to find the composition – he would telephone Aino Ackté.

Axel said he would not rest easy until the Fifth Symphony was published. The coming Sixth appeared to him bathed in Hellenic light – was it not so, the finale a *rondo hellenico*? and the Seventh

355

dark and passionately surging. He had discovered that in the finale of his Third Symphony Wilhelm Stenhammar had used French horns with upturned bells, which Axel thought was a happy inspiration.

Thereafter, the conversation moved on to the Fifth Symphony. Axel thought the first movement admirably well-formed, but felt that the second movement contained certain *longueurs*, and that the strings' statement of the principal theme was broken off too early. There were *pizzicati* lasting 24 bars in succession – wasn't that a bit monotonous? Then Janne pulled out a little notepad from the pocket of his dress-jacket (he had to go out to dinner in an hour's time) and made some notes; he said he did not trust his memory. Axel said that Axel Nyman had written a glowing notice of *Snöfrid* in *Ord och Bild*, and that Peterson-Berger wanted to hear Janne's 'wonderful' *Pohjola's Daughter* and 'Lemminkäinen's Homeward Journey'. Axel, too, now yearned for home; childhood often appeared to him in a gentle light. And were not the memories of it one of the driving forces of creative work? Then Janne gripped Axel's hand, and pressed it warmly; the memories they had were a means of preserving something, they were a sign to be deciphered, another world to look into, and he, Janne, often felt he was only an intermediary, a deliverer, a translator of a music that existed somewhere, waiting to be interpreted, a truth inside himself. Yes: the important thing was to be onself, Axel replied. Perhaps our art exists before we ourselves do, and we are here in order to conjure it out of the darkness, the way we conjure forth our actual lives. Genuine music does not proclaim, it is created in silence, in a listening to the strange voice which is the voice of everyone, everyone...

At that point Axel had to break off, and the two friends sat for a while without saying anything. Miss Rosengren came clattering in with a tray on which were a coffee pot and coffee cups. Janne produced a cigar, then put it back in his pocket again. Axel broke the silence, and said that Janne had now attained the deepest sources of his creative work: after the Fourth Symphony and *Voces* his tonal landscape stood clearly and boldly before the searching eye, the listening ear. Here a country that was bleeding could find its own true, healing reality. He himself had made attempts at composition, mostly in his head, but none of it had ever been able to compare with what he had dreamt of and shaped, during tormented, sleepless nights, with his mind alone, into a form he believed was great, pure and liberating. He had, like a Bruckner,

356

sought liberation from the personal, a heavenly light with which to express the poetic, but it had ended in chaos.

What had Axel done with it? Janne leaned towards him, and Axel's eyes, sunken and dark, looked past him. He had burned the few fragments he had managed to get down on paper in the stove. He had never been a creative person, like Janne. That had been his great sorrow. Now he wanted to return to the subject of Janne's Fifth Symphony. He felt there was a gap between the second and third movements. A shorter movement, a scherzo perhaps, would have given more weight to the development. The third movement made an overwhelming impression on him. The only thing he had with which to pay Janne back for all he had received from him was friendship. Being over-sensitive, he often exaggerated – or misconstrued – the things people said. It had given him pain when Janne had misunderstood him. All that had been linked to his feeble nerves and heart.

Axel broke off, his breath coming in rasps. Janne wanted to say something, but Axel made a gesture, wiped his forehead, continued. His doctor had warned him against excessive emotion. But how could a person protect himself against feelings? And why should he? Perhaps people had not understood his silence at decisive moments. He had been unable to speak when he had been fighting for his life and trying to avoid heart failure. But what good did it really do? Was there an inner meaning in what people called reality? He had thought a great deal about this, that he was what he was. The swan of Tuonela glided silently on dark waters. When he heard its song it was the song of death he heard. Did Janne remember the day he had conducted the *Lemminkäinen Legends* for the first time? It had been the 13th of April, 1896. He himself had not been able to be there, but had been there in spirit, had lived it. Lived the music – and Tuonela, the kingdom of the dead. And was there not in those legends, in that darkness, a yearning, and was not that yearning everything, the light which a person bore within him, which each and every one of us bears within us, giving us the power to live – and the power to depart? Was there not even in the darkest creations a consoling thought: that it had been created? That the sound of wings existed, and the yearning that seeks a heaven?

Axel had sat up, but now he leaned back in exhaustion. Janne looked at him, then looked at the floor, the carpet had such a sombre pattern. Axel was almost a shadow, yet strangely strong, Janne could feel it. Where did that strength come from? He swung the conversation round to the subject of migratory birds and their calls, the things he had observed during the autumn at Ainola and on the shores of Tusbysjö. Each year he watched them with ever-increasing melancholy – and was it not melancholy that had characterized their lives, Axel's and his own? The innermost – he had always found it hard to express it, except in music.

They sat for a while in silence together. Then Axel inquired after Aino, how she was, and after the children. Janne in his turn asked if Axel was still reading a lot. No, he wasn't any more, reading had begun to sicken him, Janne could see the way he was sitting, or lying here, slow-witted and down in the dumps!

Janne was dubious. Ever since the beginning of their friendship in 1900 he had found Axel to be the sharpest, most engaging, most deeply perceptive person when it came to his own music: there was certainly no slow-wittedness there, there was insight! Had he not written to Axel about it, that he must – must not die – that he was – invaluable – that he was counting on Axel's support from now on, as he sought his way on to new, wider expanses of water. He must go now. He had a meeting at the Academy. He would come back tomorrow. Axel must look after himself, he was precious to him. Now he must leave him.

Janne looked at his watch, he would have to hurry. No, Axel need not come out to the door with him. It had been unforgettable – all of it. He thanked Axel from the bottom of his heart. They said goodbye, embraced each other briefly, Axel held Janne's hand in his own, it was large, full of life. They looked at each other, then Janne turned and went out, paused in the doorway for a moment and looked back, raised his hand, and then he was gone. Axel remained there, standing, it was silent. Only his breathing could be heard.

From The Diary

14.2

Janne has written to thank me for 'the glorious hour' – 'you have never seemed so healthy of spirit to me as you do now.' Says he has been feeling disgusted with his 'shamefully nervous disposition', and so did not come back the following day. We both knew it, anyway.

18.2

Sent a message to Raunistula, but Rakel has moved away.

24.2

Janne now sees clearly that the first movement of the Fifth Symphony is 'one of the best I have ever composed.' So at least that movement has been rescued.

27.2

Mrs A. Lindberg wants to rent my room during the summer – don't know if I'll get my old room in Nådendal. Have written to Janne about his smoking – it leads to premature hardening of the arteries, read Vretblad, *Concert Life in Stockholm During the 1700s*. It is freezing cold.

15.3

When do the swans leave, when do they return, Janne.

Epilogue

Postcard to Herr Professor Doctor Jean Sibelius, wife & children

A terrible illness (or rather four of them) is laying me waste just
now, a so-called 'dry cardiovascular inflammation' – which has
penetrated one of my lungs, two different heart complaints inside
the same lung, dreadful torments which cannot be treated with
drugs, morphine impossible, the heart is weakened by it – others
already ineffective, etc. Strength at an end, yearn to sleep. Yes,
dear glorious Janne, one thing – farewell and thanks to Aino from
my sickbed – God's blessing now and always
                    Thank you for everything, everything!
                                                    Axel Cn
                                                Åbo 22.III 1919

Press Notice 30.3.1919

Yesterday the burial took place of Baron Axel Carpelan. The funeral
was held indoors at 1, Aningaisgatan and was attended by a large
number of the relatives and friends of the deceased. The religious
ceremony was conducted by the Reverend Dean K. Th. Grönstrand,
who took as the text of his funeral address some words from one
of the Psalms: 'Lord, thou seekest me out and knowest me', to
which was added an interpretation, as sincere as it was full of piety,
of the interesting and captivating personality of the departed noble-
man, so rich in talent and contradictions, with all its doubts and
enigmas, seeking after truth and deep originality.

The coffin was decorated with flowers to the singing of a choir
formed especially for the occasion. A number of wreaths and
bouquets were left by relatives as a last farewell. Flowers from the
Rosengren family were laid to the accompaniment of a beautiful
speech. A wreath from the Finnish Union of Composers was

presented by University Secretary Baron Tor Carpelan. Mrs Aino Sibelius laid a wreath from her husband the composer Jean Sibelius, the ribbon of which bore the striking words: 'Farewell, unforgettable friend, my art grieves.' Mention should also be made of a wreath from Professor Kajanus, as one more proof of the respect and appreciation Axel Carpelan enjoyed among the leading circles of our country's musical life.

More wreaths and flowers were laid in the name of Mrs Sibelius, the Björk and Mieritz families, from the old paternal home, and others.

From Lydia Rosengren's funeral oration

Here, beside Axel Carpelan's lifeless corpse, I want, as the person who has stood close to him for decades with a faithfully understanding friendship, to bear testimony that a fine, noble and rich spirit, enamoured of justice, has left us and gone hence!

Endowed with a rich and warm interest in the best and most beautiful things in life and a never-ceasing thirst for all knowledge, he lived the quiet and unremarkable life of a hermit, a stranger both *in* the world and *to* the world.

His infinitely great love for the world of music – especially since the time he found in Professor Jean Sibelius a friend who both wished and was able to understand the distinctive character of his being – this love and this friendship became the brightest feature of his existence, even if he *himself* had to stand outside what was the warmest interest in his life, stand outside looking yearningly towards the land of beauty he *himself* would never be able to attain!

The Goddess of Fate had given him, as a christening present, the destiny of a *musical artist*, a warm and burning *artist's soul*, but neglected to equip him physically for such a demanding career!

This was the decisive moment for the future of the deceased. All went awry! The vessel steered with slackened sails an irregular course and never reached its goal!

An inborn, inherited frailty of constitution and, in particular, weak nerves, brought about the conflict between the will to *accomplish* something good and beautiful in life, and this physical *inability* to translate his finest thoughts, ideas and musical conceptions into work and action. This was the tragedy of his life, the sorrow and despair of his youth and the reason for the resigned inactivity of his manhood!

With this disposition, and under the circumstances in which he lived out his days, his life became a true martyrdom.

Yet here in this place for which he constantly longed, here he found *so many things* which his mind in its thirst for knowledge had so long desired and which he had hitherto been compelled to do without.

A faint evening glow which cast its rays upon the final days of his life, but too late?

Now he has fought the struggle, now his suffering is at an end!...

From the diary of Jean Sibelius

24.3.1919
Axel. How empty life feels. No sun, no music, no love...How alone I am now with my compositions.

29.3.1919
Now Axel is being lowered into the earth's cold arms. It feels so deeply, deeply tragic! For whom will I compose now?

22.4.1919
Symphony no. V finally in shape. Have fought with God....Oh, that Axel is no longer alive! He thought of me to the last. $+2°$ outside, and sun. The lake still covered in ice. Of migrating birds I have seen only wood-geese, but no swans.

Translator's Notes

General note: Throughout this translation, the Swedish names of towns and places have been preserved. Thus the reader will find 'Helsingfors' in place of 'Helsinki', 'Åbo' in place of 'Turkku', 'Tammerfors' in place of 'Tampere', etc.

17   Pinello's *Puff's Almanac*: Nils Henrik Pinello (1802–79) was a writer and journalist who made frequent contributions to the newspaper *Åbo Underrättelser*, under the sobriquet of 'Captain Puff'. He founded a restaurant, 'Pinellan', in Åbo, which opened in 1848.

17   The Finnish tenement soldier: in nineteenth-century Finland 'tenement' soldiers belonged to the standing army formed by conscription under the *indelningsverket*, or 'tenement system', found in the era of Swedish rule. The officers and commanders of this army were rewarded with homes which they were allowed to keep for the duration of their whole lives, and were also granted various kinds of financial concessions.

18   Pacius: Fredrik Pacius (1809–91), Finnish composer and conductor. His works were written in the classical–romantic tradition of Spohr, though many of them focus on Finnish national themes.

20   *King Fjalar*: the title of a play by J.L. Runeberg (see below).

25   Pinellan: see above.

31   Alexander Armfelt: Alexander Armfelt (1794–1876): public functionary who studied in Uppsala, Edinburgh and Åbo, served as the director of the Bank of Finland and as Secretary of State in St Petersburg, where he advised both Tsar Nicholas I and Tsar Alexander II, acting to the latter as consultant on such matters as the reform of the Finnish currency and the restoration of the *lantdag*.

32   Alphyddan, Opris, Kapellet, Brunnshussalongen: names of

Helsingfors restaurants.

34 Johan Ludvig Runeberg: Johan Ludvig Runeberg (1804–77), Finland's national poet.

40 Rydberg: Viktor Rydberg (1822–95), Swedish romantic poet and novelist.

45 Wecksell: Josef Julius Wecksell (1838–1907), Finland–Swedish romantic poet and author of the tragic drama *Daniel Hjort* (1862). He died in a Helsingfors mental hospital.

58 Ingelius wrote to Cygnaeus: Axel G. Ingelius (1822–68), writer, composer and music critic. The recipient is Fredrik Cygnaeus (1807–81), poet, aesthetic theorist and historian.

59 K.A. Tavaststjerna's *Before Morning Breeze*: Karl-August Tavaststjerna (1860–98), writer, architect and journalist. His most famous prose work was the novel *Hard Times* (1891), which depicts the sufferings of the poor during the years of famine 1867-68. *Before Morning Breeze* (1893) was his first book of poetry.

62 Language wars: the struggle between the 'Fennomanes' (advocates of the Finnish language) and 'Suecomanes' (advocates of the Swedish language) which raged during the latter part of the 19th century. Konstantin Pobedonostsev was the head of the Russian Holy Synod.

63 The Phoenix: an Åbo restaurant.

70 Grotte: 'Grotti' – the magic mill described in the Old Icelandic *Lay of Grotti*. Victor Rydberg's *The New Lay of Grotti* made the mill into a symbol of Mammon-worship and the darker aspects of modern industrialisation.

70 'Our Land': the Finnish national anthem, a setting by Pacius of the introductory poem to J.L. Runeberg's *Fenrik Ståhl's Legends*.

81 Editor Cygnaeus: Gustaf Cygnaeus (1851–1907), educationalist and newspaper editor who founded the *Åbo Times*.

91– I grew up... Christmas '65...: this passage refers to events in
92 Finland during the reign of Tsar Alexander II (1818–81), which was a period of national development for the country. Johan Vilhelm Snellman (1806–1881) was one of the founders of the

modern Finnish state and culture. Among his many achievements were the introduction of Finnish as the language of the courts, and the organization of a new money system.

93 The postal decrees: an Imperial Russian ukase which in 1890 subordinated the Finnish postal authorities to the Russian Ministry of the Interior. As a result of the 'manifesto' letters posted from Finland abroad or to Russia had to bear Russian stamps, while only letters posted inland were allowed to bear Finnish ones.

94 Kajanus: Robert Kajanus (1856–1933), composer and conductor who had an immense influence on Finnish musical life at the beginning of the twentieth century. He founded the Helsingfors Philharmonic Society, an orchestral conservatoire and a symphonic choir. Old Topelius... Edelfelt, Ville Vallgren, Gallén. Zachris Topelius (1818–98): the writer, journalist and historian who, along with Runeberg and Snellman, was one of the creators of modern Finland. Albert Edelfelt (1854–1905): nineteenth-century Finnish painter, who concentrated mainly on historical and national-romantic themes. Ville (Carl Wilhelm) Vallgren (1855–1940): Finnish sculptor, many of whose works still stand in Helsingfors today. Axel Gallén (better known as Akseli Gallen-Kallela, (1865–1931): probably the greatest Finnish visual artist, whose works enjoy an international reputation similar to that of Sibelius.

104 Adolf Paul (1863)–1943): Finland–Swedish dramatist and theatre critic.

110 See note to p.59 above.

113 Law-speaker: the supreme judge and leader of an Old Swedish *land*. The institution was abolished in Finland in 1868.

119 Mörike: *Einem Kristall gleicht meine Seele nun, den noch kein falscher Strahl des Lichts getroffen*: 'My soul is like a crystal now, which no false ray of light has yet struck.'

124 Kivi: Aleksis Kivi (1834–72), Finnish prose writer and novelist who had very little success in his own day, but whose works are now reckoned among the major classics of Finnish literature.

137 *Jätä rauhaan! Etkö tiedä: rikkailta ei tipu?'* 'Leave him alone!

369

Don't you know? You won't get anything from the rich.'

139 the Poet Wennerbom: a reference to Fröding's poem 'Skalden Wennerbom'.

141 V. v. Heidenstam: Verner von Heidenstam (1859-1940), Swedish poet.

151 Fröding: Gustaf Fröding (1860-1911), Swedish poet. 'Daubs and Patches' (Stänk och Flikor) is the title of his best-known volume of poems. Fröding died in a mental hospital.

156 Mikael Lybeck: Karl Mikael Lybeck (1864-1925), Finland-Swedish poet and prose-writer whose work marked the transition from realism to symbolism in Finland's Swedish-language literature.

161 Flodin: Karl Theodor Flodin (1858-1925), Finland-Swedish music critic.

163 Laureatus: the title of a collection of poems by Karl August Tavaststjerna published in 1897, the year before his death.

165 'Floradagen', 13 May: traditional day of celebration for students at the universities of Åbo and Helsingfors. Estlander: Carl Gustaf Estlander (1834-1910), Finland-Swedish literary and art historian.

165 Ernst Ahlgren: the pseudonym of the Swedish woman novelist Victoria Benedictsson (1850-88).

166 The Bøyg. In Norwegian folklore, an enormous, invisible, serpentine being. In Ibsen's Peer Gynt, the Bøyg becomes a symbol of an obstacle that can be sensed but not identified.

167 Russification: the process, begun by Bobrikov in 1898, whereby Finland was brought more closely into line with Russian social, political, legal and cultural institutions, and involving the imposition of the Russian language as the medium of official discourse.

167 Bobrikov: Nikolai Ivanovich Bobrikov (1839-1904), Governor-General of the Grand Duchy of Finland from 1898 to 1904, when he was assassinated by Eugen Schauman.

169 The February Decree: Imperial decree of 1899 which introduced the period of Russification.

169 The People's Petition: an appeal made to the Tsar in March 1899 on behalf of the Finnish people, asking for the revocation of the February Decree, and containing 522,931 signatures. The deputation bearing the petition was not accepted by the Tsar, and the Decree was not revoked until 15 November 1905.

173 Oehlenschlæger: the Danish romantic poet (1779-1850).

190 Mielck: Ernst Leopold Christian Mielck (1877-1899), Finnish composer, who suffered from poor health and died at the age of 22.

194 Hospitz: a Christian private hostel.

196 Ständerhuset: large, ornate public building in the centre of Helsingfors.

200 Axel Lille (1848-1921): politican and journalist, editor-in-chief of Finland's Swedish-language newspaper *Nya Pressen*, which did much to foster Finnish national feeling during the years of Russian domination.

201 Sinebrychoff: Sinebrychoff Oy/Ab, Helsingfors brewery founded in 1819 by the merchant Nikolai Sinebrychoff.

205 Finlayson's: Finlayson Oy/Ab, Tammerfors cotton mill and textile factory, founded in 1820 by the Scot James Finlayson (1771-1852).

219 Balmashov has assassinated Sipyagin: the student S.V. Balmashov (1882-1902) assassinated the Russian Minister of the Interior, D.S. Sipyagin (b. 1853), in Kiev.

227 Vitalis Norström: Johan Vitalis Norström (1856-1916), Swedish philosopher.

230 Bobrikov's dictatorial decree: the decree of 1903 by which Bobrikov assumed more or less the powers of a dictator.

241 N. Vremya: *Novoye Vremya*, the Russian cultural and literary periodical. Suecomanes: see note to p.62 above.

245 Lennart Hohenthal, etc.: the student Lennart Hohenthal assassinated Eliel Soisalon-Soininen (b. 1856), the much-hated Procurator General of Finland, in 1905.

249 Svinhufvud: P.E. Svinhufvud, the jurist and statesman who became the third president of Finland.

252 Apostol: Aleksej Apostol (1866–1927), military band-leader and musician.

255 Yrjö Mäkelin (1875–1923): social democratic politician and journalist.

255 The November Decree: this revoked the February Decree.

256 Eero Järnefelt (1863–1937): Finnish painter, brother of the writer Arvid Järnefelt. Saarinen: Yrjö Saarinen (1899–1958), Finnish expressionist painter. Sigurd Frosterus (1876–1956): Finnish architect and essayist.

261 *Tschuhonica sunt, non placet – tschinownikis!*: 'They're Finns, the bureaucrats don't like it!'

266 *Äiti, äiti!* Finnish for 'Mother, Mother!'

270 Neckan: a mythological creature related to the German 'Nixe', or water-sprite.

272 Automat: a kind of snack-bar, where the food was kept in heated slot-machines that accepted tokens.

274 the Karamzin House: Eva Aurora Charlotta Karamzin (1808–1902), was a St Petersburg court beauty who married Colonel Andrei Karamzin. After her husband was killed in the Crimean War, she went to live in Finland in her villa Hagasund near Helsingfors.

276 Seyn: Frans Albert Seyn (1862–1918), Governor-General of Finland from 1909 until 1917.

281 Josephson: Ernst Josephson (1851–1906), famous Swedish painter.

289 Werner Söderhjelm (1859–1931): linguist, literary historian and diplomat. Ernst Lindelöf (1870–1946): Professor of Mathematics at Helsingfors University from 1903–1938. Leo Mechelin (1839–1914): Finnish philanthropist.

291 Yrjö Hirn (1870–1952): Finnish literary historian and aesthetic theorist. Guss Mattsson (1873–1914): Finnish writer, journalist and chemical technologist.

294 Ekelund: Vilhelm Ekelund (1880–1949), Swedish poet and philosopher.

305 Favén: Antti Favén (1882–1948), Finnish painter and portraitist.

315 Langhoff: Carl Fredrik August Langhoff (1856-1929), Finnish military man and public functionary who served in Russia until 1890, when he was put in command of the Finnish Army. He was appointed Secretary of State in 1906, but resigned the post in 1913.

317 A. Paloheimo: Alfred Paloheimo (1862-1949), Finnish insurance director.

321 Viktor Nováček (1873-1914): a Helsingfors music teacher of Czech origin (not to be confused with the composer Ottokar Nováček); gave the first performance of Sibelius' violin concerto in February 1904.

329 *Akseli setä*: Finnish for 'Uncle Axel'.

329 Westerholms: paintings by Victor Westerholm (1860-1919), Finnish landscape-painter.

330 Eino Leino (1878-1926): Finnish novelist, dramatist, poet and essayist in the national-romantic mould.

331 Erik Furuhhjelm (1883-1964): Finnish composer of orchestral and chamber music who published the first monograph on Sibelius (1916).

331 Otto Andersson (1879-1969): Finnish musicologist and folklorist, Professor of Musicology and Folk Poetry Research at Åbo University from 1926-1946.

332 Werner Söderström (1860-1914): Finnish publisher. His firm still flourishes to this day.

332 Gripenberg: Bertel Gripenberg (1878-1947), Finland-Swedish romantic symbolist poet.

341 Höffding and Grundtvig: Harald Høffding (1843-1931), post-Kierkegaardian Danish philosopher. N.F.S. Grundtvig (1783-1872), Danish poet, philosopher and educationalist.

344 Tokoi: Oskari Tokoi (1873-1963), leading social-democratic politician during the period leading up to 1918. He emigrated to the USA in 1920, and spent the rest of his life there.

349 Kordelin: the reference is to the execution of the businessman Alfred Kordelin (1868-1917) by Russian sailors during the 'November disturbances' of 1917.

352 General Mannerheim: Carl Gustaf Emil Mannerheim (1867–
1951), statesman and military leader who became the sixth
president of Finland. He led the Finnish armed forces to victory against the Red Army in the Winter War of 1939–40.

355 Jarl Hemmer (1893–1944): Finland–Swedish writer and poet.